ANTHONY QUINN

The Streets

JONATHAN CAPE
LONDON

Published by Jonathan Cape 2012

2 4 6 8 10 9 7 5 3 1

Copyright © Anthony Quinn 2012

Anthony Quinn has asserted his right under the Copyright, Designs
and Patents Act 1988 to be identified as the author of this work

First published in Great Britain in 2012 by
Jonathan Cape
Random House, 20 Vauxhall Bridge Road,
London SW1V 2SA

www.vintage-books.co.uk

Addresses for companies within The Random House Group Limited can be found at:
www.randomhouse.co.uk/offices.htm

The Random House Group Limited Reg. No. 954009

A CIP catalogue record for this book
is available from the British Library

Hardback ISBN 9780224096911
Trade paperback ISBN 9780224096928

The Random House Group Limited supports The Forest Stewardship Council (FSC®),
the leading international forest certification organisation. Our books carrying the FSC
label are printed on FSC® certified paper. FSC is the only forest certification scheme
endorsed by the leading environmental organisations, including Greenpeace.
Our paper procurement policy can be found at:
www.randomhouse.co.uk/environment

Typeset in Fournier MT by Palimpsest Book Production Limited,
Falkirk, Stirlingshire

Printed and bound in Great Britain by Clays Ltd, St Ives plc

Endpapers: map of St Pancras showing Somers Town, 1880, reproduced by
permission of Camden Local Studies and Archives Centre

For Sarah, my sister

More helpful than all wisdom is one draught of simple human pity that will not forsake us.

The Mill on the Floss, George Eliot

I
Coats, shirts

It was nearly half past six by the time I found Marchmont's house, a prosperous terrace on the west side of Montagu Square. An amber softness glimmered behind the leaded fanlight. I had knocked, and was still busy cleaning my boot heels on the porch's scraper when the door swung open and Rennert, his chief secretary, stood there, a vanishingly slender man whose spindly legs and beaky nose put me in mind of a heron. My breath plumed frostily as I bid him good evening. I had met this gentleman at the office, on the Monday I began my employment, and had already noted the shrewdness of his gaze as it swept the whole newsroom and almost instantly picked me out from the stragglers. Without a word he had crooked his finger, beckoned me over like a schoolmaster spotting the new boy in the assembly hall and coolly recited my instructions for the day.

Now, on the porch, those appraising eyes once again conducted a rapid inventory of my person, perhaps pausing to wonder why in such a climate – it was a bitter night in February – I had chosen not to wear a topcoat. With a jerk of his chin he admitted me to the high-ceilinged hallway, and the gas jets flared in their brackets from the sudden rush of cold I brought in. Following him down the hall, I happened to glance up the staircase and saw a girl, in a nightgown, watching us from the shadows. I did not yet know that Marchmont was, amongst other things, a father of six. Rennert led me into a reception room which evidently adjoined his master's office, for through the closed double doors could be heard a booming laughter that I instinctively identified as Marchmont's, though I had never had the acquaintance of the man before this evening. The laughter, full of rippling confidence, seemed to extend an invitation – no, an order – to join in, and by the sound of things his present company were eager to oblige him.

Rennert, who showed no sign of listening to the merriment next door, gestured for me to take a seat on the sofa. He noticed my shivering as I sat down and warmed my hands at the fire. These occasional Friday nights were meant, I gathered, to be 'at-ease' encounters between the guvnor (as Marchmont was known to everyone) and his team of inspectors, though my inward commotion of nerves at the prospect of being introduced could not be quite stilled. I had laid aside my small briefcase, which Rennert's attentive eye now fell upon.

'Your report is in there?' he asked.

I nodded, and unlocking the clasp drew out a thin sheaf of loose foolscap, closely written in my sloping and rather blotchy script that made every vowel look identical. (I was at that time inclined to believe that a gentleman's handwriting should not be altogether legible.) I handed them over and saw him frown as he riffled the pages. Without looking at me he said, 'These are the notes you took today?'

'No. They are – the whole week's.' He did look at me now. His lips started to purse, but he continued examining the contents. I shifted in my seat and stared down at my hands; I was once more transported back to the schoolroom.

Presently he raised his eyes again and said, 'Rather exiguous for five days' work.' I wasn't sure what 'exiguous' meant, but sensed it did not signify approval. He sighed, removed his spectacles and pinched the bridge of his nose. 'I take into account that this is your first week on the paper, and that the work can be . . . troublesome. But there is nonetheless a standard of reportage expected of our contributors, it requires a certain finesse –'

He was interrupted at this moment by the opening of the double-leafed doors and the emergence of two prefectorial young men, both bearded and trimly dressed, their bodies canted at a deferential angle to an older, larger fellow who swaggered urbanely between them and then paused on the threshold. This was Marchmont. Bobbing his head mischievously towards his departing guests, he muttered something about 'do as my shirt does'. Bafflingly, they all exploded into laughter once more. With an exchange of 'g'nights' they were gone, and now Rennert stepped forward.

'Sir. I have Mr Wildeblood here,' he said.

'Ah, the neophyte – come,' boomed Marchmont, retreating into his office. We followed, and almost waded into the room's conspiratorial fug of cigar smoke and alcohol. All was in affable disarray – the carpet speckled with smuts from the fire; bundles of paper totteringly stacked upon an ancient chaise longue; an unstoppered sherry decanter on a side table with smeared glasses; a chaotic desk which 'the guvnor' had just made even more untidy by throwing his short legs upon it. He was an odd-looking fellow, his stubby frame surmounted by a bald head as round and glazed as a toffee apple. Wisps of reddish-brown hair straggled over his ears. His fleshy nose and cheeks glowed pink from the sherry, and more than one chin spilled over his stand-up collar, but this dissolute aspect was counterpointed by dark little eyes that glinted with a hard, disconcerting curiosity. He was perhaps fifty, or slightly older.

Recalling the details of this introduction years later – Marchmont's name has since become famous – it is not just the man himself who seizes my mind's eye, it is the backdrop against which he sat. Across that entire wall stretched a map of London, vastly magnified, which would not have been unusual in itself but for the discrete blocks of colour that patched certain neighbourhoods of the city. These had been applied, I saw, from tiny pots of drawing ink ranged along a thin wooden shelf, itself suspended on string at waist height along the length of the wall. Parts of the map remained unmarked, but these were mostly on the city's outskirts; towards the centre a motley of colours – navy, yellow, purple, pink and red, much red – began to cluster amongst the street patterns, lining the arterial roads, the fields and parks, the river and the canals. The effect was intricately pretty, like a mosaic, though what it signified I couldn't say.

'So . . .' began Marchmont, expelling another noxious cloud of cigar smoke, 'you're Elder's nephew –'

'His godson, sir.'

'– and you've been assigned to . . . ?'

'Somers Town,' I said.

'He's had rather a slow start,' Rennert said drily. Marchmont by a slight tilt of his head seemed to ask why, and, perceiving that he was not someone easily fooled, I told him the truth.

'I had great difficulty in . . . understanding them, sir – the people, I mean. The slang they use is so very singular.'

At this he swung his legs off the desk and stood to face the map. He examined it for a few moments, and, without turning round, said, 'So you have been mainly talking to market people – street sellers, hawkers, costermongers, that sort.'

I agreed that this was the case, for I had wandered for most of that week in the Brill, the market occupying the whole south-east end of Somers Town. When he enquired as to my impressions of it I thought immediately of the bustling narrow streets, all alike, and of the Sunday morning that I first became acquainted with the place. As you enter the Brill the market sounds are barely audible, but with each step a low

3

hum, like that of a beehive, starts to gather; then, on turning a corner, a great tumult of voices assails you, as if you were standing in the sea and a monstrous wave had suddenly broken over your head. Before you the pavements are thronged with men and women, some talking and smoking, some hurrying about with their goods in bags and aprons, or else standing at carts and barrows heaped with vegetables – the cobbles are green with refuse leaves. But it is not only victuals for sale; here or there you find a magpie hoard of used articles, combs and cups, brass lamps, tinderboxes, candleholders, old jackets and trousers, fire irons, frying pans, knives and forks, boots, braces, hats, door knockers, key chains, and, in incalculable profusion, wretched 'bits and bobs' that one cannot imagine being bought once, let alone sold again. The din is astonishing, the stallholders' cries grow so importunate that the noise seems to double in your ear, and on all sides you see a press of bodies, whether young girls carrying home jugs of beer and breakfast herrings, or boys sauntering about with pet terriers under their arms, or older men with pipes in their mouths, and any number of them playing cards or shove-ha'penny on the footpath.

These were Marchmont's people, the object of his restless curiosity and the lifeblood of an investigation to which I was the latest recruit. For the last two years their habits, occupations and earnings had been chronicled in his weekly paper, *The Labouring Classes of London*, and sold to a horrified but fascinated public at bookstalls and railway stations for tuppence an issue. Marchmont, seated again, listened intently as I recounted my ventures into the Brill, nodding his head and occasionally chuckling at some detail or other. He took particular delight in the story of my being invited by certain gentlemen to play 'three-up', a game of chance that requires you to bet on all 'heads' or all 'tails' on three ha'pennies pitched into the air. I played five games straight –

'And lost every one of them?' asked Marchmont with a grin.

'Yes. All five.'

'Doubtless they saw you coming,' he said, 'and I assure you – they were no gentlemen.' Behind me Rennert stifled a snort of amusement. I added that during the game the men's talk was at its most impenetrable, and again Marchmont looked unsurprised. 'Costermongers are notorious for their slang; they are always seeking an advantage, and essential to that end is a language only they understand. They use it to fool their street rivals – the Irish, the Jews.'

I replied that I was neither Irish nor Jewish, yet they were pleased to baffle me just the same.

4

'You are a stranger to them. You know little of their ways. Therefore they would try to exploit your ignorance in a game of chance.'

'Then perhaps you could enlighten me,' I said, taking out the note-book from my breast pocket. 'I recorded certain words and phrases that recurred in their speech . . .' He settled back in his chair and spread forth his palms, as though to say, *Be my guest.* I found the page on which I had written them. 'Yenep?'

'A penny,' he replied. 'Money is often reduced to back slang. Rouf-yenep is fourpence. Net-yenep is tenpence, and so on.'

'Top o' reeb?'

'Pot of beer.'

'Cool him?'

'Look at him.'

'On doog?'

'I think you can decipher that one.'

'A couter?' I said, trying to run the word backwards in my head.

'A sovereign,' he said with a shrug. 'Not everything is reducible to the backwards rule. Gen, for some reason, is a shilling, and a bandy is a sixpence.' He watched as I noted these translations, and I must have sighed a little, because his tone softened with a kind of pity. 'Have patience. The language of the costers would take an outsider years to comprehend fully. You have been amongst them but a few days.'

I looked again at that cartographic marvel behind him; inwardly a question was forming. 'Sir, may I ask – is the paper engaged in a phil-anthropic mission? Is that the purpose of our endeavours?'

Marchmont looked down, and joined the fingertips of each hand in a meditative arch. 'How old are you, Mr Wildeblood?'

'One-and-twenty, sir.'

'This is your first time in London?'

'It is.'

He absorbed this, then pointed to the most heavily inked portion of the map. 'Behold the East End, where we began our project. Do you know the most signal fact our enquiries have uncovered? It is that nearly a third of its inhabitants live in a state of abject poverty. By this I mean they cannot raise the basic minimum – I calculate it at seventeen shillings a week – to cover the cost of rent and food for themselves and their dependants. In certain areas, such as the Old Nichol in Bethnal Green, the figure rises to over eighty per cent. Just consider – eight in ten inhabitants of that vicinity are paupers. But we are beginning to discover something even more extraordinary. Since broadening our field of interest to Blackfriars, to Holborn and Drury Lane, to Borough, to Southwark – and to Somers Town – we are learning that the East End is by no means exceptional in its state of destitution. Some years ago, when I put an estimate of the city's poor at three hundred thousand, I was abused and derided – people were angry, dismissed it as "provocation". But all the evidence thus far suggests I was too cautious – the number is likely to be closer to eight hundred thousand! Now, to answer your question, even if it were desirable to offer philanthopic relief to the poor, we have not the resources to do so. Our motive is not paternalism, or socialism, or radicalism –'

'Then . . . what is it?'

'Why, it is journalism. We go through these neighbourhoods, street by street, house by house, and in so doing we glean a systematic and impartial understanding of the causes and conditions of poverty.'

'But . . . if we expose the reality of those conditions, to whom will be the benefit?'

Marchmont frowned. 'My dear boy – the benighted public, of course! The efforts of Mr Dickens notwithstanding, the world of the London poor is a *terra incognita*, as remote to most people as those tribes that dwell at the ends of the earth. By our endeavours the public will learn precisely the nature of this great capital of ours, where the beggar and the banker rub along cheek by jowl. They will learn that slums exist a mere six hundred yards from the gates of the Palace of Westminster, that a few minutes' walk will take them from a club in Pall Mall to a dosshouse in the Seven Dials. We shall present a survey the like of which has never before been seen.'

I was still unsure as to how this might alleviate the plight of our subjects, but I didn't wish to deflate his transport of rhetorical fervour. Instead I gestured at the map. 'The different colours – what do they mean?'

At this point Rennert stood up and tapped his watch in signal to Marchmont, but the latter held forth his palms as though to hush him. 'Each designates a class of living, which you will learn as you proceed. But in Somers Town, you will encounter no more than three. The purple streets indicate a mixture of poor artisans and the respectable lower orders. The dark blues signify an impoverished class living from hand to mouth – widows, deserted wives and children, casual labourers – who might be raised from poverty by hard work. The red—' and here he paused – 'the red streets are home to loafers and criminals, street Arabs, society's dregs. They are, you might say, the outcast poor

– beyond reform. You will become well acquainted with the type.' He looked challengingly at me. 'Do you recoil at such a prospect?'

I considered this for a moment, and answered him, 'Not at all.'

The decisiveness of my tone surprised him, for hitherto I must have seemed to him diffident, and probably ignorant. At that moment a knock sounded at the door and a servant put her head round the jamb.

'Sir, Mrs Marchmont asked if you would bid the children goodnight before you go.'

'Indeed I will!' he cried, and hoisted himself from his chair. 'See that the carriage is brought round, Dawkins. Arlington Street.' He was suddenly all business, locking his desk, re-stoppering the sherry decanter, tucking a cigar case into his pocket, and muttering in a distracted way to Rennert. It seemed that I had been momentarily forgotten about, for his only concern was to find the store of 'blunt' he had secreted, and he indulged a good deal of head-scratching and pocket-patting over its whereabouts. (I deduced from this that blunt was a slang word for money.) When Rennert blithely pulled open the lower drawer of his own desk and produced a sheaf of banknotes, Marchmont almost shouted his delight.

'Baccarat night, you see,' he said with a wink, splaying the notes into a fan. 'And these fellows are sticklers for ready money – you can't write 'em a cheque!'

I tagged along behind as they sauntered out of the office and into the hallway. Marchmont, not one for ceremony, shook my hand and bounded up the stairs, evidently keen to have done with his paternal duties and make haste to his card night. I was left once more in the company of Rennert, who, opening the door and blowing his cheeks at the cold, turned another of his beady looks on me.

'This is no night to be without an overcoat.' I nodded agreement, and made a comical grimace. He continued to stare at me. 'Do you have an overcoat?'

I admitted that I did not, and his expression mingled pity with the smallest flicker of exasperation. 'You collected your pay at the office this evening?'

'I was informed that payments would be delayed – registration and so forth . . .'

He nodded, and said, 'Should you manage not to take chill and die over the weekend, come to my office first thing on Monday morning.'

I thanked him, though I didn't know what for, and stood on the step ready to leave. But something came back to me at that moment, and I said, 'One other thing, sir. A phrase Mr Marchmont used this evening, just as those two other gentlemen were leaving his office – something about "do as my shirt does". I have heard this before. What does it mean?' I remembered the explosive laughter it had provoked, and now I saw in Rennert's pale eyes a sardonic gleam that was perhaps the nearest this sombre man ever came to amusement.

'Just a phrase the governor has picked up on his travels,' he said, then dropped his voice confidentially. 'It means – "kiss my arse".'

I walked back east under the glimmering lamplight of the Marylebone Road. At King's Cross I saw an omnibus that would have carried me up to Islington, where I had my lodgings. But I reasoned that the tuppence I spent on the fare would be better saved for a bite to eat over the weekend. What I had omitted to tell Rennert was that my coat had been stolen in the Brill, and my purse with it. The story of its theft betrayed such arrant naivety on my part that I could not yet bring myself to confess it. Two days previously in Somers Town I had been footsore from tramping the streets and had chanced to rest in a tavern near the market. It was a low sort of place, crowded – so are they all in this vicinity – but I found a corner where I might eat my mutton pie in relative seclusion. I also took a pewter of ale, and soon, warmed by the fire, I loosened my collar and took off my coat. My error was to go outside to the privy, for when I returned the chair where I had hung it was bare. I looked about the room, at the costers and the pipe smokers and the stallholders, all in murmurous chat and none of them so much as glancing at me. I might as well have not been there, like my coat, which actually wasn't.

I approached the potman at the bar, who continued polishing a glass as I told him of this unaccountable disappearance. He listened politely, then tweaked his mouth to acknowledge the pity of my situation – no money, no coat – but he had nothing to offer beyond, 'Can't help yer, son. Lot o' lifters round 'ere.' Perhaps, I pursued, someone had witnessed this 'lifter' in the act, at which he gestured at the indifferent mass of drinkers crowding the room, as if to say, *You ask them.* I felt so aggrieved at this moment that I took his leave to do just that, and, swallowing, raised my voice to nobody in particular. 'My coat and money are gone. Did anybody happen to see the thief?' A few of the tavern's customers looked around, and I sensed that they did not much care for a stranger bandying the word 'thief' amongst them. It had the ring of an unwarranted accusation. Into this silence I repeated, less firmly, 'Anybody?' I heard someone make a kind of hissing noise in reproach, and then a muttered voice: 'Dunno about no coat, but 'e can do as my shirt does.' My burning ears still heard laughter as the tavern door swung behind me.

And now, two days later, I knew the meaning of that delightful phrase.

2
Nice as nip

Fleet Street was a rattling pandemonium of carts and carriages and omnibuses that I had to dodge on my way to Salisbury Square, a tiny cobblestoned enclosure where the editorial offices of Marchmont's serial occupied the upper part of the building once owned by the *Chronicle* newspaper. It faced directly onto St Bride's Church. *The Labouring Classes of London* was at that time one of the most successful weeklies in the country, and people trooped up and down those stairs at all times of the day and late into the night. As well as Marchmont's staff of copy boys, subeditors, stenographers, typesetters and illustrators, you would see a less regular (though generally more vociferous) train of cabmen, labourers, street vendors and ruffian-types passing through, at the guvnor's invitation, to tell their stories personally. Marchmont, always under the pressure of deadlines, would then redictate this material, with embellishments of his own, to a shorthand writer. It made for a somewhat chaotic workplace, since the bevy of 'bona fide' contributors from the street was not easily distinguished from that class of chancers who preyed on the paper's open-door arrangement. Thefts were not infrequent.

The office routine was supervised by the imperturbable Rennert, who would meet with his staff of inspectors (as we were called) on the Monday morning to explain that week's theme or subject – it might be 'the costermongers' diet', or 'children street sellers', or 'Sunday-morning markets' – and to distribute the 'dailies', for expenses that would be incurred whilst on the streets. Marchmont would usually be in his office, either writing or interviewing, and seldom emerged before five o'clock. But not today. He was in the main office when I arrived, yarning away to a little coven of his writers – I soon came to learn he liked nothing better than to be *attended*, like a king amongst his courtiers. Around him the office began to find its industrious rhythm, which would gather in energy as Friday loomed, the day the paper went to press.

Whilst he was occupied with entertaining his staff, Rennert summoned me to his own office that fronted onto Fleet Street: I could hear the racket of the thoroughfare below us. Rennert had taken from his desk a small metal box, which he unlocked, and proceeded to examine its contents. Without looking up, he said, 'Would it be correct to assume that you are presently – short of funds?'

I replied in the affirmative, and he fished out five sovereigns.

'This is an advance on three weeks' wages, with a little extra. Your rent is how much?'

'Seven shillings a week.'

'I advise you to open a bank account,' he said, and then wrote something on a piece of paper which he handed to me. 'Keep back thirty shillings to pay for an overcoat – go to this fellow.' He had written the name of a tailor, and his address. I thanked him, put the money in my pocket and turned to leave. 'Wait,' he said sharply. 'The governor will accompany you today. He knows Somers Town well – you should learn from him. When you make notes, write in pencil. Your reports are of no use if your hand is illegible.' He said all this in a clipped, businesslike way, as he might have done with any of his minions. But then he looked at me squarely, and there was something changed in his tone when he spoke. 'Do you like to gamble, Mr Wildeblood?'

'No,' I said, recalling then the story of the 'three-up' I had told on Friday evening. 'That is – not very often.'

He nodded, I think in approval; then he said something that greatly surprised me. 'Don't tell him you're carrying this money.' I was confounded for a moment – the identity of 'him' was plain – but the look in Rennert's pale eyes warned me not to ask his meaning. He bid me good day, and I went back into the main office, where Marchmont was still volubly enthralled by one of his own monologues. Some minutes later, having reached a rare pause, he spotted me loitering in the vestibule, and bidding his audience farewell he ambled over with that curious swaggering gait of his – he didn't walk so much as *roll*. He shrugged on his coat, with its huge fur collar, and a hat, and we proceeded down the stairs and out into the street. I asked him if we should take an omnibus, but he dismissed the idea with an impatient wave.

'The best means of discovering this city is to walk it,' he said, then happened to look round at me. 'What, no coat?' The day was murderously raw.

'I mislaid it last week. Mr Rennert has advised me as to where I might purchase another.' I took out the slip of paper with the tailor's details and showed it to him. He exclaimed on reading it.

'Regent Street!? Great heavens, does he imagine you're *made* of money?'

'He advanced me a loan on my wages,' I replied, and then wished I hadn't, as he gave me a slyly appraising look.

'I know where you might lay hands on a coat, and save yourself a few shillings.'

We continued in the direction of the Strand, with Marchmont's voice in my ear the whole time, then turned into the warren of narrow courts and alleys approaching Holborn. They were close-packed, mean-looking habitations around here, but Marchmont walked seemingly without fear. When he stopped to chat to a street seller or a char as she washed the steps, he did not for a moment talk down to them, but nor did he try to ingratiate himself by pretending to be an equal: his top hat and watch chain announced his station in life. I suppose his manner was one of convivial aloofness. His pace, leisurely up to now, became brisk as we reached one thoroughfare – I think it was Shelton Street – and he said, in an undertone, 'We need not linger around these parts.' It seemed that even the guvnor put limits on his own amiability. Once out of Drury Lane the very air seemed cleaner, the streets wider, and we took the squares to the north – Bloomsbury, Russell, Tavistock – in our stride.

He must have noticed me shivering, because once we crossed the Euston Road into Somers Town he made a beeline for a little shop selling second-hand apparel on Ossulston Street. I say 'little'; behind its narrow frontage lay a cavernous interior whose walls were lined with dishevelled rows of coats and jackets in all cuts and colours. It was a dingy sort of refuge, a waiting room of worn old clobber from which rose the astonishing smell (I would hazard) of all the bodies that had once inhabited these dismal garments. I looked at Marchmont, expecting him to remark on the ripe medley of odours, but he was already at the racks, holding the sleeve of a coat and rubbing its cloth between his stubby fingers.

A diminutive trader, appearing from behind a curtain, had sidled over, eyes darting busily behind his spectacles. Around his pate hanks of oily unkempt hair straggled from the back of his head to his collar, which did not look quite clean. Beneath his jacket he wore a waistcoat of flaming scarlet-and-green tartan.

'Morning, sirs,' he said. 'And what may I do for you?'

'This young feller requires a coat,' said Marchmont, still absorbed in his examination. The man took a cursory measurement of my chest with his grubby tailor's measure.

'Well, we does all sorts, sir – dress coats, Ulster coats, great coats, frock coats, pea coats, bob-tailed coats, pilot coats, and overcoats of a *h'aristocratic* style, though there's no great call for 'em nowadays,' he added, with a faint note of regret. He fixed a narrow-eyed look on me. 'I fancy you might suit summin' like *this* . . .' and he pulled from the rack a grand black frock coat with wide peaked lapels. He held it for me to shrug on and gave a little brush to the shoulders.

Marchmont at last deigned to cast his eye over the garment. 'It's a tidy fit,' he said, 'and decent cloth, too.'

'Oh, it's nice as nip, sir, better than what they does you in the slop trade – far better.' And he gave another little stroke to the material, as if it were the coat of a favourite dog. I rather admired it myself, until I happened to notice on the revers of the left sleeve a curious brownish stain, about the size of a wax seal. I felt a sudden inward recoil.

'What's this?'

The clothes dealer peered at it. 'Looks like dried blood. P'raps a butcher once worn it.' He appeared quite unconcerned by this possibility. I looked to Marchmont, who also took a neutral view of the stain.

'More likely a surgeon's,' he said, 'given the cloth's quality.'

This last word roused the dealer to enthusiasm. 'Oh, I'm glad you sees the quality, sir. Not many customers is very perticler about quality – they just comes 'ere for a bargain.'

But by now I was unbuttoning the coat – I couldn't get the thing off my back quickly enough. Blood!? Marchmont, his eyebrows raised in surprise, stared at me.

'I can't wear that. I'm sorry,' I said, with enough conviction in my voice to forestall any argument. The dealer looked baffled by my rejection. Marchmont only said, 'It seems you have a customer more *perticler* than most.'

I turned to the man. 'You said that you had pilot coats . . .' I did not know a pilot coat from a pilot fish, but I liked the sound of this raiment. The man went back to the racks and plucked out a double-breasted jacket with wooden buttons in dark blue serge, less fine than the frock coat, but free of incriminating stains. It was shortish in length, but the collar could be pulled up to protect your ears from the cold, and there were slash pockets at each side to warm the hands. I looked at myself in the brown-spotted glass of a cheval mirror, and thought the coat looked well. Marchmont's reflection joined mine – he seemed somehow diminished in the glass.

'You have the look of someone about to run off to sea,' he said archly.

'I had an uncle who was a sailor,' I replied. 'I believe I met him once.' And I knew that his ship had gone down with all hands somewhere on the way to Guatemala, in the 1860s.

The man had sniffed a sale. 'In good condition, too. Worth twelve shillin's of anyone's money.'

I nodded, thinking that reasonable, but Marchmont gave a theatrical sigh. 'I'm sure you can do better than that,' he said.

The man gave a defensive shrug. 'Twelve is about the card for a good thing like this, sir. You said y'self, you pays for quality.'

'Not *quite* what I said,' replied Marchmont drily, and for the next minute or so the two of them haggled over what might be a fair price. The man insisted he could not go lower than ten, but Marchmont with casual tenacity knocked him down to eight. So I had my coat, and had spared myself a few bob into the bargain. Or so I thought then.

For the rest of the morning Marchmont conducted me on a perambulation of Somers Town, which district, I learned, he had known intimately from his youth. He had once lived at Seymour Street, he said, in the days when the place still clung to its fading cloak of respectability. Before that, at the end of the last century, it had been home to a colony of 'foreign artisans', mostly from France, who sought refuge from the Reign of Terror. Whilst the wealthier sort of émigrés settled to the west, around the streets and squares of Marylebone, exiles of the poorer class found their way to St Pancras and Somers Town, where they soon established a genteel industry – of silversmiths, tailors, carpenters – to rival Clerkenwell and Spitalfields. Looking about the shabby terraces now, at the swarming streets and the rowdy taverns, it did not seem (I could not help remarking) so genteel any longer.

'On the irrational market of social reputation a place may rise and fall quickly,' said Marchmont. 'It is the way of the city. Somers Town started out as pastoral land, with its fields and flower gardens, and as money circulated it became prosperous. Streets of grand houses spread over the wild common. But then money left – who knows why? – and those houses were sold off for less than they cost to build. The neighbourhood became seedy and cheap. Another wave of immigrants poured in – the Irish notably – and the family terraces were broken up into rooms for rent. My boyhood home is now a dosshouse with beds for fourpence a night.'

I stole a glance at him then, but his expression was opaque. 'The change does not . . . trouble you?' I said.

He tweaked his mouth slightly. 'Well, I was lucky. I got out.' The reply seemed to satisfy him. We walked on, and he continued to reminisce. 'The Brill market, which you already know, used to be twice the size in my day, before the railway came.' At this, he pointed yonder to the spires and smoke stacks of St Pancras, the grand station erected about ten years before. It had necessitated a vast clearance of slums.

'So that has improved the district's character,' I said hopefully.

'A little. But clearing slums solves only half of the problem. The poor still need to be housed. Some were dispersed north to Camden, Kentish Town and beyond, but you still have many railway workers, itinerants and so on. Thus the modern scourge of overcrowding.' He looked thoughtful then, and seemed about to enlarge on this theme. But instead he asked me whether I had done any 'house-to-house' yet. I shook my head. 'Then perhaps we should begin.'

This was the part of the job I had been dreading. Hitherto I had walked the streets engaging in conversation with local tradesmen and costers and whoever else happened to be abroad that day, such as any curious visitor might do in a place unfamiliar to him. But whereas the streets were the common property of all, to go knocking at people's doors and seeking entry into their homes was surely an imposition on them, especially if one had no pretext other than 'scientific enquiry'. My brief experience of the neighbourhood (I still heard the mocking laughter of that crowded tavern) indicated that the locals did not much care for strangers. I confessed this misgiving to Marchmont, who seemed amused by such nicety of feeling.

'My dear boy, we are not "trespassing" at all – we are conducting a professional investigation, and so long as they know you're not working for the church – or the police – they will yarn away for as long as you please.'

We had come to a halt, and with a swift glance around he announced that we should start here. I refer now to my notebook of this time, to the entries I wrote on that first day. It is a fair example of the particulars upon which *The Labouring Classes of London* was founded.

No. 26 Hampden Street. On the ground floor a family of Irish costers. One large room, two beds. Husband in good health, but the wife disposed to drink. Two girls & a boy, all 'out working', according to their mother.

On the floor above a Mrs Morley, a respectable Roman Catholic lady, widowed with a daughter who gains a living in the City for both. She offered us tea, but seemed to possess so little in the way of cups, saucers, &c that we declined. The room poorly furnished but clean.

On the second floor, a married couple, both of about fifty, & very much the worse for drink. The husband is a market porter, presently unemployed; the wife given to begging & picking up odds & ends in the street. Placid when we met them, but notorious in the district for their brawling (Mrs Morley below made indignant complaint of them).

Two rooms on the third floor occupied by two or more coster families. Difficult to know anything about these people, who asked us for money & were disagreeable when refused. A man might be husband, brother, or lodger; to whom the children belonged it is impossible to judge. Mr Marchmont says there would be many such cases in the street.

Nos 24 and 22. No answer at the door.

No. 20. Empty; to be demolished.

No. 18. In one of the parlours live the Trent family. Father, mother, son of seventeen, daughters of fourteen & twelve. Have lived in this room for several years. Mr Trent is a former tailor who now does repair work on clothes – 'not a profitable line' he says. His wife goes out nursing. They make between them twenty shillings a week, with help from the son (a coster). Daughters attend the Ragged School. They are another 'good' family on the brink of poverty, their struggle against it piteous.

On the first floor, a street seller of 'small articles' lives with a woman of doubtful character – possibly a prostitute. Room entirely unfurnished save for a narrow truckle bed & an upturned crate which did service as a table on which to eat. Damp on the walls & ceiling unnoticed (or else ignored) by its occupants.

The upper floors of the house are occupied by Irish families too shifting & multitudinous to document. 'Bedlam,' says Mr M. after five minutes' converse with the landlord.

No. 16. Empty, though vagrants are said to bed down here.

No. 14 has three floors. The parlours & first floor are occupied by a shifting tenancy, mostly of a low class of costers whose wives sell watercress or flowers in the street. On the second floor live Mr & Mrs Snowdon, with five children. He works as a house painter but brings home little money; his drinking habits are unlikely to enable any long-term employment. The mother cares for the children, but is hard-pressed to keep them from starvation. Beer & a little bread the only victuals to be seen. The room they inhabit is filthy, & a home to vermin; walls leprous with damp, floor strewn with rubbish. The stench indescribable. Above the fireplace (unlit), a miserable-looking sampler, with this stitched motto: GOD BLESS OUR HOME. On the third floor, in one room, a family of six, with two beds between them. The panels of the door broken, either from negligence or a drunken mishap – not an uncommon sight. The husband, a lamplighter, suffers from asthma; the wife, quiet & steady, but forlorn in appearance; sells cress. Two children present were without shoes or stockings; whereabouts of the older two unknown.

No. 12. Empty.

No. 10. This house was, Mr M. believed, entirely abandoned, & the parlours & first & second floors showed severe dilapidation; even the grates had been stolen from the fireplaces. On the third floor back room, however, we found a Mr Duke, a former surgeon & of a very different class from the paupers & drunkards along the street. He was fifty-five, well-spoken, his attire worn but neat, & he recounted his misfortunes without bitterness. His wife & child had died in a railway accident up north ten years ago or more; unable to bear his grief he took to drink, lost his job & savings, & moved to Somers Town because it 'seemed as convenient as anywhere else' – & he could afford it. He has since stopped drinking, though he will never be able to regain his former station in life. Earns a little money in the neighbourhood as 'a quack'. A chair, a table & a mattress are the sole furnishings in the room.

Of all the interviews we conducted today this man's story touched my heart the most, & greatly alarmed me. For if someone of his education & class can fall through the net into poverty's chasm, then who is to say that it could not happen to oneself?

Such were the day's findings: an inauspicious beginning, you might think. Yet the standard of poverty and degradation I afterwards encountered in Somers Town was seldom less terrible than this, and in certain cases very much worse. But I will not burden you with too detailed a record of my investigations. I could not bear to write it down again, and in all likelihood you could not bear to read it.

Later that afternoon, Marchmont suggested we had something to eat, which I took to mean stopping at a dining room or chop house. Instead, he walked over to a street pieman with his stall of pastries and puddings ('Here's all 'ot!') and asked me what I should like: I chose a meat pie, and he the fish. As we stood there eating on the street, the local people passed us on either side, and every so often one of them would nod to Marchmont, or salute him as *Guvnor*. Again, he seemed absolutely at ease – he enjoyed 'knocking about' with them, and would even talk to the costers in their own slang. Meanwhile I had become curious about the filling in my pie.

'It's been rather highly seasoned,' I said, swallowing down another fiery mouthful.

Marchmont nodded. 'They put a lot of pepper in it so as to conceal the flavour of the meat. I'm afraid they're not very particular about what goes in.'

He had consumed his own pie ('eel, I think') in the way he did everything else – with great alacrity – and was now wiping his fingers on a kerchief.

'Well then,' he said, looking about him, 'I dare say you're in blunt after that bargain I got for your coat.'

'I've a few extra shillings,' I said cautiously.

'Perhaps you would care to chance it in a game? You could make good your losses from last week.'

He had recalled my story of the 'three-up'. I was reluctant to risk my money, but he was already striding off down a narrow lane. After turning this way and that we saw ahead a little court in front of the Brill Tavern, sequestered from the main thoroughfares on either side. A young lad, evidently keeping tout, was ready to whistle a warning, but then he seemed to recognise Marchmont and let us through. A gang of about fifteen young costers stood in a lively huddle, smoking, joshing one another and betting on the next toss. The ground before them was spangled with coppers, shillings and half-crowns: we had arrived in time for a big pot. Bets were being made and taken as rapidly as they could be spoken, and excitement thrummed amongst the little gathering. The street argot was the same I had queried the previous Friday at Montagu Square – *I'll try you a gen . . . flash it . . . say a rouf-yenep . . . say a couter . . . Cool him . . . I'm doin' dab . . . say net-yenep . . . say a gen* – but the talk went back and forth at such a pace I could barely make out one phrase in three. Every so often a raucous cheer would sound, a player would sweep up his winnings, and the betting would start again.

I glanced at Marchmont, whose eyes had assumed a kind of glassy absorption. He watched the gambling almost as if he were trying to commit the scene to memory. One of the group, a gangly, pale-skinned fellow with hooded eyes, had sidled over and appeared to be inviting us to lay a bet. Marchmont raised his eyebrows at me in an enquiring way. I was still cautious, having heard tales of men losing their earnings, stock money and even the coat off their back in less than an hour. So I paused for a moment, and said, 'Say a gen?'

'That's the spirit,' said Marchmont with a wink. I handed over my shilling, and the lad made a mark of it. Another flurry of betting followed. When the tossing began, I found myself, astonishingly, on a lucky streak. I bet 'tails' three times, and three times it came up. Emboldened, I raised my stake to a couple of shillings, bet 'heads', and won again. My good fortune had been noted by the regulars, who chaffed me good-naturedly and claimed I was an old hand at the game. It was only when I began wagering five bob on a throw that my luck seemed to turn, and as abruptly as my winnings had jingled in my pockets I now felt them emptying, until I was down to my last *couter*, then my last *gen*, then to my last row of halfpennies. At times I suspected a certain quickness of hand had determined which side the coin fell, but it was not enough evidence on which to accuse anyone – and I would not have dared to in any case. I had dropped about eighteen shillings when the tout's cry pierced the air – *Cool eslop!* – and the costers, pausing only to scoop up their coins, hurriedly dispersed down the various alleys off the court.

The reason for this sudden alarum became clear when two constables strode into view, by which time our gambling friends had scattered from sight – 'like rats up a drainpipe', chuckled Marchmont. It didn't take long to ascertain what *eslop* was back slang for. The afternoon was darkening grainily by now, and as we walked past, one of the policemen tipped his helmet and murmured *Guvnor*. It seemed there was not a soul in this neighbourhood who didn't know him. The thunderous wheel traffic of Euston Road could be heard as we headed out of Somers Town, and Marchmont suggested that I come to his office the next morning to dictate the day's report. He then asked me how I had enjoyed the three-up.

'Well enough,' and then told him how much I had dropped.

'And that was not all the money you lost today,' he said in a shrewd voice. I was not certain what he meant by this. He had come to a halt, and I saw under the gas lamp that his expression was watchful.

'That last house we visited on Hampden Street,' he said. 'The man we talked to.'

'The surgeon,' I said, nodding, though still in the dark as to his meaning.

'I saw you part with some money.' I heard reproof in his tone, and waited. 'What did you give him?'

'Not much. A few bob,' I shrugged. I didn't realise that Marchmont had seen this transaction, but I ought to have done: very little was lost on him. 'The fellow was near to destitute. He'd lost his wife and child –'

'You will hear many such tales of woe in Somers Town,' he said.

'You . . . didn't believe him?'

'Oh, I believed him entirely. That is not my point. Amongst such people you will achieve nothing by alms giving. Our mission is to observe, to enquire, to report. It is not ours to interfere.'

'To interfere?' I said, baffled. 'But – is it not our common duty to save a fellow from starvation?'

Marchmont was shaking his head. 'Mr Wildeblood, listen to me. There is but one way of relieving the poor, and that is by developing their powers of self-reliance – not in treating them like helpless children and offending their independence of character. I know whereof I speak. You will only demean a man by giving him money, and bankrupt yourself to boot.'

'I'm not sure –'

'You can do nothing,' he cut in. 'Do not attempt the impossible.'

It was the first time I had heard him express this curious philosophy, which I later came to know as *laissez-faire*, and I felt more surprised than offended. There seemed to me a contradiction in his thinking. At his encouragement, I had just lost a substantial sum in a low game of chance, yet now here he was dealing out stern advice as to why I should not waste a few shillings on a poor man. Wasn't the former actually a more reprehensible way of dissipating one's money than the latter? I should perhaps have had this out with him right there, but in those days I was still young, and impressionable, and held Henry Marchmont too much in awe to provoke.

3
In the Brill

You have perhaps been wondering about my name. Wildeblood. It carries a touch of the outlandish, does it not, a name you could imagine gracing a soldier, or an adventurer, or a desperado of some sort – not the unillustrious son of a provincial chemist, at any rate. But this was the name handed down to me, and I hope I have not dishonoured it. My father, Thomas Wildeblood, whose family came from Swaffham, in Norfolk, showed great promise as a student of biology, and eventually won a scholarship to Oxford, where his talents flourished. He might have achieved further distinction there, I believe, had not the untimely death of his own father obliged him to return home and take over the running of the family pharmacy. He inherited a little money, enough to be able to marry, and later to purchase an old rectory in a village a few miles south of the town, where I was born in the November of 1860.

Being their only child I was much loved by my parents, though I hesitate to call my boyhood a happy one, at least in the conventional sense of the word. I recall long periods of time spent in my own company, so fearful was my mother that I should mimic the habits and manners of children of an inferior class to our own – or should I say *her* own, since she was peculiarly conscious of being higher-born than our neighbours. She came of a notable family in Norwich whose money was gone, and because she felt keenly those narrowed circumstances she was the more likely to remind people of her genteel origins. My father, sadly aware of her prickly excess of pride, strove to ensure that I would not inherit it. He encouraged in me his own sensible moderation and a spirit of gregariousness, but a child brought down at dinner to meet the friends of his parents will discover that, however eagerly displayed, his lisping charm soon palls on adult company. Best were the days when he took me with him to the shop in Swaffham, and, while he was engaged with his staff, I was let loose to roam the large storeroom at the back, gazing up at the serried rows of dusty bottles and bulbous flasks, with their esoteric labels and rebarbative odours. The whiff of a sharp chemical will instantly transport me back to those days. If my father was at leisure he would sometimes take me out in the fly to spend an afternoon in the meadows hunting butterflies, whose names he would recite to me with the reverent tenderness of a poet.

These treats, alas, were rare, for he was much occupied with business and I was set to work every morning under my mother's tutelage: she had taught me to read, including some grammar and scripture, for neither of which I exhibited any aptitude. (My poor mother. Unlike my father, she was devoutly Christian, and fostered hopes that I might one day be a bishop!) Having parsed screeds of prose or recited however many psalms till midday, I could do as I wished, so long as I never trespassed beyond the fence at the bottom of our long sloping garden. How did I fill those hours? Let me own my favourite means of diversion. One was to examine the natural world, such as the swampish green depths of our pond, where fat goldfish nosed through the murk and frogs bulged pensively; or to watch a spider patiently wrapping a fly in its delicate cocoon of death. One preoccupation, though, actually had the virtue of a purpose. In the long corridor upstairs a deep alcove was set into the wall, so deep that I could fit myself within it and, silent as an icon in its niche, sit at drawing for hours, a block of paper against my knees. I must have been a bloodthirsty little cuss, for the only thing I ever drew were pictures of historic battles – bodies sprouting arrows from the longbows at Agincourt, kilted Highlanders brutally dismembered at Culloden, Nelson dying on the deck at Trafalgar – which I would then present before my mother's doubtful gaze. It was only when she heard the twang of the Swaffham commoner in my voice – I have it still – that my mother realised her efforts of social engineering had been in vain. Denied playmates of my own age, I had fallen back on the company of the only other people about, that is, our servants – John, the old gardener, and his wife Eliza, our housekeeper – whom I came to regard as my dear friends. My only friends. Even now, to think of their endless good-humoured patience with me, the brat of the house, squeezes on my heart. It will probably not strike you as any great privilege to be ferried about in a wheelbarrow, or to stand close to a bonfire and feel its crackling heat on your face, or (what would have horrified my mother) to be allowed to scrape the remains of Eliza's custard bowl. But such were they to me. I find that I miss the sight of that garden more than any other.

Belatedly, then, my mother acceded to my father's long-urged belief that I be sent to school, where I should not only benefit from a more rounded education but learn how to associate with a rowdy class of strangers, otherwise known as my peers. You would perhaps expect from the above narrative that I had grown up cosseted and unaffectionate, a creature ill-equipped for society at large. Cosseted I had certainly been (school offered a savage corrective there) but I was not unaffectionate. On the contrary, when affection at last *did* come, from a source other than my own limited sphere, it acted upon me with an exigency that was tidal, overwhelming and calamitous. I had not the buoyancy to cope with it, and, struggle though I might, it pulled me under as irresistibly as a vortex. How should I have known that I was so susceptible, I, who had been raised with no keener sense of worldliness than that fat goldfish?

But I must not run ahead of myself. The establishment to which my parents consigned me was an 'academy' in Berkshire – I shall not lower myself to name it – where young gentlemen, according to its brochure, were 'liberally boarded, fairly treated and carefully instructed in every department of useful education'. Ye Gods! It was, as I have implied, no refuge for a tender soul, especially one who talked in a bumpkin accent, had played little sport and knew almost nothing of tact, or of cunning. Institutional discipline was absolutely foreign to me, and harsh treatment came oftener from the masters than it did from the school roughs, most of whom I dwarfed. (I inherited tallness from my father, and bless him for it.) I will not exaggerate: this was not Dotheboys Hall. For most of my time there I passed beneath the notice of anyone who might really have harmed me. But to live in such an atmosphere, where gratuitous humiliation might be visited upon you at any moment, where kindness was mocked and sentiment was outlawed – it must leave its mark. I have never known a place to have been designed around such a contemptible purpose: to wit, the destruction of love. But such was the lesson the inmates had to learn.

Do you begin to see the violent contrasts that have dictated my life's course? The first ten years of my boyhood a strange idyll of loneliness, sequestered from company and raised like a greenhouse flower. The following eight, confinement to an institution whose brutish habits I was singularly ill-prepared to combat, let alone embrace. The 'useful education', I should add, barely deserved the name. The grammar and scripture I had learned by rote at my mother's side bequeathed me an advantage in those classes, but in all else, save the study of art, I was a poor student. When I ought to have been studying the collapse of the Hanseatic League or grappling with the mysteries of Euclid I was instead dreamily engaged in sketching a cumulo-nimbus, or a gnarled oak, or a plough horse. (I had graduated from the carnage of battlefields by then.) How soon my father came to acknowledge that his son would never emulate his academic distinction I cannot say. Oxford was wildly out of the question. But in the light of what followed, that may have been one of his more easily borne disappointments.

Having furnished that introduction to Somers Town and the working people of the Brill, Marchmont did not accompany me there again, though he indicated through Rennert that he would continue to take particular interest in my reports. I could not be sure if this directive was due to the guvnor's old affection for the neighbourhood or his indecision regarding my employment there; after all, I had no training in journalism, and had been hired only on the recommendation of my godfather.

So I pounded the Somers Town streets on my own, as doggedly as any vendor or hawker. Straight away I marked a difference in people's reception of me, and twigged the advantage that Marchmont's company had bestowed. His natural ease with the class we were studying was plain: they opened their doors to him, and were willingly drawn into conversation. I had no such talent, and the faces that met me were stiff with suspicion. I was a stranger, an interloper, and they knew it. Some believed I was a *slop* (the police), some a clergyman (my mother should see me now). Others accused me of being an agent of *the work'us*, which I later discovered to mean the St Pancras Workhouse. I had seen this dismal edifice up on King's Road, and was careful not to mention the place in conversation, if I could help it. However desperate people might be, there still flickered a thin flame of comfort if a meal, or a few pence, or a bed for the night was secured. But the workhouse represented the absolute terminus of hope, the staging post on a journey whose end was death. To those who mistook me thus I might have been an emissary from hell.

Even at those houses where I was admitted, danger often lay in wait. One man, a builder, unemployed and reeking of drink, had no sooner invited me in than he asked for money. I had begun to explain that payment was not part of the transaction when he stood up and called for his 'friend'. This turned out to be a brawny, ill-kempt, mean-eyed woman, who listened to the man's grievance before reaffirming his demand to be paid, 'or else we'll break your fuckin' neck'. I vacated the room speedily, their oaths ringing in my ears as I hurried down the staircase. I thought I had reached safety on the street when, of a sudden, a crash sounded behind me: a chamber pot had just missed my head and cracked on the pavement. (I later recounted this to Marchmont, who said, 'Ah, the bitter cry of penurious London,' and roared with laughter.)

I felt less inclined to be mirthful. The day's rounds were long, and they yielded scant reward. Incomprehension continued an obstacle on both sides: while I struggled with their language, *they* as often looked blank on hearing my country accent. How many times would I have to repeat a sentence before its meaning registered on a face? It disheartened me to be making so little headway, and I might have abandoned the work in despair had not a certain incident changed my fortunes entirely.

It was a market day in the Brill, about three weeks after my venture with Marchmont, and I was mooching about the stalls. It was a morning of weak sunlight and scudding clouds, and the narrow streets were humming with trade. A young fellow brushed past me roughly, and as I turned in expectation of an apology I felt the merest flutter of a hand at my back, and another man in a corduroy coat and billycock hat was passing briskly in front. It took but a few seconds to realise my purse had been prigged, and the fellow striding away was the culprit. 'Oi!' I cried, and without even bothering to look round Billycock broke into a run. I started in pursuit, dodging this way and that between traders and market folk, keeping in sight my light-fingered quarry. Light-fingered but not, I should say, light-footed; I was gaining on him, and his swift glance backwards told me he knew it.

Having got to know the layout of the Brill, I was confident there was no street he could hide down which I hadn't visited myself. On that score I was wrong. My pickpocket had taken a sharp left off Aldenham Street and then disappeared; retracing my steps I saw that I had run straight past an alley, so narrow I had to turn sideways and move crabwise along. Blackened walls reared massively overhead. I reached the end, and found a court with turnings to the left and right. Both vistas looked absolutely identical, canyons of three-storey housing whose dilapidation was severe even for Somers Town. I cocked an ear, and thought I heard footsteps echoing down the right-hand passage. I hurried along, less sure of myself now. The noise of the Brill was gone here; the crowds, not more than a minute behind me, had vanished. I came to another crossways, and stopped. I had entered a labyrinth, it seemed, and saw how easy it might be to lose oneself. Just as this thought struck me I turned into a blind court, and there was the thief, leaning against a wall with his billycock hat, a smile and – behold! – three of his mates. They all wore billycocks and cord trousers, like a uniform. I looked behind, and a fourth mate had somehow appeared to block my retreat. I remembered at this moment Marchmont's warning against 'going off the main drag', and imagined the regretful shake of his head on hearing this latest folly of mine.

These fellows had been standing around, as if in wait for me, and on my appearance the tallest of them took a step forward. 'You're a ways from home, ain't yer?'

I stood there, tensed, sorting the odds. I said nothing.

'Lost yer pipe?' he said in the cawing cockney of his tribe. He tipped his hat off his brow to take a closer look at me. 'I'm bound to tell yer, there's a charge for them who's crossin' this bit o' property. A tax, y'know?'

'How much?'

He paused, frowning at my literal-minded question, then looked round at his fellows. One of them sniggered. 'Let's see 'ow much you've got in them pockets,' he continued in an equable tone.

'My purse is gone,' I shrugged. 'Your friend there stole it.'

My interlocutor turned to the pickpocket and said, in a sarcastically quizzical voice, 'You 'ear that, Tig? This young shaver reckons you lifted his *purse*.' He mimicked this last word in my own accent – not badly.

Tig, though his shoulders still heaved from his recent sprint, brazenly shook his head. 'Dunno nothin' about it.'

I made a *tsk* sound in deprecation of this lie. The tax collector, pulling a face as if to suggest *he* didn't believe Tig either, spoke again. 'Well . . . someone's got to pay the piper, and if you ain't got the blunt, we'd best be 'avin' yer coat.'

Not again, I thought. I'd become rather fond of my pilot coat, and didn't relish explaining its loss to Marchmont, or to Rennert, for that matter.

'You can do as my shirt does,' I replied. The phrase had leapt off my tongue without troubling to consult my brain. To clear up any doubt, I fastened the top button which had come unloose. He stared at me, disbelieving; then he nodded at the man beyond my shoulder. I heard his step, and sensed that an arm would be locked around my neck at any moment – but I was prepared. As his shadow lurched in the periphery of my vision I had time for a quick backward glance that allowed me to thrust my elbow smartly into his face: I heard a snap as it connected with his nose, and then a yelp of pain as he staggered back. Hurling him aside I bolted back down the passage whence I had come, with the others at my heels. If I had the advantage in pace, they had the bulge on direction: I wanted to be getting out of there, but my pursuit of the thief had enfolded me in a warren of alleys and lanes I had no clue as to navigating. On, on I flew, hare-like, with the hounds grunting behind me. Every time I thought to reach the main drag I seemed to turn down another nameless way, and might have continued indefinitely had not my frantic zigzagging been suddenly checked. A coster's barrow, emerging from a side passage, caught me shin-high and I went for a purler across the cobbles.

My first thought, before the pain of landing had registered, was: *done for*. The coster must have been in league with Tig & co., for he had timed his intervention perfectly. Dazed and prostrate, I felt his hand at my shoulder, but the voice that accompanied it was almost clucking with concern. I was lifted tenderly to my feet, and the hand was now brushing the dust and grit from my coat. He was a tallish fellow of about my own age.

'. . . comin' through faster 'n a squirrel with a nut,' he was saying to himself, in a musing undertone. Then I realised he was talking to the donkey that pulled his cart. I had just glimpsed his face – sallow, with very dark eyebrows and a patchy stubble on his jaw – when clattering footsteps announced the arrival of my pursuers. I looked around at the coster, who seemed to take in at once what had prompted my violent haste.

The man who had demanded my coat now addressed this coster as 'Jo'.

'Gaffy,' replied Jo in greeting. 'You're in a hurry.'

Gaffy (if such was his name) nodded at me. 'Been after this feller. A regular trosseno – owes us blunt.'

'A trosseno?'

'Yeah. Owes owt-gen, exis-yenep. And cool what he done to Jags.' He jerked his thumb at the one whose nose I'd bloodied; above the hand he held to it his eyes were bright with malevolence.

Jo shot me an appraising look. 'Sez you're a bad'un as owes 'em two-and-sixpence. Know anything about that?'

I shook my head. 'I never met them before. That one –' I pointed to Tig – 'lifted my purse on Phoenix Street. So they owe *me*.'

Jo's gaze held mine for a moment – a decision had to be made – then he heaved a sigh. 'I reckons you's mistaken, Gaffy. Cool him, 'e's no cross-chap, just a gent as got hisself lost. So let's be on our way.'

'Now, Jo,' said Gaffy, his voice still reasonable, 'I tumble to you, but do the 'andsome . . . you'll not put yer bones up for this one.'

'Oh, won't I?' said Jo, a challenge in his voice. At this, one of the gang took a step forward, and the air felt abruptly charged with intent. Jo didn't appear to move a muscle, but by some quicksilver feat of dexterity he now had something in his hand, and it glinted with warning. Gaffy stared hard at him.

'Sorry to see you do that, Jo. Pullin' a chive on us. Very sorry, indeed.'

'Yeah, well. You takes another step, I mean it, you'll know what sorry is.'

Gaffy took a long moment to consider, then jerked his head at the others, who slunk back the way they had come. The last to withdraw, he scratched with his index finger just below his eye, a gesture directed at Jo. Then the court was empty but for us two, and the donkey. I examined my palms, smarting where I'd skinned them on falling.

'Scraped the enamel?' said Jo, peering at them. I nodded.

'I'm really most obliged to you for – . . . I'm David. David Wildeblood.'

Folding his knife with a magician's little flick, he pocketed it and took the hand I had proffered. He looked amused by this formality. 'Gianpaolo. People calls me Jo.' He squinted at me, and looked thoughtful. 'I seen you before, ain't I?'

'Have you?' I couldn't imagine where.

'*Yeah* . . . I seen you with that well-togged spark – the fat feller. You was eatin' hot 'taters one market day, few weeks back. That was you, wunnit?'

I agreed that it was. But his memory must be uncommonly good, I remarked, for I had only spent a morning and afternoon with Marchmont in the Brill.

'Old Jo's got all his buttons on!' he crowed delightedly. 'Old' Jo, as I later discovered, was nineteen, angular in face and frame, and dressed not unlike my recent adversaries, in cords and loose jacket, but with a merchant sailor's navy cap instead of a billycock. His eyes were as dark as raisins, which sorted with his Italian name. He had turned round his cart, and was coaxing his donkey likewise, when he looked back at me. 'Comin' along?'

I followed him, not sure of ever finding my own way out of there. As we walked, Jo smoked from a clay pipe with a long stem, and seemed happy to answer whatever questions I put to him. He had been a coster lad since the age of fourteen. No, he wasn't an Italian, but his mother and grandparents were, they'd come from over there, like, oh, years ago. He'd lived in Somers Town all his life, knew every last stone of the place, and he had never been out of London. He wrinkled his nose when I suggested he might one day visit the land of his forefathers ('Bit far, Italy, I've 'eard' was his considered view). He knew a few words of Italian, from his mother, but she had died when he was at the Ragged School. His father had been a coster and would have taught him the trade, but he had also died when Jo was only a 'nipper'. So who had raised him? His sister, he said, who once worked as a slummy – a servant girl – but now earned pin money from sewing and such.

I asked him about the brigands we had lately encountered.

'Gaffy and Tig I know a bit. The others weren't from around here – a Shoreditch mob, p'raps. You wants to be stayin' clear of 'em.'

'I'd be glad to,' I said. 'You always carry that on you?'

He nodded. 'Cool the curve on the 'andle.' The blade was again in his hand without my having seen him produce it. He stared at it proudly. 'Bought it with the first blunt I ever made – from a hawker in Bow. It's me little pal!' It occurred to me that he and his little pal had quite a reputation: those brutes had thought better of tangling with him.

By now we were back in the Brill, and Jo was calling to this or that coster as they passed by one another. 'Aw'right, Jo!' a flower girl would say, and Jo would return her greeting with a cheery halloo. Everybody appeared to know him, and like him – and it was this last perception that sparked an idea in my head. We had reached Chalton Street, his regular pitch, and he was setting out his trays of onions, cabbages, turnips, watercress and whatnot. As he did so, he began calling the prices of his wares in a sing-song voice ('Fresh woorter-cressis, penny a bunch') which I now noticed was rather hoarse for one so young.

'Yeah, well,' said Jo, shrugging, 'I'm shoutin' all the day long, so it gets a bit throaty. And some days you lose it altogether . . . *ca-a-a-m on, fine ripe plums, penny a pint.*'

'You make a good living, then?'

'Not so dusty.'

'Are you ever at leisure?'

'Course. I always 'ave time for cards and skittles – ask anyone!'

'Because I was wondering . . .' and I proceeded to explain my work for Marchmont's paper, and how difficult I had found it, first in securing the people's trust, and second, in comprehending the peculiar tongue they conversed in. With a local favourite at my side, however, I was sure they would greet my enquiries more amenably, and perhaps open up about their occupations, earnings, lodgings and so on. 'It would be such a very great help to me,' I said, and having conceived of this arrangement it felt suddenly vital to me that Jo agreed to it. He didn't say anything, but the way he gazed off into vacancy indicated his doubts about the enterprise.

'Of course, I'd be willing to pay you . . . for your time . . . if that's what –'

He asked me how much; I really had no idea what to say, and plucked a number out of the air. Jo tipped his head sideways, considering. 'Well . . . every little 'elps, as the old lady said when she pissed in the sea.'

I looked at him uncertainly. 'Does that mean you will?'

He laughed, and made a satirical little bow. 'At yer service. But it won't be every day I can spare – I 'aves to keep the old moke in work.' I understood him to be referring to his donkey. At that moment two old women were hovering about his stall, waiting to buy, and Jo gestured to me as though to say, *Back to business*. I thrust out my hand again, eager to have his pledge. He took it.

'Tomorrow, then?'

Jo gave me a little wink. '*Yeah* . . . I'll be 'ere, don't you worry, Mr, er –' He had forgotten my name already.

'David. It's David,' I said. But he had already turned away, too busy pitching his wares to the crones for any further conversation.

4
Doogheno or dabheno?

Jo proved as good as his word, and in the following weeks I came to regard his presence at my side as a kind of lucky charm. He would either take an hour off in the forenoon, leaving his barrow with some street Arab, or else, if he wasn't too fatigued, go door-to-door with me after market hours. It wasn't all plain sailing – wariness and hostility still glinted in some of the faces that answered my knock – but most of Somers Town's tenantry seemed quite willing to cooperate once they realised I didn't pose a threat. Nearly all of them knew Jo by sight, and must have assumed that I was just his eccentric friend from out of town. When we had completed a day's stint, I would repair with Jo to a taproom or eating house and ask him to clarify this or that bit of local slang I might have misunderstood.

It is true what they say about language: the best way to master it is to be always amongst those who speak it. Even without Jo's help I was becoming more adept in the argot simply by constant association with hawkers, costers, shop people. I noted down fewer phrases now, because so many of them had taken up residence in my head. Whenever I played at cards in the Brill Tavern I could understand the chat flowing across the table and no longer puzzled over the stakes – *couters* and *ewif-gens* and *flatch-ynorks* were common currency to my ears. I believe I can identify the moment I became a 'natural' speaker of back slang. There was a phrase Jo unfailingly used when talking to his fellow costers about the market. If he arrived late and found his mates already at work, or if he happened to encounter someone he hadn't seen for a while, he would say, 'A *doogheno* or *dabheno*?' meaning, Is it a good market or a bad one? One afternoon, arriving at his stall later than usual, I said, almost unknowingly, 'A doogheno or a dabheno?' Jo, who had often chaffed me for my awkward mimicking of coster language, didn't even look up from peeling his apple. 'Dab,' he said, with a little shake of his head. He hadn't even noticed! I took great heart from this.

My continuing investigation of the neighbourhood, on the other hand, gave me no such cause for cheer. That the dwellings of the poor were insanitary, and overcrowded, and unsafe, I already knew. That they were home to all manner of vice and degradation I also knew. What shocked me was discovering how much the tenants *paid* for the privilege of living there. Renting was the custom, of course; the vast majority had no home to call their own beyond the next Monday, when the rent fell due. In the dosshouses – 'the kips', Jo called them – rooms were occupied on a relay system with two or three tenants using the same bed for eight hours at a time. It was squalid, and cheap. But weekly renters paid between 2s 3d for a single room and around 7s 6d for a three-room lodging. By my calculation, this meant that a quarter and sometimes as much as half of their income was eaten up by rent. Something was amiss. When I came to London in search of a berth I had seen lodgings in Marylebone and Regent's Park offered for 8s per week – but those were decent, comfortable places, with views, not the broken slums of Somers Town. Even my modest abode, in Islington, was but seven shillings a week for rooms that looked almost luxurious in comparison with the tenements on Clarendon Street or Hampden Street.

It became clear that somebody must be making a great deal of money on property that was barely fit for human habitation. But when I asked this or that tenant who their landlord was, I was returned only blank looks. Nobody knew. All that concerned them was being able to pay 'the man' when he came round on Monday morning. Jo was no more able to enlighten me on the subject than anyone else.

'I pays me sister, an' she pays the rent man. That's all I know about it.'

'Yes, but who *owns* the property? There must be a landlord.'

He shrugged; he was not in the slightest bit interested. I had not yet seen his home, so it was impossible to judge whether his rent was fair or not. Eventually, after some pestering by me, he agreed to find out the name of his landlord. In the meantime, I continued to butt my head against this wall of ignorance. When I did chance to meet an actual rent collector, he swatted me away as he might have done a louse (an insect which, by the way, enjoyed a widespread occupancy in the tenements of Somers Town). 'What's it to yer?' he replied on my asking his employer's name. I explained my work on Marchmont's paper, and why the local rents were of interest to me. Before I had even finished speaking he turned his back and walked off. I suspected he would not take kindly to being followed.

Late one morning, towards the end of March, I was going door-to-door, alone, at the north end of Charrington Street when a second-floor window opened and a man stuck his head out. 'Oi!' I retraced my steps along the terrace. It was a house I had already knocked at and received no reply. The man was leaning on the sill, watching me. 'You the feller who's been askin' about the rents?'

I admitted that I was, and he told me to 'wait there' before disappearing from the window. Moments later the front door opened and a thickset man with close-cropped hair issued forth, his air slightly too forthright to make me feel quite at ease. Without Jo for company I was still conscious of my standing as an intruder; I had not yet suffered bodily harm by 'poking my nose' into others' affairs, but I knew that it entailed some risk. The man was on his doorstep, candidly scrutinising me. I decided to put on a bold face.

'I had assumed the house was empty – nobody answered my knock.'

'It's a Monday. I thought you might be the rent man. I won't answer when he calls.'

'I see. You have an objection to him?'

His lips emitted a little sardonic *pfff*. 'I've an objection to payin' for a house that's fallin' to bits.'

I nodded. 'Would you allow me to . . . look for myself?'

He stood aside, and I passed up the step and into the hallway. The man, whose name was Brampton, led me upstairs, where he lived with his family on the second floor. They rented two rooms, one a bedroom for him and his wife, another for his three young children – a relative luxury. This was a Regency terrace which, through neglect and overcrowding, had forsaken its erstwhile gentility and joined the downward slide towards slum living. Mr Brampton was bitterly aware of this decline, pointing out the damp which had seeped upwards through wainscoting, old plaster and exposed laths. He was a carpenter by trade, and took particular offence at the jerry-building that had kept the place upright for the last few decades.

'Look 'ere,' he said, showing me a great bulge in the front-room ceiling, as if some giant had sat upon it and left an impression of his backside. The window frames were rotten, and the sills bowed from the damp. 'I ain't payin' 'em another penny till I see the repairs they promised. I've been at 'em for that long, an' still there's nothing done.' I could not doubt the justice of his complaint, but on whom devolved the responsibility of this repair work? Who was the landlord?

Brampton sighed in weary disgust. 'Who knows? The people I've dealt with are from the vestry – they run the place.'

He was referring to the St Pancras Vestry, a cabal of local tradesmen who supervised the district's amenities and services. I had already gathered it was not a popular administration.

'A bunch of blackguards, every damned one,' said Brampton with feeling. 'They let these houses sink into rack and ruin. They refuse to build baths and wash houses, they ignore the broken drains. They'd see us drop dead before they did anythin' to help.'

'Who is the head of this vestry?'

'Moyles. Walter Moyles. You know him?'

I shook my head.

'He runs the Victory pub. A loud feller, lots of big talk – you know the sort.' I could see a vein throbbing in Brampton's neck; just the mention of this individual was darkening his mood. He watched me as I scribbled down the name in my notebook. 'What, you takin' up the matter at the Vestry Hall?' I heard the sardonic note in his question.

'I'll do my best,' I replied. He squinted at me, apparently surprised that I was speaking in earnest. 'In the meantime I will be reporting on this negligence to my guvnor.'

'Good luck,' he scowled, though I sensed an interest beneath his gruffness. That he had no expectation of receiving help acted as a spur to my better instincts. As we took the staircase down to the hall, I noticed that the walls had been recently whitewashed, and remarked on it to him.

'That's their idea of improvement. No matter as the houses are filthy and unsafe – they just patch 'em up with whitewash and cheap wall-paper.' He stopped me on the stair, and held up his finger – which he then proceeded to work into a crack in the wall. The damp plaster crumbled away like cheese. When he spoke, his tone had changed to simple resignation.

'A whited tomb – that's all this place is.'

Jo had heard of Moyles, and he knew the Victory off Phoenix Street – there wasn't a pub in Somers Town he didn't know. But when I suggested we paid a visit there, he pulled a face. I was given to under-stand that it was not an establishment famed for its friendliness, and strangers asking questions were likely to be given short shrift. Oh, so he was afraid to accompany me there? I said, teasing him. But Jo didn't respond to my light-hearted tone.

'Trust me, all the villains in town drink there,' he said, unsmiling.

So I decided to seek out Moyles in his official role as head of the St Pancras Vestry, which assembled (I learned) every other Friday at midday. The Vestry Hall itself was located in a draughty red-brick building on Pancras Road whose shabby, ill-repaired aspect was surprising; municipal bodies generally convened amidst pillared marble and panelled oak, places far superior to the neighbourhood whose affairs they managed. Later I realised that most vestrymen resided far outside the boundaries of Somers Town, and that consequently there was no urgency to make pleasant a venue so little used by any of them. The hall today held a large crowd, nonetheless, as Jo and I found seats, and a mood of expectation was abroad. However supine and ineffectual the vestry was reputed to be, their parishioners were out in force. What they hoped to gain from it I couldn't immediately say. The board, seated behind a long desk on the rostrum, were an unlovely collection of paunchy, squirish businessmen who either talked amongst themselves or were absorbed in reading a newspaper. As we settled, one of their number was droning through a report apparently with the express intention of putting his listeners to sleep.

At my side Jo yawned silently. Once the droner had finished there came a long sequence of footling exchanges about the difficulty of calculating the vestry's income and expenditure: nobody could supply a definitive view one way or the other. Now *I* yawned. The business had snailed along for a further half-hour when Jo, unexpectedly alert, nudged me out of my stupor. 'That's 'im,' he whispered, as a tall, powerfully built man with Gladstone whiskers and a casual air of command rose from his chair. From the long table a secretarial voice piped up: 'Quiet, please, for Mr Moyles, who is going to speak on the subject of drinkers' and publicans' rights.' Moyles proceeded to talk, in a booming and faintly Irish-accented voice, about the latest proposals by Parliament to have pubs closed on Sunday and to prohibit sales of alcohol to children under the age of thirteen. The first, he said, was an outrage upon the liberties of the working man, who should be allowed to drink whenever he wanted. The second proposal was just as wrong-headed, he claimed: better that children should carry out beer and spirits from the pub than their mothers, 'who would otherwise be neglecting their duties in the home'.

This counterblast against Parliament encouraged a good deal of nodding and 'hear, hear'-ing amongst the vestrymen, but down in the stalls you could feel a distinct restlessness. Private interest masquerading as piety was not what they had come to hear. At the front a man stood up and said, without preamble, 'When do you intend to address the maintenance problem? We got people living like pigs in a sty just cos you lot dither over paying for repairs.' His words were met with a kind of supportive lowing from the assembled, amongst whom I now spotted Mr Brampton, my aggrieved carpenter from Charrington Street. Moyles, in the firing line, looked unruffled, and turned the question over to a Mr Porteous, head of the vestry sanitary committee. This rotund gentleman replied that he had got wind of 'irregularities' in the drainage system and the upkeep of certain houses, and had consulted the landlords about 'setting things right'.

'So the matter is in hand?' said Moyles. Porteous replied that it was, and Moyles nodded his satisfaction.

'But when are these repairs to be made?' persisted the man in the stalls.

Moyles spread his palms in complacent surrender. 'That will be taken up with the individual landlord.' More grumbling met this, which I took as my cue. Jo looked startled as I stood up and cleared my throat.

'Sir, if that is the case, may I suggest that you and Mr Porteous lose no more time in improving the dilapidated condition of the houses on Hampden Street?'

Moyles stopped and squinted in my direction. He looked confused. 'I beg your pardon? What has this to do with the present business?'

'I believe it is quite pertinent. You indicated that the matter of repairs is to be decided between the head of the sanitary committee, Mr Porteous, and the landlord. In the case of Hampden Street, sir, that landlord is *you*.'

There was a moment of stunned silence. Moyles's features had passed through confusion and were darkening towards displeasure. 'That is a private matter —'

'On the contrary, it is a public matter,' I replied. 'I visited the Records Office on Euston Road only yesterday, and found your name entered as landlord on properties in Hampden Street, in Drummond Crescent, in Clarendon Square. That being the case, I see no reason why you should delay in addresssing the legitimate complaints of your tenants.'

By now the rising jeers of indignation amongst the parishioners had swollen into a roar of mutiny, drowning out the vestryman who was attempting to call the meeting to order. Catcalls shrilled in the air, feet drummed on the wooden floor. RESIGN! RESIGN! came the cries, and Moyles, no longer sure of his authority, had retreated to his place at the desk.

What happened next bore the appearance of spontaneity, and I flattered myself to think that my little intervention had provoked it. But the likelihood was that someone had planned it all along. An enterprising coster had wheeled a barrow up the aisle to the front, just as if it were another market day and the Vestry Hall his favourite pitch. Mr Porteous, now apoplectic, stood up and shouted, 'Get that thing out of here!' which was probably the wrong note to strike in the circumstances. Cackles honked through the room. People stood up and joined the coster at his impromptu stall: Brampton yelled out, 'You want to know what it is to live in a pigsty? – here!' and within seconds a missile sailed over the heads of the vestry board and landed *splat* against the wall. A tomato. The next instant a chaotic fusillade of fruit and vegetables coloured the air, and Porteous and his colleagues were shielding themselves from the onslaught. I thought of the village stocks, back home, where wrongdoers used to offer target practice. Moyles, I noticed, was the last of them to hold steady at the rostrum, glowering like Zeus about to hurl his thunderbolt at the impious mortals; but instead he was forced to duck another tomato, and, dignity forfeit, he scrambled off himself.

A few minutes later the double doors of the hall creaked open and – *cool eslop!* – a file of policemen poured in. The crowd's blood was up, however, and having seen off the vestrymen they faced about and started pelting the blues. Jo, laughing hysterically, grabbed my sleeve and cried, 'Davie, let's skedaddle!' We ran, half crouching, down the side aisle, dodging between the bobbies and a vegetal barrage that showed no sign of drying up. As we gained the outer entrance we saw more of them hurrying towards the hall, and Jo, who nursed an instinctive loathing of the police, steered us into the scuff of locals who were streaming up the narrow lane north towards Camden.

Once we were clear of the place he turned to me. I heard amusement, and the smallest scintilla of admiration, in his tone. 'What a riot – an' you *started* it!'

I reflected with satisfaction – I confess it – on my endeavouring to uncover the identities of the landlords, though it had required no great feat of investigative brilliance. Anyone could visit the Records Office and ask to consult the dusty old ledgers, which catalogued (in very close print) the leaseholds of every house in the parishes of St Pancras and Somers Town. Anyone could – but it seemed that nobody had. When my eye first fell upon *W. W. Moyles* written in a clerk's hand I felt surprise; then, as his name began to recur on one page after another, my blood quickened. Did anyone else suspect that this gentleman – his name painted on the Vestry Hall's board of honour – was also one of the neighbourhood's most prosperous slumlords? He was not alone, either; several of his vestry colleagues, including Mr Porteous, were listed as owning property in the parishes. No wonder they had looked so pleased with themselves: the racket must have seemed foolproof. The tenant would make a complaint to the vestry about the squalid condition of his lodgings, or some other nuisance – vandalism, violent neighbours. The vestry would pass on the complaint to the sanitary committee, who in turn were supposed to enforce the landlord's duty to make his property safe. But if that landlord *was himself* a vestryman and sanitary inspector, and could keep his anonymity intact, he would effectively be rendered unaccountable. A tenant might as well present his grievance to the pigeons that strutted up and down the Brill.

I felt my chest puffing like a turkeycock as I hurried down to Salisbury Square to file that day's report. If I could get the story down by four o'clock they might use it for publication the next day. And what a story to tell! As luck would have it, Marchmont himself was in the building that afternoon, and without even pausing to talk to the copy-taker I made a beeline for his office. His door was ajar, and I saw Rennert talking quietly and rather gravely with him; he stopped very suddenly at my knock.

'Mr Wildeblood,' said Rennert coolly. Marchmont looked at me but said nothing, and I had an intuition that the two of them had been arguing: the air in the room seemed to bristle around them. 'You have a report, I presume.'

'Indeed', I said, 'and I have taken the liberty of bringing it directly to you.' I proceeded to recount the tale of my enquiries at the Records Office, my discovery that certain vestrymen were secret rack-renters, and how my questioning of same had caused a small riot at the Vestry Hall today. As I talked, I began to sense that my narrative was not inducing those gratifying expressions of outrage and disbelief that I had anticipated; in fact, neither one of my listeners betrayed even a moment's surprise. On my first referring to Moyles I noticed Rennert shoot a look at Marchmont, who sat at his desk as still as a pasha.

I stuttered a little towards the end, at a loss to explain the apparent indifference with which my disclosures had been received. Marchmont drummed his pudgy fingers on his desk for a few moments, then turned his gaze on me.

'And this is what you expect us to run in tomorrow's edition?'

I shrank from the sneer in his voice. 'I assumed it was fit to print –'

'Fit for whom? We are not some fly-by-night satirical rag, sir, nor are we in the business of Radical pamphleteering.'

'He has defaulted in his duties as a landlord – I would say there is a case for him to answer.'

'Oh, you would?' His tone had turned sarcastic. 'And who, pray, would you hire to prosecute such a case when it comes to court? Do you imagine we can afford to lock horns with the likes of Walter Moyles?'

'If we felt sure that we could win the case –'

'But we do *not*. Moyles has made a great deal of money from his property speculations. How would a man accumulate all that without knowing precisely how far he can bend the law? Only think of the people he consorts with – Members of Parliament, magistrates, churchmen. He has so many of them in his pocket it has started to bulge.'

I was surprised. 'So . . . you knew that Moyles owned these slums? You always knew?'

Marchmont looked at me pityingly. 'Mr Wildeblood, there is very little that happens in this city I do not know about. It is in the nature of my work. So I would consider it a mark of respect if henceforth you refrain from carrying in these old scraps and laying them at my feet like some befuddled bloodhound.'

'Sir, I confess I'm dismayed by your –'

This was too much. Colour sprang to Marchmont's cheeks as he stood up and hissed, 'How dare you persist in bandying words with me! Must I remind you of our relative stations in this office? – *I* am the editor, without whom this periodical would cease to exist. *You* are a stripling, an apprentice. You are of no more account than that crossing sweep on the Strand – and I might add not *half so useful!*' He had paused, trembling with anger. Rennert had also stood up and without a word was ushering me from the guvnor's office. I felt myself blushing violently, too shocked to offer any kind of apology, even if one had been required. As Rennert marched me through the office I felt all eyes upon me. I had heard of Marchmont's Vesuvian explosions of wrath – they were a kind of legend amongst the staff – but it was still an astonishment to find how suddenly he could be provoked. I was trying even now to determine exactly what my offence had been.

We had reached the top of the narrow stairwell above the entrance hall when Rennert spoke, in a voice that sounded kind.

'You should take the rest of the afternoon off. We will start again on Monday morning.'

'I'm sorry to be the cause of – I believed I had hold of a good story.'

'You were mistaken,' he said, and I noticed then how weary he looked. One of his eyelids was twitching with fatigue. 'He has a short fuse. You ought not to take it in a personal way.'

I nodded, perhaps too complacently, for he seemed to take my equanimity as a sign that I was not altogether chastened by the recent dressing-down. 'Allow me to give you some advice,' he said. 'For your own sake, don't ever raise Moyles's name in his hearing again. It may not go so well for you a second time.' He had reverted to his brusque, impersonal manner, and I arranged my features into an expression of penitence. I would remember his advice, not because I thought it might save me, but because it was too mysterious to ignore.

5
Leary man

The following day's *Chronicle* ran a report of the tumult at the Vestry Hall, and, moreover, it named chief vestryman Walter Moyles as landlord of several slum properties in Somers Town. The anonymous reporter argued, with a distinct note of relish, that this intelligence 'should shame Mr Moyles and persuade other such landlords to address the scandalous disrepair into which so many of their properties have fallen'. So it seemed that not every newsman in London was cowed into silence by Moyles's reputation. I arrived at the office on Monday morning well aware that Marchmont would also have read the *Chronicle*, but I had sense enough not to raise the subject with him again. In fact I kept clear of the guvnor altogether. Something about his behaviour that afternoon – his disproportionate fury at my harping on the Moyles story – had put me on guard, and Rennert's subsequent warning only strengthened it.

That morning I was emerging from Salisbury Square when I noticed two men loitering on the other side of the street, watching me. As I walked west up Fleet Street I felt myself being followed, and I knew enough of London's underworld by now to be prepared for a dodge – a 'pull' – whereby a sharper, operating in concert with one or two others, would select from the crowd a likely person to rob. It was a common hazard: the sharper would approach his victim, often a countryman new to town, and engage him in conversation. Having drawn him into a pretence of friendship (the tricky part) he would then invite him to a taproom or gambling den he knew. Once installed there, he and his confederates would ensure that their gull was carrying money on his person and, either with loaded dice or marked cards, relieve him of it.

So when I paused outside a printer's shop and stood at its angled window, I was not surprised to catch in the reflection those same two men, dawdling close by. Indeed, I felt an odd satisfaction in spotting them, having suffered the indignity of daylight robbery twice in my

first month in London. I was becoming wise to the ways of the underworld. Rather than prolong the suspense of being followed, I decided
to wait for them to approach me – which they duly did. They were a
respectably attired pair, which in itself constituted a clue: sharpers knew
that anything too 'flash' would encourage suspicion. This pair both
wore dark frock coats and bowlers, like City gents, and their demeanour
of professional competence was, I had to admit, artfully managed.

'Sir,' said the shorter one, 'I wonder if you might have a moment to
spare?'

I turned and straightened, considering them. The idea of twitting
them was irresistible. 'Gentlemen,' I said, looking from one to the other,
'I should spare us all some time and effort if I tell you straight away
that I have but a few pence in my pocket. I have no watch or jewellery
of any sort to tempt you further, and I am too attached to my coat to
let it out of my sight. I regret to shun a stranger's overtures of friendship, but you must understand that they are wasted on me.'

The pair made a show of looking nonplussed by this; perhaps they
had not expected their dodge to be rumbled so precipitately.

Again it was the short, well-spoken fellow who replied. 'I think there
is a misunderstanding. My name is Clifford Paget, and this gentleman
is Mr Alfred Kenton, who has recognised you –'

'I am not the gull you suppose me to be,' I said, interrupting him,
'and I have business at hand. So if you would kindly excuse me –'

Paget held up his hands in a placating gesture. 'Hold, sir, please. We
are no magsmen! I write for the *Chronicle* – you perhaps read my article
about the riotous assembly in St Pancras Vestry Hall last Friday?' That
stopped me. As I looked at them more closely, the man continued. 'Mr
Kenton here runs the Union for Rental and Sanitary Reform. He said
it was your questioning of Mr Moyles that started it all off.'

'How do you know?' I said.

'Cos I was there,' Kenton replied. 'I seen you around – you're Jo
Garrett's mate, ain't yer?'

'Mr Garrett also obliged us with your employer's address. So you see,
Mr Wildeblood, we are here only to discuss a matter of mutual interest
with you.'

'I do beg your pardon for –' *mistaking you for a pair of sharpers*, is
what I meant but could not bring myself to say. 'But why did you not
simply call at the office? I would have received you there.'

Paget's smile was unillusioned. 'What? A writer from the *Chronicle*
calls in for a chat? Your guvnor would throw a fit.' We walked on a

little, then turned off Fleet Street and found ourselves in Temple Gardens, overlooking the Thames. Paget was a plumpish fellow, in his forties I supposed, with a bulbous nose, piercing little eyes and a quick, assertive manner. Kenton was older, grey-whiskered but hale-looking, and sported a livid bruise across the bridge of his nose. He caught me looking at it.

'A memento from the Vestry Hall. I caught a hot'un from the slops after we'd been pelting 'em'. His tone suggested he would not be reconciled with them in a hurry.

'That brings us to our purpose,' said Paget. 'Mr Kenton and I have been allies ever since the *Chronicle* took up the scandal of the Somers Town rents, which, thanks to your timely prompt last Friday, is in the news once again. Knowing of your sympathies we hoped you might lend your support to our campaign.'

'Campaign?'

Kenton drew from his coat a handbill, such as one sees distributed outside music halls, and passed it to me. But it was no bill of entertainments.

PAY NO RENT

to unscrupulous landlords who flourish and grow fat on your misery and degradation. It is time to stop the exploitation of the poor, who are poisoned by their thousands in vile, unhealthy slums. The government has failed to help you. It is time to help yourselves.

A MASS MEETING
will be held in
TRAFALGAR SQUARE, W.
on Sunday, 7 May, at 3 p.m.
Speakers will address the meeting in support of the No Rent Campaign.

I looked up to find Paget's gaze on me. 'A worthy cause?'

'Without a doubt,' I replied. 'But I'm not sure how I can help . . .'

Kenton cuffed the pamphlet I was holding. 'You can start by distributing these. We intend to rally all the poorest neighbourhoods in the city – Clerkenwell, Whitechapel, Limehouse. The Nichol, of course. We'd be most obliged if you agreed to be one of our agents in Somers Town.'

Even as I nodded my willingness to help I sensed trouble ahead. Taking the sheaf of bills Kenton handed over, I warned myself that Marchmont should not get wind of my involvement.

'Are you quite confident that people will come? For most workers the day of rest is rather precious.'

'What have they got to lose?' said Kenton. 'People are sick to death of living in slums, despite what the government thinks. And once they know that the landlord they have been making rich is a peer of the realm, or a lawyer, or a churchman – well, I believe they will come, and protest.'

'A churchman?' I said.

He nodded. 'We have discovered that the head of the Ecclesiastical Commission owns a whole swathe of slum property.'

'Hard to believe, isn't it?' said Paget in answer to my look of incredulity.

Kenton now took out his pocket watch and checked the time. 'Gents, I must press on. I have a revolution to organise! Mr Wildeblood –' he offered me his hand – 'let us hope that together we can do some good.' He nodded in a familiar way to Paget, and walked off.

'Capital fellow, that,' said Paget. 'Most energetic. You know his actual job is as a textile dyer? All the campaigning and proselytising, that's just what he does in his spare time.'

'He seems very . . . fervent. Who produces these?' I held up the pamphlets.

'He does – from a small printing press at a house in King's Cross. Near to where he keeps his wife and six children.'

'Good Lord,' I muttered. 'Just like my guvnor.'

'Ah yes,' said Paget, with a distant smile, 'and how is dear old Henry?'

I looked at him in surprise. 'You know Mr Marchmont?'

'Know him? I used to work with him. I suppose you might say we were friends.'

'But . . . no longer?'

'No,' he said crisply. 'Though I still follow his career with interest. He's done well for himself – better than I would have anticipated.' His words had been hung out like bait, and I rose to them rather defensively.

'Why would you say that? You think him an inferior writer?'

'By no means. Henry's one of the very best on Fleet Street – as he himself will tell you. No, I am only surprised by his . . . prosperity. I gather he now keeps a rather grand house in Marylebone.'

'It's a comfortable place,' I said warily. I couldn't tell if he was angling for malicious gossip or simply wanted to determine how much I knew. Loyalty kept me close-mouthed.

'He was not always so provident,' said Paget, which piqued my curiosity the more. We had begun walking back towards the Strand, and still I said nothing. I sensed him looking sidelong at me. 'Ever been gambling with him?'

'Once or twice. And yourself?'

He gave an abrupt laugh. 'Oh yes. We used to play, years ago – mostly whist, billiards, a bit of roulette. My word, he did love to gamble! He was very nearly bankrupt because of it. Did you know?'

I shook my head.

'He went abroad to escape his creditors. His wife – poor Jane – answered the door to them. He might have gone to prison for it, but somebody must have bailed him out.'

'Who?'

'Possibly his father-in-law. Jane comes from money. He owed a good many people.'

'Including yourself?' I said, wondering.

'Oh, no. Our parting was to do with – something else. It goes back to the time he conceived his Poverty Map of London. Perhaps you know it?'

I admitted I had seen it at Marchmont's house. 'It looked very much a work in progress.'

'I dare say. Henry invited me to assist him on it, seven or eight years ago. He had such high hopes of it – we both did. He once told me it would be his monument . . .'

'It may yet be,' I said, stirred to loyalty again by his doubting tone.

Paget gave a conceding shrug that showed his double chin. 'Of course. And if ever a man were capable of doing it . . . Well, his memory is prodigious. He could tell you how many knife grinders worked in Camden, or chair menders in Whitechapel. He knew the names of pubs in streets you'd never even heard of. Population shifts, living standards, every sort of data. He had it all up here.' He tapped the side of his head. 'But – it was doomed! There are too many contingencies for such a project to be realised. Not even Henry could keep up. London is always in flux – one might just as well try to grasp hold of *that* –' He gestured at a cloud of dust that had billowed grittily from behind the wheels of a passing omnibus. The Strand's mid-morning traffic was on a thunderous crescendo. We had both raised our voices to be heard.

'And that was your disagreement?'

'We had many disagreements,' he said. 'The one which finally sundered us was of a more, ah, philosophical nature.'

We dodged past carriages around St Clement's and gained the picturesque quiet of Wych Street. Paget had left the story of his estrangement interestingly poised, but something had diverted his attention as we walked along the cobbled street of ancient shops and rickety theatres. 'I love this old street. Most of it's been here since the seventeenth century.' I looked around at its timbered, higgledy-piggledy buildings, at the casement windows tilting towards each other like neighbours talking across a street. Its quaintness reminded me a little of Norwich. 'And you know the great pity?' Paget continued. 'It will all be gone in a few years' time. This street, Holywell Street – the entire neighbourhood I shouldn't wonder.'

I looked at him in puzzlement. 'What d'you mean, gone?'

'Demolished. They are planning a vast boulevard, on the Parisian model, to run straight from here up to Holborn. It is meant to be the centrepiece of a "new London", the capital city of trade and empire – a big opera house, grand restaurants, shops finer than Regent Street's. Some will make a fortune out of it, you can be sure. But little old streets like this –' he paused to look about – 'they will go. Commerce dictates it. If our omnibuses cannot trundle down them, well, what use are they? The council argue these streets have outlived their purpose, so down with 'em!'

'That's a sad prospect,' I said.

'It's the future, I'm afraid. London is going to change out of all recognition. There is too much money around to prevent it.'

'How do you know all of this?'

Paget allowed himself a mock-affronted laugh. 'My dear sir, I am a journalist. I am paid to know such things, or else to know the people who will tell me.'

As we continued west I pondered the consequences of a gigantic swathe of streets and lanes and houses being torn up. Could any good come of it? 'I suppose the slums around Clare market will be earmarked to go.'

He nodded affably. 'You do well to look on the bright side! Yes, those fetid dens won't be missed. But such clearances themselves present a difficulty. In planning this spacious imperial city they neglect something vital. If you pull down the houses of the poor, you have to find new places for them to live.'

'Mr Marchmont told me the very same thing,' I said, recalling our conversation that day in Somers Town. 'Perhaps you and he are more like-minded than you know.'

I had intended the remark light-heartedly, but Paget did not smile. After a few moments he said, 'I would not wish to consult him on the matter of the poor.'

'Why not?'

His gaze now met mine. 'Because we should always be at odds. You will discover – perhaps you already have – that we live in an age of conflicting attitudes to poverty. On the one side are those who denounce the practice of charitable giving. They believe that the poor must help themselves, must struggle on as best they can – that is the laissez-faire view propounded by Marchmont, and, I should add, Mr Gladstone's government. Then you have the well-meaning but meddlesome evangelicals who give assistance with one hand and a biblical pamphlet with the other. It is a philanthropy which reduces the pauper to the level of a needy child, and tends to the prestige of the givers more than the plight of the receivers. But surely *you* have talked with Marchmont about this?'

'We have. When I brought up the Moyles business he gave me quite a hot time of it.' An image of the guvnor's furiously congested face startled my mind's eye.

'I've no doubt,' said Paget. 'D'you know, we once had a conversation about Somers Town, he and I. The housing there has been in an atrocious state for years, and knowing of his association with the place I asked him what he would do about it, given the chance. I shall always remember his reply. He said, "As little as possible." *As little as possible*. I think they were nearly the last words we ever exchanged.' He had been talking almost to himself, his expression lost in brooding.

There was a pause before I said, 'So what *should* be done about it?'

'I don't pretend to know. But one cannot simply stand by and let the place go to rot. Property has its duties as well as its rights – do you not think so, Mr Wildeblood?'

By now we had reached Covent Garden, and were being jostled on all sides by costers and draymen and flower girls. Their whistles and cries, dinning about our ears, relieved me of the obligation to reply. This was just as well, because I felt that whatever I said would be construed as a rebuke to Marchmont. On our brief acquaintance I liked Paget, but I did not want him to assume I was his ally. There was also the difficulty of answering the question satisfactorily. Yes, property did have its 'duties' to the less fortunate; but how far did they extend, and who would ensure that they were adequately carried out? I had believed that councils and vestries would be the agents of change, but since the revelation of the rents scandal I had seen how erroneous that thinking was.

We had reached a corner somewhat beyond the bustle of the market, and Paget had stopped to buy a newspaper from a street vendor. I heard a nearby church bell strike the hour.

'I must be off,' I said.

'To the good people of Somers Town?'

'Yes, I'm going door-to-door with Jo – my associate.'

'Old Henry keeps you hard at it . . .'

I shrugged agreement, and hoped he wouldn't say anything else about my employer. I had heard more than enough in the last half-hour.

'Perhaps I will see you at Mr Kenton's meeting,' said Paget, offering a chubby hand. 'Here's to the No Rent Campaign – and the deuce take Moyles and his cronies!'

It was a busy day in the Brill, and as I walked towards Jo's stall I saw him talking animatedly with a young woman, dark-haired and sallow-skinned like him. I had an inkling that this might be his sweetheart, and held back from approaching them. I had noticed the puzzled looks we sometimes got during our perambulations in the neighbourhood, though Jo never seemed to be embarrassed by my company. Nevertheless, on this occasion I thought I should wait until he saw fit to introduce me, and I took myself on a roundabout stroll for twenty minutes.

On my return I found him alone, paring an apple with his beloved knife and eating slices off the blade.

'Doogheno or dabheno?' I said, and he laughed. My back slang still had the power to amuse him.

'Doogheno.' He picked up another apple from a tray, rubbed it on his sleeve and tossed it to me. We stood there, chewing away. I considered asking him about the young woman I'd seen, but a kind of shyness held my tongue. He was rather private when it suited him, and he had never suggested that I visit his lodgings. At first I thought he might be wary of inviting a stranger to his home, but then I realised that the idea had simply never occurred to him. He had his work, and he had his life, and the two did not overlap.

As we did our door-to-door, I handed out the 'No Rent' leaflet to certain tenants we encountered. A few people expressed interest in attending the event, having heard about the commotion at the Vestry Hall. One man said that the landlords 'had it comin''. This was the spirit of resistance Kenton was hoping to inflame. More often than not, though, they would stand at the door and look at the leaflet with bovine indifference. Some immediately handed it back without comment, which struck me at first as rather boorish. But after the third or fourth time this happened Jo explained: they couldn't read. So I asked Jo to recite the salient points of the leaflet on the doorsteps. It sounded more persuasive coming from him, but I found he soon tired of repeating himself; he was not one of nature's born revolutionaries. I suggested that we finish for the day, and he nodded his eager agreement.

We walked back to Chalton Street, where he kept his pitch, just as the last stallholders were packing up for the day. The pavements were slimed with green, leaves and spoiled fruit that would rot for weeks after. I was humming a street tune that had recently lodged in my head, and Jo, hearing it, took over. It was one of the longer canting songs, yet he seemed to know every line of it, and as he came to the final verse we improvised a harmony.

> But mummery and slummery
> You must keep in your mind
> For every day, mind what I say,
> Fresh fakements you will find.
> But stick to this while you can crawl
> To stand till you're obliged to fall
> And when you're wide awake to all
> You'll be a leary man.

Once we had finished cackling, I asked Jo what a *leary man* might be. 'Leary?' he said. 'Well, it's like . . . fly. Wise to things, as such . . . the sort of feller you're *not*,' he added with another laugh. I tried not to look hurt. Jo began another song, this time one I didn't know. His voice was as clear as a choirboy's, and he finished on a trilling note that seemed to please him. But when I asked him to sing another he shook his head.

'Nah, I 'aves to rest me pipe for tomorrer,' he said, giving his throat a little tweak. Jo dreaded losing his voice, for he thought a coster at his stall should always be pattering. 'But if you likes I can take yer to an h'establishment round our way where they's singin' all night.'

'I would like nothing better,' I replied, for lately I had felt a loneliness dogging my steps as winter turned to spring, and the city streets began to swarm with people. London crowds conspired to make me feel more of a solitary than ever. I was indeed 'wide awake to all', as the song had it, but it was melancholy to feel that I was also invisible to them. Jo said that I should meet him tomorrow evening at a public house called the Rainbow on Clarendon Street, and as I jotted the name in my pocketbook he gave a little chuckle.

'You an' yer notes. No wonder people mistakes ya for a slop!'

I had never before been invited to drink with Jo outside of what he sardonically called 'h'office hours'. For all the time we had spent in one another's company I knew very little about his personal life. I would meet people in the Brill who were familiar with him, but since Jo knew just about everyone it was difficult to distinguish who his particular friends might be. The April evening was mild as I walked down the Pentonville Road, past the looming silhouettes of King's Cross and St Pancras and into Somers Town. The Rainbow was a solid old place at the north end of Clarendon Street, and I could hear a chattering hubbub through its open door. I ascended a narrow staircase to the pub's upper room where, through the thickening veils of pipe smoke, I met a lively crowd of men, women and girls, all with pewters and glasses before them.

I had shouldered through to the bar, and was peering in a distracted way over the heads of the drinkers when I heard a familiar voice behind me.

'Cool this feller – like a tart in a trance.' Jo stood there, smirking, flanked on either side by a young girl. Both were pert-looking creatures with hair brushed straight over the brow – the factory-girl fringe – and they giggled like hyenas at his droll description. 'Nell, Nora,' he said, with a flourish of his hand, 'this is Davie, me pal up from the country.'

'How d'you do?' said Nell, or Nora.

I made a little bow, which set them off on another fit of giggles. I felt that I had to rise above my introduction – surely I cut a figure more imposing than a bumpkin? – but could think of nothing to say. Meanwhile Jo, in response to one of the girls, was standing drinks; he passed me a pewter of ale, and pointed his thumb towards a fellow who was settling at a piano hard by the bar. The evening's entertainment was about to begin. There rose a sudden anticipatory hum in the room as the pianist plonked out a few broken chords; then he was off, tinkling forth a selection of popular melodies. Now and then a man would be persuaded to stand up and sing the lyric, which, however indifferently performed, would be boisterously applauded. It was a striking phenomenon, this public hunger for music; I had never seen working people enthuse over anything so passionately, not even drink. As alcohol gradually overmastered inhibition, the singers came forward more readily. The evening looked likely to degenerate into a raucous free-for-all, but just then the pianist rose from his stool and held forth his palms in a hushing gesture.

'Is Roma in tonight?' he asked, scanning the room. His eyes alighted on Jo, who lifted his chin in reply.

'Servin' at the bar downstairs.'

The pianist asked for someone to go and fetch her, and, indicating his reluctance to play until that lady arrived, he slouched back on his seat and filled his pipe. A few minutes later his request was answered, and a dark-haired young woman entered the room, the same one I had seen Jo talking to on Chalton Street. Up close she – Roma – was rather striking, her pale forehead contrasting with very pronounced eyebrows in the Italian style; her eyes, bluish green, were misted with preoccupation, which the wide curve of her mouth seemed to accentuate. It was a strong physiognomy, beautiful in its way, but not one, I thought, to be easily moved to gaiety. She wore a dress of small-patterned print, with an embroidered linen collar. I wondered how long Jo had known her, and on what footing their relationship stood.

She was now in animated converse with the pianist, whom she seemed to be upbraiding for this frivolous summons. From his shrugging conciliatory manner (he too, I thought, was of Italian stock) it appeared he had got what he wanted. She moved to the side of the piano, and as she composed herself she caught no one's eye. The room had fallen quiet. She began singing, in a low, plaintive tone, 'The Bonny Light Horseman', which gathered in feeling as she proceeded. You could hear why her voice was so prized; it was at once husky and sweet, and whilst it ranged over the upper notes with ease you could hear a lost, lonely ache in it. At the song's conclusion a tempest of applause broke out ('That's something like, girl!') and the demand was raised for another. Roma acknowledged it with the merest twitch of her mouth, and, with a touch of perversity, she ignored the pleas for the music-hall standards and sang instead a short, mysterious ballad in Italian, or what I assumed was Italian. They cheered this one even louder when it was finished, for despite the unfamiliar words the meaning was in her voice, in a palpable warmth that spoke to the heart. The stamping and hoots and calls for more had no sway with her; she would not sing another. She lingered there for some moments, having performed a slow, grave bow to the assembled, as if to say, *I accept your thanks, and now bid you goodnight.* Then, with a brusque signal to the pianist, she made her way out of the room, deaf to the groans in her wake. I had never seen anything quite like it.

I sidled back along the bar towards Jo, who had been watching her performance with an air of nonchalant pride: he was impressed, but unsurprised. The two girls had drifted off.

'That was . . . quite something,' I said.

'Yeah. In good voice tonight, our gal.'

This affectionate moniker seemed to confirm it. 'So that young lady is your sweetheart?'

The mouthful of ale Jo had just taken exploded from his mouth in surprise. Spluttering, he stared at me, half amused, half appalled. 'You wot?! Oh, I've 'eard it all now –' He looked about him for a witness, but none was at hand. Still incredulous, he turned back to me. 'Sweetheart, my eye! That's me *sister.*'

'Oh . . . I'm sorry – I didn't –' I said, flustered.

'I said I 'ad a sister – d'ya not 'ear me?'

I was about to protest that he had never told me her name, but behind us the piano had started up again, drowning further possibility of talk. I could see Jo still shaking his head, astounded by the ignorance of his pal 'up from the country'. The musical entertainment continued at a roar, but my thoughts had gone elsewhere. I was wondering about Roma, about her singing, and her extraordinary air of self-possession. She did not look much older than Jo, so she must have been young indeed when she took on the responsibility of raising him. Perhaps that was why there had seemed in her expression something, not austere exactly, but – withheld.

It had occurred to me that Jo might, at some stage in the evening, deign to introduce us. As midnight came round and the pianist finally drew down his lid, the two of us descended the stairs to the main bar. Tables were being cleared and the more unruly elements turfed out. The dimmed gas jets and the clink of glasses on wood announced closing time. She was sitting alone at a corner table, her face a mask of absorption, and as Jo led me over I could see she was totting up the night's takings. She looked up as we approached, and her gaze met mine so penetratingly that I had to look down. Jo did a little caper in front of her.

'Smashin' turn that, tonight, Ro,' he said. 'This is David, feller I was tellin' you about.' From his sly smile I had a moment's dread that Jo was about to chaff me about my mistaking her for his sweetheart, but all he said was, 'Most h'enamoured of yer singin', 'n' all.'

She inclined her head, rather regally, in acknowledgement. 'Our mum taught it me, years ago,' she said. I heard a soft London twang that had not been discernible in her singing voice. 'So you're the feller who's been round the houses' – *owsers*, she pronounced it – 'asking about the rents and such.'

I admitted that I was. 'It's for Henry Marchmont's periodical.'

'I know, I've read it,' she said, and there came an elusive half-smile. '*The Criminal Classes of London.*'

'No, not "Criminal",' I corrected her, 'it's the *Labouring Classes.*'

'Oh, beg y' pardon,' she said, though I now sensed that her mistake was actually a little jibe. And I might have challenged her – why *criminal?* – if I hadn't felt so disconcerted by her knowing look. The unspoken implication was, *you understand what I mean, even if you won't admit it.* There followed some desultory chat between herself and Jo about what hour each would be repairing homewards; the latter declared his intention to 'make a night of it', which elicited an indulgent nod from his sister. I took this as the moment to withdraw, and bid them both good evening. Jo gave his usual cheery 'g'night'. Roma said nothing, but only raised a slow hand in farewell, or dismissal, which seemed to me the more likely.

6
An honest living

I was in the office dictating a piece about cats'-meat dealers one morning when Rennert stopped by my desk with a letter, addressed to *D. Wildeblood, Esq.*

'You ought to look in your pigeonhole more often. It's been there for days,' he said, his eye hovering quizzically over the envelope before he moved on. I was not inclined to check my pigeonhole for the simple reason that nobody ever wrote to me, but this one broke my duck in grand style: no wonder Rennert had looked curious. The creamy vellum envelope was embossed; within, the single sheet of paper I unfolded felt as crisp and unarguable as a royal summons. The discreetly printed address at its head – Kensington Palace Gardens – seemed to continue that illusion. Who would possibly know me there? The impressively exact hand, in brown ink, belonged to the private secretary of Sir Martin Elder: he wished to inform me that my company was requested for a dinner at Sir Martin's house, please to reply, &c.

I knew the name, though I had never met the man. A City banker of some renown, Martin Elder had known my father at Brasenose nearly thirty years earlier; a chance meeting at an alumni dinner had briefly renewed their friendship, and there must have been sufficient affection between them (or else strong drink had contrived a likeness) for my father to seek the honour of Elder's standing as godparent to his first-born. He had accepted, though aside from an infrequent exchange of letters with my father contact between him and the Wildeblood family was almost nil. He had never visited Swaffham, we had never visited London, and it was not until I was in my teens that I discovered I had a godfather at all. Circumstances had induced my father to write to him some months ago, requesting the favour of finding a situation for me in London, and thus came about my apprenticeship to Elder's distinguished journalist friend, Henry Marchmont.

I reread the invitation. The appointed dinner was for 19 April, which, because of my delay in picking up the letter, meant the date was rather more proximate than I had first thought. It was the next evening, in fact.

Shadows were lengthening as I stepped off the omnibus on Bayswater Road. The night sky was a blanket of indigo. Kensington Palace Gardens was cordoned off by a gatehouse, where I was obliged to explain my business to a guardian before I could pass through. The houses along this private tree-lined avenue were huge stone and stucco palazzi, each set back from the road behind a spiked palisade, and unlike any others I had seen in town – or indeed any others I had seen in my life. Sir Martin's, larger than its neighbours, loomed above a bank of elms. From its tall stone gate-piers, each surmounted by a carved eagle, a crescent path of gravel led round to the colonnaded entrance. It looked like an embassy or some important public building, and I had an abrupt intuition that I would be the only guest to arrive here by 'bus. As I was walking in, a man and boy, both in the shabby apparel of their class, were at work in the road, patiently shovelling horse dung into a cart; I supposed they would only be allowed to do so here under cover of night. The man raised his head on hearing my step, and I saw weariness dragging on his features.

I ought not have been surprised that the liveried footman who answered my knock was far better turned out than I was. ('The togs on 'im!' I imagined Jo declaring.) I had put on my one decent suit of clothes, but nervous examination of the jacket as I sat on the upper deck had revealed a telltale shininess at the elbows. My boots, which *ought* to have been shiny, were the same I wore every day on my tramps around Somers Town, and seemed to protest their fatigue. The footman and I walked, not quite abreast, across a hallway stunned with light from an enormous chandelier, its individual candlepoints doubled in the floor's gleaming marbled tiles. A wide gilt-framed mirror tracked our progress, reserving judgement. The dazzle of the hall gave way to a shadowed corridor, at the end of which another servant pulled back a door that opened to a vast drawing room. The crimson swagged curtains that reached from ceiling to floor gave the impression of a theatrical set, with thirty or so guests in converse, awaiting stage directions. The men were a loud lot, their voices pitched at a volume appropriate to their entitlement. The ladies provided a tinkling treble. None of them so much as glanced at me as I entered.

More liveried staff roamed about with drinks on a tray, and I took a glass, succour of the social castaway. Rather than drown in this flood of anonymity, I steered along the edges of the room, pausing to inspect the glazed oil paintings – of hunts and hounds, of bucolic scenes, of bewigged grandees – as if I were a seasoned gallery haunter. As the chatter boomed around me, I pondered the odds of spending an entire evening in company without once being obliged to speak.

A voice at my shoulder interrupted this reverie. 'You seem awfully fascinated by that.' I turned to find a young woman appraising me, head tilted to one side. She had an open, friendly face, pink-cheeked, snub-nosed, with piercingly blue eyes. Her blonde hair was tied back in a girlish bow.

I realised I had been staring at a portrait of a haughty-looking gentleman posed *à la mode*, a shotgun crooked under his arm and a shaggy hound at his feet. 'I've been making a keen study of all these paintings,' I admitted. 'It helps to have something to do when one doesn't know a single person in the room.'

'Well then,' she said pleasantly, extending her hand. 'Catherine Elder. Call me Kitty. But you must know Papa.' She gestured at the hunter figure I had been examining on the wall.

'That's Sir Martin?'

She looked puzzled by the question. 'Of course it is. If you don't know him, then what –' She stopped herself, perhaps aware that the question forming on her lips would sound discourteous. I hurried into an answer.

'I know *of* him. I'm his godson, you see – though I've never had the honour of an introduction. David Wildeblood.'

Her eyes widened in candid surprise. '*Godson?!* I didn't even –' She stopped herself again, blushing. 'Well, you must come and meet him.' And at that she threaded her arm through mine and walked me through the roaring throng. I felt relief inflate my chest; from being a forlorn solitary I could now hold up my head as companion to perhaps the prettiest girl in the room. She had stopped at a grouping of guests and, with a little widening of her eyes to me in reassurance, she tapped the shoulder of a man with his back to us. He turned, and as Kitty introduced us I perceived the likeness from his portrait; Sir Martin seemed too proud of his square jaw to allow a beard to disguise it. Narrow grey eyes were set deep under his brow, and there was a sportsmanlike virility in his bulk. What the painting hadn't quite conveyed was his tallness. He rose a good two inches above me. The hand he offered was dry but pawlike, with a prehensile strength.

'So we meet at last!' he said in a rumblingly deep voice, his gaze searching my face. 'Yes, I see your father in you. How is dear old Tom?'

'He's well, thank you, sir,' I replied, though in truth I didn't know. My father had not communicated with me since I had come to London.

'One of the finest minds I've ever known. He could have been, well . . .' Sir Martin seemed to consider a lost future, and then dismissed it. 'We were fast friends at college, he and I. You know, I have your father to thank for saving me.'

I tipped my head in polite enquiry. 'Saving you – from what?'

'From the Church!' he said with a disbelieving laugh. 'As a young man I once considered taking orders.'

'And now instead you just *give* orders, Papa,' said Kitty, seizing her moment with a little grin of delight.

'Ah, very good, my dear. Yes . . . it was my ambition to become an Anglican minister when I first went up to Oxford. Strange to think now,' he said, with the merest glimpse at his baronial surroundings. 'Tom Wildeblood showed me the error of my ways – and I was grateful to him.' There was meaning in his tone. I was now beginning to see how my father had ever presumed to seek a favour of Sir Martin, a man so very different from the general run of our acquaintance.

'And now Mr Wildeblood is your godson!' cried Kitty, declining to pursue the exact nature of her father's conversion. 'That makes us almost kin, doesn't it?'

'Not quite,' said Sir Martin with an indulgent chuckle. 'But you are welcome in our home, sir. Kitty, perhaps you would allow Mr – that is, David – to take you in to dinner. We shall talk again later,' he said to me, as another couple stepped forward to claim his attention.

We drew a little away from the throng. 'I'm afraid your father has burdened you with an obligation – I hope you don't mind.'

'Mind? Not at all. The men who usually walk me in to dinner are old and fat and limping with gout. You represent an improvement,' she said, with a candid up-and-down survey of me.

I smiled and bowed at her pale compliment. 'He gives many such dinners, then?'

She nodded tolerantly. 'I suppose he does, what with the charities and committees and so on. Tonight's is rather larger than we're used to.' She paused, and narrowed her eyes. 'Are you at one of the big houses?'

I looked blankly at her. 'I beg your pardon . . . ?'

'I mean, banking house. You do something in the City, yes?'

This misapprehension startled me. What moneyman of her acquaintance wore such second-rate togs, or boots with the dust of the street on them? 'Not I,' I replied with a short laugh. 'I work on a weekly paper, *The Labouring Classes of London* – perhaps you know Henry Marchmont?'

'But of course! Everyone knows Henry. He and Papa are very thick with one another. So . . .' she said, a new light of interest in her gaze, 'you're a *journalist*.'

'Not exactly. Mr Marchmont calls us his "inspectors". We go out gathering the information and report back to him – the job of writing it up is mostly his. So you see, he's the journalist, I'm just –'

'His errand boy,' she said, so carelessly that it could not have been meant to offend – but from overestimating me as a 'journalist' she had gone too far in the opposite direction. I only shrugged; it would have seemed conceited of me now to protest. At that moment someone announced that dinner would be served, and Kitty, heedless of her slight, invited me to accompany her. We passed from this vast room to another that was merely immense, dominated by a long mahogany dining table that flamed brilliantly with candelabra. As the begowned ladies and black-coated gentlemen settled themselves along the table's length, I found to my relief that I was seated right next to Kitty. And then I was plunged into dismay as I read the menu card, set before each diner's place. The catalogue of courses it described was literally more food than I would have eaten in a week, or perhaps a fortnight. Worse, it was entirely in French. Here and there I recognised a word – *caviare* I had heard of, and *saumon*, but I was at a loss to construe *tortue claire*, or *ris de veau*, or *tournedos*, or *andouillettes*. The arsenal of cutlery to be negotiated was equally inhibiting. I decided then that my best recourse was to imitate Kitty in everything she did.

At that moment, however, Sir Martin rose from his seat and tapped his wine glass to call for silence. His mouth was set in an austere slotted line, and when he spoke his voice was low and grave.

'Ladies and gentlemen, before we begin, it is my melancholy duty to report news that has lately reached us. I have learned that Mr Charles Darwin died this afternoon, suddenly, at his home in Kent.' He paused, and looked down the table. 'A great scientist, a brave social pioneer – and a loss to the world. I should consider it fitting if we honoured the gentleman with a toast.' Slowly, to the sound of scraping chair legs, the assembled rose to their feet, and mumbled in awkward echo of Sir Martin's baritone: 'Darwin.'

A silence, and then we resumed our seats. On my other side was a lady of extravagant circumference whose interest in the menu card, I sensed, was keener than her appreciation of the world's recent loss. I could not swear that I heard the lady lick her lips, but there was an audible purr of satisfaction as she laid down the card and looked about her. As the only guest not engaged in conversation I became, unavoidably, her object of study. She introduced herself as Mrs Abernathy, and gave me to understand that she was wife of the florid-faced cove diagonally opposite, the Right Honourable Member of Parliament, Augustus Abernathy.

'. . . and I suppose you know of Monsieur Charbonnier?'

'Ahm, no, I'm afraid not,' I replied, lost.

'Our chef for the evening!' she replied, tapping the card she had just been scrutinising. 'One of France's greatest. He came here some years ago from Paris – an exile from the war, you know.'

I did *not* know, either of M. Charbonnier's talents or of his exile. But my ignorance did not appear to have thrown Mrs Abernathy off her stride, for she was enlarging now upon the career of the Frenchman and his celebrated food. I was a diligent listener, though I could not contribute more than an encouraging *mm* or *really?* in between the lady's long swathes of monologue. Perhaps satisfied that she had had her say, and diverted by the arrival of the much-heralded 'cuisine', she eventually paused and asked me about my own dietary arrangements. Did I keep a cook?

'No, I – in truth, I don't have a kitchen,' I said.

Mrs Abernathy blinked at me, uncomprehending. 'Good heavens! No kitchen? Then you dine at restaurants?'

'Very seldom. I work in a neighbourhood that tends to favour public houses and cheap dining rooms. Most days I eat with a companion of mine at a baked-potato stall.'

Now she looked at me as if I had just coughed up a lump of gristle onto the table. Ironically, this reminded me of a recent occasion when I had done exactly that. Jo and I were sharing a meat pudding outside a shop on Ossulston Street. The offending lump I had bitten into was as tough as boot leather, and I had spat it out in disgust, much to Jo's amusement.

'You mean . . . you eat your dinner *on the street?*' Pity was grappling with horror in Mrs Abernathy's voice.

'It is no hardship,' I replied, deciding to sound cheerful. 'If I don't care for a baked-potato one day I can have pickled herring, or eels, meat pie, sheep's trotters, pea soup. There's always a great variety, you see.' She was nodding, rather worriedly, it seemed. It was quite possible she thought I was a derelict in disguise for the evening, and that her descanting on the majesty of M. Charbonnier's cooking might now seem unfeeling. So I quickly explained to her the nature of my employment, and the convenience of taking one's daily bread on the street.

'Somers Town, you say. I have heard – is it true? – the people there are terribly poor.'

'Yes,' I admitted, and Mrs Abernathy heaved a bosomy sigh of sorrow. 'Though I should say they would be surprised if they knew you pitied them. There is great companionship and kindness amongst the people. They take real pleasure in buying and selling, and they relish their food – when they can afford it.'

'And . . . if they cannot?' she said, sucking up a dainty spoonful of the soup – the *tortue claire*, I gathered – recently set before us.

'They starve,' I shrugged. 'Some have to survive on as little as four shillings a week. I did know an old lady –' I hesitated, and looked at my interlocutor. 'But perhaps you would prefer not to hear of such distress . . .'

'No, please continue,' she said earnestly.

'Well, I had interviewed this lady at her home – she earned a little money as a lacemaker, but one could see that her circumstances were dire. Her husband had been ill for a while, and was too old to work in any case. Some weeks later I visited them again, and found that the lady had died. I gather it was from the effects of malnutrition. The husband followed shortly after.'

'Oh! The pity of it,' cried Mrs Abernathy with feeling. Her tremulous note of lament alerted her husband.

'My dear?' he said, frowning across the table. She proceeded to repeat, with little sighs, the pathetic account of starvation I had just confided to her. Mr Abernathy listened gravely, then said, 'The lady ought to have applied to the workhouse. Then she and her husband need not have starved.'

The man seated next to Abernathy had been following the conversation, and spoke in a manner that recalled Mr Marchmont – that is, addressing no one in particular, but loud enough for everyone to hear. 'Quite right. They were undone by their own negligence. How can the state help people who won't help themselves?'

'Oh, Mr Lobbett –' protested Mrs Abernathy, but I cut in ahead of her.

'I happen to know why the lady didn't apply for help. In part it was pride – she had once known a more genteel life – but it was chiefly because the workhouse provided no accommodation for married couples. If they had gone in, they would have been separated. *That* was what they most dreaded, so the lady decided it was better to try and subsist on outdoor relief.'

Mr Lobbett, the ends of his moustache twitching, stared at me for a moment. 'It seems to me they had forfeited the right to be so particular. If people allow themselves to sink into destitution they must be prepared for the consequences.'

'That's harsh, sir,' said Mr Abernathy. 'Better provision should be made for the elderly. But your point is taken – where the vast majority of the poor are concerned, outdoor relief is wasteful. We must accept that there exists a whole underclass prey to vice and drunkenness and what have you – unfortunate, but there it is. This degraded element has to be prevented from infecting the rest of society, and the safest means of doing so is to create a place where they would be, as it were, quarantined. That place is the workhouse.'

Mr Abernathy's oration had silenced his listeners; one of them, a man with ginger hair and long whiskers, had been monitoring our conversation with noticeable interest. His watchful blue eyes were fixed upon me. In the little pause that followed Kitty leaned in our direction and said, with innocent gaiety, 'What are you all talking about?' The question was a cue, and raising my voice to a Marchmontian resonance I said, 'Oh, we have just been consigning the poor to oblivion. Whereas we once imagined that their plight was due to a lack of work, or low pay, or illness, or some other hard circumstance, it is now agreed that they are a dangerous class of criminal, and should be incarcerated in the workhouse. Very convenient, I should say!'

That secured their attention. Even Mrs Abernathy seemed to hear the satire in my tone, for she looked over at her husband for help in responding to this impudence. That gentleman's eyes were thin with displeasure. 'Do I know you, sir?' he said.

'I shouldn't think so,' I said pleasantly. 'My work takes me usually to the environs of Somers Town, where I am amongst people you would probably cross the street to avoid. Indeed, some of them are criminals, just the same as you would find in Bayswater and Kensington. But most, in my experience, are not. They are decent and hard-working and as innocent of vice as –' mischief prompted me – 'Mrs Abernathy here.'

Mrs Abernathy, who had food in her mouth, swallowed it very

quickly, alarmed to find her name suddenly conjoined with the character of the labouring classes. She looked again to her husband as the most in need of immediate appeasement. 'Augustus, dear – this young gentleman, um, works for Henry Marchmont on his weekly periodical – you know the one? . . .'

Lobbett, with a sneer in his voice, said, 'Ah. The popular press. Like the poor – always with us. I find myself increasingly at odds with the likes of Henry Marchmont. Can he not find a more edifying purpose in life than to sentimentalise the lower orders?'

Kitty allowed herself a theatrical intake of breath at this. 'Don't let Papa hear you speak ill of Henry. He is *revered* in this house.'

Lobbett gave a smile that did not travel to his eyes. 'Then in deference to our host, I shall say no more of that gentleman. But perhaps his acolyte here could explain to us the concept of the deserving poor. What *is* it that they deserve?'

A spasm of rage jolted me at this point, but I remembered where I was, and kept command of myself. 'I will tell you. They deserve to be free to enjoy their life, instead of worrying and struggling over the means to sustain it. That is the difference between the poor and the rest of us. We are at liberty to ask, "How do I wish to live?" The poor man only asks, "How can I keep myself alive?" If you had ever witnessed the sort of privations and desperate economies that go on in this city, at this very instant, you would not be tempted to wonder at what they "deserve".'

'Bravo, Mr Wildeblood,' cried Kitty next to me, 'that is well said.'

I tilted my head in thanks to her, though I could tell that approval would be in short supply across the table. Mr Abernathy was flaring his nostrils as if at a rotten fish, though the salmon with sauce mayonnaise on our plates seemed blameless. 'And who, sir,' he said, 'is to pay for this great scheme of improvement? We ourselves contribute to charities for the relief of the poor, but is gratitude their response? No, it is only complaint – about wages, about paying rent. Pauperdom is passed on, like a disease, and I say again, the best way to contain it is in the workhouse.'

'Well, on the matter of rents,' I replied, 'I have something that may interest you.' I fished out of my breast pocket a folded piece of paper and pushed it across the table towards him. He looked at this offering suspiciously, but took out his spectacles anyway and proceeded to unfold it for perusal. I added brightly, 'I should think the meeting will be greatly intrigued by your views.'

As he read the contents Abernathy's face stiffened with disdain. He looked up at me and, without speaking, handed on the piece of paper for Lobbett to read. The latter ran his eye across it, and coloured furiously. '"Pay no rent",' he quoted with a snort. 'I might have known you were in league with that rabble. This is insupportable. Sir, may I ask – what are you *doing* at this table?'

'The same thing you're doing,' I said, holding up a morsel of salmon on my fork. 'Grateful to be eating food of a quality and abundance that most people could scarcely conceive of. And enjoying company that's convivial –' I now looked from Abernathy to Lobbett – 'in the main.'

At that Lobbett snatched up his napkin and made to rise, but his movement of protest was stifled by a voice from the head of the table. Sir Martin, as if intuiting a potential outbreak of unpleasantness, boomed in Kitty's direction: 'Enjoying the salmon, my dear?'

'Yes I am, Papa,' she called back.

'I hope you don't mind that it's served with the head.'

Kitty glanced down at the cloudy-eyed fish, then smiled at her father. 'No, not really – so long as they don't serve the chicken that way.'

Sir Martin laughed loudly, and one by one everyone else did. The gathering tension suddenly dissolved, though for the remainder of dinner neither Abernathy nor Lobbett deigned to talk to me. Mrs Abernathy, caught amidships between a disobliging stranger and an offended husband, kept her conversation to a purse-lipped minimum. It did not trouble me. Kitty, oblivious to the chill from across the table, beguiled the time with merry accounts of her horse riding and theatregoing whilst yet more courses came and went. That she was heiress to the vast wealth around us did not appear to have affected her at all; there was no condescension or haughtiness in her manner. We chatted away as though we had known one another for years, and I liked her for it.

I had stopped eating by the time the second pudding was served ('Mm, *chartreuse de fraises*!' crooned Kitty), and feeling my stomach roil and swell at the unaccustomed volume it had to accommodate I was reminded of another of Jo's phrases. He often talked of dinner as 'doing the tightner', and I was about to relay this titbit to Kitty for her amusement when Sir Martin's major-domo hurried in and whispered agitatedly in the ear of his master. Sir Martin's saturnine expression did not change as he nodded to the man, rose from the table and walked to the end of the room, where he threw open the double doors overlooking the back garden. He took a step out onto the terrace before seeming to recall his responsibility as host.

'Ladies and gentlemen – my apologies,' he said. 'I have been informed that an intruder has been sighted in the garden.' A quavering murmur of shock escaped one or two of the ladies present, and Sir Martin held forth his palms in a mollifying gesture. 'There is no cause for alarm. My staff are dealing with the matter.' But whether he trusted them to do so was uncertain, for he once again stepped out into the night. His guests, glancing at one another in confusion, looked momentarily stunned. What was the etiquette for such an occasion? After a few moments, two men rose at the far end of the table and disappeared after Sir Martin; others began to follow their lead, and, prompted by curiosity more than obligation, I also stood and headed for the open doors.

Out on the flagged terrace the night was still, and the expansive garden, a few steps below us, was steeped in shadows. Sir Martin was in urgent converse with one of his staff – a gardener, it seemed – whilst those guests who had boldly poured out now hung back, unsure of what they were supposed to do. 'Outrageous – the damnable nerve of it!' I heard someone mutter behind me, and someone else mentioned a recent newspaper report of housebreaking in the area. The light from the dining room carried only so far onto the lawn, beyond which all was a moonless black. This was suddenly illumined when, from the room above us, an auxiliary bank of gaslight flooded down; it revealed to us a pair of servants who had been poking around in the bushes and, beyond them, an untidy heap of rags underneath one of the elms. 'What's that?' a voice asked. It was too far away to tell, until, without warning, the heap began to rise, provoking a small 'oh' of fright from a lady beside me. The rags had weirdly resolved themselves into a hag-like figure which had, it seemed, been crouching within the dark. Now its – his – hiding place had been exposed, and he was on the move, though not very quickly. He carried a sack on his shoulder.

'Over there!' someone cried, and as the figure scuttled behind the trees Sir Martin and several of his dinner guests set off in pursuit. One of them was holding a storm lantern.

I found Kitty at my side. 'He must have climbed the wall at the back,' she said. 'They come in from the park.'

'"They"?'

She shrugged. 'Housebreakers, I suppose. The wretch is for it if Papa gets his hands on him.'

More of the men were descending from the terrace onto the lawn, scenting drama in the air. One fellow, sweating and puce-faced from drink, had thrown off his coat and was leading a group in the direction of the trees. He bellowed back to his companions, 'Let's chase the rogue down!' and someone mimicked the parp of a hunting horn, to much laughter. I too stepped down to the lawn, velvety under foot, and began following the impromptu posse of stalking males. In the distance I could see Sir Martin's advance party fanning out in a line. I didn't give much for the trespasser's chances with this pack on his heels. All that had saved him from capture so far was the poor visibility; the swinging lantern was not luminous enough to scatter the black-blue shadows. Its narrow blade of light must have made a lucky stab, however, because a cry suddenly went up, 'That's him!' – and a figure, silhouetted against the bushes, was moving, in a laboured, half-crouching run, towards a passage at the corner of the house from where I presumed he had come. Another gardener stepped in the way of the fleeing man, and both fell in a heap.

Whatever pain the intruder had felt was immediately compounded by a savage kick to his gut from the beefy, red-faced fellow who had discarded his jacket. 'That'll serve you, you filthy beggar!' he cried. The leaders of the hunt party closed in on the scene, Sir Martin foremost amongst them, his face eerily lit by the lantern.

'That's enough, Douglas,' he said sharply to the aggressor, who had just delivered another kick to his quarry. Crumpled on the ground, the man was revealed under capture as more pitiful than menacing. He was perhaps fifty, a low, shrunken-looking character whose clothes were patched and worn; his demeanour was that of a derelict, not a housebreaker, and it seemed to have punctured the giddy mood of excitement. What was he doing here? Sir Martin was addressing the same question to him, and received a muttered reply.

'Speak up, now. How did you get in here?'

The man, breathing heavily, raised his head and pointed to the door he had been making for: the tradesmen's entrance. As his face turned to the light I felt a jolt of recognition. It took me a moment to realise that it was the fellow I had seen outside with his boy some hours earlier, shovelling horse dung on the road. Someone had picked up the man's burlap sack and handed it to Sir Martin, though from its shape it hardly seemed capacious enough for swag. Sir Martin opened the sack and peered into it – then jerked back, his nose wrinkling in distaste. Without quite knowing why I stepped forward and asked to examine it for myself. The bag was light, and its contents gave off a bitter, stale whiff of tobacco.

I turned to Sir Martin. 'Sir, this fellow is no thief – he works on the streets. I saw him as I arrived at your door this evening.'

'Then what the deuce is he doing in my garden?'

I dipped into the bag and held its miserable contents in my palm for inspection. 'Cigar ends. That is all he has in here. He collects cigar ends off the ground.'

'What?' said Sir Martin, frowning his disbelief.

'There is a trade for it. I have seen them working in other affluent quarters of town – anywhere cigars are smoked. When they have gathered a sufficiency of ends they sell them on to the large manufac- turers. Who then reconstitute them.'

'And they make a *living* from this?'

'I think so – in part. This fellow was also collecting horse dung along the road, with a boy.'

At this the wretch, prostrate on the ground, spoke up. 'That's roight, sor. I make an honest livin'. An' he's a good boy, sor.' He was addressing me, as the only person present, I suppose, who would vouch for his innocence.

'Where is the boy?' I asked.

'Just by the gate, sor,' he said. 'Me son. We makes an honest livin'.'

'Yes, I understand,' I said. Honest it surely was, though how much refuse he would have to gather to make a 'living' I could not begin to say.

By now the house was ablaze with lights, and those who had not ventured outside had their faces pressed to the windows. The trades- men's door at the side had creaked open, and through it emerged two slops – policemen, I should say – escorting the Irishman's lad between them. The circle that had formed around our trespasser opened to admit these new arrivals.

'Found 'im 'iding in the bushes outside, sir,' said the constable, tipping his helmet. 'Sez as his old man told him to wait there.'

The boy was about ten, pale, scrawny, with an angry port wine stain running from his right cheek to his neck. What bad luck, I thought, to have *that* on top of all his other disadvantages. He hurried to his father, who, standing, clasped him to his side. Sir Martin, pinching his brow, looked like a man who would have preferred somebody else to resolve the situation, which was now a domestic inconvenience rather than the villainy everyone had supposed. He turned to the onlookers. 'Ladies and gentlemen, please, let us return to the dining room. Our chef, I gather, has prepared more sweetmeats to delight us.' There followed a melting away of the guests back towards the illuminated house and the mouth-watering prospect of a gossip about the evening's drama. M. Charbonnier's sweetmeats would be the garnish.

I too was withdrawing when Sir Martin called me back. He was standing a little apart from the policemen and the forlorn pair of father and son.

'Thank you for your . . .' He wasn't sure what service I had done him, and nor was I. He had plucked from his waistcoat pocket a sovereign, and for a horrifying moment I thought he was about to tip me. 'I have told the constable I will not press charges. He will be released . . . with a warning.' He nodded to himself, perhaps impressed by his own forbearance, then handed me the coin. 'Give this to the fellow, and send him on his way.'

It was generous: a sovereign was probably more than this man earned in a month. But that he had endured such humiliation to gain it disturbed me. I followed the policemen along the narrow passageway and out towards the front of the house. The man was still holding the boy's hand. Our crunching footsteps on the gravel finally took us to the entrance, with the pair of stone eagles on guard atop the gate-piers. I waited whilst one of the constables gave the man a short finger-wagging lecture before they moved on. Beneath one of the road's tall gas lamps a cart stood; the man had left it there, I presumed, whilst he made his hopeful expedition into this Eden of choice cigar ends. He now took a step towards me, and made a humble bow. 'God bless you, sor,' he said.

I didn't know what to say, so I took his hand and put the sovereign in it. He looked at the coin in his palm, and then looked at me. His expression was one of utter confusion, and I thought I knew why. Convinced that I had saved him during the melee in Sir Martin's garden, he was now at a loss as to why I should be giving him money. The man who he imagined had been his protector suddenly stood revealed as an impersonal dispenser of charity. Our brief relationship had been reduced to hard cash. I experienced an odd bristling of shame – though of course the fellow took the sovereign, and with a distracted nod, he and his blush-faced boy collected their cart and tramped off into the night.

Back inside the house I was crossing the hall when the ginger-haired man I had noticed earlier at dinner appeared from round the corner.

I was going to walk on without a glance, and expected him to do the same, but as I approached he slowed and caught my eye. Politeness required me to halt, though I felt no great inclination to speak to him. He gave his name as Montgomery Sprule, and introduced himself as a 'social scientist'.

'You have perhaps heard of my book *The Inferior Race*?'

I confessed I had not, but he seemed unfazed by that.

'I could not help overhearing your discussion at dinner,' he continued in a lofty but not unfriendly tone. Up close his eyes gleamed an Arctic blue. 'And behold, we have seen your deserving poor man, saved from arrest!'

'I think he deserved rather more than that. As he said, he earned an honest living.'

'Ye-e-es,' he drawled, 'but I wonder how long the man can subsist on work as meagre as his, with a family to feed. I mean, cigar ends?! You must see how poverty has degraded him.'

'Certainly I do – which is why it behoves us to campaign for better working conditions, fair pay, fair rents. Poverty must be a collective responsibility, not an individual one.'

'On *that* point we are entirely agreed. But your treatment is impractical.'

'Oh. And what would you propose?'

His tone became more confiding. 'We must regulate the existence of the chronic poor – by complete segregation. No, I don't mean the workhouse – I heard what you said to Abernathy and the other fellow. That is only a temporary solution to a permanent problem. I mean we must create entire settlements, away from the city and its temptations, perhaps on the coast, or on some moorland. A healthy environment, no strong drink but plenty of fresh air, where there would be appropriate employment and rational recreation.'

I looked at him, and for a moment I wondered if he was joking. 'I don't see how such a scheme could work.'

Sprule raised an indulgent finger. 'Ah, but it would work. The families of the poor will be trained each day in self-sufficiency. They will build their own homes, farm their own food. And in helping themselves they would become servants of the state. So the whole country benefits.'

'You overlook something, Mr Sprule. What if they – the poor – don't want to leave their homes?'

'If we show them the advantages of these resettlements we believe they will be persuaded to go. Why would they wish to continue in the desolation and squalor of an urban slum?'

'You say "we" . . . ?'

He opened his hands expansively. 'A committee of like-minded professionals who have a concern about the future of society,' he replied. 'Criminal theorists, medical men, social investigators, and so on. I wondered if *you* might care to put your name down, given your evident interest in the question.'

'Thank you for the offer. But no – it seems to me you could only manage such a scheme by compulsion. And I believe a man must be free to choose where he lives.'

Sprule pulled a face to suggest his ambivalence on that particular principle. 'As you wish. Though I should tell you that Mr Marchmont has given us his backing. Perhaps he would put the matter more persuasively than I can.'

'*There* you are!' cried Kitty, bounding up to me. 'I thought we'd lost you for the evening.' Her interruption was timely, for it covered my surprise and bafflement on hearing Sprule's mention of Marchmont as one of his allies. This resettlement project hardly squared with what I knew of the guvnor's avowed belief in laissez-faire. I had managed an awkward bow in taking my leave of Sprule, but I felt his still, measuring gaze on me as Kitty, arm linked companionably in mine, led us back to the dining room, and the inexhaustible bounty of Sir Martin's table.

7

Pay No Rent

The scandal of the rents was already blazoned on the bricks and mortar of Somers Town, and the worst of the tumbledown houses belonging to Moyles now wore bill posters (NOTICE TO QUIT) across their windows, like a blindfold victim awaiting the executioner. Nobody knew when demolition would begin, but it seemed that the relief this would bring to the poorest tenants of the neighbourhood was not unanimously welcomed. I passed a dispiriting half-hour in conversation one morning with a woman who could not understand the benefits of the coming clearance. Mrs Nicholls and her two young children lived on Barclay Street in a single first-floor room afflicted with damp, rot and loose windows. Her husband had died of tuberculosis a year earlier, and it was only on account of the parish that she had been able to make up the week's rent. The broken note of doubt in her voice as she talked of vacating Barclay Street pierced me.

'I mean . . . we've lived 'ere such a long time. Why's they movin' us out?'

I could have said, plainly, that her room was not fit for human habitation, but I realised the offence this might give. 'Well, the houses hereabouts aren't always safe to live in. They must either be repaired or pulled down.'

She squinted gloomily into the distance. Her face was quite comely, though hardship had weathered it. I estimated she was about forty. 'I wish they'd just leave us be. We don't wanna go to the work'us.'

'You won't *have* to go to the workhouse, Mrs Nicholls. Once the vestry pull down these houses they'll be obliged to settle you else-where.' I wanted to give her reassurance, though in truth I was not absolutely certain of the vestry's policy towards tenants made homeless by clearances. I trusted to municipal common sense that they would make provision.

'I don't understand why they's moving us out,' she said, her talk retracing its small agitated circle, like a fly on a windowpane. My efforts of consolation frustrated, I promised to call upon her again, and left.

I had made a note of this encounter in my pocketbook and was on my way to the Brill when I saw, across the street, a woman moving at a struggle with an enormous wicker basket. Her face, vacant with concentration, was suddenly familiar to me, and I waited for a jingling horse and cart to pass before I skipped to the other side. She would have walked right by me if I had not called out 'Roma' – at which she looked up sharply, as if disturbed from a dream.

'Oh, it's you,' she said, refocusing her gaze. She shifted the basket, which I now saw was of assorted garments, to make herself more comfortable.

'That's quite a burden you're carrying. Would you allow me – ?' I stepped forward to help, but she waved me away.

'Nah, I can manage,' she said neutrally.

'May I not be of service to you? Please?'

At that she gave a resigned sort of shrug, and heaved the load from her shoulders. She then proceeded to hand over half of them to me. They were mostly dresses, of silk and tulle and cotton, a few blouses and cloaks. Faint ghosts of powder and perfume rose from the massed material. Their slipperiness made them quite difficult to hold in a bundle, and I began to see why it might have been easier for her to carry them alone.

'I'm on my way home with 'em,' she said. ''Bout five minutes' walk?'

I nodded my readiness to proceed. In the light of day I saw something flawed in the iris of one of her eyes, and wondered if she were partially blind. She noticed me staring at her and said, 'Something the matter?'

'No, please – lead the way.'

We began walking, neither of us speaking. Roma, I suspected, was not the type to start conversing for the sake of it, and she showed no curiosity in me. I looked down at the bundle in my arms.

'You own a great many dresses,' I joked.

She didn't laugh, but she did turn her head and snorted thinly in acknowledgement of my feeble sally. 'I do repairs for a tailor on Ossulston Street. They's sent him by ladies in the West End.'

'So . . . a seamstress by day and a barmaid by night.'

'You could say. I just do whatever pays.'

'That should include your singing,' I said, hoping to charm her. But

74

she only did her little shrug again; she didn't wish to be charmed. Some moments later we came to Clarendon Square, and her step slowed as we approached the Polygon, the curious circle of tenements that sat in the middle. I did not know of such an architectural composition anywhere else in London, with pairs of houses forming the external sides of the figure, like a cake cut into slices. Roma had taken out her latchkey and mounted the steps.

'D'you know, I always wondered who lived in these houses,' I said, looking up at the patchy stucco face with its iron-wrought balconies. 'They must have been very grand once.' I had spoken without thinking, and blushed at my rudeness – but Roma, perversely, found this amusing.

'An' look what sort o' people lives here now!' she said with a laugh.

'I beg your pardon. I didn't mean that.'

Shaking her head, she opened her front door, a dexterous manoeuvre given the basket that was restricting her movement. As I hesitated on the bottom step she turned back to me. 'Are you coming in?'

We ascended four flights of uncarpeted stairs, past whitewashed walls that showed ancient grime and windows warped in their frames. Roma said nothing as our steps clacked against the floorboards; it had become obvious even in this brief time that she had none of Jo's affability. Their lodgings turned out to consist of a large front parlour and two bedrooms, a more commodious arrangement than was usual in the neighbourhood. The furniture, though modest, was of a decent quality, whilst the swept hearth and air of tidiness indicated the supervision of a proud householder. Above the mantelpiece hung a crucifix, with a sampler and a small photographic portrait of a couple displayed on the facing wall. Roma, warming a kettle on the hob, had seen me looking at this last.

'Joseph and Giulietta. Our mum and dad. Tea?'

'Thank you, yes.' I turned back to the photograph. 'They look very young, your parents.'

She nodded. 'Died young, too.'

'Jo told me that you raised him.'

'Yeah, well,' she said, and I hid a smile, so exact a replica of Jo's was that *Yeah, well* and the little shrug that followed.

'That must have been hard for you.'

A shadow of something crossed Roma's face; she stopped what she was doing and stared at me. 'Hard?' she said, echoing the word sardonically. But then she seemed to recover herself. 'You wouldn't believe me if I told you.'

'I'm sure I would,' I replied, but she ignored this. She had returned to her preoccupied mood, and I felt once again that my company was of no more consequence to her than a burr that had stuck to her coat. With anyone else I would have taken the earliest opportunity to withdraw myself, but I found that Roma's indifference only sharpened my eagerness to please her.

She poured me a cup of tea, then turned to the dresses now pooled over a little couch and began sorting through them, one by one, pausing to insert a pin to mark each torn seam or frayed collar. There came a moment when, handling a close-cut purple gown, she stood and held it consideringly against the length of her body. She caught my eye as she did so.

'Very becoming,' I said.

She was absorbed in it. 'I've always wondered how it might be to wear such a thing.'

'You should try it on,' I said, looking over my teacup.

She shook her head absently. 'It's silk. D'you know how much this'd cost?'

'No. How much?'

She made a sort of *tsk* noise, as if her question were not meant to be answered. Throwing the gown back onto the pile she continued her inventory. I thought then of the recent dinner at Sir Martin Elder's and the sumptuous gowns I had seen that night. Why was it that those ladies should enjoy the privilege of wearing such raiment when they were no more deserving than any other? I sensed that the question had perhaps occurred to Roma, but that she would not care to debate it with a near-stranger. Which was all I was to her.

As I sipped the tea, I said, 'Have you seen the posters for the no-rent demonstration in Trafalgar Square next week?'

Without looking up from the dresses, she said, 'Yeah, I seen 'em.'

'And may I hope to meet you there?'

'Not likely,' she said, and after a pause added, 'I hear you didn't get much support for it.' Jo must have told her about my campaigning at the doorsteps.

'There was some reluctance,' I admitted.

Now she did look at me. 'You should try an' understand why. People don't want to fight with the rent man – it'll only get 'em a reputation for troublemaking. And the next time they need a room the landlord'll be sure not to bother with 'em.'

'But if enough tenants refused to pay these exorbitant rents then the landlords would have no choice but to yield – we could force them to make repairs, to make houses safe and habitable.'

'Fine for you to say. But a landlord can do as he pleases – if you don't pay he'll sling you out. You know what puts the fear up people? It's not the damp or the filth, or the crowdin'. What frightens them is havin' no home at all.'

'But what use is a home that hasn't a decent roof over it? With doors that have had every panel kicked out of them?'

'It's *a home*,' she said, 'an' that's better than nothing.'

I looked out of the window at the shabby terrace of Clarendon Square opposite. Like everywhere else in the vicinity, it had seen better days, and I fell to wondering, as I so often did, about why houses really became slums. The negligence and profiteering of landlords had certainly contributed, but one wondered at the character of tenants who allowed, and in some cases hastened, the spread of decay. 'The sty makes the pig' had always been my conviction, but was it inconceivable that sometimes it might be the other way about?

'I was at a dinner the other night where the opinion was decidedly in favour of putting society's unfortunates into the workhouse.'

Roma curled her lip in scorn. 'Nice company *you* keep. I've 'eard that before, from them as don't know what "poor" means. They always talk of 'em as if they were criminals.'

'D'you know, that's exactly what I said to them.'

'You did?' For the first time she gave me a look of sincere interest. 'What they say to that?'

'They didn't much like it. And they liked it even less, I fancy, when the wretch who was caught lurking in the garden turned out not to be a housebreaker after all. He and his boy had been collecting cigar ends.'

Roma wore a pensive frown, and I imagined I could see in its contours the smallest readjustment of her view of me. Or perhaps it was the way in which she moved from the couch where she had been sorting the dresses to the chair opposite mine at the table. The light slanting through the window showed up the irregularity in her iris, and, as she concentrated on her sewing and darning, I was free to stare. Curiosity finally overmastered me.

'Your eyes . . . are they different colours?'

She nodded. 'One blue, one green. Gave my parents a proper fright when I was small. My mum was that upset she took me to the quack, but 'e told her it was harmless. It's some condition – used to bother me as a girl. People *starin'* at me . . .' Her emphasis was pointed.

'I'm sorry,' I said quickly. 'It is only that they are so very – remarkable.'

'What, like a circus freak?'

'No, no . . . I mean, like – wonderful to behold.'

She responded to this, typically, with a wry twist of her mouth, as if any compliment from me could not be taken quite seriously. I had finished the tea, and there was no reason – other than my own inclination – to linger. Then I saw how I should make myself useful.

'These dresses – if they only require repair, perhaps I could be of assistance?'

She glanced up from her work. 'I don't see how, unless you can sew.'

'But I *can* sew,' I replied, and took up a gown whose seam had split at the elbow. 'May I?' Turning it inside out I then threaded a needle and calmly closed the hole with a few stitches. I handed the garment over to her for inspection. She looked at this handiwork for some moments, then tilted her head slightly.

'Not bad,' she said. 'Well, if you want to improve the shining hour . . .' She stepped over to the couch and selected those dresses that required only simple repair. I had an inkling that she was impressed, though I didn't anticipate any expression of warmth, and none came. So we sat there, in companionable silence, stitching away like a pair of Spitalfields tailors.

'Where'd you learn to sew, then?' she said presently.

After a hesitation I said, 'At school. We all learned.'

This appeared to satisfy her, and then we talked about *The Labouring Classes*, and how I had come to work there. She was particularly interested in Mr Marchmont – many were, I found – though less because of his pioneering journalism than his reputation for high living. She had heard that he liked to 'play large' at the gaming tables.

'He does enjoy a game of baccarat,' I admitted.

'And a lot more besides,' said Roma. ''Sfar as I've 'eard, he's not much of a gentleman. Don't honour his debts, they say.'

'I believe that was once the case,' I said cautiously.

'Oh,' she replied, and paused. 'Only I got this from a friend who works at a casino up west. 'Cordin' to her, your guvnor's there a lot, and he run outta credit a long time back.'

A *trosseno*, I thought, recalling Jo's word for a bad'un. Could this really be true? I had had the story from his erstwhile colleague Paget about Mr Marchmont sailing close to the wind financially, but that dated from years ago. It seemed highly improbable that he could afford the

Montagu Square house if he were 'cracked up', as they said in Somers Town. I looked at the little clock on Roma's mantelpiece, and rose to my feet.

'Well . . . talking of the guvnor, I'd better be doing my rounds. I have some tenants to interview round the corner in Sidney Street.'

Roma pulled a quizzical face. 'You'd better be quick about it. There ain't many left!'

'What d'you mean?'

'Sidney Street? They pulled down 'alf of it last week.' Seeing my look of utter surprise, she said, 'There's a load of houses with notices to quit – you must have seen 'em.'

'Yes, but . . . I didn't think they'd start immediately.' I knew Sidney Street was one of the most poorly maintained in Somers Town, and that it had probably gone beyond the help of renovation. Yet its demolition felt precipitate. 'And – the tenants?'

Roma shrugged. 'Same thing as always 'appens. They fend for themselves.' As she explained it, there would be a scramble for the few rented rooms still available. The rest would seek shelter in dosshouses already packed to bursting, or else be homeless – which meant living on the street.

'I wish you good day, then,' I said somewhat absently, and Roma, putting aside her sewing, stood up too. She was straight-backed in posture, and her chin jutted to the smallest degree, as if in challenge.

'Much obliged to you,' she said, gesturing at the repairs we had got through, and in a state of distraction I took the stairs back down to the street.

Five minutes later I was surveying the evidence for myself. One side of Sidney Street lay in rubble, whilst the other was clad in scaffolding, preparatory to its destruction. Two workmen were loitering on the site, and I asked them by whose authority the street had been earmarked for clearance. They didn't know. 'We's just 'ere to knock it dahn,' said one of them, and I didn't doubt their lack of curiosity. 'A lot more of 'em to go,' the man added.

This was perplexing. Houses that had been neglected and left to rot for years were suddenly in a queue to be pulverised. From where had this initiative sprung? Surely not the vestry, whose incumbents had grown prosperous as slumlords. I decided to return to the Public Records Office on Euston Road, where my investigation of the rents had begun. The clerk at the desk presented me with the same heavy ledger I had inspected six weeks ago, and, settled at a corner table, I turned its wide brittle pages until I came to the list of leases in Somers Town. What stood out were the multiple corrections; when a property changed hands the form was to paste the name of the new leaseholder over the old. On my previous visit I had seen but few of these alterations. Now whole pages were overlaid with pasted slips, each freshly inked. The page for Hampden Street, once part of W. W. Moyles's slum empire, was now mummified with strips bearing the same name, *Condor Holdings*. Recalling that the workmen had mentioned Medburn Street as their next port of call I looked in turn at that, and, again, most of the leases were bracketed under the company *Condor Holdings*. Moyles's name had disappeared from the columns entirely. I had an inkling of some dodge afoot, though I could not for the life of me see what it was. Without shutting the ledger I carried it back to the clerk at the main desk. I asked him about the new names recorded as leaseholders in Somers Town, and he replied that all such changes were recorded within a month.

'But – do you see? – whole streets have been taken on lease, even though they're unfit for habitation.'

'If that's what it says,' he replied with a shrug.

'Does it not surprise you – all this property changing hands?'

He looked at me in a bored way. 'Where property is concerned, nothing ever surprises me.'

Before I left the place I checked in a business directory for Condor Holdings, and took down an address in Bishopsgate, E.C.

The journalist Paget, sitting opposite, drained the last from his pewter and consulted his pocket watch. The ale had left a thin fringe of foam around his beard. Up close his blotchy skin and piggy eyes were strangely hypnotising. One might stop short of describing him as ugly, but Nature had certainly not gone out of her way to bless him. He was, I gathered, a bachelor.

'Twenty to three,' he said. 'Time to join the fray.'

We were in a public house at the foot of St Martin's Lane. Beyond the frosted window could be heard shouts and laughter and footfall, and the occasional trotting clop of a horse, all heading towards Trafalgar Square. We rose from our table and emerged via a side door into Chandos Street, and immediately I knew that this was to be no paltry show of protest. Shoaling from the direction of the Strand were scores of men, some in their Sunday togs, many carrying placards. PAY NO

RENT TO ROBBER LANDLORDS distilled the message of the day. Some carried the flags of Fair Rent Leagues and of Tenants' Protection Societies. An Italian ice-cream seller was doing brisk business with marchers wearied by their tramp from the east.

The day was murky, and close, without a glimpse of sun. Hustling our way through the straggle of bodies, we decided to skirt the perimeter of the square and thus avoid being pulled into the vortex of the crowds massing around the National Gallery. We had gained the steps of St Martin-in-the-Fields and were crossing the stone flags beneath its grand portico when, from the opposite direction, we came in view of a familiar swaggering figure. At his side was someone else I knew. An encounter between us was unfortunate, and unavoidable.

'Well, well,' said Marchmont, quickly recovering from his surprise at seeing me with his former associate. 'I had a notion you might show up here.' He was addressing Paget with the distant respect of enemy generals meeting before an action. 'This is Montgomery Sprule,' he continued, introducing his companion. 'Clifford Paget from the *Chronicle* – and one of my staff, Mr Wildeblood.'

Sprule bowed slightly at Paget, then turned to me. 'Mr Wildeblood is already known to me, sir. He and I had an exchange of views on the future of the London poor.'

Marchmont eyed me narrowly, and said, with deliberation, 'Is that so? And what conclusion did you reach?'

Sprule was urbane in his reply. 'None at all, I'm afraid – on the matter of housing them, Mr Wildeblood expressed himself very much against our resettlement scheme.'

'Quite right, too,' said Paget. 'The idea of uprooting whole neighbourhoods and relocating them to the countryside is preposterous.' He gestured at the crowds still pouring into the square. 'How willingly d'you suppose *they* would comply with such an arrangement?'

Sprule's level expression didn't change. 'There are ways and means, Mr Paget. One cannot expect the great revolutions of social engineering to pass off without a tremor. Naturally there will be disputation along the way. But five years from now, perhaps sooner, I predict that resettlement will have been embraced as a necessary measure to save society.'

'To save society? – from what?'

'Why, from the contagion of degeneracy,' said Sprule, as though the answer were obvious. 'We cannot allow the slums simply to fester on. Resettlement is the only policy that will halt the deterioration of our social and economic health. In that way we shall regulate the very existence –'

'Your missionary zeal is admirable, Sprule,' said Marchmont, cutting in sharply, 'but I fancy Paget here is on the clock. May I advise you gentlemen to have a care this afternoon? It seems –' he looked out over the sea of bodies – 'the local constabulary is out in force.'

He was not wrong. As we had been talking, long lines of policemen had appeared seemingly out of nowhere to picket the edges of the square and were now jostling the crowds contained within. The guvnor, having tipped his hat to us, walked on with Sprule, who had the slightly thwarted air of one who would like to have lectured us a good while longer. I suspected he was a man not used to being interrupted. But Marchmont would have interrupted the Queen if it suited him. Paget and I, in an effort to circumvent the crush, were heading for the junction at Northumberland Avenue, where we might plot a more convenient path towards the centre.

Paget glanced round as we edged through the press of bodies. 'There's our man,' he said, nodding towards the chief speaker as he mounted the steps of the National Gallery. It was Kenton, the leader of the Rental Reform League and the star of today's protest. I recognised him from the day Paget introduced us on Fleet Street; I particularly recalled the bruise across his nose which he had sustained during the St Pancras Vestry affray. In the weeks since, his name had scarcely been out of the newspapers, his printing works in King's Cross had been raided by the police, and in Parliament a Tory MP had accused him of 'fomenting a working-class rebellion', a charge which Kenton was only too pleased to accept. Now here he was, megaphone in hand, ready to address the assembled thousands.

'Workers,' he began, 'we have come together this afternoon for a simple reason – to put a stop to murder. Yes, murder! What else should we call that poisoning of our bodies and spirits, the result of inhabiting foul dens that are no more than living tombs? Yet not only do we endure them – we pay for them, too, over and over again, because robber landlords demand their rents. Listen to me. These slum owners are growing rich on your misery, your degradation, your slow death. We have asked the government for help, but they have failed us. So the responsibility is ours to set things right, to stand up to the rack-renters and say *No more*! You shall not have another penny from us!'

The last words of this oration were almost drowned out by the tumultuous approval that burst like a dragon's roar from the crowd. This was the stuff they had come to hear. It set the tone for the next speaker, and another after him, each of them kindling the mood of indignation that crackled in the air. As we stood there, a distant worry snagged on my consciousness, and it prompted me to consult Paget.

'That man Sprule – what do you know of him?'

'Only that he's off his nut. I gather he's embroiled in some charitable enquiry into the working classes – that's why he's been knocking about with Henry.'

'He hasn't much in common with the guvnor's view of intervention – "as little as possible", you told me.'

Paget shrugged. 'If I know Henry he'll have worked the association to his advantage. Sprule is probably paying him in some unofficial capacity.'

I brooded for some moments. 'Sprule seems very confident about this scheme of relocating the poor. It's as though he knows something we don't.'

'It has no chance of succeeding,' said Paget flatly. 'As I said, it would be impossible to persuade people to move en masse to the countryside, however temptingly it is presented. Neighbourhoods cannot be so easily dispersed.'

'Yes, but you heard what he said about "ways and means". Perhaps the state might have recourse to less congenial methods of persuasion.'

'That would not –'

Paget's reply got only so far into this expression of demur, for the words about to form on his lips were suddenly and rudely dashed. The stirrings of agitation we had felt earlier in the boisterous throng had gathered strength on the way to where we stood; it arrived first in a hefty shove to our backs, which threw us in turn against our close-packed neighbours directly in front. This barging impact set up a hugely violent ripple that carried us forwards, causing others nearby to stumble and fall to the pavement. The air rang with oaths and cries of pain. The reason for this commotion, at first unknown, was now discernible: a mounted policeman had strayed into the centre of the square, and the horse, either confused or maddened by the noise, was rearing up in terror. Next thing it bolted, charging a line of demonstrators in its path and knocking them down like skittles. Some brave soul grabbed the horse's reins, and, wrong-footed, the beast and its rider collapsed in a neighing heap.

As we later discovered, this incident was fatefully misconstrued; from the ambiguous perspective of those on the margins of the square an act of self-defence perhaps looked like an attack. In any event it acted as a provocation to the blues. Now a whole line of mounted police made a charge on the eastern flank of the demonstration, scattering some, putting others to flight; yet with barely any room to run multiple collisions ensued. Paget and I, still borne headlong by the momentum behind us, were now trying to scramble our way out of the ruck. The front ranks of the demonstrators, who had probably heard these ructions at a distance but not known their cause, were soon caught in the surge of bodies bearing down upon them, pushing them back against the temporary fencing erected in front of the gallery steps. It was lucky for all concerned that it *was* temporary, because a solid wall would have fatally crushed the oncoming wave. Instead it broke and toppled under the weight of the panicked crowd, of which we were still a helpless part. The steps were now thirty yards in front of us, and there, I calculated, safety would lie. Paget had slipped, like many others, in the melee, and without ceremony I dragged him bodily to his feet. 'Quick, man, to the steps,' I cried. But this channel of escape was abruptly closed, from the north, by another massed charge of police horses, whose aggressive intent could no longer be doubted. Some of the mounted slops were laying batons on demonstrators, whose only offence had been to break free of the chaos that had so suddenly engulfed them.

Seen from the vantage of Kenton and his fellow speakers on the steps, the spectacle must have looked baffling – and then horrifying. Bad enough that people were being trampled down by the onrushing throng; worse still that the police were picking off stragglers by coshing them about the head. One poor woman I saw found her shawl entangled with the stirrup of a mounted slop, whose momentum dragged her along in its wake before she was hurled bodily to the ground. The piteous calamity happening in front of them had moved the organisers to remonstrate with the police. When that proved futile, a group of them came down to intervene, Kenton foremost amongst them. But this was only more paraffin poured on the bonfire. Wading into one violent scuffle, he was immediately set upon by three slops, and disappeared under a blur of truncheons. With the steps blocked from access we turned back on ourselves. At this stage angry demonstrators were openly engaging the slops in running battles, and for a moment I stopped, transfixed by the chaos around us. I didn't notice the shadow at my back until I felt a cracking blow at my ear; my legs gave way, and the ground rose to meet me. I couldn't tell how long I was unconscious, but when I came round Paget had somehow got us clear and was half lifting, half walking me down a narrow alley off St Martin's Lane.

I begged for a moment's rest, and sank down with my back against the wall. As Paget squatted down and wiped the blood from my scalp, he said, almost to himself, 'Perhaps he was right after all . . .'

'Who?'

'Sprule. He's been warning of "a people's revolution" for years, putting the wind up the government. Now with the murders in Ireland yesterday there'll be a right panic.'

'What murders?'

'Chief Secretary for Ireland and his undersecretary were stabbed to death in Phoenix Park. Fenians, they suspect. But what happens over there could just as easily happen here – there is a dangerous mood abroad. The government will be hot to root out seditionaries.' He paused, and turned to me. 'And that will include anybody attending a protest like today's.'

8

Monkey on a stick

I was more shaken by my fall in Trafalgar Square than I had at first perceived. My head the next morning throbbed – my unseen assailant must have delivered a fearsome thwack – and my knees and arms were tender with abrasions. (I wondered if Paget had actually *dragged* me along the ground to safety.) I did not feel well enough to go to work, and instead shuffled to a low eating house round the corner from my lodgings for a bowl of soup. As the spoon trembled in my hand I felt sadly valetudinarian. *The Times* reported that the riot had been orchestrated by seditious elements in the crowd, though admitted that the police had been, in certain instances, 'heavy-handed'. Casualties, many of them head wounds, had been taken to the nearby Charing Cross Hospital. Over twenty demonstrators had been arrested in the disorder, including Kenton. The leader page opined that yesterday's events carried an ominous message for the government: 'Unless measures are quickly taken, a brutalised labouring class will be ready to rise up and seize control.' Dread was in the air, just as Paget had suggested.

I was back at my rooms in Hanover Street when the landlady, who rejoiced under the queer but appropriate name of Mrs Home, stopped by with a letter. The opulent texture of the envelope seemed familiar. I opened it and read:

Kensington Palace Gardens, W.

8 May, '82

Dear David,

I did so enjoy our conversations at dinner here last month, since when I have been engaged in a charitable venture in which I think – I hope – you might be interested. Perhaps you will allow me to tell you about it in person. I wonder if

87

you are at liberty on the afternoon of Saturday week? – we could meet at the house and then stroll in the park, if it pleases you.

Your affectionate *god-sister*,
Kitty

I supposed she must have got my address from the letter I had written to Sir Martin thanking him for dinner. But why did she want to tell me about this charity of hers in person? Surely she was not so deluded as to mistake me for a potential patron? No, she knew of my lowly employment under Marchmont – she probably even knew how much I earned. It was, I decided, simply an overture of friendliness, and one that I was glad to accept. We had got along pretty well on the night, certainly more than I had with the other guests. It would also give me the opportunity to discover what she knew of the mysterious Sprule, whose book I had borrowed from Mudie's. Thus far I had read only the preface of *The Inferior Race*, wherein Sprule thanked both Charles Darwin and Francis Galton. Two pages in two weeks; I could justly claim for myself the title The Inferior Reader.

In the meantime my enquiries concerning Condor Holdings had achieved precisely nothing. I had written to them some weeks ago about their taking possession of various leases, and still awaited a reply. Paget, who knew quite a lot about everything, had never heard of them. At one stage I was minded to ask Rennert – 'the oracle', as he was known at Salisbury Square – but an instinct warned me not to, and, in the light of what followed, I was glad to have obeyed it. It had come to my notice that the copy I dictated most afternoons was being used in the paper less and less often. When I mentioned this to certain more experienced inspectors I learned that a gradual whittling-down was not unusual: Marchmont was always on the lookout for unexplored neighbourhoods to incorporate into his survey, and Somers Town had perhaps yielded up most of its vital ore for now. It had also become apparent that the Poverty Map was now his chief preoccupation; Rennert was to all intents and purposes the presiding spirit behind *The Labouring Classes of London*, and it was to him I reported.

But for now I had a somewhat lighter workload, which gave me time to pursue my investigation of the Somers Town leaseholders. With no likelihood of receiving any communication from Condor Holdings, and no other information about this company forthcoming, I took it upon myself to pay them a visit in person. Bishopsgate House was a City office building occupied by shops on its ground floor, rising to a sooty terracotta facade from which huge banks of windows stared down. Such was its aspect from the far side of Bishopsgate Street, which was this morning so thunderous with carts and cabs and 'buses that merely crossing from one side of the road to the other held the air of an achievement. Inside, the board on the wall listed at least twenty businesses in occupancy, Condor Holdings amongst them. A few dark-coated City gentlemen stood about jawing in the atrium.

I took the stairs to the fifth floor, and eventually found their office at the end of a gloomy corridor. I knocked once, twice, on the mahogany panelled door, and on receiving no reply tried the doorknob. Locked. I settled on a courtesy bench seat hard by, and waited. A half-hour or more had passed when, from the next office along, a man emerged and, on seeing me, asked if I was his next appointment.

'No, my appointment is with your neighbour,' I lied, gesturing at the Condor Holdings office.

The man pulled a dubious face. 'You'll wait a long time,' he said. 'I've seen barely a soul come or go from that place. Whoever they are, they don't seem to hold with office hours.'

'D'you happen to know what hours they *do* keep?'

'Not a clue. That door's always closed – queer way to run a business, I must say.'

We exchanged a shrugging look, and he was about to withdraw when I called him back. 'You did say "barely" a soul, am I right?'

'What's that?'

'Well, you implied that you *have* seen someone here before.'

He frowned, recalling his own words. 'Yes. Once, I believe. A fellow called in at the office for twenty minutes, then left, just before the close of business. I noticed it only because it was so unusual.'

I asked him if he remembered when this occurred, and he blew out his cheeks in such a way as to suggest he could sooner recall the date of the last lunar eclipse. The time snailed by. At half past one I strolled down to the street and bought a ham sandwich from a stall; I returned to my lonely post on the fifth floor and ate it there. I must have dozed off because the next thing I knew the office worker I had spoken to woke me with a tap on my boot. It was now gone four. From the sceptical look he gave my half-eaten sandwich I suppose he must have thought I was just on the mooch.

'I fancy my appointment has been forgotten,' I said, rising to my feet and trying to sound businesslike whilst I brushed crumbs off my trousers. I gestured in resignation at the door of Condor Holdings, and echoed his earlier opinion that it was indeed 'a queer way to run a business'.

'Better luck next time,' he called, just as I reached the turning for the stairs.

In daylight the Elder mansion at Kensington Palace Gardens looked almost objectionably grand. The carved eagles on the gate-piers looked down their beaks at me, and the immaculate white stucco of the facade glowed against the obsidian gaze of the windows. To clink the brass knocker upon the door seemed in itself an act of trespass, but the footman admitted me once again without a twitch. I was halfway across the marbled expanse of the hall when I heard my name called – nearly sung – from above, and there, head and shoulders canted over the spiral of the balustrade, was Kitty.

'Come up!'

I followed the curve of the staircase to the second floor, where she greeted me with a handshake. Her sky-blue pinafore dress made her seem younger than I remembered, though I had a notion she was of an age with me. A sly, dimpled half-smile suggested some privately anticipated delight. She turned on her heel and bid me follow her.

'I want to introduce you to a new friend,' she said over her shoulder. I felt a small jolt of disappointment as I tramped after her along the corridor. Wasn't *I* her new friend? She opened a door off to the left, and I entered a vast drawing room (there was no other size in this house), its centrepiece a circular buttoned sofa upholstered in damson-coloured velvet; its tiered, segmented plumpness gave it the look of an enormous furred jelly mould. Kitty peered about the room, then said in a fondly indulgent tone, 'Now, where is the little fellow?' I was about to enquire after the identity of this diminutive when from behind the sofa rose a ghastly inhuman screech. I turned to Kitty in horror, but she responded with a merry tinkling laugh and hurried towards its source. 'Here he is!' she cooed, and came from around the sofa carrying – to my astonishment – a small, black, spindly-tailed monkey. I say black, though the fur on the neck and head were yellowish-white, and its wrinkled little face a cloudy pink. Its expression, I should say, was one of ineffable stupidity.

'Isn't he adorable?!' cried Kitty.

It was the not the word I should have reached for. The creature bore a close resemblance to the associate of an Italian organ-grinder who often passed by Jo's pitch on Chalton Street. This monkey, sitting atop the organ, would hold out a tin cup to solicit payments for his master's music, and Jo (who loved animals) would delightedly pet the thing, as Kitty was doing now, and even carry it about on his shoulder. For myself, I could discern no charm in these impudent primates, and rather shrank from their jerky movements and horrid chattering.

'This is David,' Kitty was addressing the monkey. 'Say "how do you do", Ferdinand.'

'Ferdinand? Is that really its name?'

Kitty tutted in rebuke. '*Its?!* You mustn't insult poor Ferdy. *He* is a white-headed capuchin, named after the friars – do you see that sweet little cowl on his head?' She now began to dance the monkey vigorously around the room. 'We love to waltz about the place, don't we, Ferdy?'

I sighed quietly. It was remarkable to me how a domestic pet could reduce a sound-minded person to imbecility. Keen not to be embroiled in their capering, I withdrew to the window seat. After a few more circuits of the room Kitty at last released him, and plumped down on the seat next to me. She was breathless from her exertions, and the colour that pinked her cheeks was, in spite of the idiot spectacle that caused it, rather fetching. The simian – 'Ferdy' – had perched on a side table, and was absently nibbling on a nut he had found in a silver bowl.

'He's awfully intelligent, you know,' said Kitty, perhaps sensing my want of warmth towards her pet.

'I dare say. Where did you find, er, him?'

'Papa gave him to me,' she replied. 'He's become rather interested in apes, you see, from reading Mr Darwin. He says they are making all kinds of advancements in the science of heredity and breeding and a lot of other things we don't yet understand. Mr Sprule could probably explain it all – you met him, I think?'

'Yes, I did. I've been meaning to read his book.'

'Papa says he's awfully clever – which I suppose would excuse his dreariness.'

'He does jaw on rather.'

'Hmm . . . and I can't bear to look at his long ginger whiskers. Is that terribly unkind of me?'

'Well, there's no helping an instinctive dislike,' I said, glancing again at Ferdinand. 'I ran into Mr Sprule a few days ago, as a matter of fact. He seems to think the country is on the brink of revolution.'

'Can that be true? I've not seen any barricades or flaming brands . . .'

'I think one would have to look a little further than Kensington for evidence.'

She permitted herself a sigh of philosophical complaisance and stood up to open a window. It offered a long prospect over Kensington Gardens to Hyde Park and the uneven horizon of Park Lane; down below could be heard the castanet clop of horses being exercised, and the languid threshing of treetops. My eye had drifted to a portrait on the opposite wall of a lady whose liquid gaze and sad smile recalled my young hostess.

'Is that – your mother?' I asked her.

She turned, and nodded. 'This was her favourite room. She died when I was five.' She said this in a matter-of-fact tone that had – who knows? – taken years to master.

'She looks very beautiful,' I said, meaning it as a compliment to Kitty: their resemblance was unarguable.

'Yes . . . though Papa always says she was even more beautiful in life. I can't quite remember her so well.'

I kept the silence of sympathy. It occurred to me that Kitty, without a mother's example or the companionship of siblings, might have grown up to be a rather spoiled and wilful young lady. Yet she had eluded that fate. If cheerfulness were a mask she wore, it was one that had become inseparable from her face. Rising once again, she proposed a walk.

'Come along, Ferdy,' she called to the monkey, still hunched over the silver bowl, and when he failed to respond she gathered him into her arms. He let loose a burst of staccato squeals; whether in protest or pleasure was hard to tell. I followed monkey and mistress back down to the hall and through the house. We had stepped into the garden – scene of the night's drama a month ago – when from the side of the house we heard the clatter of hooves and Sir Martin came into view astride a high-stepping hunter. By the time we had walked over he had dismounted and his groom had taken charge of the steaming horse. Sir Martin squinted at me as we approached, hands resting, teapot-like, on his hips.

'How d'ye do, sir,' he said, offering me his gloved hand. There was about him something equine, too, perhaps in the long jawline and the pronounced tendons in his arms and neck. Even his teeth looked strong and horsey.

'David and I are going to take a stroll in the Gardens, Papa,' said Kitty.

'And this is your chaperone, I suppose,' he replied, nodding at Ferdinand, who crouched mutely between us.

'Oh, I think we must leave Ferdy here. I have a distinct impression that he is *not* unanimously admired.' I couldn't mistake the pert look which accompanied this remark.

'Bring him in, then,' said Sir Martin, and we three followed him back inside the house. We passed through a suite of reception rooms on the other side of the hall before we reached a commodious study-cum-library, with an iron-framed gallery running around its walls. I had seen libraries before in which the books seemed to slumber on the shelves, perfectly undisturbed by their owner. Not this one; the atmosphere it inhabited was one of scholarly preoccupation. On a stacked trestle huge leather-tooled volumes lay open, and in one splayed text I caught sight of tiny pencilled marginalia, the evidence of close study. In one tottering cairn of books on Sir Martin's desk I spied the gilt-lettered names of Darwin and Galton, and another that had recently become inescapable: *The Inferior Race* by Montgomery Sprule. I was at liberty to absorb this whilst Sir Martin searched his desk for the key to Ferdinand's cage, situated in a far corner.

'Ah . . . careless of me,' he muttered, plucking a bunch of keys that depended from a lock in the wall. I couldn't help noticing it was a safe.

'Now David knows where the family jewels are kept!' cried Kitty in mock alarm, and we laughed. The monkey was promptly conducted to his cage and secured therein. She proffered another nut through the bars, and the creature took it without comment. We were on the way out when Sir Martin called to his daughter.

'Kitty, be back in good time. Remember we have Douglas and his family coming to dinner.'

We made our exit along the lawn and through an ancient door almost hidden from view by the curtain of russet creepers on the garden wall. We emerged into the park just as the sun began to hide itself in the clouds, though the temperature was still mild. Kitty had fallen uncharacteristically silent, and I ventured a guess as to why.

'Who's Douglas, may I ask?'

Colouring slightly, she gave me a sidelong look. 'Oh, his family and mine have known one another for years. He was at the dinner you attended — you recall a fellow of about six-and-twenty, with a pinkish complexion and blond hair brushed back off his forehead?'

I remembered him. It was the man who had aimed a violent kick at the poor devil we had run to ground in the Elder garden. 'You are particular friends?'

'Not exactly. He happens to be one of a small company of men Papa considers eligible.'

'I see. And by what standards does he judge this . . . eligibility?' I had a strong intuition that 'personal charm' would not count amongst them. Kitty sighed.

'It's mainly to do with family – breeding, I suppose. He has a dread of people marrying outside of their class.'

'Ah . . .'

Kitty perhaps heard a note of scepticism in that brief syllable, because she hurried on to explain. 'He takes the science of it rather seriously, I'm afraid. There's a word he uses – what is it? – *hypergamy.*'

'What on earth is that?'

'I think it essentially means "marrying above oneself". Papa believes that the masses should wed only amongst their own, otherwise it will damage the integrity of the superior class.'

I was starting to realise what an influence Sprule had had on her father. Theories of evolution were frequently in the news, and Darwin's death last month had reawoken debates concerning Natural Selection. But then perhaps Sir Martin's wariness admitted of a simpler explanation: a man of great wealth would naturally strive to protect his only daughter from fortune-hunters. I now recalled Kitty's light-hearted complaint that the men she usually accompanied into dinner were wizened elders with gout. She associated with no one who might take advantage of her, in other words . . . though clearly the paternal protectiveness did not extend to *me*. Probably Sir Martin thought me a youth of such inconsequence that I did not represent a danger. I felt a question being begged, nevertheless.

'And if the attraction runs the other way? That is – if the well-bred person should conceive a predilection for an inferior?'

Kitty looked thoughtful. 'Well . . . it would be sad if love were thwarted . . . But is an encounter between people of such different societies very likely?'

'It is not unheard of,' I said carefully. 'The search for love can take strange directions. And it seems to me quite difficult enough without throwing the obstacle of *breeding* before it.' She looked at me then with great solemnity, as if we were sharing in some profound truth, and I decided to laugh it off lest she turned the matter personal. 'But why talk of this? We are neither of us about to plunge into the marital abyss, I think.'

'Of course not,' she replied, though I sensed an anxiety about that prospect still clouding her horizon. Perhaps this Douglas was recommending himself to her more insistently than I knew; there seemed nothing of the shrinking violet about him. We had walked as far as the Serpentine, where a few rowdy youths on the edge were daring one another to immerse themselves. Kitty paused to watch them splash about for a few moments, and chuckled in happy amusement.

'Fresh air and fun,' I said, for want of something better.

'Mm. Actually, that's rather pertinent to what I'd like to discuss. You recall Mrs Abernathy from our dinner last month?'

'I do indeed,' I said, trying to reconcile the idea of 'fun' with the august personage she had named.

'She and her husband are patrons of several charities, as you may know. Well, she has enlisted me in her latest venture, called the Social Protection League. It's a kind of experiment, I suppose, to take the city poor on improving excursions to the country, where they may breathe fresh air and take their leisure in the open spaces. You see, I recall what you said at dinner – about the poor deserving to enjoy their lives rather than worrying about their subsistence. Even for just a day, this will surely be of benefit to them.' She was looking at me earnestly. 'Do you approve?'

'If it is as you say, I could not possibly *dis*approve. But this charity must have considerable backing.'

'Oh, it does. Mrs Abernathy's as rich as a Jew, and I know that Papa has put up some of the money, too.'

As she described it, this 'experiment' did appear to derive from a spirit of philanthropy. City-dwellers whose existence had been confined to mean, ill-ventilated tenements and close-packed streets would at last be enabled to sample the joys of open countryside, to inhale air that was clean instead of sooty. 'It seems a capital idea. But – how may *I* be of assistance in this?'

'Ah, that's just it. The charity has decided to launch the scheme in Somers Town, it being one of the most disadvantaged neighbourhoods in London. And I thought that you, having worked there, might wish to observe the salubrious effects of rural recreation on the people. If all goes well, you could write about its progress for Henry's paper.'

That did not seem an outlandish proposition. Even if it did not accord with Marchmont's laissez-faire sensibility, it would probably find an audience with Rennert. I asked her when they proposed to implement the scheme.

'The plans are already afoot! There's a list of sixty or seventy locals who have applied for the inaugural outing a few weeks hence. As I understand it, a train will take us from St Pancras Station to a meadow somewhere in Bedfordshire, where food and entertainment will be provided for the day. I would only need to tell Father Kay that we'd like to join them.'

I might have known there would be a catch. 'Father Kay?'

'He runs a parish in Somers Town – I thought you might know him. He will be taking charge of the excursions.'

'I see. Should we expect to be led in prayer?'

Kitty took the question innocently. 'I suppose we might . . . but it's not a religious charity, if that's what you're thinking. He just happens to be on the board.' She must have detected a slackening in my enthusiasm, for now she said, 'It will be quite informal, of course. You could bring that friend of yours along – the one you've talked about?'

'Jo? Unlikely, I think. He's never been outside of London.'

'What, *never?* Well then, all the more reason to invite him. And it will be on a Sunday, too, the day of rest.'

I shook my head. 'Sunday is Jo's busiest time.'

She digested this information, and said, 'Someone else, then? I'm sure you have other friends who'd enjoy a day out.' Even that modest estimation of my acquaintance was quite mistaken – in London I knew barely anyone to call a friend – but I was too proud to admit it. My hesitation seemed to alarm her, and she grasped my sleeve. 'Please say *you* will come.'

I was too touched by her supplication to refuse. 'Yours to command. We shall be company enough for one another.'

She beamed her gratitude. 'I am greatly relieved! I don't know whom I should have turned to if you'd declined.'

I knew. 'Ferdinand?' – which earned me an outraged giggle and a schoolmarmish slap on the wrist.

The following Friday was Jo's birthday, and he was holding a little celebration, as custom demanded, upstairs at the Rainbow. In the weeks preceding the event I had been puzzling over what gift I should bring. The simplest course would have been to stop at the Home and Colonial Stores and buy sweetmeats or a bottle of gin and a screw of 'baccy', but I was minded to give him something of more lasting value. He didn't read (I wasn't sure how well he *could* read) so a book would be of no use, and, his beloved knife excepted, he was unsentimental about trinkets or silver, being more inclined to sell things on than keep hold of them. I had all but forsaken this quest when, the day before, I happened to turn off Upper Street into a quaint narrow lane of shops previously unknown to me. Outside one of them stood a rocking horse, as though tethered there, and I found myself staring into the window of a most wondrous old toy shop, of a sort I never thought to exist any more. I concede that the glassed display was strictly intended for a child, but I found myself transfixed by this Aladdin's cave of jack-in-the-boxes, black-eyed dolls, mechanical gewgaws, dioramas, magic lanterns, intricate miniature galleons inside bulbous bottles, lead soldiers in the livery of redcoats and Roman legionaries, all illumined in the soft glow of the gaslight. But what captivated my gaze was an item perched high in one corner, its articulated form so enchanting – so strangely *hilarious* – that I knew instantly it was the gift I was meant to give Jo.

I did have second thoughts, on the night, with that beribboned box resting in my lap as the 'bus bumped down the hill towards Euston Road. Would Jo really see the charm of what was, incontrovertibly, a toy? Perhaps my unease derived rather from consideration of the smart togs I wore. I could not exactly fathom why I should have dressed up for the occasion, but now that I was earning a weekly screw the price of a new suit of clothes seemed no longer prohibitive. The brown worsted which the tailor had made up for me still felt like someone else's, someone smarter, and the boots with cork soles would not have disgraced Marchmont himself. I stepped off the 'bus at St Pancras to give my legs a bit of a stretch, and as I walked through the Brill the last of the stallholders were packing up for the day, the cobbles still green from their leavings. I recognised most of the costers, so often had I traipsed up and down these streets.

My misgivings were well founded. No sooner had I entered the upper room of the Rainbow than I ran straight into Jo, who hooted with laughter. 'It's Champagne Charlie!' he cried, looking me up and down. 'Some old uncle took a blinder and leave yer 'is h'estate?'

'No . . . It's just a suit, one you've not seen –' But Jo, deciding that I must have inherited a fortune, was singing over my defensive reply: '*All round the town it is the same / By Pop! Pop! Pop! I rose to fame! / I'm the idol of the ba-a-a-armaids / And Champagne Charlie is me name.*'

Nell and Nora, his giggly familiars from the last time I was here, were at his shoulder, and the pianist, overhearing a popular soubriquet, obligingly tinkled out the notes to 'Champagne Charlie'. And so the whole room joined in, and I kept my head bowed so as not to draw attention to myself as the object of Jo's chaffing. He had now picked up a tray of half-and-halfs from the bar and, over the music, was signalling me to follow him. I edged through the scrum of Friday-night revellers to reach his table, where sat a whole company of people I'd never met before, all of them singing. Jo, depositing the drinks, turned and whispered in my ear: 'They're singin' your song!' I thought he was about to continue his teasing and introduce me as 'Charlie', but he took pity instead and called out, with his mitt on my shoulder, 'This 'ere's Davie.' A beery chorus of greetings rose up. There was one amongst them, of course, I already knew, and she was watching me with her disconcerting feline stillness. 'You go and sit by me sis,' said Jo, and I needed no further prompt. Before I did so I handed Jo his box with a 'happy birthday'.

There was barely room on the bench for me, but Roma wordlessly moved along and I squeezed myself in next to her. The tiniest gleam was perceptible in her gaze, and I had the impression she was trying not to laugh. I loosened my collar, feeling suddenly warm.

'Nice togs,' she said by way of greeting, and in my surprise and relief I raised my pint of ale to her – too quickly, for it sloshed over the lip of the pewter and soaked my sleeve. She smiled slightly, and shook her head, as if she expected no better. It was a look I was beginning to know.

'Jo reckons they're a bit . . . tofficky,' I confessed.

Roma offered no reply, merely kept a level gaze, as if considering the justice of Jo's estimation. Her silences were unnerving precisely because you could never tell what she was thinking. Eventually – minutes seemed to have elapsed – she said, 'We haven't seen you round here for a while.'

'Yes . . . I think I've become of less use to the paper. Marchmont doesn't seem so interested in Somers Town any more.'

She gave a sardonic moue. 'They all lose interest in the end.'

I shrugged, and told her of my enquiries concerning the leaseholders. 'What I can't understand is how the leases have changed hands so quickly. I visited the Records Office and found that Moyles and his cronies are no longer liable as landlords – they've ceded the worst of their property to a company named Condor Holdings. And unless –'

The sombre turn of this conversation was interrupted by a strange

cackle from across the table. Jo had just then uncovered the contents of
his birthday box and was holding it up to view. The gift I had brought
was now displayed for all: a wooden monkey with articulated limbs and
an expression altogether more prepossessing than Ferdinand's. The faces
crowding round the toy and its recipient looked bemused, but not
unimpressed.

'Cool this feller!' laughed Jo, jigging the monkey about as though it
were a living creature. He looked over at me and cried *Davie!*, which I
was pleased to interpret as a lively expression of thanks. For the second
time that evening Jo was moved to sing, and (as I remember) his ditty
went thus:

> *Click, click, I'm a monkey on a stick*
> *And anyone with me can play*
> *And my antics he'll enjoy till he finds a newer toy*
> *Then he'll bid me a polite good day.*

This provoked another burst of laughter from his companions, who
were now scrutinising the monkey as if it were some creature I had
personally carried back from the Galapagos Islands. I turned to Roma,
whose open smile at Jo, different from the Mona Lisa twitch I knew,
had transformed her face: the delight on it seemed the more precious
for being so rarely glimpsed.

'Does Jo have a song for every occasion?' I asked.

'Most you'd care to mention,' she conceded. 'Our mum knew lots
of songs – ballads and such – but Jo would've been too young to
remember them.'

'Maybe it's in the blood.'

She was still looking fondly at her brother. 'He's pleased with his
new pet, anyways. Where d'you come by it?'

'A toy shop near Upper Street. I've had monkeys on the brain ever
since a friend of mine – Kitty – acquired one. A real one, I mean.'

'Oh. Kitty your girlfriend, is she?'

'No, no. She's the daughter of my godfather.' I didn't dare to enlarge
on that, sensing that Roma would not be impressed to hear of the high-
born Elders or their fabulous wealth. But I couldn't altogether ignore the
connection, now that it had been raised. 'As a matter of fact, she's invited
me to join her in a charitable venture a few weeks hence. We are to
accompany a large party of Somers Town people on a country jaunt – a
meadow somewhere in Bedfordshire, as I understand, where food and

entertainments will be provided.' I gave a slightly nervous shrug. 'A day out for those who perhaps cannot afford one . . . It seems to me a worthy cause.'

Roma considered, frowning. 'I didn't know you worked for a charity.' The way she said the word put me on guard.

'I don't – my purpose is to report on it. You have a dislike of charity?'

'No. I just don't believe it's charity that people deserve – it's justice.'

The implications of that seemed well-nigh impossible to challenge. I took a long draught of my half-and-half. 'So, I should presume that you would rather not . . . join me for the day.'

'Why should you presume that? A day in the country might be just what I fancy'.

'Is it?' I said, a rising note of hopefulness in my voice.

'I dunno,' she replied coolly. 'Depends on who arsked me.'

I blinked at her. 'Have I not just asked you?'

'No. You said that you "presumed" I'd rather not. You didn't *arsk* me.'

I was careful not to show my exasperation. 'Very well. Would you consent to accompany me?'

She bowed her head in an exaggerated gesture of graciousness, then said, 'I'll think about it.'

The rest of the evening concertinaed in a blur of ale and porter and singing. Jo, used to keeping them in a roar upstairs at the Rainbow, gave a full-throated recital of his repertoire, then Roma herself (at my request) sang 'The Leary Man'. For some reason a couple of lines from it – *For every day, mind what I say, / Fresh fakements you will find* – had lodged in my head as I accompanied Roma, arm linked with Jo's, along the midnight streets back to the Polygon. On the way I mentioned the charity outing to Jo, expecting him to decline, but to my surprise he responded with bright-eyed alacrity. He would leave his Sunday stall to the care of a pal.

'Free grog and skittles for a day – doogheno!'

'By "refreshment" I think they mean lemonade rather than grog,' I said quickly. 'It won't be like a night at the Rainbow.'

He shrugged amenably. ''S all right. I 'ear as the countryside's pretty as a pitcher, but them that lives there is a queer lot.'

'Some are a little odd,' I admitted, 'but most you will find quite friendly.'

We had stopped at their door when I happened to look up, and a shaft of moonlight glinted on something affixed to the wall of the

Polygon. Squinting, I made out a brownish memorial tablet on which was inscribed the following: *William Godwin and Mary Wollstonecraft lived at this address Anno Domini 1797*. I had never noticed it there before. I turned to Roma. 'What were they known for?'

She looked disbelieving. 'You must be joking. She was a famous author, wrote books about women and how they've been cheated and done down – by men. He was an author, too, Godwin. They'd just got married when she died, in childbirth.' She paused a moment. 'You didn't know?'

'I'm afraid not. I've never *heard* of them.'

She clicked her tongue in reproof. Now Jo spoke up, 'They sez Dickens lived 'ere too for a bit, when he was a lad, an' up at Bayham Street.'

'You've heard of Dickens, haven't you?' said Roma drily.

'Yes, of course I have,' I replied, offended. 'I will be sure to borrow a book of this Mary Woll – what's-her-name – at Mudie's, if she's indeed so famous.'

We had said our goodnights, and they were climbing the steps up to the door when I called to Jo that he should keep the Sunday week free for our trip.

'Sunday week, prime. Anyone else comin'?'

'I've asked your sister,' I said, with a glance at Roma, 'and still wait on her reply.'

Roma, jiggling her latchkey in her hand, gave me a sidelong look. 'I s'pose I should go. Keep you two out of mischief.'

Jo, emitting a series of animal grunts, hoisted his monkey onto his shoulder. '*Three*, ya mean.'

9
Bindon Fields

What is it that makes us persist in the face of fatigue, discouragement and dreariness? Or, more precisely, what made *me* persist in an endeavour that seemed utterly unprofitable? I had been knocking at the door of Condor Holdings for weeks and had received not a peep from the place or its representatives. My letters had gone unanswered. I would have been tempted to dismiss the company as a chimera, a figment, were it not for their name, inscribed in black and white, on that list of occupants at Bishopsgate House. Someone had taken the trouble to affix the plate there, so it *had* to have some material form. I was waiting as usual on the fifth floor one afternoon, my eyes glazing over, when something happened.

A man in smart checks and bowler, with a watch chain glinting on his waistcoat, came down the corridor and – to my astonishment – unlocked the office door at which I had been keeping my tiresome vigil. Without a glance at me he disappeared inside. Finally! I rose, and knocked, and waited. When no reply came I knocked again, and then repeatedly for the next five minutes. Exasperation must have compelled him to answer, because the face that appeared at the jamb contained no glimmer of a welcome.

'Good day,' I began. 'I've been trying –'

'What business have you here?' he cut in sharply.

'My name is Wildeblood and I'm pursuing an enquiry into property developments at Somers Town.'

He stared hard at me. 'On whose behalf?'

I sensed that to reply 'the renting classes' would not be to my advantage. 'A private client.'

At this the man stepped brusquely past me and looked both ways down the corridor, as if he were expecting to find a phalanx of heavies in attendance. Once he realised that I was alone, he squared up to me, so close I could see the stubble on his chin and smell the cigar on his breath. 'Don't call at this office again – understand?' he said, then turned his back and closed the door on me. For a moment I was too stunned to move. After all of my petitions and letters, all the waiting and stalking, *this* was the manner of reply I was to expect? I was about to start banging on the door again and demand satisfaction when an impulse cautioned me to hold off. If secretiveness and intimidation were the principal tools by which the company appeared to operate, then I would have to be a little shrewder in my dealings with them.

I checked my watch: it was twenty past four. The offices would close at six. I took the stairs to the atrium and walked out onto Bishopsgate Street, where I spotted a low dining room directly opposite the building I had just exited. Inside, I waited for a table by the window, and then installed myself there, twitching the dusty net curtains to get a better view of the entrance to Bishopsgate House. I worried that amidst the toing and froing of City gents and clerks I would fail to spot the check-suited fellow emerge. I waited, drinking tea and wiping the condensation from my lookout window (the noise and steam from the cooking in there was monstrous). Five o'clock came and went, and by half past I was convinced that he had somehow eluded me. Perhaps the building had a back entrance and he had slipped out that way. At ten to six I paid my bill and returned to the street, berating myself for the missed opportunity – and at that moment the Condor Holdings man came trotting down the steps in my direction. If his eyeline had strayed an inch to his left he would have seen and recognised me as the pest at his door, but it did not, and he walked right past me. It was a gift from Providence I was determined not to spurn.

My quarry had a purposeful gait, and my first anxiety was that he would outpace me and vanish into the thickening late-afternoon crowds. I dared not get closer than twenty yards to him lest he sensed his footsteps being dogged. It was fortunate that the suit he wore, with its green-and-brown checks, was sufficiently distinctive to mark him at a distance. He had turned off Bishopsgate into Cornhill, at this hour a streaming mass of toppered gents on their way home. At Cheapside he stepped onto an omnibus, and I thought he had given me the slip; but Providence was once again my friend, for another 'bus, the first one's twin, happened to be passing, and reaching for the pole I clung on as it rattled west. Towards Holborn Circus the wheel traffic began to cluster, and, halted at a crossing, I darted from my hanging post and leapt to catch the one on the 'bus in front. I spied the man sitting on the knifeboard upstairs, and, shielding my face, settled in at the back.

As the 'bus continued its bumpy course along Oxford Street – a maddening din of wheels and hooves – I considered what I should do were the fellow to be run to ground. His demeanour had argued a certain brusqueness that might turn unpleasant if provoked. I was calculating my chances when, at the junction of Baker Street, he rose and edged his way towards the stairs. Having pulled my hat over my brow, I sensed his shadow loom across me, and stop: for a moment I thought the jig was up, and he was waiting for me to look him in the face. Head down, I held my breath – and then the shadow moved on, his pause explained by the crush of other passengers waiting to alight. Down the stairs he went, and I was on his heels again as he turned up Baker Street. He stopped, once, to buy a *Standard* from a street vendor, and I loitered by a shop window before he moved on again, a left turn, then a right. We were now in a district which suddenly seemed familiar, and it took me a minute to realise why: the man was heading directly into Montagu Square, which I had last visited the week in February I had started at the paper. I dawdled around the square's railings, watching yet hardly believing, as the man stopped and knocked at the one and only residence I knew there. The door was opened, the man disappeared within. Had I made a mistake? I took out my notebook, and flipped to a list of addresses. There was no mistake. It was a house I had once entered myself – Marchmont's house.

It was an early summer's evening, and I noticed the narrow public garden in the square was still open. The tall chestnuts and hedges provided handy cover against being spotted from the house. And there I lurked, my mind as giddy as a spinning top. What business did Marchmont have with an agent for Condor Holdings? Did he know about the galloping progress of clearances in Somers Town, and, if so, why had he not made efforts to oppose it? Then I wondered if there might be a more innocent explanation. It was a Friday, which I now recalled Marchmont describing as his 'card night' before he cut short our interview. Perhaps the fellow I had pursued to his door was simply another of his gaming cronies. Ten minutes later a carriage drew up outside; the door of the house opened, and there he appeared, with his unmistakable rolling gait – Marchmont – and the check-suited man in tow. They climbed in. I was close enough to see Marchmont signal to the driver with a tap of his cane on the top, and they were gone.

Checking my watch, I knew that Paget would have finished for the day at the *Chronicle*, and that he might be found at one of his haunts off Fetter Lane. In my urgency I hailed a hansom, and soon we were clattering back across town towards the City. Within twenty minutes I was paying off the cabby at Holborn Circus and hurrying between those public houses frequented by newspapermen. At the third I tried Paget was standing at the bar with some of his familiars, and caught sight of me agitatedly beckoning him over. I realised only then that sweat was pouring off my face.

'You look as though you've been chased here,' he remarked.

I mopped my brow. 'D'you recall my asking you about a company named Condor Holdings?'

'The one listed on the leases?'

'Yes! I've been trying to hunt them down for weeks – they're more secretive than the Masons. But here is their dodge. Most of the leases are fast-expiring, so if the landlord gambles right, he will be able to get to the end of the lease without spending any money on improvements. The houses meanwhile fall into disrepair, the leases are acquired by Condor Holdings, they decide for the sake of profit to raze the lot.' Paget began to speak, but I interrupted him, gabbling through the story of how I had just stalked the agent across town to Montagu Square. 'And whose house d'you suppose he called at? Marchmont's!'

He raised his eyebrows briefly, though his expression betrayed nothing beyond thoughtfulness. After some moments he said, 'Let us not forget that Henry has many business interests. If Condor Holdings is amongst them, what of it? It's a registered company, even if it is rather particular about its privacy.'

'But you said yourself – the first time we met – property has its duties as well as its rights.'

'Indeed I did.'

'Then surely you see the conflict? They are overseeing a demolition of property that will leave many in Somers Town homeless. Marchmont's own periodical exists to report on the hardship of just those people. Now it seems that he is hand-in-glove with the destroyers.'

He sighed. 'I have seen too much of Henry's sharp practice to be surprised. It is unethical, I agree. But not illegal. The law says an Englishman is entitled to do with his property as he sees fit, and that includes knocking it down.'

'So . . . there is nothing we can do?' I asked, deflated.

'Not unless we can discover malfeasance in the handling of the leases. Don't despair, my boy. We shall get to the bottom of this affair.' He paused, and his face darkened. 'I have some news, too. You remember that Kenton was arrested at the Trafalgar Square demonstration? Well, he's disappeared.'

'I thought they had released him.'

'They did – but he never returned home. His wife came to me yesterday, said she hadn't seen him in three days.'

'Might he not simply have – left town?'

'Unlikely. Kenton's a family man. He wouldn't abandon them. I visited his printing press in King's Cross and found the place had been turned over. The man is in trouble, I fear.'

'D'you suppose the police are behind it?'

He shrugged gravely. 'He's been a thorn in their side . . .'

A silence fell between us. I thought of the last time I had seen Kenton, wading into the melee at Trafalgar Square and being set upon by the slops. He had spearheaded a movement to change living conditions, not just in Somers Town but in other downtrodden neighbourhoods of London. In reward for his efforts he had somehow become an enemy of the state. Paget cleared his throat again. 'I don't wish to alarm you, David, but you would do well to be on your guard,' he said. 'Kenton told me some weeks ago he was being followed. It's conceivable that you and I are also under scrutiny.'

'I hardly think –'.

'Listen to me – this government has a morbid fear of revolution, and Kenton has been identified as one of its possible fomenters. Even as distant associates of his we should be on our guard.'

'But Kenton's only gone missing, he's not *dead*. Chances are he's just lying low somewhere.'

Paget nodded, but he looked very far from convinced.

The day of the Bedfordshire outing, a Sunday in the middle of June, began fair, and gradually melted into sultriness. The prospect of this rural venture, too eagerly awaited, had disturbed my sleep, and I woke early enough to hear the milk seller's cart horse clopping on the street below. My landlady had not yet risen, so I dressed and set off with a view to having breakfast on the way to the station. I called at an eating house on the edge of the Brill called Casti's, a place that opened early to serve the market traders and railway workers. I drank coffee at the counter and marvelled silently as the coster next to me drank off a glass of short with his saveloy. Gin, at this hour! I was taking my leave when I saw from the corner of my eye two ruffian fellows hunkered over their breakfast. There was nothing unusual about such types, not in Somers Town, only that I had the disagreeable sensation of having seen them before. I managed to slip away without their noticing me.

Five minutes later I was standing at the concourse of St Pancras Station amidst swarming crowds of travellers such as Mr Frith might have painted. It soon became apparent that most of them were bound on the same excursion as I. Here and there charity employees bustled about, identified by scarlet sashes on which was emblazoned 'Social Protection League'. Beneath the giant vaulted roof hissing swathes of steam rose from an incoming train, and the waiting throng turned like a herd of cattle towards the platforms.

'Davie,' said a voice behind me, and I turned to find Jo, in his Sunday togs, and Roma next to him. She was wearing a navy dress with a yoke collar, and had braided her dark hair. I stuttered out a greeting.

'Looks like every coster in the Brill is 'avin' a day out,' he said, swivelling his gaze around us. 'They'd have to make a lot o' sandwiches to feed this mob.'

'I imagine so. Shall we find a carriage?' I led the way along the platform, hoping to spot Kitty, though I guessed that she'd be occupied with looking after the board members and patrons. After giving our names to one of the registrars, we stepped onto the train and found an empty compartment. Roma and I sat opposite one another by the window, whilst Jo stood outside in the corridor, smoking his pipe and chatting to a couple of his mates. I gazed from under my brow at Roma, and wondered what she was thinking.

A sudden jolt shook me out of this reverie. The train had begun to move off, slowly, so slowly at first that it seemed the platform outside was shifting, not the carriage. As it gathered speed, the window showed the backs of houses, cramped yards, belching chimneys, and odd perspectives on buildings which only a railway journey ever provided. We passed through back-to-front Camden and Kentish Town, a monotony of suburban terraces, then the city began to straggle and thin out; instead of houses and pubs and factories we began to see fields and hedges. I turned to Roma, who had also been absorbed in our progress.

'D'you think you will like the countryside?'

She glanced at me, then turned back to the window. 'Maybe. Friends who lived there say how quiet it is, without the noise of traffic – or people. I remember my mum sayin' when she was a girl, in Italy, you could have whole days when you 'eard nothin' but birdsong.'

'So she was a country girl herself?'

Roma nodded. 'Yeah. She adored the place, but, as I heard it, the life got so hard in their village – Monty-somethin' – her parents reckoned they should starve if they didn't leave quick. How they ended up in Somers Town I don't know. An' with them gone I s'pose I never will.' Her tone became musing. 'It's an odd thing, ain't it, that my mum should've come all that way, through all those countries in Europe, yet here we are, Jo and me, never once been out of London.'

'Aren't you curious to know where she came from?'

'I try to imagine it,' she said, and a rare smile formed on her lips. 'It's very beautiful, they say. I should have liked to visit, one day . . . Florence, that was the nearest city to them. They used to show me little pictures of it.'

'But they called you "Roma" instead,' I said.

'Yeah, well . . . p'raps they thought it easier to spell! *Un paese bellissimo, parole non potranno descrivere la sua bellezza . . . Dio si stava mettendo in mostra quando ha creato l'Italia.* That's what my mum would've said.'

'Good Lord! What does that mean?'

'Oh – "A beautiful country, more beautiful than anyone could describe it – God was showing off when He made Italy."' She laughed at that, though there was something wistful in the sigh that followed it.

'But really,' I continued, 'should you not like to go? The land of your forefathers?'

'What I should like to do ain't the same as what I can afford to do. Believe me. Not much chance of my goin' abroad when I spends my days tottin' up ha'pennies.'

I wanted then to say that *I* would pay for her to go, if I were able. But of course I didn't dare. I could picture only too well her look of scornful pride as she declined such an offer. It was a point of principle to her that she would not accept charity, and even today's venture she had only undertaken as a favour to me. At that moment there came a tap on the glass of our compartment door and Kitty, wearing one of the charity sashes over her dress, pushed it open.

'David! I've been searching the whole train for you,' she said gaily, turning an expectant look upon my companion opposite.

'Kitty, this is Roma,' I said. Jo, who was loitering in the corridor as Kitty arrived, now hovered behind her, widening his eyes comically. 'And this is Jo.'

She clutched Jo's hand with enthusiasm. 'Now *you* I've heard all about,' she cried. Jo, bemused, looked from Kitty to me as though to say, *Who's this?* I invited her to sit down, and explained our connection to one another.

'. . . I didn't even know Papa *had* a godson, in truth, but we've become fast friends ever since,' Kitty supplied, before directing her helpless charm upon Roma. 'Such a lovely name,' she cooed, searching her face. 'Are you Italian?'

Roma shook her head. 'I was born in Camden Town, like my pa. But my mother was Italian.'

'We've lately been talking of Italy,' I said, endeavouring to oil the social wheels. 'Have you ever been there, Kitty?'

'Only the Lakes,' she replied breezily. 'But I do long to go to Venice, and Naples – and Rome, of course!' She beamed at each of us, as if in hope of securing our approval. Roma watched her, but said nothing.

'I served a cove from Naples at the stall a while back,' Jo piped up. 'Merchant sailor, he was. Very fond of peaches. Used to sell 'em to him by the plasket. I learned somethin' from 'im too – before that I always thought Naples was in *India*.'

Kitty burst out laughing at this, and Jo, delighted to tweak anyone's funny bone, even by accident, joined in.

'I'm sorry not to be sitting with you,' said Kitty, 'but I've been told to look after the board's patrons in First – and a stuffy lot they are! Only, I should like you to meet Father Kay, he's rather an interesting character. He's vicar at the Church of St Columba in Somers Town – do you know it?'

'I've passed by it,' said Roma. 'Anglican place, ain't it?'

'It is. I suppose you must be . . . Roman Catholic?'

'Well, Ro here is,' said Jo. 'I don't much care for churchgoin' meself.'

'A vicar who calls himself Father?' I said.

'He's very High Church, all incense, candles and whatnot. I gather some of his parishioners are rather disturbed by his Romish tendencies. But he's been a stalwart of the Social Protection League, and he's always collecting money for it.'

'That sounds like a Catholic,' said Roma drily. Kitty shot an anxious look at her.

'We look forward to being introduced, I'm sure,' I said. Green fields and copses slid by the window, now glinting from the rays of a high-hoisted sun. It was becoming quite warm in the carriage. Kitty stood and said that she'd better be getting back. 'But I'll see you once we arrive at Bindon Fields.'

'Yeah. We could 'ave our wittles together,' said Jo brightly. Kitty looked blank, and turned to me for elucidation.

'Perhaps you could join us for luncheon,' I supplied.

'Oh, I do hope so!' she said in a tone of breathless sincerity; and, with a little wave, she was gone. I felt Roma's eyes on me as I plumped back down on the seat. Kitty's brief appearance had left us unexpectedly tongue-tied, and the rhythmic clacking of the rails below filled in the silence. It was Jo who at length was moved to comment on our recent visitor.

'Snappy gal, that,' he mused approvingly. 'I never knowed you 'ad *h'aristocratic* relations, Davie!'

'She's not a relation,' I replied, 'she's the daughter of my godfather.'

Jo, who didn't quite comprehend the nature of a godfather, only shrugged. I looked to Roma enquiringly, but her expression was just as inscrutable as ever. 'I liked that diamond on her finger,' she said quietly. 'Very handsome.'

'Yeah,' agreed Jo, 'don't see sparklers like that down Chalton Street . . .' He tilted his head, and then whistled a few bars. '*'Twas a diamond as bright as a harvest moon . . .* How does that one go, Ro?'

Roma smiled, and shook her head.

Jo was still testing the words of his half-remembered ditty when the train began to slow, then came to a shuddering halt at a tiny railway station, Bindon, whose modest proportions seemed barely ready to accommodate more than a handful of visitors at a time. Its white-painted fences and dainty windows bearded with flowerboxes lent it a quaintness very alien to the monstrous black halls of smoke and clangour that we knew from the railway termini of London. This rural backwater had surely never seen such crowds disgorged onto its platform. The League's stewards were directing the press of bodies out through the station's surprised vestibule and thence up a narrow lane with hedgerows on either side. At the front of what was now a long queue I could see Kitty gamely assisting one of the less mobile patrons, whilst further along the lane a five-bar gate was being opened in welcome. My idly roving gaze was arrested, quite abruptly, by the sight of the two men whose faces I had lately spied over breakfast in Casti's. They were strolling about twenty yards ahead of us, and now I recalled the last occasion I had met them: one was the fellow who had lifted my purse that day in the Brill, the other was the gang leader from whose further depredations Jo had saved me.

I nudged Jo at my side, and directed his attention towards the pair: I saw his dark eyes widen, momentarily, as he took them in.

'Gaffy, an' his mate Tig. He was the dab tros—'

'I know, I remember.' I also remembered Gaffy's murderous look when Jo brandished his knife in warning. 'What are they doing here?'

Jo hoisted his eyebrows, as though to say, *You have to ask?* Crowds would always attract that rank of the criminal fraternity who tended to work in close quarters – the priggers and lifters and dippers. Whilst race meetings and prizefights were their usual haunts, an outing such as today's would be regarded as 'prime', for who would think of their pocket being picked on an occasion sponsored by a charity?

In a nervous reflex I felt for the purse in my coat, and found it secure. After some minutes of dawdling at a bottleneck in the crowd, we were finally ushered into Bindon Fields, a wide expanse of meadowland bordered by lines of mature trees with a little wood sloping off at its far end. The sun, reclining on the pillowy clouds, burned down majestically. Shielding their eyes against the glare, Jo and Roma both appeared at a loss, stunned by so much open sky and a world quite empty of buildings and traffic. We were evidently the second trainload to have arrived from London, for the fields were already host to a large crowd. Little parties of folk sat on picnic blankets or else roamed about the place, which resembled nothing so much as a country fair. Young men and women threw quoits in contest, or shied at coconuts in stalls; a little knot of them had started a game of rounders. Most of the children were sitting cross-legged and entranced by a Punch and Judy show. It was the very picture of bucolic contentment.

Long trestles had been set up for serving refreshments, cold fowl, potted herrings and mutton pies, crusty bread, bowls of fruit, ginger beer and lemonade. One of the volunteers handed us a blanket, which we took and spread on a spot at the edge of the wood. The overhanging beeches provided a cool shade from the noonday sun. Roma took a bite of an apple, and stared into the distance, bemused.

'The Social Protection League,' she said, reciting the name blazoned across the stewards' sashes. 'Never heard of 'em. Have you?'

I shook my head. 'I know of it only through Kitty. She's very keen on charitable works.'

I expected a sardonic response to this, but Roma's expression was only thoughtful. After a few moments she fixed her gaze upon me. 'Don't you come from a place like this?'

'You mean the country? Yes . . . I was raised in a quiet, out-of-the-way sort of village, in Norfolk.'

'Norfolk,' repeated Jo. 'I've 'eard that name. Where is it?'

'Oh, it's a county in the east, a good few miles –'

'Nah, I mean, where is it from *here?*'

Jo's grasp of geography was based simply on an estimation of distances from wherever he stood. I looked up to check from where the sun was coming. 'Over that way,' I said, pointing in an easterly direction. It seemed to satisfy him. Roma's curiosity, however, was more searching.

'So – did you not like the life in Norfolk?'

'I liked it . . . well enough. But circumstances obliged me to seek employment elsewhere. My godfather used his influence to secure a position for me at Marchmont's periodical, and so I came to London.'

'Circumstances . . .' she said in echo. Her gaze had become very shrewd.

At that moment our conversation was interrupted by the approach of Kitty, with a companion. As we went through the introductions, I sensed Roma's curiosity still directed upon me, but I didn't trust myself to catch her eye. The gentleman at Kitty's side was Father Kay, a thickset, muscular fellow in his forties with a pugilist's nose and a penetrating sharpness in his gaze. His dark hair was oiled neatly back from his forehead.

'Do be seated,' he said, for we had all stood to greet him. 'Catherine here tells me this is your first time out of London. Does it please you?' He addressed this question mainly to Jo, who had been idly peeling an apple with his knife.

'Very well, sir,' said Jo, levering a slice from the blade to his mouth. 'Though the country's a queer sort of place. Not a single 'ouse in it!'

'Quite a chive you have there,' said Father Kay, squinting at Jo's knife. His voice carried the faint trace of an Irish brogue. 'I hadn't expected a man of the cloth to know a flash word like *chive*.

'Oh, just for parin' an' whatnot,' replied Jo equably, though he now folded away his knife to spare himself further scrutiny. The reverend stared at him for some moments, considering, then turned to survey the leisurely scene before us.

'A gratifying sight, is it not? The working people of London at last granted an opportunity to drink in the clean air of the country . . . What I would give to whisk away every parishioner of mine from the polluted city streets and establish them here. The changes we should see!'

'Your parishioners might not thank you for it,' I said after a pause. 'From my experience the people of Somers Town like where they live. There is a familiarity, even in hardship, that binds them to the place.'

'David is one of Mr Marchmont's inspectors,' said Kitty to Father Kay, who listened in perfect stillness to my counter-argument, before replying.

'Well, there is a troublesome ignorance at large. Which of us would choose to abide in a degraded urban district rather than enjoy a wholesome, healthy life in such a place as this?' He spread his palms in a gesture of saintly reasonableness. He spoke as one apparently unaware of the fact that Roma and Jo were denizens of the very place he had just called degraded.

I cleared my throat. 'With respect, one could better serve people by an improvement of their living standards. The streets are only "polluted" because those who govern us allow them to be. If the state provided decent housing and sanitation there would be no need to uproot whole neighbourhoods and resettle them in the country.'

Father Kay was shaking his head in regret. 'Such a scheme of amelioration would take years, decades, to become effectual. In the meantime the criminal elements of society will go unchecked, adding to the sum of human misery.'

I had heard this line of reasoning before. 'May I ask, Father, do you know Montgomery Sprule?'

A flicker of surprise registered in the rector's eyes. 'I do indeed. Monty – Mr Sprule – is on our advisory board. We have congenial views on certain social questions.'

'That I can believe,' I said. Kitty, alert to something adversarial in the tenor of this conversation, smoothly interposed herself.

'Father, time presses. There are several trustees to whom I should like to introduce you before the day is through.' Father Kay rose to his feet without demur, and, clearing his throat, addressed us in a blandly formal tone.

'Bow your heads for God's blessing,' he said, and began muttering some phrases in Latin and then in English. I was rather dumbfounded by this, but out of some mechanical deference I cast my gaze to the ground. Just as she lowered her head I caught Roma's frowning expression of incredulity and was obliged to bite back the laughter rising in my throat. Jo fidgeted uncomfortably, though he did at least stop chewing his apple. Father Kay finished his prayer, and having wafted a beatific sign of the cross over us he allowed Kitty to lead him away.

When they were out of earshot, Roma said wryly, 'I'da thought it was polite to *arsk* whether we wanted his blessing or not.'

'Perhaps we should mention that to him next time,' I said. 'I'll go and fetch us something to drink.' As I crossed the field I noticed the disreputable pair of Gaffy and Tig deep in talk with one of the charity stewards, and hoped that the latter wasn't carrying any valuables on his person. Weaving through the crowds, I reached a trestle where drinks were being served and collected three glasses of ginger beer. On returning to our spot I found Roma sitting alone; Jo, typically restless, had gone off to look for his coster pals.

I folded myself down onto the blanket and handed her a glass, and we sat there for a few moments in silence, gazing over the fields. I couldn't exactly tell what had changed – perhaps it was only the effect of the day's pleasant warmth – but Roma had softened to the point where I appeared to have become an object of interest to her.

'Is something the matter?' I asked.

She smiled and shook her head. She was not one to look embarrassed at being caught staring. 'I'm a little surprised.'

'Oh . . . by what?'

'By you. It bothers you, doesn't it? When we first met I 'ad you down as another of 'em who comes from up west to walk round the 'ouses and stare at the poor. Or the sort that's always handin' out tracts and callin' it charity.'

'So . . . you thought I just went slumming?' I could not hide the hurt in my voice.

'Maybe. But – from the way you talked to his holiness before, it's like – I dunno, like you care too much.'

'How can anyone care too much?' I said.

She shrugged. 'You're different, that's all. Most as come to Somers Town just 'spect it to be a den of thieves.'

I was about to savour this morsel of approbation when my eye was distracted by an extraordinary flash of colour. Poised, quivering, on the edge of our blanket, was a butterfly, glossily flushed; the sight of its deep maroon wings, bordered with cream and a hem of light blue spots, caused me a little intake of breath. It was a matter of inches from where Roma sat.

'Don't move,' I said to her. She followed my gaze to where the dainty creature had composed itself. Holding my breath, I got up on my haunches and shifted forward, crab-like; just as I reached a hand to the butterfly it stirred its wings and rose, fluttering upwards like a miniature kite, and fled into the trees. 'Quickly,' I said to Roma. She rose willingly enough, though her expression frowned bemusement.

'What's your hurry?' she asked. We were now striding amongst the trees.

'I think I have just seen . . . a most uncommon thing!' Twigs cracked drily beneath our feet as we stalked further into the wood, with light from the sun sparkling through the interstices of the branches. The secretive woodland scent of moss and leaves rose to our nostrils. We waded through bracken, and a frantic rustling in the undergrowth caused Roma to jump in fright.

'Don't worry, it's only a rabbit. Or a pheasant.' I took her hand; I had forgotten how the country and its underlife might alarm her. We walked on, looking to the left and right of us, and I found myself praying – to whom, to what? – that I would get a second chance with my quarry.

'So it's . . . rare?'

'Intensely rare,' I replied. 'Some years a small number of them reach England, generally from Scandinavia. I have only ever seen it before under a glass – ah . . .' At that moment I had caught sight of it again. It was nearly camouflaged against the trunk of a willow, but its yellowish-cream trim gave it away; I stepped closer, hardly daring to breathe, and scooped it up in the cage of my hands. I felt its velvety wings beat madly, and then stop. I took another peek, and knew its identity for certain.

'Come, look,' I said to Roma, who stepped up close and peered into my cupped palms. She gave a little gasp of admiration.

'That it?'

I nodded. 'The Camberwell Beauty. Also known as the mourning cloak – you see the cream border, like a lady's petticoat drooping beneath its dark velvet cloak?'

'Yes!' she cried, and her delighted expression touched me.

'Here, cup your palms against mine,' I said. She looked doubtful, but at my encouragement she did so, and I carefully released the butterfly into her hands. We stood there, silent, fascinated, whilst it flitted and bumped its infinitely light body against Roma's cool, pale hands. Eventually she looked up at me and said, 'To think it's from Camberwell . . .'

'Camberwell used to be a village, middle of the last century. They spotted it first in a place called Cool Arbour Lane.'

'How d'you know all this?'

'Oh. My father was – is – a keen aurelian – that is, he collects butterflies and studies them. He showed me the Camberwell Beauty in a cabinet. He had never seen a live one himself.'

'What would he have done with this?'

'I dare say he would have put it in his specimen jar.'

'You mean – killed it?'

I nodded. 'Put it under his microscope, drawn it, then framed it on his wall. They are his passion.'

Her expression became considering. 'You arsk me,' she said presently, 'it's too beautiful to keep.' I took a long look at the vibrating insect. What my father would have given to see it. I picked up the butterfly between my thumb and finger – that fragile thorax! – and set it on my open hand. It paused there for a moment, unknowing of its freedom, before it lifted, almost floated upwards, wheeling and toppling through the soft air. I felt a sudden piercing sadness, for I knew in all likelihood I would reach the end of my days without seeing another.

We ambled on deeper into the wood. There was a silence between us, but not like the awkward silence of our earliest meetings. The excitement of the butterfly had somehow bound us together; we had just experienced a vision of Nature at its most transient and delicate. We crossed a little brook by means of stepping stones, walked through a glade, then climbed a winding path that skirted the farthest edge of the wood. A half-hour or more may have passed before Roma spoke.

'I've not heard you mention your father before. Why's that?'

I sighed, and paused. 'We are estranged. I've been . . . a disappointment to him, and to my mother.'

'That why you left Norfolk?'

'Yes. It was thought – my continuing there – it became clear . . .' I had stuttered my way to a halt. Then: 'It was best for all concerned that I left.'

Roma possibly heard in those broken phrases a reluctance to elaborate, and I was grateful that she did not persist in her questioning. We had emerged on the other side of the woods, and stopped on seeing, in the distance, a site of construction – three or four houses were halfway to being built. There was no movement around them; the builders would not have worked on a Sunday. The very idea of a house – of a building – in such a remote place seemed incongruous, and vaguely offensive. Who would dare violate such a charming scene?

The sun had dropped low in the sky. I consulted my watch, and was surprised to see that it was gone four o'clock. The hours had melted away since we had pursued our butterfly into the wood. Roma looked about her, wonderingly.

'The quiet of the place . . .'

'I know. After the city it seems uncanny. So tell me, now that you've seen it, where should you choose to live – London, or the country?'

She gave a shrugging look. 'Well, it *is* beautiful . . . but London is all I've ever known. Maybe I'd miss the noise!' she said, squinting into the distance. 'I s'pose I shouldn't mind where my home was, s'long as it were shared with someone who loved me.' I may have imagined it (perhaps the exertion of our walk was to blame) but as I stole a glance at her face I thought I saw the very faintest trace of a blush.

It was agreed that we should return, for the train back to St Pancras was scheduled to depart at five o'clock. I chose what seemed to be a more direct path to the Fields, and, on reaching a tall stile, Roma allowed herself to be lifted down by me. It was the first time I had touched any part of her but her hand, and as I felt the narrow anchor of her hips through her thin dress I was ambushed by a sharp spasm of longing. On the walk back, with Roma at my side in an unusually voluble mood, I fell to hoping that the pink I had seen on her cheek might have some material connection to me.

In retrospect the day must have been too perfect to last. The novelty of the outing, the fine weather, the sighting of the Camberwell beauty and the long walk through the wood with Roma had, by the time of our departure, assumed the magical enchantment of a spell. With the last stragglers having boarded the train and the Bindon guard's whistle blown, we were being agreeably rocked along in a carriage back to London. Roma and I again sat opposite one another, whilst Jo, his face sunburnt from a day in the open, was merrily joshing away with a couple of friends, a gangly cove named Jed and a sweet-faced girl named Liddy. They had just started up a favourite canting song –

> *Oh! where will be the culls of the bing*
> *A hundred stretches hence?*
> *The bene morts who sweetly sing,*
> *A hundred stretches hence?*

– when our carriage door flew open and Kitty burst in, her eyes wild with distress. I had barely risen to my feet before she threw her arms about me and hid her face on my shoulder. The song had died in Jo's throat as we listened to her pitiful sobbing.

'What on earth is it?' For some moments there came no reply, but then she at last lifted her face, and said, between heaving breaths, 'My ring – a diamond – is gone. Stolen.'

Now why, on that last word, my eyes should have found Roma's I cannot rightly say. Perhaps it was because she had noticed the ring earlier – called it 'handsome', indeed – that I sought a complicit understanding of the gravity of this theft. But that meeting of gazes was unfortunately timed. To have followed the word 'stolen' with an instant glance towards her must have given Roma the impression that I had already fixed upon a suspect. Too late I saw my mistake, and coloured deeply, which in itself only damned me further.

This all lasted but a moment. My immediate responsibility was with Kitty, whose expression conveyed an inconsolable misery. (It transpired that the diamond had once belonged to her mother.) No, she had not removed it at any time during the day. She was certain that it was on her hand when she boarded the train. I tried to sound reassuring as I proposed that we repair to her carriage and start our investigation from there: it may simply have slipped from her finger unnoticed, or else might have been picked up from the floor by a passenger. Of course I did not believe any of these mollifications for an instant, but I felt so pained on Kitty's behalf that I clutched at straws. Jo, who had been looking on anxiously, offered his services as co-investigator, and disappeared with Jed to search the other carriages. Before I too left with Kitty I looked over at Roma, but she pointedly refused to meet my eye. For the remainder of the journey to London we scoured every compartment, inventing scenarios as to where Kitty might have mislaid the precious object. But my foreboding that it would not be recovered was confirmed by the time the train pulled into St Pancras.

10
The hereditary taint

A few nights after the Bindon Fields outing I dreamed of my father. I suppose talking to Roma about him and the butterflies must have set it off. I had not seen either of my parents in more than a year, and aside from two letters from my father the previous November concerning my prospective employment through the good offices of Sir Martin, I had had no communication with him. Shame had hitherto stopped my hand from writing (I saw no profit at all in appealing to my mother) but now the apparition of his kindly features during my hours of unconsciousness had stirred me to break the silence. I kept the letter brief, and used the episode of the Camberwell Beauty as my pretext. To a devoted aurelian the report of its sighting would seem a small miracle.

His reply, which followed promptly, was in tone more gracious than I had anticipated, considering what had passed between us. He enquired as to my well-being, and expressed a sincere interest in my progress under Marchmont. And I could almost believe he was touched by the account I had presented of the Camberwell beauty: 'I rejoiced to read of your sighting, as I did in your felicitous description of its markings. Its Latin name, which you do not recall, is *Nymphalis antiopa* . . .' His beautifully even cursive on the page was, I felt, an unspoken rebuke to my own blotchy scrawl. What I had dreaded to read – the history of our estrangement – was delicately swathed in qualifications, like bandages applied to a cut: 'Let us not rehearse the events of a time that cannot be too soon forgotten. What was done will not be undone. You must allow me, however, to challenge one particular offence you have laid, albeit implicitly, to my charge. I have never considered you beyond the reach of forgiveness – nor would I ever. If by the severity of my first response to your wrongdoing I conveyed a determination to "disown" you, I am heartily sorry for it. It was not my intention. My heart was stricken – I confess it – but much more with sorrow than with anger. I hope that this long silence has afforded us both a period of reflection, and perhaps fostered an equal willingness to discover our better selves . . .'

He added in a postscript that a certain academic conference to be held in Bloomsbury a few weeks hence might compel him to come up to town. If so, he hoped that we might be able to meet during whatever brief moments of leisure this professional obligation might spare him. Knowing of his reluctance to visit London – both he and my mother had a horror of the place – I reasoned that either this conference really was unavoidable or else he might be dissembling an actual wish to see me.

Meanwhile I felt the burden of a more recent estrangement. I still winced to recall the look I had directed at Roma on Kitty's tearful report of her stolen ring. Was it more accusing than I had first imagined? The necessity of searching through the train had separated us for the remainder of the journey, but on arriving at St Pancras I had hurried back to our carriage in the hope of intercepting Roma and resolving the misapprehension that I had read in her eyes. Alas, she had gone, and Jo with her. That I had affronted her, however unwittingly, was put beyond any doubt on my turning up – cap in hand, so to speak – at the Polygon the following evening. I had never seen Jo look so embarrassed as he came out to greet me on the doorstep.

'She's really got the hump,' he said with a doleful grimace. 'I dunno what you said to her, but she ain't comin' down.'

I glanced up to the top-floor window, and saw that there was a light in her room. 'Jo, I didn't say anything to her, I swear. She must have thought I gave her, I don't know, a *look* . . .'

'A look? Whatja mean?'

I sighed and shook my head, and Jo, who had his own delicacy of feeling, didn't press me for an answer. We stood there brooding for a few moments. Eventually he said, 'Yor friend's diamond. You didn't find it?'

'Kitty said she remembered a scuff around her as she was boarding the train. One or two fellers shook hands with her – she thought it was by way of a thank-you.'

Jo gave a little snort. 'Yeah – "thanks for slippin' us yor sparkler". We should've warned her . . . Gaffy'd be quick as a snake to spy that.'

'You think it was him?'

'I'll lay yer twenty shiners on it.'

'Poor Kitty. It was her mother's, you know.'

Jo gave a cautious squint, then said, 'There's ways of gettin' it back.'

'How?'

'Well, there's a Jew fence I knows – an h'acquaintance, like – runs a dolly shop not far from 'ere. But you'll 'ave to pay some.'

He agreed to take me to this fence, then sheepishly said goodnight without asking me inside. As close as Jo was to his sister, he had an acute sense of when not to cross her. I sometimes wondered if he were a little afraid of her. I wouldn't have blamed him. Walking away through Clarendon Square I glanced up at the top window and thought I saw a face there. But it may have been my own fancy, deceived by the shadows.

A few days later I found myself on Barclay Street, and felt a needling of my conscience in having avoided Mrs Nicholls for a while. It was not so much the way her plaintive manner dragged on my spirits; it was more to do with comprehending her plight and being at a loss to help. I could give her money (I *had* given her money, in defiance of Marchmont's principles) but it had almost no effect in alleviating her situation. She and her two children continued to subsist on the parish, but deprived of her late husband's regular income there was no likelihood of her getting clear of poverty's quicksand. When she answered the door to me today, however, she seemed more sanguine than usual, and I wondered at first if the alcohol on her breath might explain it. The same forlorn air of dilapidation hung over the first-floor room, and the ticking upon the filthy mattress in the corner was alive with fleas. Yet Mrs Nicholls had had another visitor to her home that week, one whom she seemed to regard as a rescuer-in-waiting.

'A priest, you say?' I was baffled for a moment.

'Yes, I forget his name, Irish – fine figure he 'ad . . .'

'Not – Father Kay?'

'That's 'im! I been askin' what we was supposed to do now all the 'ouses roundabouts are bein' cleared. An' he told me not to fret cos his church, see, will help them as can't manage the rent.'

'Is that so? And what does he propose to do?'

She paused at this, and her thin face clouded over with worry. 'Oh, I'm not s'posed to say. 'E said it's not built yet.'

'What's not built?'

She looked uncertain, wary of confiding to me. I could not imagine what kind of pledge Kay had made, but I hoped for her sake it proved to have some foundation in truth. Evidently it was serious enough to compel her silence. I asked her again, more gently, but she shook her head, and seemed quite sorry not to have been more obliging.

* * *

Jo had given me instructions about what apparel I should wear for our visit to the fence. 'Nothin' tofficky. If 'e sees you's well-togg'd he'll mark ya for a gull.' In truth I had nothing of that sort to boast of, only the suit I had worn on Jo's birthday, and I knew well enough not to wear *that* in his company again. Every other item of clothing I owned was now so worn that I could pass through the lowest parts of Somers Town without notice.

In those days you saw whole streets of shops there offering shabby old clothes for sale; trousers, coats, shirts, waistcoats and whatnot hung on wooden rods before the door, or else were displayed in the grimy windows. Old boots and shoes might be ranged outside on the pavement, often without laces, and tongues hanging out of them like thirsty dogs. Most of the shopkeepers were Jews, or Irish. What I didn't know, until Jo informed me, was that some of them were in the business of receiving stolen property. Thieves who could not offload their haul on licensed pawnbrokers would take it to one of these 'dolly shops' and dispose of their articles at a vastly reduced price, perhaps only a sixth or an eighth part of their value. If they were so minded they could come back to redeem them, as they would in a pawn shop, but very few did.

So one afternoon Jo led me down an alleyway off Ossulston Street and thence to a shop as I have just described, with no sign above the door, but thickly hung about with articles of female dress, most of doubtful vintage. As we went inside Jo flapped his hand at some enormous off-white petticoats and muttered, 'Could make a sailcloth outta them,' and the sound of my laughter brought forth a tall cove from round the back; he was somewhere in his thirties, wore a white shirt and black waistcoat, and a skullcap. His manner was casually professional with Jo, whom he seemed to recognise. They both instantly fell into slang, a quick back-and-forth dialogue I struggled to construe. The only part of it I caught was the repeated word 'fawney', which I knew to mean a ring. The man flicked his eyes interrogatively from Jo to me.

'Oh, he's with me. He's called David, too!' cried Jo, though the coincidence did not seem to impress my namesake. He stared at me narrowly for a few moments, then nodded as if to say, *It's no matter*. Or perhaps, *He's* no matter. He invited us to come through to the back, where his manner visibly lightened, and he became almost genial. We sat on decrepit armchairs that were coming to the end of their natural life, the horsehair poking through like mortal wounds. David – the fence – had opened a wooden case on his desk and was displaying its contents over a faded velvet cloth. Jo leaned forward and examined each ring as it was laid down. Having done so he looked away, his mouth in a pout of disappointment.

'Come on,' he said, 'don't give us snide.'

David stared at him for a moment, then smiled, as if he had been caught out. 'It fetches a good price, my friend.'

'Yeah. But it's still snide.' They were fakes, it seemed. Jo shifted in his chair, and dropped his voice confidingly. 'See, the one we's arfter belongs to his –' he gestured at me – 'h'intended.'

I didn't much care for this little fiction, but I trusted Jo's instincts for negotiation. David stared at me pityingly, as if the loss of it could only have been my fault. Sighing, he produced a key and opened a drawer of his desk. From this he lifted a strongbox, which he unlocked with another key. Without letting us see what was in there, he placed one ring after another in a row upon the velvet strip, as if he were about to perform a trick. Five diamonds winked against the dingy light of the room. The fence handed a dainty magnifying glass to Jo for his closer perusal. He picked one of them up, eyed it, then handed over the glass for me to do the same. The gem sparkled with a brilliancy even I could tell was genuine. It shone so brightly as to seem almost on fire. But I also knew it wasn't Kitty's ring.

'You sure of it?' said Jo, scrutinising it again.

I nodded, and turned to the man. 'The ring – the one that was sto—the one she lost – it had a different shape. Cut into a sort of crown . . .'

'What shape? Oval?'

'No . . . a hexagon.'

'Ah,' he said shrewdly. 'An Antwerp Rose. Quite rare, I should say.'

'You seen one recent?' said Jo.

'Maybe,' said the fence, his expression unmoving.

'Don't you fret, David. We ain't no narks.'

The fence sat very still for a moment, then seemed to relax. 'Let's say – I might've seen one such, just lately.'

'But you wasn't buyin'?'

'Not at his price.'

'How much?'

David gave a little shake of his head. 'A monkey.'

'Pardon me?' I asked, as an image of Kitty's disagreeable pet seized upon my mind's eye.

'A cool five hundred,' supplied Jo. An involuntary exclamation escaped me. The street price, as of any prigged jewellery, was much less than its actual value, reflecting both the eagerness of the seller and the calculation of the fence, who was after all taking his own risk in receiving stolen valuables. Dumbstruck, I had not even thought of asking the vital question, but Jo had.

'The cove who flashed it. Was 'e about so tall, with a jail crop and ears stickin' out like that?'

Our host gave a wry snort in response to the description. He left a sly beat before saying, 'I couldn't rightly say, it was that dark.'

I looked to Jo, thinking he would challenge him on this evasion, but he only nodded and extended his hand across the desk. The two of them shook, but as I rose, preparing to leave, David leaned forward to mutter something in Jo's ear. It seems he wanted assurances as to my discretion, for I heard Jo tell him, sotto voce, that I could be trusted – that I was 'proper leary'.

We were out on the street again as I sighingly regretted David's failure to identify the man who tried to sell him the ring.

Jo looked at me. 'Whatja mean? It's Gaffy, no question.'

'But . . . your man said he couldn't recognise him, it was too dark.'

'Nah. You gotta listen. 'E said *I couldn't rightly say* . . . meanin' – yeah, that's the trosseno, but you didn't hear it from me cos I didn't say nothin'. He just didn't want it traced back to 'im. See?'

We walked on, and I pondered the interview just gone. If Gaffy did indeed have the ring in his possession, it would require nerve as well as money to get it back. I recalled his murderous look that day in the Brill when Jo had pulled the knife on him and saved my skin. I was not sure if he had recognised me again at Bindon Fields, but he surely would have seen Jo. A little shiver of dread passed through me as I considered the peril to which I might be exposing him.

'Jo,' I began, and he blinked of a sudden, as one whose train of thought had been interrupted. Perhaps his preoccupation had been running along similar lines to my own. 'Don't take this wrong, but I'm minded to pursue this matter alone. She's my friend, Kitty – I don't want you sticking your neck out for her.'

'Oh yeah?' He looked amused by my unburdening him of responsibility. 'And how d'you mean to *pursue* it h'exactly? You know where Gaffy hangs out, do ya?'

'I could find out,' I said, shrugging.

He stopped and gave me a pitying stare. 'You ain't *that* leary.'

* * *

I had just let myself in at Hanover Street when Mrs Home, my landlady, poked her head round the parlour door. She said that a gentleman had stopped by an hour ago with a message to meet him at his office. And the gentleman's name? I enquired. She couldn't recall – so sorry – but he was fattish, with a beard, and had 'piggy' eyes. She added, gnomically, 'If 'e wus hanged for his beauty, 'e'd be hanged innocent.' 'From the *Chronicle*, was he?' 'That's it!' she cried. '*Thank* you, Mrs Home – most helpful.'

Ten minutes later I had hailed a cab on the City Road and was heading through Clerkenwell. It was not like Paget to have called in person, which inclined me to think the summons was urgent. Overhead, thunder mumbled distantly. As I looked out of the window the sky seemed to bulge, purplish and grey, and the early-evening light turned grainy. I paid off the cabman at Fetter Lane, and took the stairs two at a time up to the *Chronicle*'s offices. Paget was at his desk, an odd expression on his face.

'I came straight away,' I said, answering his look.

'I've had word from a police station in Chelsea,' he said. 'They've found a body – fished it out of the Thames a few hours ago.'

I swallowed hard. 'Whose?'

'They believe it's Alfred Kenton. Care to join me?'

By the time we had walked to the Strand the rain was merciless; it beat down on the cobbles so ferociously that the droplets leapt back up. We sloshed along the pavement until we managed to stop a hansom going westwards, and damply hauled ourselves inside. Paget's mood was tense, and trying to distract myself from the business ahead of us I said, 'You made quite an impression on my landlady.'

Paget acknowledged this with a grunt, then looked out of the window. We didn't exchange another word until the cab clattered to a halt at the station off Oakley Street. The constable standing at the front desk took our names, then another officer conducted us down the stairs and along a gloomy, green-tiled corridor. The gas jets burned dimly in their brackets. As we proceeded I felt an unpleasant constriction in my chest, and my heart seemed to be trying to escape through my gullet. We had reached an iron-bound door, behind which lay, I suppose, what was coming to us all.

The constable heaved open the door and we entered a long, cold vault of whitewashed brick walls, reeking of carbolic acid, cigar smoke and, just beneath it, putrefaction. I felt a warning lurch deep in my stomach. An aproned attendant, whose cigar it was, greeted us with a genial detachment.

'Gents. This way, if you please.' His voice echoed off the walls.

We followed him past a row of metal trolleys, all unoccupied but for the last in the line, where he paused. Something – someone – formed a lumpy contour beneath the brown hessian shroud. The man put his cigar between his teeth, and taking the cloth in his meaty hands, he drew it back. Kenton lay there, bloated, grey-skinned and fully clothed. His mouth was a narrow, slotted grimace. Small unsightly cuts cross-hatched the eyelids – it was suggested that a gull had pecked at his eyeballs. I stared aghast for a moment, then looked away. A rank river smell of decay filled my nostrils, and I dry-retched once, twice. As I half crouched, hands on my knees, Paget lowered his head to mine and said quietly, 'Do you wish to leave?'

I shook my head, waited for my stomach to settle, then straightened to face the company. 'I do beg your pardon. I've never seen a dead – um, corpse before.'

'Well, you'll never see one deader than that,' mused the attendant casually. I was surprised that Kenton's face did not excite pity in me; death had wrought such an emptiness upon it that, for the moment, I felt nothing very much at all. 'From the bloat on him I'd say he was in the river at least a week. No marks, apart from his eyes, no sign of a struggle. Looks like he done himself in.'

At this I glanced at Paget, whose gaze thinned just perceptibly. After a silent contemplation he lifted up the corpse's left hand and examined the wrist; then he walked round to the other side and did the same with the right. Something seemed to be bothering him. He looked over to the attendant.

'Has anyone, I mean yourself and the men who dragged him out, rearranged the man's clothing?'

'Not that I know of,' he replied.

'So this is *exactly* how he was found?'

'Yeah. We haven't had time to strip him. Though I believe there was a pocketbook found on the, er, deceased. They'll show it to you at the desk.'

Paget brooded a little while longer, then with a lift of his chin indicated to the attendant that he had seen enough. The man pulled the shroud back over Kenton's poor, lifeless shape, and to my relief we filed out of that grim chamber. Back at the desk, a sergeant brought out a wooden box containing the personal effects of the dead man: a watch and chain, a few coins, a clay pipe and a waterlogged pocketbook. This last Paget took up and opened. Whatever papers had been secured within were now a sodden mess. He prised out some damp wallet litter, including a card of his own – which would explain the police's summoning him. There was one other item in there, a photographic reproduction about the size of a *carte de visite*, curling with the damp. It was a country scene which, to my shock, I recognised.

'That's Bindon Fields,' I said.

Paget turned the card over. 'You're quite right,' he replied, showing me its name printed on the reverse. 'You know it?'

I told him briefly of my recent excursion to the place. 'It was organised by a charity – the Social Protection League.'

'Never heard of them,' said Paget. 'Sounds not at all the sort of thing Kenton would have backed. You know how he detested charity-mongers.'

I held the card up. 'Then why was he carrying this?'

Paget was about to reply when he noticed the sergeant earwigging our conversation. Assuming a gracious front he thanked the policeman for his trouble, and led me out of the place. We stood at the top of the steps, watching the rain thrash the pavement. I could smell the odour of the mortuary attendant's cigar on my damp coat.

'Poor Kenton,' I murmured. 'Have they told his wife?'

'That is my next call,' he said, consulting his watch. 'And I wish to heaven it were not.' Something in his preoccupied gaze suggested he had more on his mind than that sombre duty. As the noise of wheel traffic cleared for a moment, I said, 'Did you ever suppose the fellow a suicide?'

'No – nor was he. Of course one can never speak with certainty where the mind is concerned, but I'd swear on my life that Kenton would not have done away with himself.'

'How then? No sign of a struggle, they said.'

'No, and I checked for rope burns on his wrists. But there *was* a sign.' His tone was steady and unsurprised, as he continued. 'It struck me almost immediately. Kenton was no dandy, but he knew how to button a double-breasted coat. That's why I asked if anyone had disturbed his clothing when they brought him in. The coat we saw on him just now had been fastened the wrong way – from which I deduce that someone else had put it on him, possibly after he was drugged. Or already dead.'

'But . . . who?'

He gave a little shrug. 'The police will not mourn him, not after the Trafalgar Square riot. And as leader of the Rental Reform people he's been a nuisance to those slum landlords . . . His demise is rather convenient for a lot of people.' I now realised why he had asked me to attend that horrible place. 'Do you begin to believe me now? Be on your guard – this isn't the end of it.'

I kept thinking of that postcard of Bindon Fields found on Kenton's drowned body. What interest did it have for him? As Paget said, the Social Protection League were exactly the sort of moralistic meddlers Kenton had loathed. I decided that if I were to make sense of it I should start with the SPL's most prominent board member, Father Kay. I recalled now his keen advocacy of country air for his 'flock'. It did not seem to me an ignoble mission, giving working people a day in the country that might otherwise be beyond their means. Perhaps Kenton had thought so, too.

St Columba's was an undistinguished church on Lancing Street, approached via a small courtyard hedged with gravestones of a much older age. Yew trees formed an archway over the path. Having written to Kay seeking an interview, he had invited me to call on him before he did his morning rounds of the parish. A charlady washing the church steps directed me past the vestry and along a flagstoned corridor, at the end of which I knocked upon an oak-panelled door, and waited. A voice sounded within ('Come') and I entered to find the rector seated at his desk. It was a modestly appointed office; a glass-fronted bookcase stood to one side, whilst on a table to his right rested a coloured globe of the world. On the wall behind him was a large plaster crucifix, with Christ's wounds painted a livid crimson where the nails and thorns had pierced him. The image of Kenton's pecked eyes came unbidden to my thoughts.

'Mr Wildeblood, is it?' said Kay in his crooning Irish lilt, directing me to take a seat opposite. His manner seemed less formal now that he was in his own domain. 'Catherine's friend,' he added, and it took a moment for the penny to drop – he meant Kitty.

'That's right, Father.'

'You enjoyed our day at Bindon Fields, I hope? It was thought a great success.'

'Indeed. Though I'm sorry to say it ended rather badly for Ki– for Catherine. Her ring was stolen.'

'Yes, I gather. Most unfortunate. Though amongst this class of people . . .' He spread his hands, as though the rest of the sentence was implicitly understood – only my expression of curiosity prompted him to finish it – '. . . well, thieving is endemic.' He seemed to offer this as a matter of fact, and before I could reply he had moved mellifluously on. 'So, there was something you wished to discuss?'

'Er, yes. Have you ever had dealings with a man named Alfred Kenton?'

'The rent-reform man? No, not that I recall. But I do know he was rather hostile to the Social Protection League. A friend of yours?'

'An acquaintance. He was found dead earlier this week. Drowned.'

'Ah,' said Kay with a slump of his shoulders. 'I'm very sorry to hear it. An accident?'

'That is unclear. The reason I ask is – an item was found on his body that appeared to have come from the offices of your League. A promotional photograph, about so big, of Bindon Fields.'

Kay had opened a drawer in his desk and pulled out an envelope, which he handed over to me. Inside was a card, the exact replica of the one recovered from Kenton. 'The same?' he asked.

I nodded, and said, 'Do you know how Kenton came to have it in his possession?'

He shook his head. 'These cards are not officially in circulation. Either Mr Kenton was given it by some influential friend or else it might have been – stolen.'

'May I keep this?' I said, holding the card in its envelope.

He looked at me oddly. 'As you wish.'

I stared at the picture for a moment, and a sudden flash of intuition sparked within my brain. 'Does the League have plans for Bindon Fields, Father? I mean, to build upon it?'

Kay leaned back in his chair, and a cautious smirk formed on his lips. 'Whatever would have given you that idea?'

I sensed that my blind throw had hit its mark, but I kept my voice casual. 'Oh, I was talking to one of your parishioners – Mrs Nicholls, on Barclay Street – who seems to believe you are going to lead her into the Promised Land. I wondered if Bindon Fields might be its location.'

'Mrs Nicholls,' he said, shaking his head. 'Poor woman. Too feeble-minded even to keep a confidence. And those two young children of hers . . .' He leaned forward now, and his tone became quietly earnest. 'You see it very strongly in children – that taint in the blood. There is a school of thought, I'm sure you know, that says allowing our weakest elements to breed will lead to the degeneration of humankind.'

'Not a very Christian school, I should say.'

He gave a little dismissive shake of his head. 'It is a grave challenge to society, Mr Wildeblood. The children of the very poor are not born but damned into this world. Their only inheritance is a weak mind and a deformed physique – have you *noticed* how defective is their hearing, their sight? They are stunted in their growth. Consider this: the British Army is preparing to lower its minimum height for recruits from five feet six inches to five feet three. Can we allow *this* to be the physical standard of the future?'

'I gather your friend Mr Sprule argues the same in his book.'

'Indeed he does. This is the hereditary taint, and unless something is done to check it, evolution itself will be reversed.'

'And you propose to save society from this "taint" by – what – isolating the poor?'

His look turned shrewd. 'Between ourselves, there is such a scheme in hand.'

'At Bindon Fields.' I no longer posed it as a question.

'There is much to say for it. Fresh air, comfortable conditions, appropriate employment for all. They will farm their own food and manufacture their own goods. A self-sufficient community. We hope it will constitute a more, well, salubrious home than Mrs Nicholls and her like would otherwise enjoy.'

I stared at him. 'There is one thing you overlook. Not all the poor of Somers Town are as pliant as Mrs Nicholls. How will you deal with those who decline to be resettled? By force?'

'It will not come to that. You must understand, in a few years hence Somers Town will cease to exist in the form we have known it. Those wretched houses will be swept away, but the occupants will not be forsaken as of old. We will offer them shelter in a secure environment.'

'Secure? That makes it sound –'

'Every form of society requires its protection. There will be a superintendent and a staff to keep the place in order – but we must not get ahead of ourselves. The plans are still being drawn up.' He looked at his watch, a gold hunter, and rose from his desk. 'Much as I would like to continue this, sir, I have obligations elsewhere . . .'

'You have been most generous with your time,' I said, rising, and as he led me to the door he talked of more day excursions he had planned for Somers Town. He believed that a gradual approach would help people adjust to the prospect of resettlement. It appeared that the Social

Protection League had done some careful preparation. His sharp, not quite friendly eyes were on me as he shook my hand. 'As I said, this matter is between ourselves. I hope I have your word as a gentleman?'

'Of course, Father . . . though, there *is* one thing that puzzles me. It's your "hereditary taint" theory. Even if the poorest elements are persuaded to resettle in Bindon Fields, there is still nothing to prevent them from – breeding.'

Father Kay returned a frowning look, as if I had missed the whole point of his argument. 'My dear sir, the settlements we are talking about – I thought this was made clear – they will be separated by sex. Men only, or women only.'

I cannot say whether I concealed my astonishment or not. I hope that I did. But as I retraced my steps down the corridor and out into the yew-shaded churchyard I had begun to conceive the unsettling possibility that this benign-seeming clergyman was not entirely sane.

11
Dark horse

The newspapers' reports of Kenton's death were, in the main, generous towards his achievements as a union organiser and social reformer. They acknowledged his tireless work on behalf of the renting classes, and several praised his fierce oratorical power in public debate, 'most recently evinced at the Trafalgar Square disturbances in May'. Yet barely one of them troubled to doubt the official verdict of suicide, or the coroner's explanation: according to *The Times* Kenton had been 'temporarily of unsound mind' when he had taken his plunge into the cold Thames, and no evidence of foul play had been discovered.

'Rot,' said Paget, tossing the newspaper aside. 'Kenton was as sound as Lloyd's. I'm sorry to see the *Thunderer* doing the police's work for them.'

We sat in the booth of a dimly lit chop house round the corner from the *Chronicle*.

'I notice that your own paper declined to air any suspicions,' I replied.

'I don't believe the misbuttoning of the deceased's coat will carry much weight in a court of law. And at least our report refused to call it a suicide.' He shrugged, his expression disgruntled. 'Until we have more persuasive evidence it would be better for us to lie low. I have no wish to follow poor Kenton into the morgue.'

The Bindon Fields postcard lay on the table. Its discovery in Kenton's pocket still tantalised us: Paget believed that someone had passed him information about Father Kay and the Social Protection League, but whatever it was we could only guess. If continuous staring at an object could yield its secret I would have possessed it by now.

'The disturbing part of it is that Kay appeared quite serious about the idea of male–female segregation.'

'He and Sprule both,' said Paget. 'And they are not without support in Parliament either. I know a fellow, an underling of the Home Secretary, who has told me things that would raise the hairs on your neck. He's heard members talk openly of measures to prevent the lowest classes from breeding – as though it's a danger to humanity!'

'Kay said something about appointing a superintendent at Bindon Fields. Would your man be privy to that sort of information?'

'Perhaps,' he replied, 'though I really don't see how such a scheme is practicable. You may separate the sexes in a workhouse, but on a larger scale nobody would stand for it. You cannot "engineer" the race.'

A waiter interrupted us, and Paget's beady eyes brightened as he contemplated the beefsteak and mound of boiled carrots set before him. Steam rose off it, and he gave the satisfied sigh of a trencherman. 'Hearty fare they do here,' he said unnecessarily. 'Are you sure you won't join me?'

'Thank you, but no.'

He looked more closely at me. 'You look rather pasty, my boy. Is all well?'

'I'm . . . out of sorts, I confess.' To his enquiring look I gave a small grimace. 'I have an engagement, this afternoon. With someone I have not spoken to in more than a year.'

'And may I ask . . . ?'

'My father. A long story,' I said, instantly regretting my candour. 'But he's attending a pharmacology conference in town today, and has asked to see me.'

Paget gave a wry, faraway smile. 'I was seldom on good terms with my old man. When I told him that I was considering a career in journalism he threatened to disown me.'

'What did you do?'

'Oh, that decided me for certain. Two years later I was working down here for the *Evening News*.' He laughed, and took a swig from his pewter.

'I think my father would have approved such ambition. He never expressed the smallest belief that I would amount to anything at all.'

Paget briefly stopped chewing, and eyed me with sympathy. 'That's harsh. You strike me as just the chap a father would be proud of!' His words were kindly meant, but they made me sad. I glanced up at the wall clock – ten past three – and got to my feet.

'I must away. May I take a pinch of this before I go?' I pointed to Paget's snuffbox, and he opened it for me in invitation. I held a dab on my wrist, snorted it up – then sneezed volcanically.

'By the way,' he said, taking another gulp of ale, 'something I meant to ask you – about Condor Holdings. When did you last consult the register of leases?'

I tried to recall my last visit to the Records Office. 'I suppose it was about two months ago,' I replied.

'*Interesting*. Because I sent one of our boys to check the Somers Town section and he told me that Condor Holdings is not listed anywhere.'

I gaped at him. 'What? He must be mistaken. Their name was all over the ledger. I saw it with my own eyes!'

Paget tweaked a side of his mouth in philosophical resignation. 'Well, look again – it's not there any more.'

As I hurried through Holborn I felt myself to be a drowning man, sucked under by a riptide of perplexities. Every time I seemed to grasp a spar of verifiable fact the ground beneath me gave way and I was whelmed in deep waters again. Had Condor Holdings really managed to disappear from the list of leases? If so, it indicated that they – whoever 'they' were – knew they were under suspicion. But how? A few moments' thought solved it. They had surmised that somebody was on to them; indeed, they knew his name – it was *mine*. Pondering the episode at their office in Bishopsgate, and the brusque reception by the man in the checked coat – the one I had followed to Marchmont's door – I recalled now that I must have given him my name. Alas . . . there was my error. And I had to presume that Marchmont himself was now apprised of a certain Wildeblood poking around the Condor Holdings business. Under my breath I cursed my want of guile. With their name removed from the leases, there was nothing at all now to connect the company with the Somers Town clearances.

This anxious cogitation had so preoccupied me that I was hardly aware of having reached Gordon Square. I crossed the public garden and mounted the steps of the Gothic-fronted collegiate building, my heartbeat picking up the pace. A cavernous entrance hall was aswarm with dark-coated gentlemen of the pharmacological profession, their voices echoing in the gloom. It seemed that a lecture had just ended and disgorged the delegates hither. On enquiry I was directed up a balustraded staircase to the library, not today a place of quiet study but another meeting room where refreshments were being taken. An odour of cigars and sherry suffused the air.

It took me a moment to recognise him. He stood alone at one of the mullioned windows, gazing out, a lean, tall man lost in thought. His hands, held across his chest, absently entwined one another; it was a pose that lent him the faintly worried aspect of a clergyman. I approached him, and 'Papa' was almost on my lips before I stopped myself. The appellation seemed no longer appropriate. Of course, he was still my father, that would not change, and he had never been as severe with me as Paget's sire with him. But the affectionate word belonged to another age – childhood – when relations between us were without strife or strain. Now it smacked of a presumptuous familiarity. I cleared my throat, and he turned.

'David,' he said with a pained smile, and offered his hand.

'Sir,' I said, trying to sound assured. He didn't blink at this formal address, and I felt a little stab to my heart. 'I hope I find you well?'

'Oh,' he murmured, as if waving away the enquiry, his well-being of no consequence to anyone. A year had marked a change, I couldn't say what. An air of distracted authority still hung on him, and in his wandering gaze one sensed, not a shyness – for he could be gregarious when it pleased him – but a reluctance to be amongst crowds. To be anywhere, indeed, apart from in his library, alone and undisturbed. His melancholy brown eyes rarely met mine. He gestured me to a vacant table and we sat in matching armchairs, facing one another. 'Would you care . . . ?'

'Some coffee, thank you.' We waited in silence until a man came to take our order, and then we were left with nowhere to hide from each other's company.

'Well then, tell me of your journalistic endeavours. Even in the benighted territories of Norfolk we have heard of Henry Marchmont.'

He maintained his look of polite attention as I recounted my time in the guvnor's employ, and I even embroidered it a little to suggest a greater influence at the office than I commanded. I told him about my friendship with Paget, though avoided the subject of Kenton's death and the rents scandal. I felt his interest quicken only when I brought up the Camberwell Beauty we had seen at Bindon Fields, and again I elaborated the story, such was my eagerness to impress him. This led me naturally to talk of Kitty, and her father.

'I recall from your letter that Elder – Sir Martin, I should say – invited you to dinner. I dare say he lives in grand style?'

'He does. A large house in Kensington. He talked of you, of course – said you were one of the finest minds he'd ever known.'

My father, who was quite without intellectual vanity, or any other sort, merely raised his eyebrows, then said, 'I recall a holiday up in

Scotland, it must have been our last year at Oxford. We both of us were keen birdwatchers . . . though much of the time was spent in theological debate.'

'He told me that you "saved" him from taking orders.'

His rueful half-smile neither confirmed nor denied it. 'I don't believe a career in the Church would have benefited either party.' His gaze returned to the ceiling, and the mention of Church inevitably brought to my mind one of its most devoted adherents. My father's thoughts must have been tending likewise, for he now said, 'Your mother – as you would imagine – still does her charitable work in the parish. Her sense of duty is quite . . . selfless.' He spoke haltingly, and I realised that this was his way of talking around the unmentionable subject of our estrangement. It occurred to me that he had not actually told my mother of this meeting between us, and I felt goaded by a renewed sense of hurt to say, 'I wonder if she has ever been minded to dispense her charity closer to home – towards her son, for example.' My father flinched as though he had been slapped on the cheek. He had not expected me to bandy words. His look of dismay was painful, but my blood was up, and leaning forward I spoke without premeditation. 'It is too hard, this silence of hers . . . How can my own mother be so implacable – she who prides herself on Christian values? Surely *you* see the contradiction in it?'

My voice had risen under the pressure of indignation, and my father, aware of the public room, made a conciliatory patting motion with his hand. I sat back again, trembling, and watched him pinch finger and thumb over his closed eyelids – a long-suffering look I knew well. The silence felt charged between us. 'Your mother has a good heart,' he began, then sighed – 'but it lacks understanding. Be patient. The shock to her, to both of us, was grievous –'

'But you found it in you to forgive! Why cannot she?'

He opened his eyes again, and suddenly looked wearier. That was the change in him, I now saw – a shading below the eyes, a hollowness in his cheek. 'She has too much pride. That is her cross, if she only knew it. One day she will learn forgiveness.'

'And then I should ask it of her?'

'No. She will ask it of you.'

I looked away, and we fell silent. I wanted to clear the air between us, but I could not speak candidly without causing him distress. Around us in affable colloquy were my father's fellow delegates, scientists from all over the country eager to exchange new ideas, propound new theories and enlarge their already well-stocked minds. Through the forest of bodies my eye alighted upon two august-looking gents absorbed in discussion, one listening, nodding in agreement with his interlocutor, whose talk was emphatic with hand gestures. Of what they spoke it was impossible to say, but one could fairly speculate it did not concern trivialities. The whole mood of the room felt gravid with erudition, and it suddenly daunted me to think of the volume of knowledge packed within these walls. What mystery could these men of science not unravel? What darkness could they not illumine? Then, as I looked again at my father's melancholy countenance, a line came to me: *What is knowledge but grieving?*

'Sir, may I ask you – about something that has troubled me?'

His brow lifted enquiringly. 'Of course.'

'I wonder if you have heard of the Social Protection League?' He shook his head, and I continued. 'They are a charity, run by certain well-to-do gentlemen with an interest in matters of heredity. They take their theme from Darwin, and, as far as I understand, believe it would be beneficial to society if the weaker elements – the mentally defective, the shiftless, and so on – were prevented from breeding.'

He gave a quick nod. 'I am familiar with the theory – though it rather traduces Darwin. He did not prescribe meddling with the constitution of the race.'

'And yet I hear it said – by an Anglican rector, amongst others – that the pitiful conditions in which the poor live is retarding evolution and endangering the race. Can this be true?'

My father frowned, considering. 'There is no conclusive proof of progressive degeneration. Even if there were, we cannot simply *dispose* of these weaker elements. What distinguishes man as a species is his capacity for love of all creatures – other races, other animals – however lowly.'

'So you do not hold with the theory of tainted blood? That certain people are born without hope of being anything but bad?'

Again he paused before answering, perhaps struck by the singularity of this conversation. 'I am inclined to believe – who can say for sure? – the criminal is made, not born. Those "pitiful conditions" you mention are at the heart of it. Some endure such extremes of penury and want that their succumbing to drink, or to theft, seems nearly unavoidable. Personally, I think it a wonder that they are not ten times more depraved than they might be.'

At that moment, a bell sounded from the entrance hall, and a clerk entered the room to announce the beginning of another session. My father lowered his head, and pinched his eyelids closed again.

'I'm awfully sorry, David, but my time is circumscribed by —' He waved a vague hand to indicate his professional obligation. Around us, the dark-clad delegates had begun their obedient shuffle towards the door, tobacco smoke trailing in their wake. We followed them out and had reached the top of the staircase when he said, in an undertone, 'This subject we discussed just now — you said it was a cause of "trouble" to you?'

'Yes . . . I have long wondered whether a criminal — a thief, say — was naturally born. But your words put me on the side of optimism.' We stared at one another, aware of so much unsaid between us. I offered my hand, which he took. 'So — I am grateful.'

I was turning away when he called me back. Another half-smile came to his tired, bone-shadowed face. 'By the bye, I must beg your leave not to address me so formally. *Papa* was good enough once — is it not still?'

I nodded, our eyes met, and I muttered a farewell.

A throbbing sun glinted through Bloomsbury's foliage, its fierce heat slowing the world about me. A cart horse had been parked by a public fountain to slake its thirst, and a sluggish hansom kicked up a cloud of dust as it ambled by. Flower sellers were fanning themselves on the concourse outside Euston Station. An Italian organ-grinder wiped the back of his neck with a rag, and cranked out a desultory, half-hearted tune. London was wilting.

Curiosity, mingled with alarm, drew my steps back to the Records Office where I had made my original discoveries — first of Moyles's slum monopoly, then of the leases transferred to Condor Holdings. I still clung to a vague hope that Paget's copy boy had somehow been mistaken, that he had perhaps consulted the wrong listing. I had the Somers Town ledger in front of me now, and turning its lined pages I knew straight away there had been no mistake. As the boy had reported, the names on the leases had been changed for a second time: Condor Holdings had been whited out, replaced by multiple strips bearing the names of new leaseholders. Who on earth were these people?

'Who on earth are these people?' I asked the desk clerk, the disobliging one I had encountered on my previous visit. He lifted his head, very slowly.

'They are the new leaseholders,' he replied in a profoundly uninterested tone. He didn't recognise me, which was just as well.

'So all of these leases,' I said, riffling the pages, 'have changed hands in the last six weeks, but nobody thinks it . . . unusual.' Again, he raised his eyes to mine, and his expression made it clear that a verbal reply would not be forthcoming. He returned to his work. I waited for a moment and then, just to vex him, said in an innocent voice, 'May I borrow this volume?'

'Sir – this is a Records Office, not a lending library,' he snapped. I had succeeded in exasperating him. Taking the ledger round the corner to another desk, out of his sight, I ran my eye down the first page of fresh corrections. They listed houses on Johnson Street, and the leases were divided amongst five names:

Annie O'Brien
Harriet Shepherd
George Harding
Edith Arkell
Thomas Bowland-Darke

I stared at them for some moments. I knew Johnson Street; it was in a state of near collapse. The question was this: why would people risk their money on condemned properties? All they would have needed to do was inspect the house and see the NOTICE TO QUIT sign in the window. Baffling. I had to remember these names . . .

There was nobody occupying the desks either side of me. As long as a clerk didn't suddenly appear I was invisible to the room. Gripping the edge of the page I stealthily began tearing along its margin; halfway down, the rasping noise sounded like a firework's crackle, so I gave the chair I was sitting upon a sudden jerk. The squeal of wood on parquet muffled the final liberating rip. The desk clerk gave a loud tut, but he didn't stand up to investigate the chair-scraper. I folded the torn page into my coat pocket, handed in the ledger at the desk, and strolled out.

Each day of the following week I set off early for Somers Town, and spent the mornings checking on which houses had been earmarked for destruction. Generally I would find two or three in a street; but sometimes a whole terrace had been boarded up in preparation for the wrecking ball. My mind was not, I confess, exclusively focused upon this task. It was no longer possible to walk these pavements without thinking of Roma, and I was always half hopeful, half fearful of running into her. Yet however much I haunted the place, I caught no sight of her. It felt as though she knew I was on the lookout, and so had deliberately made herself scarce.

Our paths did finally cross, on the Friday evening. I had arranged to meet Jo for a bite to eat at Casti's, but nearly an hour had passed and still there was no sign of him. I had just convinced myself that he had forgotten our appointment when into the dining room came Roma, and I flinched as her gaze sought me out. When I looked up she was opposite me, her arms folded.

'No need for that,' she said, as I made to rise. 'I'm just here to say that Jo's not comin'. He's in bed, coughin' like a horse.'

'I'm sorry to hear it,' I said, '. . . and I'm sorrier still that you've been avoiding me. Would you . . . ?' I gestured at the vacant chair. She stood, considering, her expression proudly aloof.

'Why?'

'Because I want to apologise, and win back your good opinion.'

'Oh. What made you think you *had* my good opinion?'

There was nothing in that for me, and I shrank from her lowering gaze. Then I heard the slight scrape of chair legs. She had sat down, silent, with the air of one whose time was given up on sufferance. After a moment she said coolly, 'So?'

'When Kitty came into that train carriage to tell us – about the ring – I believe that an involuntary glance I directed at you conveyed the impression – that is, it may have appeared that I suspected you of . . .'

'*Stealing*,' she prompted.

'– but I did not. I would never accuse you –'

'You didn't have to accuse me. I seen it on your face. You thought I was a thief.'

I shook my head. 'No, Roma, I did not think that. I looked at you only because you had noticed the ring earlier, and had remarked upon it. I would know if you were a thief.'

She snorted her disbelief. 'Oh, yeah? And how's that?'

'Because I am one,' I replied. 'Indeed, I have served time in prison for it.'

Her sceptical expression had gone: she squinted uncertainly. 'What? You – a thief? I don't believe it.'

I made a thin *tsk*. 'That, I recall, is precisely what my landlady said on seeing the police clap me in handcuffs.' As I spoke, I felt both remorse and a curious liberation. 'Whether you care to believe me or not, it's the truth. I was charged, I was convicted – and I was sent down. It is not a part of my life I would happily confess. You are the first person I have told since my release.'

She was frowning, unsure of how to respond. Around us the indistinct mumble of other diners continued, not caring. I had always imagined my shameful history as something lying in wait for me, ready to spring an ambush with its fangs bared. The secret had stalked me since the day I came out – from Reading, the previous November – and it had seemed only a matter of time before I was exposed, once the son of a respectable family, now a convicted felon. It had never occurred to me that I would confess it voluntarily. But I would rather that Roma knew the worst of me than to think I had suspected her a thief. I considered her now, her almond-shaped eyes, the tiny mole set at about twenty past four from her nose. The expressive arch of her eyebrows.

'What happened?' she said, searching my face.

And so I told her the whole story, beginning with my arrival at Fowler's College. You must take into account my ingenuous nature, coddled by my parents till the age of thirteen, entirely unsocialised apart from companionship with our sixty-year-old gardener and his wife, then without warning plunged into the brutish atmosphere of this academy for 'young gentlemen' in rural Berkshire. I was not so badly bullied as some, though over five years the necessities of survival surely coarsened me. Aged nearly eighteen I left the place, without prospects, but rather than return home a failure I determined I should make something of myself. The town of Caversham, the nearest to the academy, was my next port of call, and with a little money my father had given me, I found rooms there. I found a job, too, assistant at a printer's, ill-paid and dreary, but tolerable withal.

And there I might have remained, keeping the 'noiseless tenor' of my way like so many others, but for an ache that spurred me onwards. That ache, simply put, was loneliness. The few friends I had made at school were already dispersed, and I fell back on the company of the only decent fellow who had stayed in the vicinity of Caversham. We would sometimes meet for dinner at a hotel on the high street, and on one such evening found ourselves conversing in a jolly way with the young woman who served at the table. Her name was Amy, a pretty, dark-haired creature of about one-and-twenty whose ready laugh fell most engagingly on the ear. I recall she gave us drinks on the house.

Later, I walked her home, and she told me a little of her history – she was born and raised in Stamford, Lincolnshire, and had come here two years earlier after a certain Mr Fenton had offered to secure her a position as governess. But the man kept prevaricating, and the arrangement was continually delayed. Needing to pay her rent, she had taken a series of menial jobs to tide her over, thus accounting for her present employment at the hotel. By the time we had bidden each other goodnight at her door I was – you have guessed it – helplessly besotted. Perhaps it is the fate of someone unaccustomed to warmth that he will grab too precipitately at the merest wisp of human affection. I was that susceptible.

I began to seek out Amy's company to the exclusion of all else. She in turn seemed happy to be sought after, and we spent an occasional day out wandering over fields and stiles. It was perfectly chaste, I should say; it did not occur to me to play any role but that of attentive swain. Yet I soon noticed in her manner a hesitancy, and a sudden inclination to fearfulness that provoked my concern. Time and again I asked her to tell me what the matter was, but she refused. Finally, after an absence of some weeks, she reappeared at the hotel, with a bruise down the side of her face. Even I was not so naive as to swallow her explanation of it as an accident. This time I insisted that she tell me the truth, and, amidst a flood of tears, out it poured. It transpired that the man Fenton was a creditor of her mother's – a widow – and had some hold upon her daughter in consequence. In return for clandestine 'favours' from Amy – here the story took a sinister turn – Fenton would write off a portion of the family's debt. Amy had decided to comply with this transaction until such a time as the slate had been wiped clean. But Fenton by now had become unwilling to relinquish her, and, instead of using debt as his leverage, he threatened to ruin her if she dared to break from him. Lately she had tried to end the repulsive arrangement by fleeing to London. The attempt was doomed: she had no friends there, and no money to enable her to disappear. The bruise on her face was Fenton's warning against her trying such a flit again.

A heart of stone would have been pierced to hear this. My own heart, infinitely more permeable, was moved to outrage. I promised there and then to do everything in my power to help her. She smiled at that, and joked, in a broken way, that she was fortunate to have such a knight errant. But how would she ever escape this blackmailer? The tears she had managed to hold back came once more. I could not bear to see her in distress, and resolved upon a scheme. What if – what if I were to find a means of spiriting her away from the town to some place of refuge? *He would track me down*, she replied. In other words, she was trapped here.

I brooded on this for a few days, trying to devise a plan. The friend in whose company I had first met Amy was a Scotsman named Robert, whose advice I believed I could depend on. One night I went to his lodgings and told him the whole story, of Amy's plight, and of my determination to rescue her. He looked very dubious about my intervening, though once he realised I was not to be dissuaded he agreed that the safest course would be to take her out of the country. But where? His first suggestion was Norway, a name that sounded rebarbative to my untutored ear – a dismal place full of elks and snow. Robert then got to talking of a holiday he had once enjoyed in the Low Countries, which chimed with my own imagining of them as an affable, accommodating territory. By chance he also knew of someone in Amsterdam who would be able to provide board and lodging. There was a steamer which ran from Harwich to the Netherlands . . . It could be done. It had to be done.

A vertiginous excitement seized me as I contemplated this bold step, and before I could change my mind I sought Amy at the hotel. Her initial look of anxiety only spurred me on, and once I had explained to her where the Netherlands were she seemed to take courage. Perhaps she began to see it as I did; that is, romantically. She would be a fugitive, and I her protector. There remained, alas, a very obvious stumbling block. The cost of the ferry from Harwich for two would be – I knew not what – whilst food and lodging and other expenses had to be accounted for. Amy had no savings, not from the pittance she earned, and my own were negligible. Robert would lend me a little, though he was hardly in funds himself. That early surge of excitement was receding, and I felt for the first time what a desperate thing it was to need money. The obvious recourse I had was to apply to my father, who, I knew, would have come to my aid. But he would also have asked why I required such a large sum, and I did not have it in me to deceive him.

When the moment demands, however, it is surprising to learn exactly what one is capable of. It had become clear that selling off possessions would not raise the necessary. A signet ring (given to me by my mother) extracted from the pawnbroker about a quarter of what I'd hoped. A few other oddments – silver, books, clothes – made a few pounds, but not nearly enough. I was coming close to despair when fate tossed me a solution. One day I was at work in the front shop of the printer's offices, on my own and quite probably in a daydream of Amy. I heard a carriage halt on the street and a customer stepped briskly inside. He had come to settle an account, but since the manager was not present I told him I was authorised (which was true) to handle the transaction. The man, evidently in a hurry, nodded his acquiescence and handed over a stiff envelope, which I opened and counted out the banknotes. It came to £120, plus a few shillings. I wrote out a receipt, signed it, and the man went on his way.

Ordinarily I would have put the envelope on the manager's desk and thought nothing more of it. But now the finger of opportunism was prodding me. The banknotes were in my charge, and, with drumming heart, I saw in an instant how I should take advantage. Nobody else was in the shop. I peeled off two £10 notes and hid them in my pocket. Opening the till – it was sometimes my job to count the day's takings – I placed the remaining hundred or so therein, thus hiding the deficit in the pool of cash already accumulated. I burnt the envelope in which the customer had presented his payment, thus creating an excuse for locking the money in the till: when, later that day, the manager asked me why I hadn't put it on his desk, I explained – in a responsible tone – that I thought it best not leave so much cash lying about unguarded. Whoever did the 'totting up' that evening reported no discrepancy. Back in my rooms I stared at the pair of banknotes; our escape fund had tripled at a stroke.

The ease with which I had managed it emboldened me. Individual sums of money passing through the business were not often as large as that day's, but the accounting was sufficiently lax for someone of reasonable cunning to skim a little off the top. A pound here, a pound there, it mounted up. Sometimes, a sudden look or hesitation on the part of an office senior had convinced me that the jig was up, and I braced myself for the unmasking. But it never came. Having concealed what I had been doing from Amy, one night I finally broke under the nervous thrill and confessed my descent into larceny. She was shocked, of course, and urged me to stop – that is, until I showed her how much I had already pilfered. *I promised I would help you escape*, I said. *Here is how.* We spoke in low voices, looking at the hoard of notes and coins emptied across my bed, where Amy, bright-eyed, now flopped, and pulled me on top of her . . . If I had once scrupled to continue this reckless plan, after that night I never did so again.

With money in promising accumulation we decided upon the date of our removal, a week hence. By this time I had seen the blackmailer

Fenton at the hotel – a younger-looking man than I had imagined – and though we never spoke I had no difficulty in tracing knavery in his very profile. It was agony to watch Amy behave so equably towards him in the hotel's taproom, but we had agreed that her manner should remain absolutely unchanged, lest his suspicions be aroused. The day I purchased our ferry passage from Harwich to Rotterdam was the first time Amy briefly lost heart: she had been in Fenton's thrall for so long that the reality of deliverance suddenly overwhelmed her. But I was quick to assuage these fears, showing her the little store of cash that would enable our escape. As she stared at it, I saw an eagerness for the plan rekindle in her eyes. We clasped hands, and swore to hold our nerve.

The day arrived, a working day like any other, except that we both knew it to be the last ever of our residence in Caversham, and perhaps in England, too. I had given Amy the key to my rooms, where she would change in undisturbed preparation for our journey. I would join her immediately on leaving the printer's, where they were still blessedly unaware of the thief in their midst. All day I watched the clock's hands snailing around their circuit, each minute seeming to last an hour – the bastinado could not have been a more exquisite torture. Five o'clock finally came around (relief!) and with feigned nonchalance I took the day's takings from the till into the back room to be counted. I knew immediately that something was afoot on meeting there the firm's wizened accountant who, to my knowledge, had never been spotted anywhere outside of his tumbledown office on the floor above. My employer, Mr Flegg, stood next to him, and another gentleman I had not seen before. He turned out to be the arresting police officer. Though they found nothing in my pockets – ironically, it was one of the few days I had kept my hand out of the till – Flegg's accountant had already accumulated sufficient evidence to damn me. But why had they chosen this of all days to pounce?

I found out. Conducting me in cuffs to my lodgings, the police discovered the place in tumultuous disarray, drawers emptied, the bed and mattress torn apart, every last stitch I owned strewn across the floor. Whoever had broken in must have known there was loot to be had, and had turned the room upside down looking for it. This was plainly not the scene the chief detective had anticipated. At his quizzical look I gestured to a small storeroom where I kept a travelling trunk and other unwieldy items. The trunk's lock had been jemmied, its innocent contents upended. It was upon seeing the disturbed wedge of floorboard beneath it that I knew, instinctively, that the burglar was no stranger to me. *She* had seen me go in there, and perhaps had noticed the slight delay in my re-emergence. I thought I had been crafty. But she had outdone me, had she not? The policeman lowered a candle to the hole in the floor: my haul had gone. 'Been bested at your own game, lad,' he muttered. 'Any idea who?' I shook my head.

Whilst I was in prison awaiting trial I learned what had become of my ill-gotten gains. A man and a woman had been arrested, in Paddington, London, and after some paltry dissembling had confessed their crime. They had worked the trick several times before, with success, the woman befriending a needy stranger (never a shortage of them, I gathered), ensnaring him with a story of woe, then finagling money on the pretext of being 'rescued'. The woman's name was Amy – an alias, I believe. The man was Fenton. It transpired that he had provided the anonymous tip to Flegg and co. that I was about to leave town, my pockets bulging. Meanwhile, with the key I had given Amy, the couple entered my rooms and set about their search.

The only part of their scheme that continued to puzzle me was how Amy came to have that bruise down the side of her face, the one she said he had given her for trying to escape. During those first weeks of incarceration, staring at the limewashed brick wall of my cell, I pondered the idea of Amy – or whatever her name was – agreeing to submit herself to a blow from him, leaving such a mark as would induce a sympathetic observer to action. Yet that bit of fakery didn't sit quite right with me. I could not believe that bruise was premeditated, and instead of cursing her name I would contrive a different scenario, of Amy acting under duress. She had been his accomplice often enough before, but this time she could not go through with the deception, tormented as she was by a secret tender feeling for their dupe. Her professions of love to him were perhaps not counterfeit after all. She had begged Fenton to stop, to spare just this one from all the rest. I imagined her reasoning with him, then begging him, and finally provoking the violent reaction that everyone would see on her face. Yes, that must have been how it happened . . . For a while I clung to this fantasy of her regret, nurtured it of a lonely night, until it met the fate of so many illusions, and withered in the foul prison air.

The gaslight in Casti's had been dimmed to a brownish glow since I had begun my tale. Roma's expression, steeped in shadow, was unreadable, whilst her dark eyes, fixed on me, were as still and opaque as a cat's. I did not feel shame, or remorse, or bitterness; only a kind of vacant exhaustion from recounting my folly.

'How long did you get?' she said eventually.

'Four months. Though it felt more like four years.' There was another long pause before she spoke again.

'The sewing. I should have guessed.'

'Beg your pardon?'

'That day you helped me repairin' those dresses. I remember you told me you learned to sew at school. But that's not true, is it?'

I shook my head. 'Sewing was the one thing I learned to do in prison – apart from surviving. I can never look at a mailbag now without wondering if it's one of mine.'

A slight dimpling in her cheek suggested she was trying not to smile. 'You're a dark'un, ain't ya? A real dark horse.'

'Am I?' I shrugged. 'I only told that story to clear myself of the charge – I never believed *you* a thief.'

'Yeah, well . . . I s'pose I got that wrong.'

'Then we are friends again, you and I?'

Her face leaned out of the shadow, and I saw upon it the beam, half rueful, half playful, that secretly touched me even more than those green and blue eyes of hers. She was holding out her hand, and I took it right willingly.

12
Noser

I once fancied I knew Somers Town better than I did. It was now September, which meant that I had been nearly seven months employed there on behalf of *The Labouring Classes of London*. Yet though it was one of London's smaller districts, its topography was dense. No map of it I ever saw did justice to that warren of lanes and alleys, those turnings so obscure that they failed to merit the courtesy of a name. You will recall my earliest experience of its labyrinthine intricacy was the day I found myself ambushed somewhere in the Brill, and Jo saved me from a mugging by Gaffy and co.

Late one afternoon I happened to find myself in that very same little maze. It was perhaps not advisable to be there alone, but Jo was still abed with a hacking cough, and by now I felt no need of a protector. It was the sign above a public house that first jolted my memory: the Victory. I knew it to be a dangerous den from Jo and others, a meeting place for most of the neighbourhood villians – the sharpers and snide-pitchers, the busters and screwsmen, the priggers and cracksmen. The name of the pub seemed an irony in itself. The Victory, with its carious brickwork and smeared windows, wore a look of sullen defeat. A few drinkers stood outside its doors, while a starved-looking dog slunk about, sniffing the cobbles as if they might yield some sustenance.

I loitered on the other side of the street for a while, and watched as the pub began to fill up. Every so often a child would walk in, emerging some minutes later with a jug of beer to carry home, I presumed for parents too incapacitated to fetch it themselves. I had heard that meas-ures were afoot in Parliament to prevent drink being sold to children under the age of thirteen, though even if that became law I could not imagine it being enforced around here. The rare police constable one saw patrolling hereabouts would be more likely to call in for an ale himself than to stop anybody else purchasing it. Judging the place sufficiently busy for me to go unnoticed, I crossed the street and sidled into the taproom, dimly illumined at this hour by flickering gas jets.

Most of the clientele sat at tables playing cards or chatting; in certain gazes I saw the cheerless determination of drinkers who would not leave this room without being well and truly soused.

I stood at the bar drinking a half-and-half and took advantage of a lull to ask the potman if Gaffy had been in lately. The man curled his lip, as if such a question were pure impudence. He turned away and strolled to the other end of the bar, where I soon saw him conversing quite genially with a 'reg'lar'. At about seven, people began pouring through the doors, signalling the end of market day at the Brill. The room became so smoky and crowded that I didn't notice the shortish cove until he was at my elbow. He wore a billycock hat and a cord jacket so deeply engrained with dirt that it almost gleamed under the yolky pub light. His stubbled jaw and ferrety features confirmed him as a trosseno. He mumbled something, and leaning down – he really was quite short – I said, 'Beg your pardon?'

'I said *move yer trotters*,' he hissed, and hoicked his thumb over his shoulder. I followed him out of the taproom, down a narrow passage and into a backyard, where he told me to wait. I looked about me. The yard was enclosed on all sides, the only exit being the door I had just come through. Most of this tiny space was occupied by giant kegs and crates of ale stacked against the side wall. I was just testing the strength of a drain-pipe (I could shinny up this at a pinch) when the door swung open and three figures ambled through, then a fourth, my diminutive host from before. Gaffy stood there, nasty, brutish and tall, staring at me.

'This 'im?' he said, and Shorty nodded. At an invisible signal the two slab-faced youths at his side stepped forward and grabbed me, one by the arm, one by the scruff of the neck. They walked me Spanish, feet off the ground, to Gaffy, whose face was now so close to mine I could smell porter on his breath. As he stared, his expression changed to a frown. 'Don't I know you?'

I suppose the beard I had grown since our first encounter had caused him this uncertainty – or perhaps I simply had an unmemorable face. I shook my head, not daring to speak.

'You've been sniffin' around in my bisniss, I've 'eard,' he continued. 'At the dolly shop, now 'ere. I reckons you're a *noser*.' I knew this word for a police spy. And I also knew it was an invidious thing to be in these parts.

'No, I'm not. I've nothing to do with the police.'

Gaffy seemed not to have heard me. 'Yeah . . . a noser. And ya know what 'appens to nosers?' By a snake-quick movement of his arm I realised what he had just taken out, and I saw my reflection in its thin blade as he held it before my eye. 'Well, *do ya?*' Having drawn the flat of the knife down my cheek, he pressed its point against the inside of my nostril. My heart was now going like a racehorse. I wanted to struggle, but realised an abrupt movement could be perilous.

'No, I don't,' I breathed. My voice, with the knife up my nose, sounded queerly metallic, which in other circumstances might have been humorous.

'Don't what?'

'Don't know . . . what happens to nosers.'

For answer he jerked the blade, and I yelped like a dog. An unutterable molten pain burned inside my nose, and a Niagara of blood was purling down my chin and turning my shirt front crimson. I sank to the floor, moaning, my hands cupped over my poor sliced nostril. I sensed them talking, but heard only a high keening of distress in my ears. (I realised later that this was my own voice.) A few minutes passed, then someone else came into the yard. I was picked up beneath the arms and seated on a crate. My nose had become a flaming agonised throb in the centre of my face, and my trembling hands could not staunch the flow. Someone was lightly shaking my shoulder, but when I looked up my eyes were watering too much to see.

'I said, who are ye?' asked the voice, a newcomer.

I whimpered my name, and then he must have turned back to remonstrate with Gaffy. I overheard vexed phrases: ' . . . cut him for? . . . bleedin' like a stuck pig . . . get him in here'. He stalked off in a fury, and I was helped inside by the two young bruisers. They took me into a washroom, where I was left with a rag and a basin of cold water. I cleaned myself up as best I could, still moaning piteously. I glanced at a speckled looking glass, and started at the reflection; blotched cheeks, red-raw eyes and a nose that looked like a bit of bloody liver. Even to dab at it was agony. They returned for me some minutes later, and I was led into a snug at the back of the pub. The man whose voice I had heard sat there: it was the owner and slumlord Moyles, whom I had not seen since the day I had harangued him to advantage in the St Pancras Vestry Hall. Unlike Gaffy, who leaned against the fireplace, Moyles knew who I was.

'Mr Wildeblood,' he said, gesturing me to a chair at his table. 'Takes some nerve to come round here after the trouble you've caused. Your little stunt at the Vestry Hall cost me, I can tell ye. So, speak up – what're you doing here?' His glowering deep-set eyes and saturnine brow might have caused me unease were I not preoccupied by my wound.

I lowered the rag from my face. 'An item of jewellery was mislaid by a friend of mine. I was led to believe that this might be the place I should recover it. For a price.'

'This is a public house, not a dolly shop,' he said, and turned a look of undisguised scorn on Gaffy. 'What d'you know about this?'

Gaffy shrugged. 'He's been to the Jew fence off Ossulston Street. Some talk about a lost fawney – dunno what it has to do with me.'

'I have money,' I said carefully. 'I can pay a . . . reward for its return.'

Moyles, still frowning with displeasure, exchanged a look with Gaffy. After some silent contemplation the former addressed me again. 'You're one of Marchmont's lot, ain't you? Your guvnor's got himself in some rare trouble.'

I had no idea what 'trouble' he meant, but I had learned a method of wheedling out information during my time as an interviewer: pretend to know. Prompt your interlocutor. *Wait to see how the cat will jump* – I had got that from Paget. 'You mean the business with Condor Holdings?'

I saw a flicker of surprise momentarily cross Moyles's face before he composed himself, and I knew I had hit a nerve. 'Ye'd think a man on his beam ends would be more circumspect about money. But now he's cutting up rough, objecting to how the League intends to run the place.' I didn't altogether understand this. I guessed he meant the Social Protection League, and his reference to 'the place' was Bindon Fields. I waited for him to continue, but his expression had changed to narrow-eyed cunning. 'You know Marchmont well, I dare say?'

'Pretty well,' I agreed.

'And you have access to his records and such?'

I sensed where he was tending with this enquiry. 'I can get it very easily,' I lied.

Moyles leaned back in his chair and considered me. 'He's become quite a liability, the guvnor. Believes himself above it all. I know certain fellows in the organisation would like rid of him. But they'd need something, from the inside . . . if you take my meaning'.

I did not take his meaning. What organisation? And what information on Marchmont were they after? I betrayed none of this, only sat there, listening, nodding. I had to keep him thinking I was on *the inside*.

'I am on good terms with Mr Rennert, his secretary,' I said. 'If there is something in particular you require . . .' Moyles stared hard at me. I could tell he was calculating the odds on my being useful to him. Whilst he did so I thought back to what he had just said about Marchmont's 'cutting up rough'. With as much nonchalance as I could feign, I returned to this question. 'So what's Marchmont's beef with the League . . . ?'

Moyles, distracted, spoke loosely. 'It's still the appointment of the superintendent. Threatens to kick up a stink.'

'Superintendent? Who would that be?' My curiosity was too obvious, and his gaze sharpened on me.

'You don't know?'

'I – heard rumours . . .'

That was my mistake, the moment Moyles seemed to twig I had been groping in the dark. His expression asked the question: How much about this *do* you know? The tentative mood of intrigue between us suddenly dissolved, and when he spoke again his tone was brisk and businesslike. 'You said you had money, for the ring. On you?'

'No,' I replied, feeling the insult to my worldliness, 'not on me. But I can get it.'

Moyles looked round at Gaffy, his silent sentinel. 'I'm sure my associate knows where it can be found, at a price. I leave that for you to arrange.' Our interview was at an end. Gaffy gave a small lift of his chin in acknowledgement, and I rose from the table, dismissed. As I walked to the door, Moyles said at my back, 'You'd be well advised to keep away from here, Mr Wildeblood. And look after that nose. Next time you could lose the whole thing.'

My landlady squawked in horror when I came through the door later that evening. When I saw myself in the looking glass I used for shaving I understood why. From my misadventure at the Victory I had made my way to a hospital on the City Road, ignoring the surprised look of the lady I sat next to on the 'bus. Even at the hospital's receiving room, where one would suppose they were used to such sights, my injured nose had provoked an audible gasp of dismay from one young nurse. When the doctor had explained the procedure he was about to perform, I had lost my nerve and bleated to him, 'Is there really no other way?'

The doctor, a squat, jovial fellow with extravagant whiskers, had smirked at my cowardice. 'Do you wish to continue breathing through your nose?' he had asked.

I admitted that I did.

'Then there is no other way.'

Thus followed a half-hour of suturing that felt as though the wing of my nostril were being liberally employed as a pincushion. Now, in the glass, the face that had frightened my landlady stared back in all its repulsive absurdity. The hospital nurses had been nothing if not clinical. A thick wad of white dressing criss-crossed my nose, overwhelming it. I looked like a muzzled dog, or a sinister clown from a *commedia dell'arte*. Purplish-black rings had formed beneath my eyes, adding an extra dab of ugliness. As I discovered the next morning, I could not have drawn more startled looks from passers-by if I had worn a leper's bell around my neck.

My appearance at the office prompted sniggers, and not a few guffaws. One of the copy editors, Timms, capered in front of me, rolling his fists like a boxer. I had only just sat down when Rennert appeared at his office door and wordlessly summoned me within. He must have been quite distracted, because it was only when I sat down opposite him that his expression tightened into a frown.

'What on earth is that on your face?' he asked.

I spun him the tale of a domestic accident, though he showed scant interest in listening to it. He seemed in an oddly remote mood, so different from his usual hawkish vigilance. I was proceeding through an account of a recent interview with a street ballad singer when he held up his hand to silence me. He brooded for some moments, then puffed out his cheeks. 'Mr Wildeblood,' he began, 'the paper is to make a number of changes, mostly to do with cutting costs. It has come to the point, alas, where we must dispense with the services of certain contributors, and I regret to say that you are amongst them.'

I gaped at him. 'You're – sacking me?'

He made a regretful moue at the word. 'Please understand, this is entirely a matter of business. It is not intended to reflect upon the standard of your work here. But I should be grateful if you were to clear out your desk.'

I was momentarily at a loss. 'Is it not traditional for employees to serve out a period of notice?'

'Traditional, but not mandatory. It would be in everyone's interest if your position was . . . resolved immediately.'

'"*Everyone's* interest"? Not mine, I do assure you.' I was seized by an abrupt and unmanly urge to cry; but, keeping my eyes down, I took command of myself. A minute or so passed before I looked up at Rennert. 'May I ask – did this decision originate from Mr Marchmont?'

'I would rather not discuss the private –'

'Mr Rennert, please,' I cut in. 'Did he want me out?'

He paused, narrowing his eyes on me. I sensed a concession about to be made. 'I dare say you know on whose authority the running of this paper depends.'

'I thought as much. Though I'm surprised at the manner of it. If the guvnor is determined to dismiss me he ought to do so face to face.'

'Mr Wildeblood,' he said with a reluctant sigh, 'pray, don't take that tone. This is the same man who took a risk in hiring you.'

'A risk?'

He tilted his head knowingly. 'It is not every editor who would employ an untried youth, still less a convicted felon.'

Again, I was taken aback. 'You knew . . . about that?' He held his steady look, affirming it. I suppose I should have been grateful. Yes, Marchmont had taken a chance on me back then – but his dismissal of me now smacked of a desperate effort to cover his tracks. He had sensed that I was on to him. Perhaps Rennert suspected it, too. 'Did he imagine that I would expose his connection with Condor Holdings?'

Rennert stared back at me. 'I don't take your meaning.'

Wait to see how the cat jumps, I thought . . . but Rennert was much too wily to play that game. He would never jump first. I had to take a guess. 'I think our guvnor has run into trouble with some very unscrupulous people – slumlords, rack-renters, that sort. Maybe they have been underwriting his debts, and now they want some return on their money.'

He was still staring at me, only now his expression had hardened into something more serious. When he spoke his voice had dropped a fraction. 'Listen to me, sir. You may think you know what is going on, but you do not. You have *no idea*. Pursue this any further and –' He stopped, as though mindful of trespassing against his own rules of close-mouthed discretion. 'You are a bright fellow. You have prospects. Do not squander them. I am saying this now for your own good: stay out of Somers Town.'

'Somebody said the same thing to me yesterday. I'm afraid it only makes me more curious to know.'

Rennert had risen from his chair, and pushed an envelope across the desk towards me. I stood and picked it up, unimpressed.

'Six weeks' wages, by way of compensation,' he said. I gave a little *tsk* of disappointment, and he squinted at me. 'It is not enough?'

'On the contrary. It's generous,' I replied. 'But I object to being fobbed off. There is something afoot. Somers Town is being cleared, street by street, its poorest inhabitants forced out of their homes and hidden from sight in the country. The scheme is fronted by a private charity. Alfred Kenton knew something of it, and he ended up drowned in the Thames. I cannot yet say how far the guvnor is implicated, but I intend to find out.'

'Mr Wildeblood, you would be wise not to meddle in this. The governor is innocent of –'

'If he is innocent then he should have no fear of being investigated. Thank you for the money, Mr Rennert. Good day.' I raised my hat, and walked out of his office.

Kitty had written to me, expressing a desire to meet. Ordinarily I would have been happy to oblige her, but her involvement with Father Kay and the Social Protection League had given me pause. As matters stood, I didn't wish to compromise her position as one of Kay's trusted associates, and I remained suspicious enough of the charity to make sure that no utterance of mine should be reported to them, however innocently. I had written back to her pleading pressure of work – it was true but a short time ago – though I confess a less noble reason was keeping me within doors. The bandage across my nose, and the bruising beneath my eyes – now a livid purplish-yellow – continued to lend me an aspect nothing short of grotesque. So you may add 'vanity' to the roster of my shortcomings.

In the end, my efforts to avoid her came to naught. I was idling in my rooms one morning when the clop and clatter of a carriage pulling up on the street drew me to the window. I peered down to see the driver dismount, whilst a lady, face obscured by an elaborate hat, remained seated behind him. When I heard a knock at the door I guessed the visitor was mine, and sure enough Mrs Home was hurrying up the stairs calling my name. 'A lady,' she said in a voice hushed with deference. I just had time to put on a collar and my most presentable coat, forgetting for a moment as I emerged from the house the ridiculous excrescence that disfigured my face.

'Good heavens,' cried Kitty, staring at me in genuine alarm. 'What has happened to you?'

'Oh,' I said, reflexively covering it with my hand. 'I, um, poked my nose where it wasn't welcome. What are you doing here?'

'Why, you've been hiding yourself away! It occurred to me that you might be ill or – I don't know what. Then I enquired at the paper, and was told that you didn't work there any more.' She glanced about her, seeming to take in the street for the first time. Mrs Home was still watching our visitor from the doorstep, her gaze stunned with pride, and perhaps a little envy. 'I always wondered where you lived,' Kitty continued with a quick smile. 'I hope you'll join me for a drive, now that I've come all this way.'

'So long as you don't mind having a griffin as your companion.'

She laughed at that, and pushed open the door in invitation. 'Thank you, John,' she called to her carriage man, and we were off. The sleek conveyance drew sidelong glances from passers-by – it was not a type much seen in this part of Islington – though Kitty seemed oblivious. As we sailed down Rosebery Avenue towards Holborn, she turned the full beam of her attention on me. '*So* . . . why have you parted company with Henry?'

'I didn't have any choice in the matter.'

'You mean – he *dismissed* you?' she said, aghast.

'A matter of economy was the official reason. But I believe he had other motives for wanting rid of me.' I saw her eyes widen in curiosity, and immediately I regretted my unguarded speech.

She made to speak, but then checked herself. After a while I felt her watching me again. 'Your poor face!' she began. 'At least tell me this – you didn't get into a fight with Henry, did you? I know he used to box –'

'What? No, of course not. He wasn't even there to give me the bag – his secretary did it for him. No . . . this was sustained in another business altogether.' I palpated the wound gingerly, hoping the subject would be dropped.

'How very mysterious you're being,' she said, clicking her tongue in annoyance. Still I kept silent. 'What is the matter? Have I offended in some way that has made you unwilling to talk to me?'

'I would merely prefer to *be quiet*,' I said testily.

She stiffened. 'Now you're just being disagreeable,' she said, and cast down her eyes in hurt. I listened to the brisk clacking of the wheels and John's muttered *hyup*s to the horses and the surrounding noise of the street until I could bear it no longer.

'Kitty, forgive me. I fear I am not myself . . . You will hear how I came by this wretched thing – and understand why I didn't wish to burden you with it.'

She slowly deigned to look up, her mouth set in a reproving pout. 'Well?'

I sighed, and began the story of my stumbling upon Moyles's public house, my encounter with Gaffy in the yard, and what befell me there. Her hand flew to her mouth as she took in the precise nature of my injury. 'How *horrible*,' she said, in a voice tremulous with feeling. 'But I don't – I don't understand . . . what you were *doing* there?' She blinked at me in plaintive puzzlement.

It was the reason I had not wanted to discuss the matter in the first place, but now that I had come this far I could see no use in dissembling. 'I had reason to believe I might recover . . . a certain diamond ring, which had been stolen from a friend of mine some weeks ago. I hoped to be able to surprise her without having to explain how I came by it . . .'

I sensed her go very still at my side. When I at last ventured a look, tears were bulging in her eyes. 'Oh, David . . . what a perfectly gallant thing to do! I'm sorry to have . . .' She grasped my hand tightly. '*Thank* you.'

'Don't thank me yet,' I replied with a shrug. 'Its return is by no means secured. I am obliged to wait until that blackguard who cut me decides upon a deal.'

'He will set an extortionate price, I suppose.'

'I'm afraid so.'

'I shall pay whatever he demands,' she said decisively. 'But promise me you will not put yourself in danger again.'

I could not offer any such guarantee, but I made a placatory gesture that implied caution without committing to anything. The tale of my perilous adventure appeared to have impressed Kitty, for she became quite nervously animated about the possibility of redeeming the ring ('it was my mother's, you know', which I already did). Her talk turned skittish, inclining me to wonder if she had something else on her mind. The carriage had slowed up in the dense traffic of the West End, heading towards Piccadilly, when she broke off from her latest monologue and looked at me directly.

'There is something I must tell you,' she said, abruptly earnest. 'Indeed, I have been rather fearful of telling you.'

'Oh?' I could not imagine what it might be, and waited.

'I am engaged to be married.' She spoke in a tone of uncertain defiance, as if she anticipated objection from me. But I felt only surprise.

'I'm – that is – I congratulate you. May I presume your intended –'

'It's Douglas. The man I told you about. Our families have been intimate friends for years.' Her face had coloured, and her mouth twitched with the anxiety of one who had said too much, or perhaps too little.

'Your father must be delighted,' I said. 'I remember your remarking how seriously he takes lineage and so on.'

'Yes, he does – and he is. Delighted, I mean.' She fell silent at that, and looked thoughtful. I sensed a more enthusiastic note was in order.

'And the lady herself? I fancy you are overjoyed!'

Her answer came after a pause, and in a small voice. 'Yes, of course.' I waited for something more, but after her recent stream of chatter she seemed now to withhold. Perhaps this was maidenly modesty, I couldn't tell, but it felt possible that I should tease her out of it. 'Only think, the manly hearts that will break on hearing that Miss Catherine Elder is to marry!'

She looked very queerly at me then, as though there were a hidden implication in my light-hearted words. 'Do you think the news of my betrothal would really . . . grieve someone, then?' She spoke quite seriously, and I wondered if I had somehow mistaken her mood. Less certain of myself, I replied in a careful but affectionate way.

'I think whenever a young lady makes herself unavailable through marriage it will always cause regret amongst her admirers.'

'"Admirers" . . .' she repeated the word, almost dejectedly, then returned to her scrutiny of me. 'I have sometimes wondered about them – about what they think of me.' I smiled at her in a vague, rueful way, as if to suggest the dashed dreams of so many, but again she rather bemused me by saying, 'I could have wished that one or two of them had been more – forthright.'

I hesitated, before saying, 'Kitty, forgive me – you seem not entirely happy –'

'Is that how I seem?' she cut in airily. 'At present I hardly know *what* I am about.' She dropped her gaze, and fell silent.

The carriage had come to a halt at the south-east corner of Hyde Park, and the driver looked round to ask how he should proceed. Kitty, as though roused from a trance of preoccupation, said, 'We'll go home through the park, John – but wait a moment.' She regarded me again, with a smile of slightly forced carelessness. 'I have an appointment at hand, David. Would you mind my dropping you here?' I tried to hide my astonishment at this sudden dismissal, and was making to rise when she checked me. 'I shall not forget your bravery,' she said, and put her hand to my cheek. Then she leaned back, with nothing more to say; I opened the carriage door and stepped down. John made a clicking sound with his mouth, the horses clopped off, and I watched Kitty, bolt upright in her seat, recede into the distance. She did not turn to look back at me.

13
Fresh fakements

Jo was on the mend from his illness, which had turned out to be a case of pneumonia. He was swaddled in blankets like a little old woman when I called at the Polygon one morning, whilst Roma, plainly cheered by his recovery, had just prepared a toddy of hot lemon and brandy for him. As I entered his bedchamber he hooted with laughter at my injured phiz.

'Last time I seen a nose band thick as that was on a horse!'

Roma gave me a sympathetic look. 'Been in a fight?' she asked.

'Not a fair one,' I said, and on recounting my misadventure at the Victory Jo stopped laughing very abruptly.

'Get the fuck out of it,' he said in a voice tight with outrage. 'How could ya? How could ya be such a fool to go there *on yor own?*'

'Jo,' said Roma in sharp rebuke, whether of his language or his ill temper I wasn't sure. I had heard him swear before, many times, but never at me. He looked away, scowling, and Roma stepped forward to examine the bandage. She peeled back a corner of it and I flinched as the gauze came away from the wound. 'I could clean that for you. Looks a bit . . . crusted.'

Jo made a sort of hissing noise through his teeth at her solicitude. 'Lucky it was just your snout they cut,' he muttered. I was going to make a facetious reply, but he looked so angry I thought better of it. Roma told me to go into the parlour, and followed shortly after, carrying a little tin of medicines. From it she plucked a thin brown-glassed bottle, removed the stopper and sniffed the top. My nose smarted wildly as she lifted the old bandage away and dabbed the stitched cut ('Sorry,' she murmured) with a little rag soaked in iodine. She stood close to me, so close I could smell the soap she had used on her skin. Her dark hair, still damp from washing, was brushed back from her forehead, leaving her face oddly open and vulnerable; its contours were even more vivid in their detail than I had previously allowed. Her eyes, with their counterpoint of green and blue, unsettled me enough to wonder if they were the outward expression of a temperamental divide – green, perhaps, for all that was ardent and unyielding, blue for the quiet, melancholy side of her character. I was still entertaining this fancy when she gave a short laugh and, drawing back her head appraisingly, said, 'Like a good stare, don't you?'

Jo had calmed down by the time we returned to his room, and talked happily of his imminent return to the market on Chalton Street. A coster pal had managed his stall whilst he was ill. 'Yeah, well, Harry's a rum cull, but his patter ain't up to much. I needs to get bisniss up again . . . Course, the old moke's missed me, too.' I had seen Jo's donkey in the interim, but had failed to note any sign of the creature's yearning for his master. Roma's ministrations had freed my nose from its cone of plaster but exposed anew the unsightliness of the wound. It had none of the glamour of a Heidelberg duelling scar – it was just raw and ugly and spiked with stitches. Jo stared at it. 'Gaffy . . .' he said, then shook his head disgustedly. 'What's he say to you arfter – I mean, 'bout the fawney?'

'Only that he'd arrange a drop somewhere. I bring the money, he gives me the ring. But I haven't heard from him.'

'And you might never, neither. He knows you not got the blunt to buy it back.'

'No, but Kitty has,' I said, recalling our bemusing conversation of the previous week: I was still troubled by an inkling that I had offended her in some way.

Jo looked dubious at this. 'That won't solve it. You can't call the odds with Gaffy. He'd offer you a rat's arsehole and swear it was a ring – an' you're the sort who'd buy it off him.'

'Are you determined to keep insulting me?'

'Oh, I've 'ardly begun –'

'Right, that's enough,' said Roma. 'I'm not havin' you two at each other's throats. Jo, I'm off out. And *you*,' she said, fixing her eyes on mine, 'are comin' with me.'

Jo flopped down in an armchair, folded his arms and fumed quietly. I stared out of the parlour window until Roma had put on her coat and boots, ready to leave. Without looking at him I called 'goodbye', but heard no response as I exited. Five minutes later we had left behind the Polygon and were walking north. It was typical of her that she refrained from commenting on the little scene of discord just gone; she always had a much keener sense of when to speak and when to withhold than I ever did.

'Don't know why Jo's got the hump – wasn't *his* nose,' I said eventually, unable to suppress a sense of hurt. A pause followed, before she replied.

'It's only cos he was worried for you – just got a different way of showin' it.'

Right enough, I thought. And perhaps he's not the only one. We reverted to silence: her step was purposeful, but I didn't ask where she was heading, nor why she stopped at a flower stall to buy lilies. As we continued on our way I noted again the proliferation of scaffolding on the houses. Development's hand, once slow to action in Somers Town, was closing its grip with remorseless intent. Children still played in these fetid streets; women hauled their bundles and baskets to and from the wash house, probably unaware of the day when these tenements and workshops would be reduced to rubble. But it was coming.

The day was dullish but mild, halfway through September, its mood undecided between the vanishing warmth of the summer and the approaching bristle of autumn. To my surprise, Roma had entered the graveyard of old St Pancras Church and was navigating a path amongst the slanting headstones. She made for the far wall, where a line of tall yews had formed a screen against the hollow clank of the railway works beyond. The gravestones in this corner were of a more recent age, their faces not yet bearded with lichen. She had come to a halt before a simple stone with an arched head, and laid the lilies against it. *In Loving Memory of* . . . Two names were carved into the granite.

JOSEPH GARRETT
GIULIETTA GARRETT

Her parents. Each carried the dates of their earthly span, though it took me some moments to realise the significance in the latter's: Giulietta had died, two years after her husband, on 18 September 1872. Ten years gone, to the day.

'It's a nice spot,' I remarked, for want of something unpessimistic to say.

Roma nodded. 'Didn't have much of a life. Thirty-three when she died. Consumption – same thing *he* died of. Tell the truth, I half thought Jo might have had it these past weeks.' Now I realised why she had looked so relieved.

I considered the dates again. 'You must have been quite young yourself – when they died.'

She shrugged. 'I was fourteen when our mum went, Jo was nine.'

'So you became –' I was going to say 'like his mother', but instead chose a less poignant designation – 'the head of the household.'

'No one else was gonna take care of us,' she said, looking at me.

'How did you manage – I mean, for money?'

She gave a rueful little snort. 'We got by.'

She withdrew into silence, staring fixedly at the headstone. Her preoccupation was so abrupt and enveloping that I supposed she might be praying, and I retreated a few steps to allow her privacy. I could hear rooks cawing somewhere, complaining to each other. She had brought me to a melancholy place, yet I also sensed that she was glad to have my company. Had she not asked me to join her? I wandered along the row of new plots, glancing at this or that inscription, the dearly beloveds, the departed-this-lifes, the pray-for-the-souls . . . and of a sudden I stopped. Passing the previous headstone I had seen a name from the corner of my eye, and it had set off a chime in some remote byway of my brain. I retraced my steps and looked at it again.

THOMAS BOWLAND-DARKE

It was freshly carved on the stone. Why did I know that name? I stared at it, trying to grasp at the thread as it wormed inside memory's labyrinth. Thomas Bowland-Darke. I recognised it, but how, from where? Roma had come up beside me.

'What is it?' she asked.

'This. This name. I feel sure that I know it, but I can't think why.'

She considered the modest inscription. 'Died 3 June 1882 . . . Alone, by the look of it. No mention of a wife.'

'Thomas Bowland-Darke. Thomas –' Perhaps it was saying the name aloud that triggered it. I felt in my breast pocket and pulled out a folded piece of paper. It was the page I had secretly torn from the ledger of leaseholdings on my previous visit to the Records Office. I opened it, and listed there, in a formal cursive, were the names of the five lease-holders in Johnson Street, Somers Town, N.

Annie O'Brien
Harriet Shepherd
George Harding
Edith Arkell
Thomas Bowland-Darke

'There he is,' I said, showing her the page. 'It must be the same man.'

She pursed her mouth thoughtfully. 'Don't s'pose there'd be more than one with a name like that.'

I looked at the date of the signatories' purchase. According to this, Condor Holdings had sold the leases on Johnson Street only six weeks ago.

'This doesn't make sense,' I said.

'Why? A man dyin' isn't uncommon, not round here.'

'No, but a man dying in June and then purchasing a lease in August, I'd say that *is* uncommon.'

Now her face reflected my own look of puzzlement. 'How's that?'

'It's written here, look. Thomas Bowland-Darke bought three properties on the 7th of August 1882. But according to this gravestone he was already two months dead . . .'

'Maybe it's just a mistake,' she said. Maybe it was – but I didn't think so. Lines from Jo's song coursed around my head: *For every day, mind what I say, / Fresh fakements you will find . . .*

At that moment, over Roma's shoulder, I saw a man open the lychgate at the far end of the churchyard. He was carrying a spade. I strode off towards him, with Roma hurrying after, and we met halfway along the flagstone path leading to the church. I hailed him – he was a wiry little fellow with sunken, furtive eyes – and asked about the recently dug plots by the wall.

'There's one grave of particular interest to me. The deceased's name is Thomas Bowland-Darke. D'you recall it?'

'Not likely, sir. I digs the 'ole, I buries 'em – ain't my bisniss to remember 'em!'

'Would you be able to supply some information concerning the deceased?'

'Well, the verger's got a bill o' works up at the church. Wot's it to ya?'

I explained that I was pursuing a story for Henry Marchmont's newspaper: the name prompted a nod of recognition. Leaning his spade against a beech tree near by, the man told us to wait 'half a mo'' whilst he went off to fetch his records. Roma cocked her head to one side.

'I thought you said Marchmont gave you the boot.'

'He did. But our friend here isn't to know.'

She took the page I had ripped from the ledger and studied it. 'Johnson Street – who'd want to buy a lease there?'

'A dead man, apparently. Something's amiss here.'

'And these others – Annie O'Brien, Harriet Shepherd . . . who are they?'

'Heaven knows. But they don't sound like property speculators, that's for sure.'

Presently, the gravedigger came scuttling back, an antiquated bound register in his hand. I reminded him of the name as he opened it and riffled the pages. It did not take him long. 'Here he is. Thomas Bowland-Darke. Born 1805, died the 4th of June this year. Bachelor; no next of kin. Buried him on the 10th of June.'

I looked at him, waiting. 'Is that all? I mean, where did he live?'

The man consulted the page once more. 'No address,' he shrugged.

'What d'you mean?' I said. 'He must have been *some*where when he died.'

'Right enough,' the man conceded with a grimace, 'but it weren't *his* address.' He hoisted a thumb over his shoulder at the outline of the tall brick edifice glowering beyond the church. 'Poor feller's last home was the work'us.' And, thrusting the book beneath my gaze, he pointed to the brief entry for *Bowland-Darke, Thomas,* and the site of his final days on earth: *W/H.* Workhouse. He had died a pauper.

Before leaving the graveyard I asked the man about the other four names, wondering if they too had been buried hereabouts. But they were not in his register. As we headed back to the Polygon I confessed to Roma that this business of the phantom leaseholder had me flummoxed.

'I mean, if Bowland-Darke did own property on Johnson Street, what was he doing in the workhouse?'

Roma shook her head. 'But he didn't own it, bein' as he was, like, *dead.*' I had to concede that point.

'So . . . why would Condor Holdings sell off leases to a man known to be dead and buried?'

She gave a sardonic chuckle at this. 'Handy for the real owner, I s'pose. You can't complain to a landlord that ain't there!'

I stopped in my tracks. 'That's it! You've got it.' I slapped my forehead, aghast at my own slowness. 'They didn't sell the leases at all. They kept them, but under someone else's name – someone who couldn't be applied to.'

'Why would they do that?' she asked.

'The usual reason – money. Landlords in Somers Town are always trying to shirk responsibility to their tenants. The houses there have been crying out for repairs, and the landlords contrive to obstruct them, either by appealing to the courts or else gambling on a short-term lease that will expire before they have to cough up. But what if the landlord found a way of escaping liability altogether – by filing properties under a false name?'

'But they'd be found out –'

'Not if they attach the leases to names of people nobody can trace – like a pauper, or a derelict. *That's the dodge.* When Moyles got found out as a slum landlord – you remember the riot at the Vestry Hall? – he disposed of those leases double quick. A company named Condor Holdings took them on, a company I've spent months trying to run to ground. Just when I caught up with them, the leases were moved on again, this time to complete strangers – like Thomas Bowland-Darke. Now most of the houses are going to be destroyed, and the landlords have got away with it – all that neglect.'

Roma absorbed this in her silent way, and we walked on a little further.

'I must hunt down the other Johnson Street leaseholders,' I said, plucking the list again from my breast pocket and reading the names. 'I dare say the simplest thing to do is consult the census. Wasn't there one taken last year?'

She nodded, but there was a squint of doubt, too. 'Mightn't be easy. I reckon there's about 'alf of Somers Town would never get near that census. All them as move around dosshouses – you s'pose anyone bothered to count 'em?'

She was right. There were many ways for the poor to fall between the cracks of public notice, and the most obvious was that of homelessness. They would sleep on the street, or, if they could afford the 2d per night, in a dosshouse, four or five to a room. The itinerant poor by their very nature would be difficult for a census-taker to pin down, and with no sense of obligation on the part of the subject it would be virtually impossible.

'I've not spent much time in a dosshouse,' I admitted.

'You'd never want to, believe me,' she said.

'Rather a desperate manner of living, I gather.'

She spoke quietly, and sadly. 'It's not livin', though. It's just lingerin'.'

We had reached the top of Ossulston Street when the wail of protesting voices was caught on the air. Turning the corner of Aldenham Street we found a crowd of about two hundred jostling against a picket of police.

They were concentrated outside a row of tumbledown terraces which had been earmarked for clearance. A banner held aloft amidst the crush of bodies proclaimed SAVE OUR STREETS, a somewhat belated plea given that a quarter of this one already stood in rubble and ashes. As we skirted the melee we saw an object being flung from a top-floor window onto the police below; a chamber pot crashed and splintered on the flags, causing the nearest constable to jump in fright. Certain of his colleagues were hammering at the house from which the missile had been hurled, but without success: the door had been replaced with a stout shield of metal cladding. I looked to Roma, who only bit her lip, apparently as confounded by the spectacle as I was.

A moment later I spotted, on the edges of the crowd, a portly figure absorbed in taking notes, and I cupped my hands either side of my mouth to hail him. Paget looked round, and returned my wave. He pocketed his notebook as he dodged his way across the street.

'What's happening?' I asked him.

'An open siege, it would appear. Notices have gone up about compulsory clearances, from here to Barclay Street. The occupants of *that* house –' he pointed to the one surrounded by the police – 'are refusing to vacate it. The bailiffs called in the police about an hour ago.'

'Quite a crowd . . .'

'Once the Rental Reform people got wind of it, they turned up mob-handed. Now the whole neighbourhood's come out to support 'em. Looks like a hot 'un for the police.' As if to demonstrate the point a wooden chair came flying out of the window and dropped to the street with a clatter. A raucous cheer went up. Paget, meanwhile, was staring from beneath his brow at Roma.

'I beg your pardon,' I said. 'Allow me to introduce you. This is Roma Garrett – Clifford Paget, from the *Chronicle*.'

Paget, narrowing his gaze, said, 'Have we – met before?'

Roma met his stare for a moment, then said, 'I don't think so.'

'I thought – you seem familiar – have I seen you in a dining room, hereabouts?' His tone was friendly, but Roma's shrug of indifference did not seem to welcome the enquiry.

'I've worked 'ere all my life, in shops and pubs.' She perhaps heard her own brusqueness, for she added, in slight concession, 'I've served at tables in dining rooms, too.'

Paget nodded, and mumbled, 'Yes, yes, thought so,' but his imperfect recognition had created an awkwardness, and only the unruly hordes milling about us covered for the conversation's dead end. Roma looked rather fatigued, and I offered to accompany her back to the Polygon. She declined, however.

'I have to go by the Brill, get Jo his supper,' she said. I nodded, and went to give her my hand, but she ignored it and did something I wasn't expecting: she leaned in and briefly pressed her lips against my cheek. It was over and done with in a moment, and I was too startled to respond; she had already turned and walked off by the time I called goodbye.

Paget was looking at me. 'Old friend of yours?'

'Not so old,' I said. 'I was first friends with her brother.'

He looked narrowly after her. 'Thought I knew her – my mistake.' I was still reflecting upon the kiss she had bestowed. It had not been a frivolous gesture – flirtation was alien to Roma – but seemed to contain in it something more bonding. Like something I had earned. My head felt suddenly, pleasingly light.

Our attention just then was seized by more ragged cheers from the crowd. A man had appeared at the window of the besieged house, shaking his fist in triumphant defiance. The fracas seemed to be settling into deadlock, with the protesters on the street baulking the police's efforts to storm the house. Paget took out his notebook, jotted down a few words, then snapped it shut.

'Kenton would have been proud of 'em. I should get this story out for the late edition. Shall we?'

We began walking away from the crowds towards the Euston Road. Paget only now noticed my scarred nose, and sharply sucked in air through his teeth.

'Good Lord . . .'

'You would have laughed to see it with the bandage on.' I explained the circumstances that had led to the assault at the Victory. Paget shook his head in dismay as he listened.

'These streets . . . you have to be on your guard, David, I've told you that before. Has it occurred to you to go out armed?'

'Armed – with what? A shooter?'

'Not that. But ever since Kenton's demise I've felt a distinct unease as I go about the place. Which is why –' he stopped, and looked about the street before opening his coat and drawing from it a short black stick – 'I've taken to carrying *this* in my pocket.' He passed it to me, and I hefted its mean weight in my hand, imagining its impact upon a skull.

'Looks like a slop's truncheon,' I said, handing it back.

'It's called a life-preserver. A fellow at Smith's on New Oxford Street sold it to me – said they've become quite popular amongst gentlemen seeking to defend themselves against garrotters.'

'Has there been a fashion for garrotting lately?'

'I'm surprised you'd joke, my boy. One of these might have saved you from those brutes the other night.' He tested it with a relishing little thwack against his palm, then returned it to his coat. 'So Moyles got his revenge on you at last . . .'

'I suppose he did. But he seemed far more vexed about Marchmont than anything I'd done. I've a notion that all is not quite going to plan with the Bindon Fields project. Before he clammed up he said something about the guvnor "cutting up rough" over a superintendent. That conversation must have got back to Marchmont, because a few days later I was given the boot from the paper.'

'Well, I dare say Henry was alarmed that one of his staff had tumbled to him. He couldn't afford to have you poking your nose – sorry! – any further into his connection with Condor Holdings.'

'Talking of which, I've reason to think they are party to a most egregious fraud.' I recounted my recent discovery of Thomas Bowland-Darke's grave in St Pancras Churchyard, and showed him the Johnson Street list I had fortuitously ripped from the Records Office ledger. By now we had reached the choked thoroughfare of Euston Road and had to raise our voices to be heard above the skitter and din of wheel traffic.

Paget, frowning, said, 'So they've been using paupers' names as cover until the leases run their term . . . That's about as despicable a ruse as I've heard.'

'I have to find those other names. I thought that last year's census might give a clue to their whereabouts, but my friend thought not – if they were destitute, like Bowland-Darke, they may have been overlooked.'

'Quite probably. The poor are . . . elusive. No census could take account of them all.'

'But if – if just one of these leaseholders can be located, the entire fakery might be exposed.'

'Yes . . . unless they have all gone the way of Mr Bowland-Darke. Condor Holdings appear not to scruple as to whether their leases are distributed amongst the living or the dead.'

An omnibus had shuddered to a halt, and Paget stepped onto the splashboard. As the vehicle dawdled before pulling away, he gave me a shrewd look. 'If we do draw a blank from the census, you ought to look through the work you did in Somers Town for Henry. Think of how many people you interviewed for *The Labouring Classes* – might you not have *met* one of them?'

I was about to reply when the 'bus jolted away, with Paget leaning on the rail. He doffed his hat to me, and I raised my arm in farewell. As I continued east on foot, I thought back to the weeks and months of going door-to-door with Jo. The number of people I had interviewed must have run to well over a thousand. Paget was right, I *could* have met Annie O'Brien, or George Harding, or Harriet Shepherd, or Edith Arkell, but they may have been amongst those who declined to give me their names. How then would I know? There were simply too many dispersed around Somers Town's labyrinthine streets and courts for a comprehensive survey to be made – one might as well set about trying to monitor an anthill.

And then a new obstacle reared up before me. The notebooks I had used in Somers Town to collate all those names and addresses were no longer in my possession. I had kept them under lock and key in my desk at Marchmont's office. I had not envisaged ever needing them again. I was wrong.

14
Not to harm

The next day's *Chronicle* carried a report of the house siege in Somers Town. I could tell it was written by Paget from its veiled disparagement of police tactics and its open attack upon the slumlords who 'allow their properties to fall into ruin and bring untold misery upon the lives of their tenants'. It was as I read this that I recalled something Paget had told me yesterday about the compulsory clearances: notices had been posted by the vestry, he said, from here to Barclay Street. It was Mrs Nicholls, resident of Barclay Street, whose anxious features now rose to mind. Having seen notices to quit plastered along the walls, she would fly into a panic about where her family were supposed to live. Part of me wished I had never shown any interest in her chaotic existence. How could I possibly right the wrongs fostered by a lifetime of terrible housing and negligent charity, not to mention the endemic ills of drink, illiteracy and fecklessness?

These thoughts were my mournful company as I sat in the offices of the *Evening News*, where I had taken a temporary job. Money was rather tight, and there was nothing else I was qualified to do – 'the definition of a journalist', as Marchmont once told me. Though disgrace still hung about his name, my time in the guvnor's employ had set me in good stead as a reliable news gatherer; indeed, I felt I had earned a shabby sort of kudos for having worked on *The Labouring Classes of London*. It was possibly instrumental in my persuading the editor to follow up the story of the riot. I would go back into Somers Town to report on those streets earmarked for destruction. I had realised the probability that Mrs Nicholls and her like would be compelled to seek shelter in the workhouse, at least whilst the Bindon Fields scheme was pending. A feeling of unease steered me towards Barclay Street – and there I found what I had most feared. A handful of neighbours were standing outside the house where Mrs Nicholls and her two children had a room. The front door stood open. There was an air about these bystanders I had come to know, and a gathering dread followed me through that door and up the cheerless stairs.

A policeman stood outside the Nicholls' room. 'Dead, mother of two,' he replied to my enquiry. 'Found 'er early this mornin'. Scragged herself, they sez. You from the vestry?'

'No. Just a friend,' I said, almost swallowing the last word. Some friend I had been. 'May I . . . ?'

The bobby shook his head. 'Pathologist's in there – not to be disturbed.' As he talked on in his clipped half-sentences, a hopelessness seemed to numb my tongue. Mrs Nicholls had hanged herself. I hardly needed to ask why. It was the same reason any woman of her class might – because she was poor, and ignorant, and doomed.

'What of the children?' I asked.

'With one of the neighbours. She sez their mother got in a right state 'bout what's been comin' – the demolishments an' that. She'd took in a lot of sewin' from neighbours – tryin' to earn some h'extra, I understand, and pawned one of these bundles of clothes for a couple o' bob. Well, the parish stopped her relief money, so she's short on the rent and now can't get that bundle outta hock neither. Neighbour sez she found her this mornin' – hanged 'gainst the wall with a bit o' string.'

'What?' I said, baulking at this grotesque detail.

'Well, I 'spect she knew it'd be no good hangin' 'erself from the ceilin' – beams are so rotten it'd come down with ya!'

At that moment the door opened, and a neat, rosy-faced fellow wearing a dark suit and an air of abstraction emerged, followed by a senior policeman. The bobby I'd been talking to introduced him as the pathologist. 'This gent was a friend of the deceased.'

He canted his head slightly in condolence. 'You were familiar with her situation?'

I shook my head, and admitted that I hadn't seen her in weeks.

'Then you probably didn't know that she'd been starving to death. If it hadn't been the noose, malnutrition would have done for her.'

I hardly knew what to say. 'I didn't know that. That is – she was always short of money, but I never for a moment . . .' I stopped, and sensed the man looking at me. He was not my accuser; he had no need to be. My faltering words carried their own note of self-blame. I could have helped Mrs Nicholls, but I had been too thoughtless, and now I was too late. Where the poor are concerned one is always too late. 'I wonder – if I may pay for the funeral arrangements?'

The pathologist's mouth tweaked wryly beneath his moustache. 'No need. I gather the only money that Mrs – Nicholls? – had left in the world was expressly set aside for her burial. It seems the woman was not entirely improvident.' He shrugged, and tipping his hat said, 'Good day to you, gentlemen.' I stood there, immobile, watching his back retreat down the stairs.

I followed shortly after, still absorbing the double shock of Mrs Nicholls' self-destruction and of her uncharacteristic forethought. I had heard, but never quite believed, that the poor would starve themselves rather than sacrifice a penny of the funds saved for their funeral. An unmarked grave was a cause for dread. Perhaps it was that having known such extremes of want in this life they were unwilling to jeopardise their passage to the next, with its promise of plenty. 'The only money she had left in the world,' the pathologist had said. My God, the pity of it! If you contemplated the significance of money for too long you could go mad. I fell to wondering at the sum – the shameful pittance – that might have saved Mrs Nicholls from her last act of despair. How much per week would it have required for her and her children to maintain a modest, respectable life, with food on the table and coals for the fire? How much for a home where comfort wasn't outlawed, where vermin hadn't invaded, where the ceiling didn't leak and the drains didn't block? Arithmetic calculations pestered my brain for a few useless minutes as I walked on, oblivious to all. In the end I shrank from making an exact estimation, but of one thing I felt absolutely certain: I could have afforded it.

The next day a note came from Paget. He had consulted the London census of 1881 and found no reference to any of the names on the list. It was probable, then, that the Johnson Street leaseholders had not been of any fixed abode. Of the five on the list the only one who could be proven to have existed was Thomas Bowland-Darke – and he was now in his grave. *Scour your notebooks – the names might be there*, wrote Paget. Unfortunately those notebooks remained in a desk at the office of my erstwhile employers. Ordinarily I would have applied to Rennert for permission to consult them, but following my summary dismissal I no longer trusted him. Rennert's loyalty was to Marchmont, and I reckoned my safest course was to circumvent both of them.

I have described before the rackety offices in Salisbury Square, where the traffic of Marchmont's staff mingled round the clock with an irregular train of street people – cabmen, hawkers, bootblacks and the like – who had been invited to tell their stories personally. Add to this a third

177

class of chancers and light-fingered rogues who took advantage of the paper's open-door policy to help themselves, and you have one of the most porous workplaces imaginable. Needing to make an inconspicuous entry into the building, I realised my best hope would be to arrive at the end of the working day when no one would be very particular about the comings and goings of the paper's informants. I ascended the stairs, unnoticed, and sidled into the long office where I used to work. It was clear straight away that something was wrong. At most hours a gregarious atmosphere usually held sway, as editors took down copy or gossiped with one another. This evening I found hardly a soul about.

The untypical quiet at least allowed me to hunt without fear of interruption. I first rifled through what was once my own desk, pulling drawers that opened their mouths in an impudent show of vacancy. There was nobody in Rennert's office – unusual in itself – so I took advantage and had a thorough snoop around; but here too I found no trace of my notebooks. I returned to the main room, baffled. Where was everyone? I glanced over at the guvnor's office, his door closed, and wondered whether I should dare . . . I knocked, and receiving no reply turned the doorknob to look within. Where once there had been loaded shelves and careless stacks of books was now a wilderness of dusty fingerprints. The only items that remained on the guvnor's desk were an old lamp and a blotter. I walked around it, subjecting the drawers to the same investigation as my own, to identical effect. Someone had cleared the room in an unseemly haste: I could see groove marks on the parquet where the desk legs had been been dragged. The walls wore fresh-coloured rectangles where paintings and photographs had been snatched off their hooks.

'Wildeblood. What are you doing here?' I turned to find Timms standing in the doorway.

'Oh, I happened to be passing and – thought I'd drop by. Where is everyone?'

'You haven't heard? It's all to smash. The paper's been surviving on borrowed money, and the creditors have had enough. Bankrupt.' He pushed back his sawdust-coloured hair from his forehead and sighed.

'And the guvnor?'

'Done a bunk. I gather quite a lot of the debt was his own. And a nice mess he's left us in, I must say.' We silently considered the emptied office for a moment.

'I wonder – there are certain notebooks of mine I'm looking for. Would you know what's become of them?'

Timms pursed his mouth unhappily. 'Hardly. The place has been picked clean. I saw Rennert disappearing with a crate of books –'

'When?'

'Few hours ago. Probably just the accounts. Of course, *he* must have known trouble was on the way . . .'

'Yes, I dare say,' I mumbled, absently, moving past him and out through the door. 'I do beg your pardon, Timms, I must away.' He looked surprised by the suddenness of my departure, as though I might have just stolen something – though of course there was nothing to steal. I took the stairs two at a time, and once outside I sprinted onto Fleet Street. I hadn't the money for a cab, so I jumped on an omnibus heading west. As the 'bus jolted along I took out the *Chronicle*, and found a report of Mrs Nicholls' suicide. It included the fact that she had hanged herself with string from a nail on the wall. I imagined the little ripple of shock that detail would make as it broke upon the reader's consciousness, before it was forgotten about and, like the woman herself, never mentioned again. There was something else in the report I hadn't known: having studied her face, worn down like an old coin, I had judged Mrs Nicholls to be about forty years old. In fact, she was twenty-six.

At Oxford Circus a horse had collapsed on the street, blocking the traffic both ways, so I took the remainder of the journey on foot. Lamplighters had just begun their rounds by the time I reached Montagu Square. It was but a matter of months since I had first presented myself, shivering, at Marchmont's door: 'the neophyte', he had called me then. I wondered what epithet he might choose for me this evening, once I had denounced him. As I approached the house two vehicles stood in wait, one of them a cab, the other a trap still being loaded with suitcases and travelling trunks. A lady was consulting anxiously with one of the removal men; only the young girl loitering on the step had noticed me. I recalled her face from last time, peering down from the top of the staircase, and I tipped my hat as I passed her. The front door was open, and, ignored amidst the comings and goings of the help, I walked in. The whole house was in a flurry of evacuation. The dining room I looked into had been denuded of its ornaments and paintings; dust sheets covered the furniture, and on a long mahogany table dining chairs had been stacked upside down, their curved legs raised like imploring supplicants into the air. A man on a stepladder was taking down the brocade curtains.

I continued into Rennert's office, where he had interviewed me in

February, and saw that the double-leafed doors to Marchmont's inner sanctum were slightly ajar. With a soft tread I stepped up to the gap and watched as Rennert busily sorted through books, glancing at each spine to determine whether it should be packed or discarded. Marchmont, his back to the room, was staring fixedly at the map on his wall, the one he had shown me so proudly that evening. There was something forlorn in the stillness of his posture. I accidentally announced myself with an ill-placed step; the protesting groan of the floorboard caused both men to turn their heads, and Rennert pulled back the panelled door.

'Mr Wildeblood, what on earth —' There was no welcome in his voice. He looked grey and drawn, and old.

'The front door was open,' I explained, directing my gaze at Marchmont, who seemed perfectly unsurprised by this intrusion. He gave a quick snorting sigh before he spoke.

'An untimely entrance. As you see, we are rather preoccupied . . .' His tone was unruffled, in contrast to the disarray of his surroundings. It seemed not in his nature to panic. I took a deep breath to steady myself.

'I have come to collect a set of notebooks containing information I gathered during my employment in Somers Town. I believe there is evidence in there that Walter Moyles intends to use as blackmail against you.'

Marchmont absorbed this, though his expression betrayed amusement rather than consternation. He picked out a cigar from his case, clipped its end and lit it, emitting a pungent cloud of smoke. 'I fear you are on a fool's errand, sir. I am acquainted with Mr Moyles — a scoundrel, as you suggest — but he is in no position to blackmail me.'

'He said you reneged on a financial arrangement he had with you, regarding Condor Holdings . . . your "cutting up rough" about an appointment —'

'Good Lord,' said Marchmont with a chuckle, 'you *have* done some doughty digging, haven't you? Rennert, I wonder if you've any notion of what Mr Wildeblood is accusing me of.'

Rennert, who showed little relish for our conversation, looked gravely at me. 'None at all. We are pressed for time, sir, so kindly state your business here.'

'Very well. I believe Mr Marchmont is engaged in an illegal property speculation with Condor Holdings and the Social Protection League. You are privy to the resettlement scheme in Bindon Fields, and therefore must know of the fraudulent sale of leases that has enabled it. I happened to stumble on this conspiracy, Moyles got wind of it, and shortly afterwards you sacked me from the paper, lest any further revelations came to light.'

Marchmont glanced at Rennert, though his expression did not in the least hint at complicity in what I had just described. He took another long pull on his cigar, and said mildly, 'Mr Wildeblood, it no longer matters, but I will try nevertheless to extract some fragments of sense from your deposition. My arrangement with Moyles and the League was not shady in the way you suggest. In return for a fee I agreed to deliver one or two lectures on Somers Town, should there have been a need to present the Bindon Fields scheme before Parliament. That scheme still awaits approval. As to the fraudulent leases, you may well be right, but I must plead ignorance of them. I had quite other reasons for withdrawing my services.'

Something calm and matter-of-fact in his voice was beginning to sow doubts in my head. 'What reasons were they?'

He paused, and Rennert gave an impatient little cough. 'Sir, I really must –'

'We have time enough,' Marchmont cut in, and turned again to the Poverty Map, with its blaze of coded colours. 'Eight years! Eight years I have been at work on this map. All those thousands of houses, of streets and tenements, all of those teeming lives investigated and encoded here. Nothing like it ever seen before! I had imagined this would be my legacy –' he splayed his hand in a magician's flourish – 'and that every future survey of the London poor would take account of it.' He stopped, and gave a philosophical sigh.

'But you ran out of money,' I supplied.

'Indeed I did – *mea culpa*. Money has flowed through my hands like water. I ought to have cupped them more tightly. We all of us have our weaknesses . . . mine has been the casino and the card table. I thought I could keep the paper going – it had nearly closed before – but my lucky streak deserted me. I'm afraid you were a casualty of that. I was no longer able to pay my own staff.'

'And Bindon Fields? Why did you withdraw your support?'

He looked measuringly at me through his cigar smoke. 'I suppose you will find out soon enough . . . *Primum non nocere*, Mr Wildeblood. Do you have Latin?'

I shrugged my ignorance.

'"The first principle is not to harm." I recall your shock on that first day we visited Somers Town, when I warned you not to involve yourself in the plight of the poor. You thought me heartless, but charitable giving, as I warned you then, demeans both the donor and the recipient.'

'. . . *as little as possible*,' I murmured. 'I had it from Paget – you said that to him once.'

Marchmont tilted his head sideways in admission. 'Ah, that is a sundering I do regret. If Paget had stuck with me, well, who knows what we might have achieved . . .' He paused, abstracted for a moment, before he returned to his theme. 'Not to harm – and the safest way to do no harm *is* to do as little as possible. Alas, I broke my own rule. I allowed myself to be persuaded by Mr Sprule, and others, that Bindon Fields would be a model for rehabilitating the urban poor. Oh, it was meant to be first-class, "A1", this pastoral refuge for the dispossessed. Then I learned that they intended to appoint a superintendent, a Mr Jonas Harrigan – heard of him?'

I shook my head.

'His previous office was governor at Maidstone Gaol.'

'What?' I felt my insides begin to run cold.

'Yes. A prison governor. Bindon Fields is to be a labour colony, and the inmates employed as servants of the state. It's a segregational scheme designed to defend social purity . . . One oughtn't to be surprised – after all, this is the country that drafted the Poor Law.' Now I understood what Father Kay had meant. *Every form of society requires its protection.* Bindon Fields was not a shelter to keep the poor from harm; it was a place to keep society from being harmed by the poor.

'But . . . they couldn't. No government of any decency would allow it,' I said, mostly to myself.

'I gather it has a cabal of supporters in Parliament, led by Mr Abernathy. You know their arguments. To them, the poor are essentially a criminal class that must be contained for the sake of public health.'

'Abernathy . . . we met once at dinner –'

'Yes, and I hear you gravely offended him, *and* his wife'. Again, I detected a kind of amused approval in his tone. 'Father Kay and his Social Protection League are a determined lot. You have a fight ahead of you.'

I looked searchingly at him. 'But you yourself must condemn the idea. I mean, a *labour colony* – surely it is *your* fight, too.'

Marchmont held up his hands and looked about his stripped office. 'Alas, one that I must decline. You see a man on his beam ends! It's either exile for me or a prison cell. Out of consideration to my family I choose the former.' I now recalled Paget telling me of the guvnor's previous bankruptcy, years ago, when he bolted abroad and left his wife to face the music. So it seemed that he had acquired a sense of duty in the meantime, if no better luck as a gambler. At that moment, the girl I had passed on the step sidled into the room. She glanced about shyly, then said, 'Papa, the man says the trap is ready to leave . . .'

Marchmont winked at her. 'Thank you, my dear. I shall be there presently.' The girl, shooting her father an uncertain look, withdrew.

Rennert, consulting his hunter, said with quiet urgency, 'Sir, you really should – there's no telling when they'll show up.' I presumed 'they' were his creditors, or did he mean the police? I had no clue as to the real extent of his debts, and now was not the time to ask. The guvnor sighed absently, and took his coat and hat from the stand in the corner. He looked up suddenly and caught me watching him, a rueful gleam in his eye.

'I could have wished for a more satisfactory leave-taking,' he said. 'But the fault is mine, as I say. Exit, pursued by a bailiff.' He clapped a trilby on his bulbous head, then took the silver-topped cane Rennert held out to him. 'Mr Wildeblood –' He extended his hand, and I took it. 'One more word of caution. Steer clear of Moyles. You have been a stone in his shoe, and he'll not think twice about dispatching you from it. As for those notebooks you came for, I'm sure Rennert knows their whereabouts. He knows everything else!'

He took a final resigned look around his office, and then padded out in that lazy rolling gait of his. Rennert followed him into the hall; I remained on the threshold, reluctant to intrude upon their farewell scene but unable to stop myself eavesdropping. I listened to Marchmont's voice, briskly consoling a lady whose distress emerged in little gasping lamentations – his wife? After a few moments, the lady's voice receded, and then Marchmont was in converse with Rennert, a spoken duet in which I could hear the notes but not the words, the one's self-assured boom playing off the other's low, discreet phrases. It was not long before they ceased, and then Marchmont's voice sounded from the street, where he was barking instructions to the cabby, or else to the removal men. There came the sharp smack of a whip, and the slow commotion of departing horses and grinding wheels. I stepped back into the office, fuggy with tobacco smoke. Marchmont had carelessly left his cigar burning in the desk ashtray; I picked it up and crushed out its fiery tip against the pewter.

When Rennert returned to the office he looked somewhat enervated, as though the guvnor's departure had drained him of vital juices. It may have been a trick of the light (the room itself seemed to have shrunk) but his face looked gaunter, and his figure even spindlier: he reminded me of a wounded egret I had once found on a riverbank near home. He lifted a stack of books from the worn chaise longue, then set them down again, seeming to have forgotten what he was meant to do. He turned, and started slightly on seeing me, as if he had expected to find himself alone. I suddenly felt very sorry for him.

'Would you – care for some help? Tidying . . .'

'Your notebooks,' he said, ignoring my offer. 'I took them because I hoped the governor might one day put them to use. He is a man whose sense of purpose depends on his work. Take that away from him and –' He stopped, unwilling to articulate his gloomy prognosis.

'Where will he go?' I asked.

'Belgium, to begin with. He has close ties in Bruges. Then – I don't know – he speaks good French, and German . . . a man of his calibre will always find a welcome.' He looked thoughtful for a moment, then, blinking away his reverie, he stepped over to one of the open crates. After some rummaging he plucked out three bound notebooks whose navy boards I recognised, and handed them to me.

'I shall return them to you once I am finished.'

'Keep them,' he replied. 'A memento of Somers Town.'

'But you said the guvnor might require them one day –'

'The governor will not be coming back. Not in a long time. Perhaps not ever.'

I looked at him, wondering if he would elaborate upon this speculation, but his face was unreadable. It occurred to me that Rennert would have made a good poker player, with his cool impassive front, but I also knew that, unlike Marchmont, he never gambled. It was possibly that which had made their partnership work, the one's steady diligence matched to the other's combustible audacity. But it was not something that could last.

I was about to offer my hand in farewell, but he had withdrawn to the other side of the desk and was taking down the great coloured map, on which had been pinned such high ambitions. 'Goodbye, sir,' I said. Still with his back to me he stopped what he was doing, and turned his head slightly. I could not swear to it, but in the fleeting moment the light fell on his eye I thought I saw a glint of moisture. His voice, when it came, was as dead as ashes.

'Goodbye, Mr Wildeblood,' he said, in such a way that suggested we would not meet again.

One evening, later that week, I lay on my bed and opened the third and final notebook from my period as inspector at Somers Town. I silently thanked Rennert for instructing me back then to write in pencil, for my atrocious penmanship was often illegible even to me. I turned up the gas lamp on the bedside table, and retraced my time on the streets.

> . . . the second-floor room occupied by a family of Irish costers. Man of 60, quiet, steady type & afflicted with asthma; the wife drinks; children out at work. Could not see a single chair to sit upon. Broken parts of windows are stuffed with rags . . . A couple, Mr & Mrs Standish, married for 20 years, earned a living by making toys in the form of mice, which are set to run around a wooden plate by the manipulation of a wire beneath. He said they made about 2 shillings a week. Polite but wary, seemed anxious that I might steal his trade secrets. Their room clean but small, & one damaged table at which they worked and ate . . .
> No. 15. A 'disorderly house', viz. home to prostitutes & their bullies, but also frequented by thieves & vagrants; most of the occupants, about 20 in number, were drunk, & filthily clothed; at least three people asked me for money . . . On the first-floor front live the Mountjoy family. The man was formerly a soldier & now worked at St Pancras as a porter; the wife in a dreadful state, nearly insensible with drink; their 20-year-old son in advanced stages of consumption; the daughter, also grown up, sold flowers in the street. All four live & sleep in this room . . .
> No. 32. Another common lodging house for women, of which there are many in this neighbourhood; a horrible, crowded place that could only be home to those in unimaginably low condition, victims of drink or folly or misfortune . . . this a long, narrow street offering a vista of dismal penury, which I had not visited before & would not choose to again. A crowd had gathered round a drunken man lying white-faced in the gutter – he was bleeding from a stab wound in his stomach – & a rowdy argument going on as to who should have the care of the wretch. Eventually, some friends carried him off to a nearby house, amidst bellowed imprecations. A little later, when I

passed this way again, the crowd had dispersed & only a few children remained, & a pool of blood glistening almost black on the cobbles . . .

It was all like this, page after page of it, though it would be impossible to convey the day-by-day experience of what Marchmont called 'outcast London' – the sudden shrieks, the casual viciousness, the roaming drunks and derelicts, the appalling stench of blocked drains. It was lowering to retrace the chaos, set down in my own hand, and rather surprising, too: it unnerved me to realise that I had forgotten many of the encounters I had recorded here. That toymaker and his wife, yes, I recalled them quite vividly . . . but most other faces from those teeming houses of the poor were already lost to me.

I read past midnight, eyes itching with fatigue. My trawl through the first two notebooks had turned up nothing. A grey mood of hopelessness dragged on me. I looked at those four names on the torn sheet of Johnson Street leaseholders, almost certainly undiscoverable, even if they were still alive. So what was the sense in trying? I must have dozed off then, for I dreamed of standing in a room that resembled a gambling den but turned out to be part of someone's house. A man in a top hat who recalled Marchmont in manner but not in appearance was explaining the rules of some abstruse game, which, even as he talked, I found myself playing – and doing rather well. 'Beginner's luck!' he cried pleasantly. It seemed that we were great friends, this not-Marchmont character and I, for once my pockets were bulging with coins I began to press my winnings on him. Which I noticed he was only too pleased to take.

The next time I woke, with a start, the lamp was gleaming weakly. A quarter to four in the morning. The notebook lay open next to me, though not (I thought) at the page I had last perused. And, quite spontaneously, my eye fell upon the name 'Arkell'. It stood off the page so suddenly that at first I imagined myself to be dreaming still, and stared in bemusement. Edith Arkell. Not a dream at all. It had arrived like an arrow out of nowhere, right at my eye.

No. 12 Goldington Street. Front parlour occupied by family of three, the man a railway worker, his wife takes in washing. One son, ill-looking, in irregular employment. In the upper room, an old widow, poor but respectable, introduced herself as Mrs Arkell (E.). Has lived there for five years, she said.

I had met her, I noted, on 14 May. In June, according to the Records Office, this poor widow had bought the lease to several houses on Johnson Street, transferred to her name by Condor Holdings. It was quite obvious to me that Mrs Arkell had no idea of her recent elevation to property owner. But I was going to make sure that she found out.

15
Lights out

The following morning, light-headed from my nocturnal astonishment, I was in the middle of writing to Paget about my fortuitous discovery of 'Mrs Arkell' when I heard raised voices on the doorstep. Mrs Home, my landlady, was addressing someone in a peevish tone, and from the sound of it receiving a fair amount of impudence in return. I ambled down to the hall in time to hear her snap 'Be off with you! This is a respectable 'ouse –'

'May I be of assistance, Mrs Home?' I asked in a calming, responsible voice.

'This cheeky Arab knocks 'ere and starts talkin' t'me like I'm his *char*,' she replied, hot-faced with indignation. I had to look around her wide girth blocking the hallway to see the 'Arab' in question, a skinny boy of about fourteen whose sharp, feral features and cocky posture spoke of a rogue-in-training. Ignoring her complaint, he smirkingly addressed me.

'You the man o' the 'ouse?'

'Er, no. What business have you here?'

'Don't you start,' he snorted. 'Yor name Wildeblood?'

I replied that it was.

'Message for ya,' he said, and flicked his gaze at my aggrieved landlady, indicating he was not prepared to continue with her in attendance.

'Mrs Home, so sorry for your trouble. I'll deal with this . . . person.'

She pursed her lips in proud disdain and, shooting another sour look at our caller, withdrew. I had witnessed other such altercations between Mrs Home and 'street people' – window cleaners, dustmen, chimney sweepers – to whom she condescended appallingly. She was the more snobbish for being so close in status to the class she despised. It sometimes occurred to me that I had only been accepted as her lodger because I didn't speak with a cockney accent. The boy, who stood with hand pertly against his hip, threw down an answering look of condescension at odds with his worn togs and scrawny frame.

'Right, message for ya,' he said again, jutting his chin. 'About a fawney yous been lookin' to buy. Meetin' with yor mate Jo tonight at Hungerford Buildings, by the canal. Know it?'

I nodded. It was a disused warehouse off King's Road. 'What hour?'

'Eight. An' Gaffy sez —' his eyes narrowed slyly — 'bring the blunt.'

Jo must have arranged with Gaffy to buy back Kitty's ring. I asked the boy how much money it would require. He hesitated for a moment, as if trying to decide. 'A hundred.'

The price was low for a diamond ring, and I wondered then if the boy had any idea of what was at stake. 'I'm not sure about this —'

'It's a hundred,' he shrugged, 'or you don't see the fawney. So, eight o'clock. Got that?' The insolence of his manner was a little provoking — I began to see why Mrs Home had been so affronted.

'Got it,' I replied. He stood there, delaying, and I almost laughed at the half-expectant gleam dancing in his eye. He was waiting for a tip! With a little gasp of incredulity I said 'Good day', and closed the door on him.

A few minutes after the boy had gone I realised that I would not be able to meet Jo's rendezvous precisely at eight, having forgotten I would be working a late shift at the *Evening News*. I decided to go via Chalton Street that afternoon so as to adjust our meeting time. As it happened, Jo was away from his stall when I stopped by. I asked Jed, one of his coster mates, what time he was due back, but he didn't know. Being in a hurry I decided to leave him a note, not quite trusting Jed to do the job.

Jo — Can't get away till half past eight. Will meet you at Hungerford Buildings at nine. Gaffy wants l.100 for the ring. DW.

I folded the message up and wedged it in an angle between two trays on his barrow. This improvisation seemed very far from satisfactory, but I hurried on, eager to follow through on the matter of Edith Arkell. Goldington Street was a long terrace whose grimy stucco and clouded windows presented a familiar aspect in these parts. At number 12 my knock was met by a thickset man whom I half recognised from the last time I visited the street. Of course he knew Mrs Arkell. She had lived in the room above, for years, he said.

'But no longer?'

He shook his head. 'Oh, she was a right age,' he said, in a tone that suggested age to be an affliction — which I suppose it was.

'So she's — dead?'

'Nah. Just her 'elf gave out. Had to go to the work'us.'

I felt at once moved to pity and quietly ecstatic – not dead! 'Are you sure about that?' I said, and the man looked vaguely offended.

'You can go and arsk her yerself,' he said, pointing down the street to where the battlements of St Pancras Workhouse loomed over the rooftops. I thanked him, and walked on to King's Road, which offered a full view of the building. It was a rebarbative place, constructed on a scale that baffled the eye and shrivelled the soul. The meanness of the windows and the grimy brickwork reminded me of Reading – I mean the prison. Awful to think that Thomas Bowland-Darke had breathed his last here. One of many: Marchmont had once told me that fourteen Londoners in every thousand were in workhouses. About such matters he was seldom wrong.

Behind those walls lived Edith Arkell. If my theory was right, Condor Holdings had concealed their ownership of Somers Town housing by a fraudulent transfer of leases to persons either at death's door or else forgotten in the workhouse. And those persons had been selected because they had no next of kin, no dependants who might enquire after them. Once they were dead the ownership of the lease would be untraceable. Perfect in its cynicism, and almost foolproof in its application. Almost. If I could get inside the place and talk to Mrs Arkell, the subterfuge might be found out.

I was out of the *Evening News* office and sprinting up Fleet Street by a quarter to nine. The late-September evening was steeped in long inky shadows, and the glimmer of gaslight was reflected on the puddled pavements. It must have been raining since I had begun my shift. At the top of Chancery Lane I flagged down a cab, and was thence carried joltingly through St Giles and Bloomsbury. The clock atop St Pancras Station chimed nine as we crossed the Euston Road, and my anxiety redoubled on remembering the paltry note I had left for Jo that afternoon. It was perfectly possible that he hadn't even read it, in which case he would have been waiting for more than an hour.

I paid off the cab at the top of a narrow cobbled lane leading down to the Regent's Canal. Hungerford Buildings was part of an old brewery whose canalside premises had long fallen into disuse. A few of its windows had been holed, and the ground-floor walls sported an untidy girdle of hoardings with advertisements for quack medicines and knife polish. But the building itself, dominating the horizon, argued an irreproachable solidity, its brick bays and vaulting storeys seeming to announce they would still be here in another hundred years. Gas lamps, blurred by the damp night, offered slender bands of illumination as I patrolled the lonely length of the facade. I knew it to be a place favoured by drunks and derelicts, but I could see nobody through the curtain of dark, and all I could hear was the distant metalled clank of the trains from St Pancras.

I decided to try round the other side. Here I would have been swallowed utterly into blackness had I not, on setting forth, equipped myself with a tiny lantern, of a kind first shown to me by one of my *Labouring Classes* informants. (I only discovered later that the man used it professionally, as a housebreaker.) I struck a match to the wick, and a light flared feebly behind the glass. Adjusting my eyes I moved with the stiff-legged caution of one who could feel rather than see the cobbles beneath him. But whilst I could congratulate myself about the lantern, I realised also how foolhardy it was to enter such a place without an escape plan. It was dangerous to be alone around here, and if you were also carrying money . . . I swallowed hard, and at that moment heard a peremptory hiss from the shadows. At first I mistook it for the prowling cat I had seen some moments earlier, but as I held up my lantern I jumped in fright to see a face loom suddenly from out of a doorway.

'Jo!' I said, all relief.

'*Shhh,*' he replied, a monitory finger to his lips. 'Stash the glim.'

'What?' I whispered.

'The glim – *the light,*' he hissed. I quickly snuffed the flame, and felt Jo tug me by the arm into the doorway's embrasure. Plunged again into darkness I could discern only the ghostly outline of his face. 'Gimme a minute with this sket,' he said, waggling what I assumed to be a skeleton key in his hand before dropping to a crouch at the door handle. I could hear his exploratory twists as he worked the sket inside the lock; after a few abortive scrapings and jigglings, and a muttered curse, he caught the teeth of the inner mechanism with a screwsman's expertise and pushed the door open; we were through. Inside the building all was musty, unstirred, black – as black as a dead man's dream. I sensed Jo stepping in front of me, then coming to an abrupt halt.

'Can't see a bleedin' thing,' he said, and a moment later I heard the rasp of a match. A tiny flame showed his face in an eerie play of refulgence and shadow. I bumped his shoulder with the lantern, which he took, and lit. We stood in our pool of light opposite one another, and he gasped out a friendly little laugh, as though he couldn't quite believe the shifty circumstances in which we found ourselves.

'Is this where Gaffy usually conducts his business?' I said.

'Dunno. When did you meet him?' said Jo, holding the lantern above his head.

'I didn't. I just got the message from the boy you sent.'

He looked at me queerly. 'The boy *I* sent? What d'you mean?'

'The scrawny-looking specimen who called at my lodgings this morning, said you'd arranged to buy back the ring from Gaffy.'

He shook his head. 'I never sent no one. First I 'eard about this was the message you left on me stall.'

We looked at each other, with the dawning awareness that we had been duped, and a further tacit acceptance that we were now quite possibly in danger. The boy had claimed to be Jo's messenger as a means of luring me here, alone, with money on my person. Seeming to read my thoughts, Jo said, 'How much blunt you got on you?'

'Not enough,' I admitted. I had cleared out my bank account that day, reasoning I could negotiate the price with Gaffy. A sudden terrible surge of guilt moved me to blurt, 'Jo, I'm sorry about this. I ought to have been a bit more . . . leary.'

Jo gave a dismissive snort. 'Frettin' won't help,' he said, as though to a child. 'I know what's o'clock. Just keep yer tread soft.' And at that he jerked his head to one side, meaning for me to follow him. As I did so I had a sense of the warehouse rearing darkly, vertiginously around us, and an ominous phrase recalled from my mother's scripture teaching caused me to shudder – *Yea, though I walk through the valley* . . . Enough, I rebuked myself; it was quite likely we were walking through an empty building, for we had arrived more than an hour late for Gaffy's rendezvous. The floor beneath was gritty to the tread, and the lantern light, butterflying ahead of us, showed a forlorn carpet of weeds, broken glass and mouse droppings. There really wasn't anything here.

After a few minutes of silent tramping Jo stopped, and I could sense his body straighten up, not in alarm so much as curiosity. 'Can you smell somethin'?' he said, no longer whispering. I sniffed the air doggishly.

'Like smoke . . . ?'

Jo nodded, and swung the lantern in a wide semicircle. It seemed we had been moving in parallel to another gallery, dimly disclosed through an aperture in the wall to our left. The smoke was emanating from this direction. We turned at a right angle towards it, and as we drew nearer the sliver of illumination was revealed to be a narrow passageway. Jo handed the lantern back to me, and in a quicksilver flourish had his knife in his hand. He leaned towards my ear and said beneath his breath, 'Stay close.' We moved at a slight crouch down the passage, its brickwork clammy to the touch. The smoke carried on it something else, not only burning dust but the stale reek of tallow; ahead of me I heard Jo's sidelong dry retch of disgust. A little more creeping along and we had reached the gallery, where about thirty yards away, marooned in the empty expanse, a brazier glowed eerily orange through the updraught of smoke. A hunched figure stood near to it, turning a long stick over the flame. As we approached a look of animal wariness sprang from his dark eyes.

'Evenin',' called Jo affably.

The man lifted his shaggy head, and in the firelight we saw his filthy matted beard; for a moment I wondered if what we could smell was him. He seemed to be wearing a great quantity of old clothing – a ragged apron, jacket, perhaps two coats. I could not guess his age – it might have been anything between fifty and eighty – but he had a strange saturnine aura about him, a sense that he had occupied this place for many years, and would remain for many after. In the dim illumination his gaunt, bearded aspect unaccountably recalled a photograph I had once seen of the Poet Laureate. Jo had stepped round the brazier and was warming his hands in a companionable way. The man continued to rotate his stick, which I now realised was a toasting fork. I glanced over the lip of the brazier and saw – could it be? – a small shoe on the prongs. I had heard of people in the throes of starvation boiling shoes to eat the hide. But cooking them? Jo, bemused, I think, offered another overture.

'Dinner, is it?' he said, nodding at the thing on the fork.

The man looked up abruptly, as if he feared we might be inviting ourselves to his meagre repast. He grunted something that sounded like 'All I've 'ad today', though I couldn't be sure.

Jo tucked in his chin, his way of saying we had no intention of muscling in on a private meal, before adding, with a show of cheerfulness, 'My pal and I, we's supposed to meet, well, an h'acquaintance of ours – only we's awful late. You seen anyone . . . 'ereabouts?'

He looked to one side, thoughtful, then muttered, 'Three fellers. Stopped by 'ere. Gone now.'

'Three, was it? They say anythin'?'

He looked into the fire, and the ghost of a smile twitched his mouth. 'Same thing you said.'

Jo cocked his head to one side. 'Yeah, well . . . When's this – an hour ago?'

The man shrugged, blankly, as though it might have been a year ago for all he cared. He then withdrew his roasted whatever it was from the fire and inspected it. It seemed that our brief converse was at an end. Jo bit his lip uncertainly, and steered his gaze about the dark gallery for a few moments. Then with a lift of his brow he indicated that we should go.

'Much obliged to ya,' he called back to the man, who didn't reply. I followed Jo across the gallery to another door, which he seemed about to open and then paused, his hand on the doorknob. He took the lantern again. 'They went this way,' he said, pointing out footprints in the dust. 'So . . .' he dropped his voice to a mutter, 'we go back the way we come in – then round the outside of 'em.'

I nodded, and followed him back through the passageway and thence into the first room we had crossed. Curiosity at last got the better of me.

'D'you have any idea what he was, um, cooking back there?'

'What, Old Nick?' In the dark I could hear Jo's smile rather than see it.

'It looked like, I dunno, a *shoe*.'

Jo snorted, and said, quite matter-of-factly, 'Nah. 'E was cookin' a rat.' I felt an inward shudder as I thought again of that roasting lump on the fork.

'Well,' I said after a moment, 'I'm glad he didn't ask us to dine with him.'

For some reason this tickled Jo, and he was still chuckling away as we reached the door he had unlocked with the sket. 'You're a caution to snakes,' he said, the laugh still in his voice, and I suppose I remember the line because it was the last he said to me before it happened, before the memory of the night broke into pieces. We had just re-entered the enveloping black outside when shadows seemed to leap and fall on us. Jo was first under the cosh, I heard him swear as he was wrestled to the ground, but in the instant I stepped towards him I was suddenly and violently taken about the neck by a loop of rope. Garrotted! This is it, I thought, and clawed against the constricting pressure at my throat, struggling for air. Time seemed to slow up and stretch out whilst my hands scrabbled blindly against the choking cord – and just when the talons were closing about my neck the infernal noose went slack. Like a swimmer under water too long I burst to the surface, coughing, lungs sobbing for air. A scream of pain had torn past my ear, and the brute who'd been strangling me wheeled away – only later did I realise that Jo had slashed him along his flank. At that moment two other figures were circling Jo, watching the knife in his hand.

'Davie, the stick!' he cried, and in my breathless fuddle I saw a cosh, its promising heft, on the ground at my feet. I snatched it up and launched myself at the nearer one – from his height I knew him to be Gaffy – and by luck rather than skill I felled him with a glancing blow to his head. The keening cries of the man Jo had cut were evidently distracting the third assailant, who must have been calculating the odds of sustaining an injury of like severity. As Jo moved towards him with the blade glinting in his hand, the man backed up a few steps and, with a hissed imprecation, took to his heels. His wounded companion limped after him.

Still dizzy from my recent throttling, I sank to my knees, gagging and coughing. I felt Jo come up behind me – brave Jo – and put his hand on my shoulder. He patted me softly, rather as he had the first time I ever met him with his 'old moke' in the Brill, murmuring, 'Easy does it – deep breaths now.' I was still kneeling there, gasping out my relief, when I heard swift footsteps coming up behind us, then a collision and a quick effortful grunt, before Gaffy careened away into the night. '*Ow*,' said Jo, as though he'd just been bitten by an insect, and he sucked in his breath sharply. I didn't know what had happened until I rose and looked around. A few yards away Jo was examining something on his coat, it seemed, with an expression of irritated interest. I picked up the fallen lantern and went to him; he raised his head, and the light showed his face blurred with confusion. 'Davie, cool this, will ya . . . ?' He was breathing hard as I bent my head to the dark stain blooming on his coat, which was viscous to the touch. 'Must've speared me on the way through,' he added, and lifting up his shirt tail I saw a raw wet puncture in his flank. It was leaking an astonishing amount of black blood, and when I put a covering hand to staunch the flow it seeped through my fingers. Yes, Gaffy had got him for sure, a coward's thrust at his back as he fled past us.

Some sound of dismay must have escaped my lips, for Jo narrowed his eyes on me. 'Doogheno or dabheno?' he asked in a low voice, unable to diagnose it for himself.

'Doogheno,' I reassured him, my hand slippery with his blood. I felt him stagger against me, and knew then that I must get him to a hospital straight away. Folding up my kerchief I pressed it against the fountaining hole, and ducked round his other side. 'Put that arm around me, here,' I said, and with unwonted obedience he did so. I told him that we'd make for the main road and hail a cab, and my voice, surprising me with its steadiness, seemed to console him. I shouldered him along as best I could, but he kept slumping down, and mumbling about his need for a rest.

'Jo, please walk,' I kept repeating, and, touchingly, he would try to keep upright. A fearful urgency drove me on, for I realised our hobbling progress could not favour his chances. So I bent down and heaved him up beneath the arms. I staggered for a moment, then broke into an awkward trotting run, with Jo slung over my shoulder like a sack of coal. He was a weight, but it didn't matter: dread lent a lightness to my steps. I imagined the amusing story this would make one day, and the embarrassment Jo would feel on hearing it – like his sister, he was proudly self-sufficient, with a natural aversion to accepting favours. We had reached King's Road, almost deserted at this hour. *A cab, for God's sake*, I pleaded silently, though I knew this to be no place for casual traffic. We pressed on, drawing curious glances from passers-by. On my shoulder Jo let out a low moan, and I stopped for a moment, propping him against a low brick wall spiked with railings. Under the refulgent yellow of the street lamp his face was beaded with sweat, and his eyes did not seem able to focus when I spoke to him. The kerchief I had held to his cut was soaked through.

He had become feverish, muttering something about a hand, or a handshake, but in my rising panic I couldn't attend to anything he said. And then – a mercy – at the turn in the road a horse and trap cantered into sight, and I leapt to my feet and sprinted towards it, waving my hands. I fancied the driver might suspect this was a brazen dodge to rob him, for he refused to adjust his pace as I made my wild approach. 'Stop, I beg you!' I cried, and perhaps the shrill desperation in my voice persuaded him to pull up. In haste I gabbled out Jo's plight, with assurances that I could pay him for his trouble.

'I don't ask for your money,' said he, an old man as I now saw, and told me to help my friend aboard. Quickly, I hauled Jo onto the back of the cart, where he lay, and with a click of his reins the fellow set off again. 'There's the Temperance Hospital a few streets away,' he called over his shoulder. At the junction we turned into Crowndale Road, and then cut through the tall terraces of Oakley Square. With every jolt of the cart more blood spurted from Jo's side. He mumbled something about being cold; I looked around for a blanket but there wasn't one, so I tore off my coat and wrapped it about his shivering frame. No, he mustn't, not like this – I banished the thought before it could seize hold of my brain. Of a sudden he looked up and plucked at my arm, indicating he had a vital message to impart. I bent my head down, straining to hear him above the rattling commotion.

'Davie . . . always cool the hands,' he panted, teeth chattering. 'That's why they used – they used to shake hands – did ya know? – to show you wasn't holdin' a chive –'

'I understand, Jo. We're taking you to the hospital, see?'

But Jo only shook his head, as though it were more important for me to heed the lesson that he had just imparted. 'Cool the hands,' he repeated in a mumble. I looked again at the sodden cloth I held to his side, its white turned black under the wan moonlight. We were coming down Hampstead Road, and there ahead of us was the looming silhouette of the hospital. 'Whoa,' I heard the man call to his nag, and we clattered to a halt on the cobbled forecourt. He got down from his seat and helped me lift Jo, pale as bone, off the cart. He clucked in a sympathetic way as he stared at my stricken friend.

'These young 'uns got a lot o' blood in them,' he said, and I flinched at his callous observation; but then I thought it was perhaps meant to reassure me. I gasped out my thanks, and would have shaken his hand if I had not been so distracted with the effort of carrying Jo. By chance two attendants had just emerged at the entrance, and one of them hurried forward to relieve me as the other went for help. As we carried Jo between us into that place the attendant kept telling me to calm myself, and though my voice was raised in pleading I cannot recall any of the things I said. We got him into the receiving room, and onto the table. A flurry of footsteps around us heightened the sense of purposeful alarm. Under the gas jets' glare Jo, lying there, looked thin and sad and terribly alone. A doctor arrived, his black tailcoat flapping behind him like bat wings; I felt someone trying to pull me away, and I shrugged them off. My throat had gone hoarse, but I called out 'Jo' and gripped his bloody hand in mine. *Cool the hands*, he had told me in the cart, and I couldn't bear them to be the last words ever spoken between us. I choked out his name again, and then my eyes were blinded in an uprushing salt flood.

I lay my head by Jo's, and stared. I touched his hair, and inhaled a smell of burnt dust and smoke. I thought I should cut a lock of it to keep. I don't know how long I was there before someone patted me with infinite gentleness on the shoulder, as Jo had once done, but never would again.

16
Out of the past

Of the hours following I have no certain memory. Shortly after Jo breathed his last I gather I suffered some kind of nervous collapse, and fell where I had stood in the hospital's receiving room. Whether it was guilt, or grief, or exhaustion that did for me – or else some compound of all three – I cannot say; I only sense that it was the body's way of absorbing a calamity which the mind refused to accommodate. On waking in a darkened ward, utterly disorientated, I found a guttering candle at my bedside casting phantasmal shadows on the wall, and cried out. A nurse came to my aid, and listened patiently to my forlorn ramblings. I was racked with anguish for Roma – it was my responsibility to tell her about Jo – but the nurse explained that I was in no fit state to do so. The police had gone to Clarendon Square, she said, to inform the lady of her brother's death; she had been to the mortuary to identify the body.

I think I talked on brokenly for some minutes more; then the nurse administered a chloral, and I swooned back into unconsciousness. When I woke next the shadows had fled, and it was morning. I struggled upright, and groggily perceived an outline at the foot of my bed, a seated figure dressed in a dark cloak and bonnet. Her face when it swam into focus was spectre-pale, with eyes sunken deep, like a death's head. She held herself uncannily still, and in those first moments of recognition I felt a shiver of fear. Roma. I had an impression that she had been sitting there for some time. I said her name, my voice a raw-throated whisper.

Her gaze didn't waver. 'They said you were delirious. You carried him in?'

I nodded, still unnerved by her dreadful calm. I started to recount the events of the night, our meeting at Hungerford Buildings and the ambush laid against us, but she cut me short in a toneless voice. 'The end – tell me about the end.'

'We were in the cart. He was only half conscious. He'd lost such a lot of blood.'

'Did he speak?'

I paused. I could have said that Jo had asked for her. I felt sure he would have done, if he'd known how little time was left. But Roma wasn't to be fooled. 'He kept talking about hands – how men shook hands to show they weren't concealing a weapon. I remember he told me this once before – I don't know why.'

She took this in with the merest flicker of her eyes, then turned her face to one side. We sat there for what seemed a long while, not looking at one another, my throat numbed into silence. I felt Jo's absence as an almost palpable thing, like an ache. He was gone, gone from this place, from all places, forever. I felt another paralysing seizure of grief, and the words formed on my tongue before I was able to command myself. 'He was the best friend I ever had.'

She lifted her eyes to me again, and in a low, inconsolable tone said, 'He was the only one I ever had.' Her face seemed to suffer an inward collapse: she leaned her head on the edge of my cot and gave way to sobbing that harrowed me – long, piteous, childlike gasps of dismay quite startling in one whose manner was always proud self-containment. I had heard people weeping out their sorrow, but not like this. She seemed to be weeping out her very soul. I touched my hand to her arm, but she gave no sign of awareness, and remained hunched in that same attitude of broken supplication. At some point her sobs slowed, became longer-spaced; still she did not raise her head. I called her name once, softly, to no avail. It was the arrival of a matron that finally roused her from the daze of immobility; the woman had whispered something at her ear, and with a professional air of purpose helped her to her feet. Without a word Roma blotted her eyes with the heel of her hand, collecting herself. I thought (I hoped) she would speak to me then, to ask something more about Jo. But she did not. She only gave me a look, in which I read neither pity nor fellow feeling – just her own infinite desolation. Abashed, I averted my gaze; when I looked back, she was gone.

Later in the day I had a second visitor. Paget advanced, almost tiptoed, to my bedside with an air of mournful solicitude and a bundle under his arm.

'Your landlady was reluctant to admit me,' he said, 'until I showed her your note. Even then she watched me like a hawk whilst I collected your things.' At my request he had gone to Islington to fetch a clean suit of clothes, for the ones I had worn the previous night were in atrocious dishevelment. I thanked him, and sank back on the pillow. He stared at me a little, grimacing.

'Your throat . . .' he said, palpating his own with stubby fingers. I could still feel the burn of the rope around my neck.

'A garrotte. I should have heeded you about the life-preserver.'

He gave a rueful smile. 'You were lucky –' he said, and seemed to hear the blunder in his words. 'I'm so very sorry . . . about your friend. A stab wound, was it . . . ?'

'It pierced a major artery, the doctor said. That's why there was so much –' I felt my eyes go glassy, and tipped my head up to blink at the ceiling – the only way to stop it.

'There, there, old fellow,' he murmured feelingly, and waited for me to compose myself. It took a little while. 'The police will investigate it, I suppose.'

I nodded, though we both knew that a street stabbing, even a fatal one, would hardly exercise the police in Somers Town. Gaffy would be gone by now, lying low somewhere. 'Jo shouldn't even have been there. It was me they intended to do in – Moyles's thugs.'

I fell to brooding, which Paget observed from beneath his brow. After some moments he said, 'The woman you've tracked down – Mrs Arkell – how do you propose communicating with her?'

'I suppose I'll – visit her at the workhouse.'

He tucked in his chin at that. 'I don't think you understand. They won't allow you simply to *walk in* – it's not a social club. You need a reason to enter the place.'

'I could send her a note,' I said.

'That would be to assume that she can read.'

I shrugged; this was an obstacle I hadn't anticipated. 'What would you do?'

He looked at me levelly. 'Only one thing for it. You'll have to go on the spike.'

'You mean – as a pauper?'

'Yes. You queue for a ticket at the door – once you're in, you start looking for her.'

The idea of entering a workhouse was almost as abhorrent to me as returning to prison – something I had vowed never to do. But I trusted Paget enough to believe he was right. There was probably no other way.

'Some imposture will be required,' he continued, reading my thoughts. He peered more closely at me. 'Though – don't be offended

– you look quite knocked about enough to pass for an indigent.'

At that moment I felt too sick within to be bothered by how I looked without. My mind's eye kept returning, unbidden, to the flashing tumult of last night and Jo's helpless face in the cart, silently pleading with me. Leaning in, Paget said quietly, 'Would you like me to leave . . . ?'

I shook my head, and brushed at my streaming eyes. 'Please could you – ask the matron for my things?' He went off, and returned some minutes later with my apparel of the previous night, laying it on the cot. The coat smelt bitterly of smoke, and as I unfolded it I heard Paget gasp a little. Its dark flannel was matted from collar to hem with rust-coloured blood; the trousers, too, were similarly stained. The shirt, which had lost its collar, looked like it had been used to wipe down a butcher's block. I wound it up into a ball. 'This, I don't think I can wear again – but these others –' I picked up the coat, and felt in the lining: the money I had sewn into it was still there. Unbuttoning the side pocket I drew out the knife – Jo's knife – which had fallen out of his pocket during that purgatorial ride to the hospital. I ran my finger along its blade. Paget frowned at it, and looked about us cautiously.

'David – you weren't thinking . . . ?'

I shook my head. 'Just a memento.' And folding up the blade I put it back in my coat.

'By the way,' said Paget eventually, 'I suppose you heard about Marchmont. They are saying his debts ran to over ten thousand.'

'Impressive,' I murmured, 'even by his standards. I wonder where he is now . . .'

'I fancy his creditors are asking the very same question. You said you saw him before he fled –'

'Twenty minutes later and I would have missed him. He was packed up and ready to leave.'

'And how did he seem, *the guvnor?*' There was a prickle of contempt in his voice.

'Oh, cheerful, I suppose – and unrepentant. It was almost as if he were off on holiday rather than scarpering. I think Mr Rennert had to pay for the removal men.'

Paget snorted. 'That sounds like Henry. Always a talent for spending other people's money.'

'There was something he said,' I added, 'about the Social Protection League. I hardly know if it can be true or not – apparently there's a lobby in Parliament, led by Abernathy, to make Bindon Fields a labour camp. They intend to appoint a man to run it who's a former governor of Maidstone Gaol.'

He held my gaze for a moment. 'I heard such a rumour a while ago, and dismissed it as foolery. Well . . . I'm quite thick with a chap in Harcourt's office. He'll know, one way or the other.'

'Is it really – possible?'

'Well, the fear of the poor runs so deep at present one may envisage *anything* as possible. Though herding them into a labour camp is surely a measure beyond even the most draconian state.' He paused, and stared ahead with an air of puzzled abstraction. 'I mean, where would it end?'

I discharged myself from the hospital that evening, unable to find any peace whilst thoughts of Jo excruciated my waking hours. I was on my way to the Polygon when I faltered, irresolute. I couldn't bear the idea of Roma grieving alone in her room; and yet if I knew her at all that would be as she preferred it, aloof from intrusion, however well meaning. Changing direction I called in at the Rainbow, where the mood – did I imagine this? – felt queerly subdued. It was as though the place knew it had lost one of its own. I took a pewter of half-and-half, and drank it in silent salute to him. Then, on the back of an old menu card I wrote a short note to Roma, assuring her that I was at her service, and posted it through her door. I assumed that she would reply at some point, if only to communicate particulars of the funeral.

That assumption was erroneous. As each day passed I waited for the post, and no word from her came. I was half paralysed with suspense, desperate to hear from her but unwilling to impose myself. By Thursday I had gone to Chalton Street in search of Jo's pal, Jed, who told me that the funeral was arranged for tomorrow, at noon. Next to him Jo's pitch stood empty. I asked him whether he had seen Roma, but he shook his head. 'Poor gal – got nobody now,' he added feelingly. I supposed he knew the circumstances of Jo's death, but he betrayed no curiosity as to my part in it.

The next morning, which was overcast with a nipping little wind, I set out for Somers Town on foot. St Aloysius, a Roman Catholic relic from the beginning of the century, stood on Phoenix Street, and before I had even climbed the steps I could hear singing. I went in by the side door, inhaling a dusty bouquet of incense and candle wax. The congregation was so numerous that even in the entrance hall there was barely room to move amidst the press of bodies. At the top of the nave, over a sea of heads, I could see a coffin, accusingly alone. The hymn's melody was unknown to me, but I recognised its words.

Perverse and foolish oft I strayed,
But yet in love he sought me
And on his shoulder gently laid
And home rejoicing brought me.

An usher sidled over to whisper that there were seats to be had in 'the Lady Chapel' (whatever that was) and, with a look, I indicated my willingness to follow him. He led me down a side aisle and thence by a gloomy passageway into a small whitewashed enclosure with benches, situated at a right angle to the altar. From behind a pillar I had a spy's view of proceedings, the wreathed coffin, the officiating priest, the altar boys cassocked in black with a white collar at the neck. The hymn ended, its last notes echoing around the vaulting ribs and arches of the ceiling. The densely packed rows settled and squared themselves to the trembling pause that followed. The whole neighbourhood seemed to have turned out to say farewell to Jo. It took me a moment to recognise Roma, for though she stood in the front pew her face was veiled. She remained unnervingly poised and still, and as I watched her it dawned on me that my invitation had not been 'forgotten' at all – I had been excluded. She blamed me for her brother's death. Nor could I feel righteously indignant at this rebuff, for did I not to some degree blame myself?

I stood there, in creeping awareness of my being unwelcome. The forthright peals of the church's organ, alternating with the sedate drone of the priest's Latin, enfolded me in a trance of unhappiness. My distraction must have been severe, because when I came to attention Roma had lifted her veil and seemed to be looking directly at me. I shrank back into the shadows, wondering if I had been spotted or not. Outside I could hear the hammering clanks and thuds of building work, its brazen but muffled volume a sudden sad reminder of life going on, heedless of us, heedless of Jo.

As the recessional hymn began I rose from the kneeler and slipped away via a back door. I didn't want to risk being seen by Roma. Outside, a funeral carriage stood waiting on the street, the blinkered horse adorned with a glossy black plume. I crossed to the other side, where the noises I had heard from the chapel were revealed to be a new tenement block under construction. Part of the street had been broken up and vast trenches excavated. Engines and boilers sent up great clouds of throat-scouring smoke, and workmen were heaving loads of timber from waiting carts. The bricks, as was increasingly the fashion, were glazed terracotta. Another gritty billow of smoke belched from within the site, and I noticed that my coat already wore a light feathering of dust. Stepping away, I situated myself a little distance from the mourners now emerging from the church opposite. They huddled around the coffin as it was shouldered down the steps to the carriage; the pall-bearers were hard pressed to negotiate it. Amongst them were faces I recognised, from the Brill, from the Rainbow, from the streets where he had worked.

Before long a dense crowd had clustered about the carriage in readiness for the march to the cemetery. Whilst the priest intoned another prayer, people reached out to touch the bier, then conspiratorially crossed themselves. Roma, her face veiled once more, looked utterly alone amidst the sea of dark-clad companions ranged about her. I was almost moved to go to her – but I didn't have to, for in a dreamlike moment of surprise she detached herself from the throng and began to cross the road towards me. A friend instinctively hurried to accompany her, but Roma stopped and leaned to say something into her ear – the building noise was just then cacophonous – at which the woman nodded, and withdrew. Having thought myself unnoticed I was ill-prepared for this encounter, and dropped my gaze. She lifted her veil; her face was as pale as plaster, though her eyes, which I had supposed to be glossed with tears, were merely bruised-looking.

'You are well again?' she said, and I imagined then what a fright I had looked that morning in the hospital ward.

'Thank you, yes,' I said. 'The service,' I began, feeling a blush rise up my neck, 'I wanted to pay my respects . . .' – *but you didn't want me there*, I thought. She spoke in a distant way.

'When our mum died, they were set on takin' him away – an orphanage. He was nine years old . . .' She shook her head. 'I might've lost him.'

'You were very brave, I know –'

'No, you *don't* know – you have no idea what I did.' The sudden hard anger in her voice startled me. 'How d'you think I managed to keep him – me, at fourteen?' I wasn't sure what she was asking me, but my look of confusion only seemed to sharpen her hostility. 'How d'you think I paid for it all – our food, our rent?'

'Well, you did dressmaking, needlework . . .' I faltered, stopped, quite in the dark as to her meaning. She snorted thinly, and her gaze narrowed in pitying disdain.

'If you think *needlework* could keep the both of us, you must be – Try a bit harder. You don't know? Then arsk your friend Paget – about the night house off the Haymarket. He wasn't sure he remembered me the other day. But I remembered him.'

'A night house,' I said, my voice hollow.

'That's right. A girl can earn a livin' if she knows how.' A defiant note of pride mingled with her bitterness. 'Don't look so shocked. I thought my heart would break to do it, but it didn't – it just turned to stone. I had something to sell, an' there was plenty of *gentlemen* out there to pay for it.'

I didn't know what to say. I stood there, stunned, and my muteness seemed to provoke her. Her mouth trembled with rage. 'I should curse the day you ever came into his life. If you'd – if you'd just left us alone . . . After all I'd done, to keep him and me together –' Her voice gave out at that, and she turned her face away.

'Roma, I'm so –' A hard slap across the cheek silenced me. Her eyes widened, as though surprised by her abrupt violence. She took a breath as though about to say something, then checked herself. I dropped my gaze, not daring another word, and after some moments of seeming deliberation she turned and walked back to the waiting company. My cheek stung hot from the blow; one or two onlookers had seen it and were staring at me in puzzlement. Roma was engulfed within the inky mass of mourners, and I did not see her again once the carriage slowly creaked away, with the crowd in step. I followed at the back of the march as they turned left at St Pancras Road, and then I stopped at the corner, until the jingle of the horse's harness dissolved into the dusty air.

The following Monday I received a note from Paget urgently requesting a meeting. It seemed that his man at the Home Secretary's office had expressed an interest in the Bindon Fields case and wished to meet. The mere sight of Paget's handwriting revolted me, and crushing his letter into a ball I hurled it across the room. I stalked about my rooms in an impotent fury. I envisaged the vicious things I might do were I to come face to face with him. Then I tormented myself a little further by recalling the awkward scene in Somers Town when Paget thought he had recognised Roma but could not place her. Had he later realised who she was? No surprise to me that she had remembered *him*, and I shrank at what she must have felt as this ghost had materialised before her. Certain phrases oppressed me like fragments from a horrible dream. *A girl can earn a living if she knows how . . . plenty of gentlemen out there . . . the night house off the Haymarket.*

My impulse was to ignore his letter altogether, but once rationality regained a hold I knew that a meeting with him was unavoidable. If Moyles and the Social Protection League were to be thwarted it was imperative that I should talk to someone whose influence might count. Our assignation was at a public house in Westminster, where I found myself the next evening, almost wading through the fog-drowned streets. Figures lurched out of the clinging gloom as I passed through a neighbourhood every bit as disreputable-looking as Seven Dials or Drury Lane. The noise of the traffic rose like a distant rumour, then faded. Entering the taproom the noisome odour of damp clothes and rank tobacco almost overpowered me. As I stooged around the mid-evening drinkers I heard my name called, and there was Paget beckoning me to his corner booth.

'Fine night to come out!' he said in jovial irony. I met his eye but said nothing. 'David, this is Robert Tallis.' He gestured to a dark-browed, clean-shaven man sitting opposite, dressed in a severely tailored suit, with a thick-knotted tie surmounted by a pin. I supposed him to be about thirty. He tipped his head in greeting.

'Mr Wildeblood. I trust you're . . . recovered?'

'Entirely, thank you.'

'Poor fellow looked half dead when I last –'

'May we proceed to business,' I cut in, silencing Paget. Tallis looked quizzical for a moment, then spread his hands as though to say, *By all means.*

'I gather from Paget here you have been privy to confidences – I won't ask from whom – regarding the resettlement scheme at Bindon Fields.'

'I have. I was told by . . . my informant that the Social Protection League intend to establish it as a labour camp for the so-called "criminal" poor. You know of an MP named Abernathy?'

Tallis nodded.

'He's leading the lobby, with the support of a cleric, Father Kay, and a social scientist named Sprule.'

'I've met them. This encampment – is it legal?'

'They could make it so, if Harcourt can be persuaded that society is under threat of contamination. Their ultimate aim is to stop the degraded poor from breeding. It's a radical scheme.'

'Infamous, more like,' muttered Paget.

'You'd be surprised how quickly ideas can gain purchase. Today's "infamous" proposition may be tomorrow's accepted principle. That is why we cannot afford to stand by.' He looked at me. 'If you have information that might compromise the charity's standing . . .'

'What if it could be proven that their backers have forced hundreds of people into homelessness through the bogus allocation of leases?'

Tallis raised his eyebrows. 'Then we would be in a strong position to discredit them and put the lobby to rout. You have evidence?'

'I have hopes of – securing it. Do you happen to know of a company named Condor Holdings?'

Tallis shook his head. 'Are they involved?'

'Up to their necks,' Paget supplied. 'But they're deuced secretive.'

'Well, if you do unearth something, you should waste no time. Here,' he said, taking out a card and handing it to me. 'I've written my home address on the reverse. I hardly need tell you to be careful. They plainly have no scruples about dealing with their enemies.' His look indicated that he had been fully apprised of my recent brush with mortality. 'And now, gentlemen, with your leave, I must return to my masters at the Home Office . . .'

He rose, clapped on his hat and shook our hands in departing. I was sorry to see him go, for it left me inescapably alone with Paget. A girl had just set down more drinks at the table, giving me no option but to remain.

'Here's how!' said Paget, raising his glass with a wink. 'Glad that you could meet Tallis. He's a good man to have batting for us.'

'I hope so.'

'Well, he's helped me before when I was in a pinch. A trustworthy sort.'

I considered this for a moment. 'Not too many of those about.'

He paused, his glass halfway to his mouth. 'No. I suppose not.'

'One can never tell, I think.'

He squinted uncertainly. 'Tell . . . what, exactly?'

'The trustworthy sort, as you call them. I mean, you think you know a fellow – work with him, drink with him, believe him a gentleman – and then, without warning, he shows himself to be . . . the most appalling *blackguard*. A real bad hat.'

Paget was staring at me now, his face clouded with suspicion. 'I sense something . . . amiss. Are you implying –'

'What? That I know such lowlife scum?'

There was another pause. 'I'm not sure I like your tone. If you have something to say to me, then out with it.'

I felt my lip curling as I pondered a reply. 'Very well. Allow me to tell you a story – a brief one. A fourteen-year-old girl lives in a Somers Town tenement with her widowed mother and young brother. The mother dies, of consumption, leaving her children to survive as best they can. The girl is determined not to have her brother taken into the parish's care, but the pittance she earns from needlework will not be enough to keep them both. And so she resorts to a line of work that will always pay a young girl, if she's desperate enough. I'm sure I don't need to explain, do I?'

Paget's face had gone pale. His eyes were fixed, unseeing, at a point off to my left. 'No, you don't,' he said, almost under his breath.

'And may I further suppose you will be familiar with a certain night house off the Haymarket?'

'Why are you saying this?' he said, his voice deathly quiet.

'The woman you saw with me that day in Somers Town. Roma. You thought you'd met her before, but you weren't sure.'

His eyes lifted to mine, seeming to enquire. 'Her? But – I don't know any woman called Roma.'

'You think she told you her real name? It was her, though. She remembered you, from all those years ago.'

Paget kept staring, as though at some horrific distortion in a looking glass. Then he shook his head, defeated. 'I didn't . . . I didn't know.'

'What – that she was fourteen?'

He was shaking his head. 'I didn't *know*,' he repeated. 'It wasn't that kind of place. She – the girl – I swear to you I would never have –'

'*Don't* swear anything, not to me. You observed the age of consent. I'm sure that Roma was grateful for your fine moral discrimination.'

He sat there, eyes cast down, and for a long time neither of us said anything. I waited, choked with revulsion, and yet there was melancholy in it, too, for I realised this would be our last time together as friends. I took miserable gulps from my pewter as I waited for him to speak.

'I know my asking forgiveness is useless, but if I try to explain something – would you listen?' I glanced at him, and he read my silence as assent. 'Ten years ago I was a different man. I had been a long time recovering from a personal disaster – someone I had loved. I won't burden you with the story, but it had nearly killed me. I saw no one, went nowhere, yet I yearned for the touch of . . . Can you understand, David? I had learned to accept the disadvantage of my looks –' (I felt a dreadful quiver of sympathy then, though I refused to meet his eye) – 'but I had never thought to endure such soul-crushing loneliness. It became so intolerable that I told myself I would go out into the street and beg the first woman I met to marry me. Utter madness! But that was the pass I had reached.' He paused, and seemed to shudder at the memory. 'Of course, I did no such thing. Somehow I dragged myself through the daily round, hardly caring whether I lived or died. Then a friend invited me to dine with him one evening. He perceived my wretchedness almost immediately – I suppose it was obvious to see – and took me off to various dens he knew, hoping to raise my spirits. One of them was . . . well, you know the rest –'

'How many times did you go there?'

'My dear fellow –'

'How many?'

He shrugged hopelessly. 'I don't know – half a dozen? It was a transaction, nothing more. And she didn't look fourteen . . . I never thought to meet her again, and I dare say she imagined the same. I'm sorrier than I can say that she was driven to it, and that I . . .'

Whilst he was telling his story, his head had drooped lower, by degrees. Now he looked up again, enquiring.

'You are –' he faltered, 'fond of her, I think?'

'As though you care,' I said sullenly, but could no longer rouse myself to anger. All I really felt was pity. Ours was a world of loneliness and struggle and disillusion, and none of us would get out of it alive. I took another deep draught of ale. 'The friend I carried to the hospital, the one whose blood was on my coat. It was Jo – her brother. I tried to save him, but I couldn't.' And she will never forgive me for it.

'You mustn't blame yourself,' he said earnestly. 'Remember poor Kenton. These are violent times we live in.'

It was true, and yet I was still too sick at heart to be consoled. We sat there for some while longer, lost in our own thoughts as other drinkers mumbled around us. Eventually I rose to my feet, and Paget did likewise.

'David –'

'I must go,' I said. A look of despairing appeal was in his eyes.

'I hope, after all – I hope you will shake my hand?'

He had thrust out his hand, and I hesitated, just for a moment, before I took it. His palm was clammy to the touch. I felt his relief as I did so, but those earlier intimations still fluttered within me, like a wounded bird. Our friendship was gasping out its last. It would never recover from the poisoned arrow that had sailed out of the past and made its fatal piercing.

17
On the spike

It was time. I no more wished to see the inside of a workhouse than jump off a bridge into the Thames, but this was where the trail had led me, and holding back now would be to squander all those days and weeks of investigative toil. So I climbed back into my old clothes, trying not to think about whose blood stiffened the fabric, like old glue, and hauled on a pair of boots so worn from tramping it would have been an act of mercy to retire them.

I bent to the looking glass, and beheld an image of disrepute that had required no counterfeiting on my part. My face, with its straggly beard and scarred nostril, belonged to one as might steal a purse or start a fight. It seemed the streets had claimed me for their own. I waited for the sound of my landlady leaving the house – I had avoided her sight in recent days lest my dishevelment caused her to take fright – then slipped out into Hanover Street. I walked up to Angel and thence down the hill to St Pancras Workhouse, my brain already aswirl with gloomy presentiments. During my time at the paper I had conversed with several people who had, at one time or another, sought shelter 'on the spike', and their accounts of the experience, whilst distinct in the particulars, were unanimous on one point: it was a last resort.

The autumn afternoon was beginning to darken as I approached the building. Men loafed about the entrance, not talking, or even looking at one another. These were 'casuals', vagrants who applied for the statutory two-night stay. Some were quite respectable-looking, their affliction not illness but age: they had become too old for any kind of paid labour. Others lay slumped beneath flimsy burlap sacking, either in fuddled stupor or simple exhaustion. The gates would open, I gathered, at six in the evening, but before that you were obliged to queue at an office where they doled out tickets for admission. I adopted the same whipped-cur expression as the rest, careful not to catch anybody's eye as we shuffled in a line alongside the wall. As it inched forward, I glanced at the bills and notices haphazardly plastered against the brickwork. One announced a reward – twenty pounds – for the safe recovery of a pet pug, its owner serious enough to have had the notice printed up in different fonts. A little further along was another plea, this one for the return of a lost four-year-old boy. A brief description of the child was appended, and beneath it the promised reward – two pounds. I could almost hear Marchmont's booming, ironic laughter.

The man in front had noticed me reading, perhaps in itself enough to excite attention. He was about forty, bedraggled, unshaven, with prominent yellow incisors that lent his face a ferrety slyness – but the smile was friendly, and his voice, too. 'Been on the road?'

I nodded.

'Where'd you come from?'

'Um . . . Norfolk.'

He looked blank, and I realised then that his question referred to which *workhouse* I'd come from – he had naturally assumed I was an itinerant like himself.

'I mean, Islington,' I corrected myself.

His eyes lit up. 'Good skilly there.'

'Yeah,' I agreed, not sure what skilly was. It didn't matter, because the man was off on a long gabbling monologue about spikes he frequented – Poplar, Mile End, Islington – and the variable quality of their food and 'kip'. He talked of each workhouse with the intimate knowledge of a connoisseur. When he eventually paused I asked him about his situation; he replied that he had been employed in his earlier years making lucifer matches and white lead, but then his health gave out, he lost the work and had to quit his lodgings. He had been 'on the doss' ever since. Just then a couple of his companions arrived, travel-stained like him, and I was forgotten amidst the raucous bonhomie of their reunion.

Having at last secured a ticket, I crossed the road and found a low brick wall on which to lean. The early-evening temperature was brisk but not unpleasant, which perhaps accounted for the small crowd of casuals, about thirty in all. In winter one might see a hundred or more. Loafing there, I kept my head down and was almost entirely ignored. Almost. Someone had noticed me: he was a queer-looking cove, sporting a top hat and leaning on a stick as though he were waiting on a royal summons instead of a workhouse opening for business. I met his eye for only an instant, but it was enough. He sauntered over and, with a rakish little movement, tipped his hat.

'Mind if I join you?' he asked, indicating the wall.

214

From a distance he had looked like some racecourse swell, but up close his dandyish garb indicated its survival from better days. His mauve brocade waistcoat had held up, but the check trews were patched and worn, the boots were scuffed, and the seams of his tailcoat looked precarious. The collar of his shirt was putty-coloured, and his top hat had a dulled sheen, like the coat of a stray dog. None of this, however, seemed to impinge on his magisterial air of self-assurance. Indeed, his amused gleam suggested that he had conducted a thorough scrutiny of *my own* attire and found it, frankly, not up to snuff.

'Don't believe we've met,' he said in a light, well-spoken voice that seemed on the verge of laughter. 'William Caleb Duckenfield.'

I took his proffered hand and mumbled my name. He squinted at me, hearing something in my accent.

'Out of – hmm – Norfolk, perhaps?'

'You can tell?'

'I have a fine-tuned ear,' he said with a twinkle. 'Stopped at Norwich on my travels. Burnham Market, Wells-next-the-Sea, Cromer . . .'

'I come from Swaffham.'

'Swaffham! I know Swaffham. No shame in that.' He took off his hat and scraped long oily strands of grey hair back from his skull. The stubble on his jaw showed flecks of white, and his throat was wattled, yet in spite of these signs of age his gaze was quick and oddly youthful. 'So – what brings you here? From your dial I'd judge you're no more than twenty and despite the disrepair yours are *not* the togs of a travelling gentleman.' I smiled, disarmed by his perspicacity. He seemed to have looked right through me.

'Are you such a . . . gentleman yourself?' I asked, fencing a little. He shot me an arch look that acknowledged my little deflection.

'I've rambled about these isles a fair bit,' he drawled. 'My own forebears came from Cheshire – the Duckenfields were a notable family there once – and I came to know the north-west pretty well in my younger years. But fate has blown me hither and thither since. To find myself today at the door of St Pancras Workhouse, in health but out of pocket, one might say I was on *the crest of a slump*.' He brightened at this last phrase, and dipping into his waistcoat pocket produced a short clay pipe. As he stuffed the bowl and lit it, he said, 'If you've baccy, better hide it now, else they'll take it off you at the gate. Money and matches, too.'

I checked my pocket and found a couple of bob and some pennies – and a sovereign, which Duckenfield saw. 'A couter! You really haven't been on the spike before, have you?' I shook my head and faced his appraising look. 'Anything else on you? Diamond ring? Deeds to an estate?'

'Only this,' I said, and from my pocket I flashed Jo's knife at him.

At that moment the bell of St Pancras Church rang out – six o'clock – and he sighed, stroking his chin the while. 'Look sharp,' he said, indicating that I should follow him. We walked round the back of the wall on which we had been settled. With a surreptitious glance about him he bent down and tugged out a loosened brick. He looked at me, holding out his hand. 'Empty your pockets,' he said, and when I hesitated he gave an impatient *tsk*. 'There'll be hell to pay if they find something on you.' I handed over my coins, but he kept his palm open, 'The chive?'

'The money I don't care about, but I'm not letting this out of my sight.'

He shook his head disbelievingly, then squirrelled the cash away in the wall and replaced the brick as scrupulously as a bank clerk. He stood up, and said, 'Give it to me. Otherwise you'll never get past 'em.' He saw my reluctance. 'I'm doing you a favour,' he said. So I handed him the knife, and it vanished somewhere inside his coat.

Then he strolled back towards the workhouse, and I hurried in his wake. The line was on the move, and it now comprised only men. The few women had been directed to another entrance. Someone ahead of us had spotted the superintendent who kept the door. 'I know 'im. He's a right bastard.'

We were admitted in groups of three, and our clothing searched just as my companion had warned. The fellow in front of me was nearly turned upside down and shaken. The superintendent, Mr Scotton, had a face as wide as a shovel and the bulked physique of a recruiting sergeant. He pushed the men around with no more ceremony than a keeper at the dog pound. Sometimes he would raise his hand as though to strike, and as the wretch cowered in fright, Scotton would merely fix him with a glare of contempt and walk on. When it came to my turn, he bent his head and scrutinised me as if I might have emerged from a jungle.

'Like a fight, do ya?' he said, patting me down the while.

'No.'

'No *what?*'

'No . . . sir?'

He came up close to my face, close enough to smell his foul tobacco breath. 'Any fightin' in 'ere and *you* are *out* on your *arse*. Got it?'

'Yes, sir.'

Then he shoved me out into a sort of holding pen, where we waited. I heard him speak even more unpleasantly to others, the older men, too, who you might have thought had earned themselves a little courtesy by dint of their advanced years. But he yelled in their faces just like the rest. We then trooped off, as docile as cattle, to the wash house. The animal stink of all those bodies disrobing was indescribable. Clothes untouched by soap or water for weeks on end were dropped on the tiled floor, their vile miasma almost a palpable entity. Men, one pair at a time, were dunking themselves in the wooden tubs. The warders told us to hurry it along, and kept the line moving as though we might have been sheep through a dip. I needed no chivvying; the lukewarm bath-water, cloudy with the others' muck, was the last place I wished to linger.

A towel, worn to a thin napless rag, was thrust into my hand, and I dried myself off as best I could. Other pale bodies, pale as a fish's underbelly, shivered in the gloom, and I caught terrible glimpses of raw flesh, vermin-scourged or rash-tormented, and skin stretched taut over knobby shanks and ribs. I felt suddenly embarrassed for looking properly fed. Then we were given workhouse shirts to put on, and packed off to a dismal-looking hall traversed by two long tables, lined with benches on either side. Here we sat, and from tin plates ate an atrocious concoction we had been served out of enormous vats – this, I gathered, was skilly, and nothing like it had I tasted before, not even in prison. Some were chawing it down with bread. My first mouthful was lumpy and bitter, and almost impossible to swallow. Sitting opposite, Duckenfield looked pityingly on me and handed across a jug of water. I drank from it, sluicing the coarse dry stodge down my gullet. I mashed up another mouthful, forced it down and then pushed my plate aside. The man next to me, a startled look in his eyes, said, 'You done with that?'

I nodded, and, without bothering to transfer it to his own plate, he wolfed it clean in less than a minute, then wiped his mouth on his sleeve. He still looked ravenous. Duckenfield, apparently undisturbed in his attire, top hat included, was lecturing a few casuals about something or other; they stared back as if he were Moses himself. They all addressed him as 'Dux', which, he archly explained, was Latin for 'chief'. Not since Marchmont had I heard anyone so relish the command of his own voice.

Dinner time over, about thirty of us were herded out of the hall and thence to a dormitory whose meagre light came from tiny, barred windows high up in the wall. Low beds were ranged along either side. I flopped down on a cot. The superintendent returned and, glowering up and down the room, bellowed out a woe-betide to the men. To one unfortunate who had caught his eye he hissed, 'One peep outta you and I'll scrag your scrawny neck.' Then, satisfied by the cowed silence, he stalked out. Plunged into blackness, the shadows of the men did not stir – were they listening for his footsteps? – and a long minute passed before I heard the rasp of a match and a candle, two candles, bloomed in the dark. The whole room seemed to unbend with relief, and a low mutter of conversation began. On the next cot Duckenfield was hauling off his boots and rolling down his sock, wherein he had stashed his baccy. Others were doing the same.

'They never look in your socks,' he said in a wondering tone, lifting his thin legs onto the bed. He filled up his pipe again and lit it. 'So – your first night here. Ever seen anything like it?'

'Only once,' I replied. 'Who's the ogre, by the way?'

'Ah, Mr Scotton, the tartar, the terror, the tyrant of the two-nighter! A legend in this parish, I should say.'

I leaned in, lowering my voice. 'The men seem – *petrified* by him.'

He gave me a quizzical look. 'And you are surprised? They are absolutely at his mercy. One back answer and he'd haul you out by the hair and throw you into the gutter. For them he stands between a bed for the night and carrying the banner.'

'Carrying – ?'

'Walking the streets. The Scottons of this world are employed to keep the poor man in a state of morbid fear – a fear that even the little he has may be taken from him. The government operates on the same principle.'

'You don't seem very frightened of him,' I said.

He exhaled a languid curl of pipe smoke. 'He has a crude sort of respect for gentlemen, or what he *perceives* as gentlemen – thinks only "the swine" are fit for bullying. Of course he could toss me out like all the rest, but I've never given him cause.'

At that moment a man sidled up to my cot – he was the one who'd eaten my skilly – and handed me a squat brown bottle. I hefted it in my palm. Though it was being offered in the spirit of 'one good turn deserves another', I secretly dreaded touching my lips to a bottle other men had passed around. But it would be an insult to refuse, and I tipped my head back to swallow. Something burned down my throat, a liquid bolus of fire, and I lurched upright, trying to cough it back out of me. It was a dose of acid scouring my insides. Still gasping for breath, eyes watering, I returned the bottle to the man, who nodded as though to say, *That's the stuff.* Duckenfield took his own draught without a tremor.

'What was that?' I asked him.

'Local moonshine. It's mostly French polish, stolen from upstairs.'

'My God,' I groaned.

'What did you expect – brandy and soda?'

He lay back, chuckling, and for a while neither of us said anything. Along the row someone had begun, very quietly, a crooning lament. I thought then of Roma, and of the first time I saw her sing to a whole room, upstairs at the Rainbow, the whole place falling mute just to listen to her, and that great uproar of applause at the end. Roma: even the sound of her name made her seem far away. There was no eruption when this man's song concluded; on the contrary, the mood folded sadly within itself.

'Mr Duckenfield,' I whispered eventually, 'where do the women go?'

He was carefully removing his coat – he had already split a seam on the arm – but stopped to peer through the expiring light. 'The women? Other side of the courtyard. What, not pining for company already?'

'No, nothing like that. How would it be –'

'They catch you in there you'll get fourteen days, so think about something else.' There was another long hiatus before he said, with a shake of his head, 'I've been turning it over for a while, and *still* I can't fathom it. Please to tell me what on earth you're doing in here?'

So I laid out the story for him, beginning with my time in Marchmont's employ, the rents scandal in Somers Town, my discovery of the falsified leases and then the tracking down of Edith Arkell. Duckenfield's face was obscured in shadow as he listened, and the only sign of his consciousness I could depend on was the glowing eye of his pipe bowl and the occasional cloud of smoke, like a resting dragon. The dormitory had fallen quiet by now; our fellow casuals had reached an exhausted truce with sleep, broken only by the querulous muttering of a man in his dreams.

'And what do you hope to achieve by this?' he said, once I had finished.

'To right a wrong – a grievous wrong. Surely you see the need?'

He shifted his weight to one side, and the candle flame showed his gaunt, watchful features. 'Oh, I see *need* all the time, etched in the faces of these poor devils. Need is the engine that keeps the entire system spinning. You cannot frequent the spike without coming up against the plain fact that one part of our society connives at the deprivation of another part. Without the poor, there could be no rich. It has never been more apparent than in this city, where they are thoroughly degraded and sweated for labour. And once they have served their miserable purpose and are too old to work? Why, they are consigned to such a place as this, that decent people may not be offended by their sight! So if you believe that your plucking this *one pauper* from oblivion might bring down the giant edifice of inequity, then please, by all means, pursue her to the end.'

The satiric twang of those last words vibrated harshly on my ears, for I realised now I had been in error. I had taken him for a dandy of indifference, and found instead a mordant critic of the abyss.

'The edifice you mentioned is strong indeed,' I said at length. 'There is a temptation to do nothing. But if you saw that one brick might be loosened from its walls – just one – would you not do your utmost to drag it out?'

He stared dead ahead, eyes absorbed in thought, seeming to turn my hypothesis over. After some moments he let out a long sigh, as though wearied by the utter foolishness of thinking about it at all. 'They will run you in if you're caught. Fourteen days in quod, like I said. Does it mean that much to you?'

'I'm afraid it does.'

He blew out his cheeks. 'Well, carry me out and bury me decent . . . A Daniel come to judgement –'

'It's David,' I said meekly.

'It's Shakespeare, as a matter of fact. And it didn't end well for the feller who said it. Get some kip,' he said, drawing his blanket around him. 'We must ready ourselves for tomorrow's adventure.'

'*We?*'

His voice was crafty. 'Of course. You didn't think I'd send you out alone?'

The reveille next morning came in two stages, first the workhouse bell splitting the air outside, then the stentorian blast of the superintendent's voice rousting us out of our cots. 'Show a leg, ya lazy curs,' he boomed (he actually addressed us as 'curs'). As I searched for my boots, I glanced around at Duckenfield, who was already dressed, right down to his collar and tie.

'Your boots are under my bed,' he said, and indeed they were, each anchored by a leg of his cot.

'What are they doing here?' I asked, lifting up the cot to get at them.

'I put them there last night – after you fell asleep. If you don't pin 'em down they'll be gone by morning.'

I thanked him, and as I dressed I fell to wondering how many nights of the year Duckenfield stopped on the spike. He appeared to have such a deep familiarity with every sleight and dodge of the workhouse that you might have thought he'd been raised in one. Yet from his accent and manners, from his fancy but threadbare finery, it was clear he had been born to better things. He somehow stood aloof from the others, though he treated them with equal affability; I could see why the men were drawn to him.

We assembled once again in the dining hall, which in the wan light of dawn presented an even drearier aspect than it had the previous night. The deal tables rang dully to the clank of our tin plates. The limewashed walls offered no respite to the eye, only a yellowing notice that listed the ward regulations and the punishments that would be visited on any miscreant. The warders patrolled the room like prison guards – as if our lot had any fight in them. The breakfast skilly was served with tea, thin, dun-coloured stuff, hardly deserving of the name, but at least it was hot. In this place you quickly became grateful for any sort of warmth. Around me, the men talked of exactly the same things as they had the night before: the food and the kip, and how it compared with the food and the kip at the previous spike. Once this narrow field of interest had been tramped, over and over, this way and that, they fell to brooding, or mere vacancy. The conversation was exhausted, and they had no other.

Duckenfield had not sat with me at breakfast, but as we queued to leave I saw him in converse with one of the warders. At the head of the hall, the brute Scotton was assigning parties to this or that task – some to work in the garden, some in the infirmary, some (this was met with grumbling and silenced with a glare) to scrub down the stable. One old cove, his frame bent like a question mark, was moving at a sad shuffle towards his appointed task when Scotton ghosted up behind him and delivered a crack to his head. The man executed a painful about-face ('Oi!') but on seeing his assailant instantly swallowed his outrage and continued on his wizened way. At this, something boiled within me – something black and hateful and murderous – but I bit it back.

The warder I had seen with Duckenfield had come across to consult with Scotton, the result of which was a brusque summons from the man. He informed me that I was on kitchen duty, and that I should consider myself 'damned lucky' too – it was a plum job in the workhouse. I was bidden to follow him, and on turning into the corridor found Duckenfield lounging against the wall. The warder escorted us both down the stairs and into the bowels of the kitchen; as he left us, I saw him exchange a look with my companion: some bargain had been struck. The kitchen was a hive of huge reeking vats, hissing geysers of steam, and a deafening clangour of pots and pans that sounded like some giant being clapped in irons. Porters scurried through the roaring fug, oblivious to us, their footsteps echoing along the stone flags. Eventually, one of the cooks spotted us skulking there, and thrust a mop and pail at us. Duckenfield assumed an air of lordly indifference – as though he barely recognised such domestic paraphernalia – so I took hold of them myself, and we went off in search of something to clean.

'How did you swing this?' I asked him, once we'd gained a back parlour in which we might safely dawdle.

'Oh . . . that warder owed me. I recovered a watch one of the men had prigged from him. Useful to have some favours to call in.' He stepped up to the window to check something, and, satisfied, sank back against the wall.

'So what do we now?' I said, perching on the window ledge.

'We wait. On the other side of that courtyard are the women's dormitories. Your old Mrs whatsit may be resting her feet there even now. Though of course she may not . . .'

'You mean –'

'She may be resting in peace. You must understand, it is by and large the *old* who apply to the workhouse. They are frail and often ill when they arrive here – most of them know this will be their last home.'

I looked down. 'That's a bleak notion.'

He shrugged. 'My dear sir, what can I say? The poor are an army of strangers we have no intention of joining. But the old . . . in *their* ranks we shall all find ourselves, sooner or later, and unless fate has provided us with money, or a kindly relative on whom to depend, *this* is the ignominy that awaits. Society has no use for the old, because they are no longer of use to society.'

I watched him as he spoke, and the question which had been circling my brain from the first hour we had met now forced its way to my lips. 'Forgive me, I must ask – you are plainly an educated fellow, of good stock – how – how did *you* end up here?'

He paused, and looked amused by the question: he had not expected it. He opened his mouth to speak, and then checked himself. 'I was about to recount my life story, but an altruistic instinct seized me at the last moment, and I spared you. Ha. Suffice to say I have made and lost fortunes, and felt no remorse. My only ambition was to live by my wits – and thus far I have contrived to do so. There is no cause to look glum!'

That was intended for me. 'But . . . how can you bear it? You have no need to stop here,' I said, wanting it to be true.

He looked briefly pained by this line of questioning, then recovered his droll demeanour. 'Where else should I go? I have never owned a home, and at my age I am not likely to. For a man of modest require-ments, the food and the kip aren't so bad – and as you see I am well regarded –'

'Yet you have just denounced the place – said how ignoble the system–'

'So it is. I stop here because I choose to. The poor come because they have nowhere else but the streets. That is the pity of it.'

I searched his face for some twitch of regret, and found none. Perhaps he really was the jolly rover he claimed to be. But I wondered about him, still, for I could not fathom how a man of his natural sympathy and intelligence could endure such a place. What had his life once been, that he could relinquish it with such indifference? He had taken out a watch – he appeared to have smuggled in anything he pleased – and, a few moments later, the workhouse bell began to toll the hour. He rose to his feet.

'The bell invites us. Scotton takes out his crew of drudges to work in the cemetery at this hour. Thus we may navigate the courtyard without fear of encountering the Scylla of St Pancras – or do I mean the Charybdis? Come!'

I followed at his heels as he took the stairs by which we had earlier descended, and then we were heading towards an oak-framed, iron-studded door. Without pausing, Duckenfield drew back the bolt, which gave a foundry-shriek such as might have roused a workhouse in the next parish.

'A good thing I never took to housebreaking,' he said with a rueful smirk, and heaved the door open. We entered an irregular-shaped courtyard, surrounded on all sides by vaulting walls of charcoal-coloured brick. Overhead the sky was the colour of pewter, threat-ening rain. Sunshine in this place would have been a poor joke. It was as we were passing alongside a row of barred windows that

Duckenfield suddenly hauled me down by the collar and hissed a command to stay there. We were crouched behind a line of dustbins, and I could hear my companion's breathing at my ear. When I turned to speak he had his finger pressed to his lips. I sensed activity at the window in front of us, and angling my head at a gap in our cover I saw Scotton's profile; he was talking to someone, though had he glanced out on the courtyard a moment earlier he would have seen us ambling past. Had he heard the iron thunderclap of that bolt drawn back? My heart beat like a clenched fist against a door. I felt a tug at my sleeve. Duckenfield was scuttling away on his haunches, and signalled me to follow.

Once we had gained the shield of the wall he tilted his head to peek round the corner. 'That was a narrow squeak,' he said, brushing himself down. We crept on, close to the wall, until we reached a door at the far end of the yard. To my surprise, though evidently not to his, it was unlocked, and we passed through. Duckenfield halted here, and removed something from his pocket. It was a silk tie, which he told me to put on.

'If anybody asks, we are visitors here.' I did up the tie, and on seeing my handiwork he gave a long-suffering sigh. He fiddled around with the knot for a moment, then squinted at me, unimpressed. 'Not quite the picture of respectability I was aiming for . . .'

Just then a voice hailed us from down the corridor. 'Are you the entertainers? It's Friday today, isn't it?' An old lady approached, her eyes darting inquisitively between the pair of us. She was wearing a plain brown smock, with a little lace cap on her head.

'It *is* Friday, madam,' replied Duckenfield gaily.

'We always used to have an entertainment on a Friday – but not so much of late,' she explained. She was slightly stooped, and wheezing, though her voice carried confidently.

'Indeed? Well, my young friend and I,' he said with a glance at me, 'would be honoured to oblige you. Perhaps you could direct us to – ?'

She blinked at him appraisingly, then seemed to come to a decision. Who else in here would be sporting a top hat, brocade waistcoat and tie *but* an 'entertainer'? 'The hall is this way,' she said, and beckoned us with a waggle of her hand. As we followed, she told us her name was Miss Finch, and that she was one of the house trustees. Duckenfield leaned to my ear and whispered, 'I hope you have a party piece at the ready.'

I signalled to him frantically that I had no such thing, and he laughed behind his sleeve. The hall was a more convivial place than its counterpart across the yard, either because authority here was almost unnoticed or because the women had a keener instinct for communal living. Perhaps fifty inmates – all wearing the institutional brown – sat about talking, or else wandered in a daze. Our guide clapped her hands together and asked for quiet. We waited on the threshold whilst she explained that 'two gentlemen from the local theatre' (when had she conceived this idea?) had arrived and would be pleased to entertain them. Duckenfield's face as he listened was a picture of mischievous glee.

'What are we to do?' I asked him in a panicked whisper.

'Why, we must entertain them.' He left a pause, then added winningly, 'Or at least *I* must. *You* should try to find the lady.'

'Thank you,' I said, more relieved than I could admit. Just then Miss Finch put her head round the door and asked us if we were ready. With a wink, Duckenfield drew himself up and sauntered into the room. I watched through the half-open door as he bowed before his audience, thanked Miss Finch for her introduction and explained that his associate was temporarily indisposed – 'a ticklish cough' – but that he himself was perfectly able to perform solo. A hush had fallen on the room, and I held my breath. The silence lengthened as he stood there, and I wondered what on earth he intended to do, with so many eyes upon him.

Then, without further preamble, he began.

> *When I have fears that I may cease to be*
> *Before my pen has glean'd my teeming brain*
> *Before high-piled books, in charactery,*
> *Hold like rich garners the full ripen'd grain . . .*

His voice, beautifully supple, seemed to dance with the verse, nonchalant yet commanding, with a lilt so natural one might have thought the words had just sprung, fully formed, from his own teeming brain rather than Keats's. It was the sound of a man in his element, and when he reached the end of the sonnet there was a stunned pause before the audience broke into applause.

Miss Finch, deeming herself superfluous, had edged into the wings next to me. In response I pulled a wondering face, as though to say, *We are in the presence of a master.* Duckenfield had already launched himself into some Tennyson when I leaned in and asked, in a whisper, if she knew of a lady named Edith, or rather Mrs Arkell, in residence.

She shook her head slowly. 'It is a large house, as you see. There are a great many here I could not name.' She saw my disappointment, and added, 'Perhaps you might try the sewing room.' She evidently assumed I knew the layout of the house, and without disabusing her I sloped off down the corridor. Whenever I encountered a trustee, distinguished by their white caps, I asked the same question, but no, they'd never heard of Edith. What struck me was the social promiscuity of the inmates, here a hollow-cheeked waif, and there a jabbering imbecile; here a genteel-looking lady trying to read a book, there a loud-mouthed dolly-mop holding court nearby. Many were close in years to Miss Finch, possibly older, yet round the next turn I saw a young girl nursing a baby. No attempt had been made to discriminate, no concessions made to class or to age. It was not cruelty that predominated here, but indifference.

Eventually I found another hall, where several old ladies sat with heads bowed, unspeaking. At first I thought it might be a prayer meeting, so intense was their concentration, but then I realised that they were each absorbed in needlework. To interrupt the genteel mood seemed discourteous, and I was about to withdraw when one of the ladies glanced up, and, catching my eye, offered a shy smile. It was a face that had known hardship, but had not forgotten what it was to be gracious. Touched, I sidled over to her table, and saw that she was making a sampler, with a border of foxgloves and forget-me-nots. Her needle had just completed a word, all delicate loops and curlicues. It read EDITH. I stared for a moment at her.

'Edith,' I said in wonder. She raised her head again. I knew the answer before I had even asked her. 'Is your name – Edith Arkell?'

She frowned uncertainly. 'Yes . . . is there something – ?'

'I have news for you.' I took off my coat, turned it inside out and began to tear at the lining. 'You don't know this, but you are the owner of a row of houses not far from here.'

Her smile had faded now, replaced by alarm. 'I think there is some mistake. I don't own – any house. I never have.'

I had opened up the lining along the coat's hem, and removed from it the folded page I had taken from the ledger at St Pancras Records Office all those months ago. Smoothing it out on the table in front of her, I explained that her name had been used under false pretences and that, by default, she was now leaseholder of five separate properties. She still looked doubtful. Who could blame her?

'Mrs Arkell, please – hear me out. My name is David Wildeblood. I have come here only because I want to help you. I met you once before. You lived at Goldington Street in Somers Town. You left there and came to the workhouse, because your health had failed. I am here to assure you that this does not have to be your home. You can live in a house of your own. Is that something you would like?'

She hesitated, bewildered, but now with a faint inkling that I was not, after all, a madman. 'Well, I don't know – I'm rather old, you see, and I've no children. Who would look after me?'

'Whoever you wish – you can afford it. All you have to do is come with me. Would you do that?'

By now our conversation had drawn curious looks from other seamstresses. Mrs Arkell looked about her, as though *they* might know the answer. Her gaze returned to me once more, and perhaps she discerned some grain of possibility in my pleading look. She smiled again, and held out a bony, almost weightless hand for me to help her to her feet. Now I knew how Stanley felt when he found Dr Livingstone.

I walked her out of there, stepping back up the corridor and onwards to the main hall. The door stood open. More inmates had since crowded into the room, drawn by the siren call of Duckenfield's mellifluous voice. It took me a few moments to identify the piece he was then declaiming: '. . . *a foul and pestilent congregation of vapours. What a piece of work is a man! How noble in reason, how infinite in faculty, in form and moving how express and admirable, in action how like an angel, in apprehension how like a god! The beauty of the world, the paragon of animals – and yet, to me, what is this quintessence of dust? Man delights not me – no, nor woman neither –*'

And on that line he paused, having spotted me, with an old lady leaning on my arm. He gave a wry little laugh of understanding, and said, in his own voice, 'Though I am always prepared to make an exception.'

The newspapers had a field day. I was pleased to see that the *Chronicle* led the charge, though Paget and I, a brief exchange of letters aside, avoided one another. Once the existence of the 'phantom' leaseholder was brought to light the whole house of cards came down. Moyles and several other St Pancras vestrymen were arraigned for conspiracy to defraud. They had been caught once, in April, for neglecting the repair of insanitary and dangerous tenements in Somers Town. Instead of carrying out those repairs they had attempted to conceal their ownership of the leases, first behind the shield of a puppet company, and then under a series of borrowed names. It had enabled them to charge exorbitant rents without being answerable to the protest from their tenants. This last subterfuge might have gone undetected, the reports noted, but for the accidental discovery that one of the listed owners, Thomas Bowland-Darke, was two months dead when he 'bought' the lease on houses in Johnson Street. Another leaseholder was revealed to be a seventy-eight-year-old widow, Edith Arkell, resident in St Pancras Workhouse and quite unaware of her accession to the property-owning classes.

The exposure of the fraud reverberated through Parliament, where a lobby led by the Liberal MP Augustus Abernathy had been calling for the 'unregenerate slum classes' of Somers Town to be resettled at Bindon Fields, Bedfordshire. The lobby had been organised by a charity, the Social Protection League, several of whose members were, unbeknownst to the public, the very slumlords responsible for the shocking condition of that neighbourhood's housing. Legal action would be taken against them. The plans for any enforced relocation, let alone the pilot scheme of a so-called 'labour camp', were thrown out. The Home Secretary announced that there would be an investigation into how the St Pancras Vestry – supposed 'guardians of the poor' – had been allowed to run the parish as their personal fiefdom. What I hadn't known was that the cleared land in Somers Town had been sold to an association of property speculators. One of them was a company named Condor Holdings, which, on investigation, was found to have been recently dissolved.

A few days after the storm had broken I received a letter written on House of Commons paper. It was from Paget's friend, Robert Tallis, and included this afterthought:

> Whilst it will be a source of satisfaction to know that Mrs Arkell has been restored to a private residence and her former respectability, one pities the fate of those others amongst the 'deserving poor' left homeless by the clearances at Somers Town. I fear it very likely that some who profited from the illegal sale of the land will escape without consequences.

The morning after I had taken Mrs Arkell out of St Pancras Workhouse I returned to stand watch at its gate, in time for the emergence of the men. He looked only mildly surprised to see me, as though he were out on a stroll and had spotted an agreeable acquaintance whose name he couldn't quite recall.

'Mr Duckenfield!' I called in greeting. The other casuals, dazed by the prospect of another day's tramping, were dispersing in his wake.

'Ah, Daniel the judge,' he said with a tip of his hat, and I wondered then if he really had forgotten my name, or was quoting again. 'All well with the old dear?'

I assured him it was, having installed her at my lodgings for the time being. (Mrs Home, doubtful when I introduced Mrs Arkell as my 'aunt', came round to the idea once she sniffed the extra rent money.)

'I have something of yours,' he said, holding up a forefinger. He dipped into his voluminous coat, like a stage magician, and drew out my knife – if I could call it mine. It would always be a thing I was looking after for Jo. I thanked him and pocketed it.

'There is something I have for *you*,' I said, taking out a cloth-bound volume, blunted at the edges and somewhat knocked about since my schooldays. 'Now that I know how much you like to read . . .'

He took it, with a bemused smile, and opened it at the title page. '"*The Diary of an Aurelian*",' he read, '"by . . . Thomas Wildeblood". I've heard of that name.'

'My father. His first book – he wrote it when I was a boy.'

'But this must be a treasured – look, an inscription, "to my dear son David". This is really too much!' His pleased expression was touched with doubt.

'I would like you to have it. A token. Had it not been for you, I'd never have been able to find her. And your impromptu recital was, well – it won't be forgotten, by me *or* the distressed ladies of St Pancras.'

He waved a hand in dismissal of his good deeds.

'And you made sure that nobody stole my boots,' I added.

He smiled then. 'Well, for that I will take some small credit. I would not have you go *bootless*.' He returned his scrutiny to the book. 'And for this, I thank you. By the next time we meet I shall be an authority on butterflies of the world!'

I wondered about that – not his expertise in butterflies, but about the likelihood of our meeting again. It was too sad to think of him out here day and night, 'carrying the banner', in his own phrase. I would miss his company, but I didn't know why, or how to tell him. 'It's an odd thing,' I began, 'after such a brief acquaintance – I have a feeling that once we part we may never . . . set eyes on each other again.'

He shrugged, smiling. 'Who is to say that we won't? In this city you would be surprised at how often the same faces rise to meet you.'

'But the streets – they're dangerous . . .'

Duckenfield shook his head. 'Pray, don't alarm yourself. I know what's o'clock. I have walked the streets too long not to be leary.'

A leary man, I thought, in echo. Yes, that was what he was. 'Where will you go?'

He tipped his head to one side, and pouted his lower lip. 'The winter's coming in. I dare say I'll find a suitable hole to hibernate – somewhere I can read in peace.' He held up my father's book in illustration.

We stood facing one another for a few moments, before he said, 'One more thing. Your money – hidden in the wall over there.'

'Please,' I replied, shaking my head. It would have mortified me to take it. 'Buy yourself a decent dinner. Or – I don't know – a new pair of boots.'

He looked down at his present battered pair, as though he had never really noticed them before. 'Hmm. Perhaps I will,' he said thoughtfully. I had a sudden inexplicable urge to keep him talking there a while longer, but he had already thrust out a hand. 'Goodbye, then. I'll see you on the road.' It sounded like a valediction he had uttered often, amongst his own.

I returned his goodbye, and felt a numbness rise into my throat. I started south. Before I got to the turn in the avenue I paused, thinking I would take a last look at him tramping in the distance, a wisp of smoke rising from the pipe in his mouth. But then I couldn't bear to see whether he would stop to retrieve the money or not, and I walked on.

18
Reckoning

November had swamped the city in choking brown fogs and rainstorms, basting the streets until every building was blurred and the gutters rose like rivers in flood. Carters with lanterns on their horses ghosted out of the dark, and the air would ring with sharp cries and a screeching of wheels as some poor fool tried to cross the road. Gas lamps looked on blearily, their orange eyes blindfolded by the murk. Returning home at night, I would sometimes pass a little huddle of vagrants and hear them coughing like hags.

Arrangements at Hanover Street had reverted to normality after I had found lodgings for Mrs Arkell and a lady companion in Marylebone. I had visited her there once, and been graciously received. Otherwise, my society had dwindled almost to nothing. I no longer saw Paget, and the few colleagues from my time with Marchmont had fallen away. The *Evening News* had kept me on as a copy editor, and I settled into the dreary diurnal round of office life. As for Roma, after what happened at Jo's funeral I considered myself an outcast, and had not ventured into Somers Town since. Of course my banishment did not prevent me from thinking about her, and whenever my steps led me towards Camden or along the Euston Road I half hoped, and half dreaded, running into her. I imagined the various things I might say, if ever we did meet, but the memory of her implacable dark eyes burning through me eventually put a stop to that. She was gone, and there was an end of it.

I had not been entirely forsaken, though. On my chimney piece stood an invitation card whose severe gilt edges looked askance at the dusty night lamp and the slouching row of books. On first reading the words *Sir Martin Elder requests* I was convinced it was a wedding invitation, but it turned out to be a party at the Elder mansion to celebrate Kitty's coming of age. That I had been invited at all surprised me, for we had not seen one another since the day of that carriage ride in September when she had told me of her engagement. I suspected that something in my response at the time had disappointed or displeased her, though

I couldn't fathom what it might be – I had congratulated her, and meant it. A note, written in brown ink, had been included with the card.

My dear David,

Such ages since we last met. Where have you been? I do sincerely entreat you to come to this. Papa, forgetful of consulting me, has invited most of the guests, and a dull lot they are! But I have slipped this one out personally – I would so much prefer to spend the evening in talk with you. Please say you will come.

Yours, ever,

Kitty

She asked me where I had been, and what could I say? Impossible even to hint at the story of her diamond ring and the murder of my dearest friend. The misadventure had robbed me of any inclination to be gregarious. I would probably have held to my reclusive habits were it not for the sincerity of feeling I discerned in Kitty's note. We had taken to one another on first meeting, and our friendship had continued thereafter, not least because I was so plainly unqualified to angle for her fortune. She regarded me without suspicion, I regarded her without illusion. It suited us both.

On the appointed evening, however, as I descended from a cab at the foot of Kensington Palace Gardens, my feelings were not so sanguine. Certain intimates of the Elder circle were sure to be present. Abernathy and his Social Protection League, for example, smarting from the public assault on their charitable endeavours, would spit bile at the sight of me. Indeed, I wondered why Sir Martin had not simply declared me *persona non grata* (I had learned that much Latin). It could only be that he rose above such things – that was the privilege of the rich.

In deference to Kitty I had made myself as presentable as could be contrived. A proper old soak and a shave at the Turkish baths in Northumberland Avenue had an emollient effect on my appearance, and my mood was lifted by a fearnought of brandy and water at a hotel in Piccadilly. I had even acquired a new pair of boots, in an oblique sort of tribute to Duckenfield. The curving gravel drive of the Elder mansion was lined with braziers, kindling warmth in defiance of the wintry climate. The stately elms frowned in outrage to find their leaves torn from them. The sight of the magnificent white house itself induced a regretful longing, for the last time I had been here, in spring, there was nothing of the future I could see but intrigue and possibility. Ahead of me in the blazing hall two tall men had divested themselves of heavy evening capes and hats without a glance at the servant who accepted the burden. Other arrivals were pouring in, the cold of the night gusting behind them. My own coat was whisked off my shoulders and out of sight before I was directed by another minion – so many staff! – across the marble prairie of the hall and into an ambling line of guests. The men's uniform white shirt fronts and black tailcoats offered a frowning rebuke to the coloured silks of the ladies.

The line was filtering down a short corridor and into the ballroom, where the crowd had doubled and trebled as if it were a species reproducing at will. The noise was already remarkable; people were raising their voices to be heard against the roar. Navigating the surge of bodies I gained one of the French windows, half open to the night air. I had managed to pluck a flute of champagne from a passing tray, and was making short work of it.

'Thirsty business, eh?' A foxy-eyed man with long side whiskers had just sidled into the sanctuary of the alcove, and nodded amusedly at the glass I had just drained. He had taken out a thin cigar. 'Care for a smoke?'

I shook my head and regarded him more closely. He was well built, and carried himself with a negligent air of authority; a signet ring glinted on his pinkie. I decided to introduce myself, and he offered me his hand.

'Hardwick,' he said, drawing back slightly to get another angle on me. 'A friend of the young lady's?' There was a dry but amicable curiosity in his tone.

'Yes, I am. Sir Martin is my, um, godfather.'

He raised an eyebrow at that. 'That so? I dare say you've been hunting with him, then . . .'

'Oh, no, actually – my connection with him is not intimate. He was at Oxford with my father, back in the 'forties.'

'Indeed? I was at the varsity around that time – Wildeblood, did you say?'

I mentioned my father's first name, and college, but Hardwick only squinted through his smoke, not recalling. 'But you met Sir Martin there?' I said.

'I did,' he admitted, 'and you will not be surprised to hear that he was a formidable character even then.'

As I looked round at the cavalcade of guests, I caught a tumbling flash of diamonds at a lady's throat, their brightness so piercing I almost had to shield my eyes. Hardwick had seen them too, and said, 'Must be about ten thousand pounds she's wearing on her neck.'

'A prigger's paradise,' I remarked jokingly, but the look he returned did not partake of my nonchalance.

'*Prigger*? Now where would you know a flash word like that from?'

I quickly explained my study of slang as it related to *The Labouring Classes of London*. It appeared to satisfy him. 'Somers Town . . . I once worked there myself. Met my share of priggers – pickpockets – what you will.'

Curious in my turn, I was about to ask him what he did for a living when, like a jack-in-the-box, Kitty sprang up before me.

'David! At last!' She was wearing an oyster-grey evening gown with diaphanous tulle sleeves and lace gloves. Her hair had been pinned up, emphasising the sculptural curve of her neck. She also appeared to have gained about a foot in height.

'Happy birthday,' I said, grazing her hand with my lips, stunned for a moment by the transfiguration. When – *how* – had she become this confoundingly beautiful creature?

'What are you hiding here for?' she said, with a little frown that suggested the inconvenience of having to search, for anything. With a quick nod to Hardwick, who bowed in turn, she grasped my arm and steered me through the room. I caught the rise and fall of her voice as we walked, though not the words, still pondering her emergence from the chrysalis of girlishness into this luminous specimen of womanhood.

'I'm sorry,' I said, catching her prompt, 'I can't hear above this noise.'

'I said, I've put you on my card for the first dance this evening – you must promise me.' She registered my doubt. 'You *do* dance?'

'I would have thought that privilege belonged to your intended.'

She pouted her bottom lip, and was briefly a girl once more. 'Douglas is smoking a vile cigar with his cronies in the billiard room. He said, "Caesar doesn't dance," and laughed.' A plaintive note sounded beneath her annoyance.

'Then I am at your service,' I said, and felt an approving squeeze on my arm. 'By the way, who was that gentleman I was just talking to?'

'Oh, Francis Hardwick. He's the Assistant Commissioner of the Metropolitan Police. One of my father's old friends.' She threw an arm airily about us. 'They all are.'

We were almost out of the room when, from behind a clump of guests, Montgomery Sprule stepped in front of us. At my side I felt rather than heard Kitty's sigh of exasperation. Sprule wore a smile of strained tolerance as he bowed to Kitty but stopped short of offering his hand to me.

'Mr Wildeblood. We meet again. You will excuse me if I don't bestow my congratulations on your investigative triumph.'

'I wasn't expecting any, Mr Sprule,' I replied. 'I'm here to celebrate my friend's birthday – as you must be.'

'Quite so,' he said suavely. 'Though I feel obliged to remark that your little stunt, whilst temporarily effective, will only delay progress, not retard it. You really ought to have read my book.'

'As a matter of fact I *did* read your book, and I found your idea of progress to be as flawed as your idea of the poor. It is not that they have less moral capacity than the rest of us – just less money.'

He gave a slight shake of his head. 'You show an imperfect understanding of the way society is heading, sir. In its present constitution it simply cannot be sustained –'

'Mr Sprule,' Kitty interrupted, in her most acidly polite voice, 'fascinating though this is, the evening runs on and I must not allow Mr Wildeblood to occupy your time exclusively. Would you pardon us?'

He swooped into an exaggerated bow. 'Miss Elder, of course,' he purred, his gaze still holding mine as he backed away. Kitty was directing me towards the doors onto the terrace, which some guests had found preferable to the heaving throng within. The moon was dispensing a silvery light over the vigilant trees, and the long crescent garden stretched into blackness.

'You seemed very eager to get away just then,' I said.

Kitty allowed herself another sigh. 'I have nothing against Mr Sprule – other than that he is completely tiresome.' She then canted her head to one side and then to the other, appraising me. 'You are rather slow with your compliments tonight, David. Does my appearance not please you?'

'On the contrary, I'm not sure I've ever seen you looking so – agreeable.' It was a feeble word to end upon, but I'd clutched at it in a vague apprehension that a more meaningful one would invite trouble.

'"Agreeable"?' said Kitty, pulling a face. 'That's the sort of word a nervous curate might use to his bishop. I hoped on my birthday I might at least coax a phrase with more feeling than *agreeable*. It wasn't so long ago you were dashing off on a quest to recover a diamond ring –'

'– which ended in failure, as you know.' I had told her this in my reply to her invitation, without mentioning what had happened to Jo.

'But the impulse was noble,' she said. Her voice was light, but in her eyes I caught a glint of something intense, almost pleading, and it disconcerted me. The mood between us felt suddenly charged, and I knew I should try to defuse it. I smiled at her and adopted the light-hearted but cautious tone of a fond schoolteacher.

'I ought to have said – you look radiant, and Douglas should consider himself a most fortunate man.'

She stared disbelievingly at me for a few moments, then shook her head. 'You really don't understand, do you? I thought once you might have, but now I'm not sure . . . perhaps I've –' She had paused, her eyes searching my face again, when a sudden sharp detonation made us both jump. A moment later a pair of blonde-haired girls – cousins of Kitty, I think – were hurrying up to us, shivering slightly in the cold air.

'Kitty,' cried one of them, 'come quick – they've started the fireworks!'

'Yes, yes, I'll follow you directly,' she replied, evidently unwilling to end our conversation on an inconclusive note. But straight away another figure emerged from the ballroom, trailed by a cortège of guests, and hailed Kitty in a more peremptory manner. It was Sir Martin himself, his expression of narrow-eyed puzzlement clearing as he recognised me.

'Ah, I heard you were in the house,' he said in a tone that was not unfriendly but made clear that my invitation had had nothing to do with him. 'Well, we are assembling in the front garden – for the display.'

Kitty darted a rueful smile at me before joining Sir Martin's train on its ambling progress towards the garden. I held back for a moment, alert to the presumption of including myself in the Elder retinue. Instead, I re-entered the house via a side door I remembered from the last time I had been here, the day Kitty told me about the Bindon Fields outing. The gas jets, turned low, showed corridor walls hung with paintings in morose gilt frames, most of them hunting scenes – hare-coursing, deer-stalking, men on horses leaping across a beck. One large oil depicted an eagle in mid-pounce, the foreshortened perspective lending its yellow talons a hideous rapacity. I wondered vaguely at the terror of the field mouse or rabbit in those final seconds of its life. The distant *pop-pop* of the whizz-bangs broke into my reverie. Without a guide the house was labyrinthine, and a wrong turn obliged me to negotiate more vast and unexpected rooms. In one of them I encountered a servant lighting a lamp, and we exchanged brief looks of embarrassment – at least mine was, in seeming (and indeed being) a guest without friends. At length I happened upon the entrance hall, and fell in with the last of the stragglers on their way out to the front lawn.

People stood about in groups, their faces garishly illumined as a rocket flared and tore off skywards with a great whoosh. The ripping white starburst prompted coos of wonder. A woman in the dark next to me couldn't stop giggling, and the loud male voice at her side ('Oh dear, she's off again!') only fuelled the mood of hilarity about us. More rockets followed, whistling and screaming, each climaxing in an explosive crump that scribbled the blue-black sky with luminous gibberish. Laughter and applause tinkled on the air. The last in the display was also the longest, one refulgent burst catching and overleaping another, their phosphorescent trails reaching to the heavens, fountaining, then toppling, slowly, to nothing. And I wondered if its dying fall – all that brilliant activity gone to smoke – made anyone there feel as melancholy as I did.

Still blinking out the rocket's imprint from my eyes, I roamed about the garden. Guests recently transfixed by the spectacle seemed reluctant to return indoors, so waiters had begun to ferry trays of drinks onto the lawn. I almost ran into Sprule again, now occupied with Abernathy, but managed by a stealthy about-face to evade them. A curtain of sulphurous smog had descended, the fireworks' final bequest to the party. I had reached the outer edges of the crowd, just by the stone gate-piers, when a man detached himself from his circle of familiars and hailed me. It was Hardwick, the man from the Met.

'Quite a show, eh?' he said. 'Haven't seen one like that since they closed the Cremorne Gardens.'

'I never had the pleasure,' I replied, and he laughed as though I'd made a joke.

'Oh, we had some rorty old times down there . . . talking of which, I thought back to Oxford – you said your father was there – and, d'you know, I *do* remember him. I think we met when he and Elder were on holiday together in Scotland.'

'That would be right. He told me they used to go birdwatching there. I was lost in the house a few minutes ago and came across a quite terrifying picture of an eagle.'

Hardwick chuckled again. 'Hmm. Our host has always had a

predilection for birds of prey. There, for example.' He pointed with his eyes to the pair of carved predators that stood sentry on either gate-pier.

'Yes – I always fancy those eagles are *watching* me.'

'Rather baleful, aren't they?' he mused. 'And they're not eagles, by the way. I was told that they're condors.'

'I'm sorry?'

'Condors,' he repeated. 'Elder had them specially made. A South American vulture, I gather. But I'm no expert.'

I stood there, my whole body seized by a dreadful creeping chill. 'A condor,' I heard myself say. 'Is it . . . a particular favourite of his?'

'I suppose it must be,' he shrugged, then craned forward a little. 'Um, is something the matter? You've gone awfully pale . . .'

I stared back at him, putting it all together in my head, unable to speak. *Of course* . . . I had the queer sensation of the party around us as a submerged, incoherent babble, whilst the ground I stood on appeared to slide, dreamlike, from beneath my feet.

'*Whoa*, mind the paint!' Hardwick laughed, holding me upright by the shoulders. 'Not going to faint, are we?' No, I thought, but I might be going to vomit. I sensed a need to pull myself together, and quickly.

'I'm fine, thank you, really,' I said, forcing a tight smile to my lips. His gaze was still cautious, but he let his arms drop from me. 'I need – I've just remembered an important thing I should tell Sir Martin. I ought to do it now.'

'Of course – if you must,' he said. I was walking away before I even realised I was moving, conscious that the strangled apology I left in my wake ('Sorry to have –') was a poor return for his friendliness. When I glanced back he was still watching me. I seemed to be following my own heartbeat as I gravitated through the crowds and back through the colonnaded entrance. I was in the house again. Despite the exodus to the garden the revellers in the ballroom were still keeping their end up, the noise almost rising to hysteria as the drinks flowed on. At the far end of the room a string quartet was tuning up, and near them I spotted Kitty in animated converse with one of the senior staff. She had turned and, seeing me approach, broke into a smile so eager it was like a flag being waved. At that moment I knew I would hate myself for going through with this – and that I couldn't live with myself if I didn't.

She grasped my arm and raised herself to say at my ear, 'They're going to start – the dancing. Are you ready?'

'Kitty, will you listen to me for one moment?' She instantly read in my manner a withdrawing, for her eyes darkened anxiously.

'David – you *promised*, remember? The first dance!'

'I know I did. But first, I beg you, please do me this favour. I must – absolutely must – speak to your father in private.'

Her features closed into a frown. 'Why?'

I looked at her, and shook my head. 'I can't say – it's something important. I wouldn't ask you unless it was.'

The trusting look she returned should have broken my heart. 'But you will dance with me, once you're finished – yes?'

'I would be honoured to,' I replied, sadly aware that the promise would never be kept.

'Very well,' she said, brightening, 'I shall tell him that you'll be in his study – you remember where it is?'

I nodded, and in a spontaneous gesture – she couldn't have known it was my apology – I took up her hand and pressed it to my mouth. In her face pleasure duelled with uncertainty, and she lingered a moment before going off in search of her father. With purpose in my step I exited the ballroom, crossed the hall and turned down a side corridor. The oak-panelled door at the end of it was unlocked, and I pushed through to find the master's study, steeped in gloom but for a lamp burning low on the desk. It was as I had first seen it: the iron-wrought gallery, the cliff faces of bookshelves, the trestle stacked higgledy-piggledy with scholarly volumes. A sudden movement at the corner of my eye made me jump; then I relaxed on seeing what it was – the gormless, turnip-shaped face of Kitty's monkey, Ferdinand, peering through the bars of his cage. I wandered over, and his head lifted enquiringly, perhaps in anticipation of a feed. A tasselled velvet night curtain sat atop the cage in folds, and with a flick of my hand it dropped down, concealing the creature from my sight. I heard a muffled chattering of protest behind the cloth.

I walked back to the desk and turned up the lamp. The room swam into focus, and I had the impression of myself as a character just sidling onto a stage, about to speak. Presently I heard footsteps outside, the door swung open and Sir Martin entered. He had a cigar in blast and the air of a man who could spare no more than a businesslike five minutes. The humourless virility he projected, the wide-stepping gait and his long aristocratic jawbone were so commanding as to make me rather afraid.

'There you are. Kitty said you wished to speak to me.' He walked to his desk, and opened the clasp on a silver box. 'Cigar?'

I shook my head.

He settled, and opened his palms expansively. 'So?'

'There's a question I've been pondering. How much are you worth?'

Elder tucked in his chin, puzzled. 'I beg your pardon?'

'What do you estimate your personal fortune to be?'

'I have no idea.'

'You've made a great deal of money, though, from property?'

'Amongst other things, yes,' he replied, cautious amusement in his voice. 'May I ask what is —'

'And I imagine that whilst money accrues from this property, the rights and the well-being of your tenants — those in Somers Town, say — would not be of particular consequence to you.'

He said, a little haughtily, 'I think you misunderstand. It is not my business to collect the rents.'

'I know. You have others to do that for you — Walter Moyles, for instance, and his crew of bullies.'

He shrugged. 'I have a great many in my employ. Their names are not all known to me.'

'Allow me to try another. Condor Holdings — is that name known to you?'

He paused at that. He was surprised, but not greatly. 'What *exactly* have you in mind to say to me, sir?'

I took a breath. 'That you launched a plan of clearances to make yourself a fortune. That you concealed your ownership behind a puppet company and, after that was discovered, a series of fake names. That you colluded with the Social Protection League to segregate the poor you had displaced into rural labour camps. I think that is all, in outline.'

He betrayed nothing beyond a small tightening in his jaw. Seeing the monkey's cage he moved to it and flipped back the cloth, reintroducing its occupant. But when he next spoke something had altered in his tone. 'That cut on your nose. Did you ever consider how easily it might have been your throat instead?'

'I saw what happened to Alfred Kenton, drowned in the Thames. And my own dear friend was murdered in front of me, on the street. I realise I've had a narrow escape.'

'That you did so was out of my respect to your father. Others were not inclined to be so lenient. What you hoped to achieve — well, the safe progress of society —'

'Please,' I said, 'I've already heard your friend Sprule's thoughts on that subject.'

'You have heard, but evidently not understood.' He stared at me, and gave a little shake of his head. 'Sprule is too zealous, but he is essentially right in his prognosis. In time a great majority of the city's poor will die out, as a failed subspecies. It is inevitable. Until then, it behoves us to guard against their degrading and contaminating the general health of society. They must not drag down the rest. That is a central imperative of our survival.'

'Society will survive without having to imprison the poorest elements of it. You regard the indigent of Somers Town as a criminal class – that is your mistake.'

'Ah . . . how then do you regard them?'

I held his gaze. 'As vulnerable people preyed on and destroyed by those who should most have helped them.'

He took a long pull on his cigar, and pushed himself up from the desk on which he had been leaning. 'Well. On that we must differ. If that is all –'

'No, that is *not* all. There is blood on your hands. I intend to make known the infamies you have licensed.'

He sighed with impatience – this was too much. 'How? You think I have signed my name to anything?'

'Probably not. But I dare say you have documents that link you to Condor Holdings. In your safe there. You oughtn't to leave your keys lying about,' I added, throwing them onto his desk. He straightened up. He must have known I had found them in the lock of Ferdinand's cage. 'Please to open it,' I said.

'Nothing would induce me,' he replied with contemptuous calm.

'This might.' Jo's knife was already in my hand, pointed at him. 'I anticipated your resistance. Be assured, I would gladly use it.'

His eyes gleamed hard. 'You must be insane. I will not –' He stopped himself there, seeming to reconsider his position. His corrugated brow cleared. 'Very well then . . .'

He picked up the ring of keys, and went round behind his desk to remove the painting that shielded the wall safe. I detected an odd alacrity in his movements, as though he were actually keen to open it. He had just clicked through the combination when I suddenly realised why – *Cool the hands* – and vaulted over his desk in the instant he was pulling back the door. I held the knife to the side of his neck. 'I'll take that,' I said. He had his hand on a pistol, which I had recalled some burglar once telling me was a common appurtenance of Kensington safes – they generally held more to protect. With my other hand I relieved him of the weapon, a double-barrelled thing with a plain wooden stock. I took a few steps back.

'Now – empty it,' I said, and cocked the pistol to make sure he understood. The coldness of his glare could have frozen the Thames in summer. He reached inside and withdrew a strongbox, a quantity of folded banknotes and yellow kidskin bags that clinked. (Why did I think of doubloons?) I looked past him at what remained in there. 'Those too, if you please.'

Out came a sheaf of documents, the top one sealed with wax and tied in a black ribbon. For the first time he looked ill at ease. He kept the papers in his hand, saying, 'These things are of no value –'

'Then you will not mind surrendering them to me,' I replied, pocketing the knife and holding out my free hand. Instead he threw the papers onto the desk; his expression, his tense posture, suggested a strong reluctance to have their contents disclosed. I was going to pick them up when there came an abrupt knock at the door. Kitty breezed in – and pulled up. I watched her face pass very rapidly from dumbstruck to disbelieving.

'*David* – ?'

Of course I saw how grotesque was the scene she had stumbled on: the friend she thought she knew training a pistol on her father, the contents of his safe emptied upon the desk. I might as well have been wearing a mask and holding a bag marked SWAG. Elder gestured innocence with his raised hands, and said to her, in a tone touched with sorrow, 'Kitty. I'm afraid this young man has deceived us – he has come here intending to rob the place.'

Kitty, colour draining from her cheeks, stared at me. 'What are you – have you gone mad? Please tell me what's happening.'

Elder tried to interpose himself, but I repelled him with a straightening of my gun arm. Kitty gasped in surprise. 'I see how this looks,' I said, 'but I'm no thief. I am here for evidence relating to your father's property company – papers that will reveal his unscrupulous dealings and the exploitation of many hundreds of his tenants. I'm sorry, Kitty, but – your father is a wicked man.'

'"A wicked man"?' repeated Elder, wounded dignity in his voice. 'Sir, you are talking to *my own daughter* – d'you imagine she would for a minute entertain such gross absurdity?'

I looked in appeal to Kitty, who (my hopes rose at this moment) looked very unsure as to whether my accusation were absurd or not. 'David, would you, please, put that thing down – I implore you,' she said with a gulp.

I wish I could have obliged her, but matters had advanced too far. I only shook my head, and in the hiatus Elder spoke up urgently.

'My dear, listen to me. Go and fetch Mr Hardwick. He's in the garden. Tell him a robbery has been foiled – and the culprit awaits arrest.'

Kitty's indecision was writ in agony on her face. Any thought of a peaceable resolution to the impasse had been scuppered by the word *arrest*. I held a gun; her father held his ground. What to do?

'Catherine! Fetch Mr Hardwick,' he repeated, '*now.*'

She flinched at the sudden asperity of his voice, and I knew that my fate was narrowing. Our eyes met again, and compassion glistened in hers. But mostly what I saw there was horrified dismay. 'I'm sorry, David,' she said quietly, and as she turned away I said her name; without looking back, she faltered, and then hurried on.

And how those small moments would cost me. With my body half turned I had slackened my guard for an instant, and now Elder stood, like a duellist, squinting along the barrel of a revolver.

'I always keep another one to hand,' he said with the philosophical air of a man used to outwitting his opponents. 'Now. Step towards me, here, and put the gun on the desk. That's the way.' Over at the cage Ferdinand, perhaps scenting disruption in the air, made short hostile grunts. He shushed him. 'The game is up, Mr Wildeblood.'

'I should wait to hear what Hardwick has to say about those papers first.'

Elder gave a pitying laugh. 'It's quite beyond you, isn't it? The police will do what I pay them for – as I said, there are many in my employ.'

'You think that putting me in prison will save you? The truth is going to come out.'

He shook his head. 'I see too well that prison will put no trammel on your tongue. Alas, it will grieve your poor father, but . . . your destination is elsewhere. I should say the river's a fine and private place.'

So there it was. They would dispatch me the same way as Kenton, perhaps to be washed up at low tide some day, a bloated bundle of flesh with eyeballs pecked from their sockets. Whilst he had been speaking, the racket from Ferdinand's cage had waxed in agitation. There was a pause, then the creature – as if its tail had been bitten – gave vent to a full-throated screech. Elder, still pointing the revolver but distracted, took his eye off me, and without thinking I snatched up the table lamp and hurled it at his head. He ducked and it crashed against the cage; in the seconds it took him to right himself I had darted across the room and out the door.

I tried to make myself think at the same time as I was bolting helter-skelter along the corridor and thence by a sharp right turn into the rooms I'd traversed earlier that evening. I blessed the serendipity that had obliged me to discover their layout, for I was soon in front of the side door by which I'd entered. I twisted the knob. Locked!

'Sir?' came an enquiring voice. It was the servant I'd seen lighting the lamp before.

'This door,' I cried, 'have you the key?'

He nodded, tensing at my wild-eyed panic.

'Then quick, man, open it – an emergency outside!'

We both heard the alarums sounding within the house – the hunt for the thief had begun – but the servant fortunately assumed I was running towards the 'emergency' rather than away from it, and obliged me by unlocking the door. I was through there like a scorched ferret before I heard the first warning cry. The back garden swallowed me up in its velvety blackness, but there was no use in hiding here – I'd seen that fail once already. *Quick, quick, decide!* I told myself, careening onwards. The lawn was damp and hard underfoot, and my panting breath whitened against the dark. Here was the wall, with the park on the other side, and I looked for the ancient garden door that Kitty and I had once passed through. As I felt my way along the clammy brick and its tangled curtain of creepers I heard male voices calling to one another from the house; looking back I could see figures with lanterns, glimmering down the lawn. My fingers clutched the iron handle of the gate and I pulled on it. It was shut fast, with a deadlock.

I looked up at the wall, which I suppose was about fifteen feet high. Grasping the wizened and leafless creeper in both hands I began to shinny upwards, finding toeholds in the brickwork. I had no time to check whether it would hold my weight, nor did I care that the gnarled branches were cutting into my palms. I was still climbing when a shout went up, 'That's him, there! On the wall,' and other voices rose in excited support. Desperation made me scramble the rest of its height, and as I was clambering onto the ledge I heard another booming command from below. 'Stop there!' A pistol shot cracked through the air. I straddled the wall for a moment and looked down to see Elder himself, drawing a bead on me. 'Get down, sir, or the next one will be through you,' he called. I peered over the side, considering the drop. It was either this way, or the Thames.

I swung my leg round, bracing myself to jump, when a woman's beseeching cry of *No!* pierced the night. Without looking I knew it to be Kitty. At the same instant I heard another shot, much closer to me, and I jumped. The ground below seemed to rise very abruptly to meet my plummeting weight, and a flash of terror – at broken bones, or a broken neck – was gone almost before it had registered. Landing on a fortuitous flower bed snatched the air from my lungs, but aside from a throbbing in my side – a jagged branch, probably – I was unharmed. I brushed off the dirt from my hands and knees. Ahead lay the inky expanse of Kensington Gardens, with a screening line of trees distantly picked out by the moonlight. I plunged forward, reckoning it only a matter of minutes before the key to that door was found and Elder would be on my heels. As I ran all I could hear was the sound of my own agitated breathing. I lost my footing a couple of times as the parkland dipped without warning, then I was up again and heading for the firefly tips of gas lamps a few hundred yards away to the right.

The pain in my side still troubled me – perhaps the cut was deeper than I first thought – but I pressed on heedless, listening for sounds of pursuit. My pace had fallen off by the time I reached the row of lamps, which showed a long carriage path quite empty of traffic. Hard by, the Serpentine glittered black. I checked the wound under my shirt, and found it slick to the touch; not a pricking branch after all, but a puncture from a lead ball. I should have known Elder would not miss, even in poor light. I was breathing heavily. I walked on a few paces until I heard the distant clop of horses coming through the dark. I hesitated, wondering if I should flag them down to ask for help, but then an instinct warned against it. I hurried off the road and concealed myself behind a thick-waisted oak tree – and listened as the two horsemen slowed to a trot. A voice said, 'I thought I spied him here,' and there followed a short exchange between them. The other's voice, unmistakably, was Elder's. 'He can't get far with that wound – and the police have his description.'

Once they had jogged out of sight I took stock. Where should I go? The police would make for my lodgings in Islington, so that was out. A hotel might be dangerous, and probably unaffordable in any case. I was keeping to the dirt footpath alongside the trees, fearful of Elder's doubling back up the road. As I approached the gates at Hyde Park I saw the silhouettes of helmeted figures, a picket of bobbies evidently about to disperse through the park in search of a fugitive. Over the road and beyond the wall I could hear passing traffic on Knightsbridge. I judged the road dark enough to shroud me – wrongly, as it transpired. Halfway across one of the policemen raised his lantern.

It was enough. 'Oi – over there!' A whistle blew, and he started to run towards me. I covered the last stretch of parkland at a sprint, vaulted the hip-high wall and cried in agony as I landed on the pavement: the wound was a white-hot poker in my side, and each step seemed to suck it in more deeply. No matter – keep moving. On reaching Hyde Park Corner I simply dashed into the road, provoking an outraged oath from a 'bus driver as he swerved past me. A glance back suggested I had lost my pursuer – no, there he was, looking about – and then I was dodging the traffic as it flowed from out of the dark. Lungs aching, I urged myself along the thoroughfare until – a mercy! – a cabby spotted my frantic signal and pulled up. I climbed aboard and said, 'Somers Town,' before I changed my mind and told him to head for Seven Dials. No policeman would be looking for me there.

I pulled the doors to, and sank back into the seat. I didn't know whether the police had spotted me or not; more troubling was the way every jolt of the vehicle thrust into my side. Blood was leaking through my shirt and down my leg. A hospital? No – Elder would have men searching there, too. I must have dozed on the journey, for in a matter of minutes the cabby was rapping on the roof. I managed to climb out.

'Sure you're all right, sir?' he asked.

We were at the top of St Martin's Lane, in the thick of the swarming night hordes. I staggered a little, and I suppose he thought I was drunk. I paid the man off, not trusting myself to speak, and began to walk. To where? I had no idea. I turned left and found myself in a dreadful winding street of tumbledown tenements and grog shops. Strangers paid me no heed – wandering drunks were unremarkable in this neighbourhood. I was shivering like a greyhound (my coat was back at the Elder mansion) and sweating at the same time. A terrible and immediate urge to lie down had seized me, it was the only thing that could possibly salve the molten hole burning through my side. Please God . . . I stumbled against a doorway, and saw that it was a dosshouse. They would have a bed I could lie upon. A knock brought a sunken-eyed keeper to the door, and once he had taken my money ('fourpence the night') I was conducted up two flights of stairs to a room overlooking the street. Two of the four beds were already occupied by slumbering forms. He pointed to a cot in the corner, with a little truckle underneath. 'You won't mind sharin',' the man said, but I already had my head on the pillow. He didn't appear to notice I was bleeding on his floor.

* * *

At first I thought I was dreaming. My tongue was so dry it had fossilised in my mouth. I called out for water. From beneath my cot I heard a rustling – the truckle bed had been taken since I had fallen asleep – and a face appeared at my side, a face that was inconceivably familiar. The boy was pale, malnourished, perhaps ten or eleven years old. He had lit a stub of candle, and I reached out a hand to touch him. It was no dream.

His face seemed to be in shadow; then I saw that it was disfigured by a livid port wine stain running from cheek to neck. Having stared fixedly at me, he walked off, returning shortly with a jug of water. He held it for me as I raised myself to drink, sluicing the dried scabbard of my mouth.

'Do I know you?' I said to him.

The boy nodded. 'You gave me dad a sov once. Outside the big house.' The Irish accent did it. It was the son of the cigar-end collector, whose unwitting trespass into Elder's garden I had recalled only an hour before.

'Where's your dad now?'

'Out worken,' he shrugged, as though to say, *What else would he be doing in the middle of the night?* 'Your face is drippen wet,' he added.

I looked across the room at the untidy heaps of the other sleepers. I called out, but neither of them stirred. Where was I to get help? 'Do you know of a doctor near here?'

The boy shook his head, and said, quite casually, 'Are you gonna die?'

I pulled back the blanket to examine the wound; the sheet was dark with blood. 'I believe I am,' I said, and he nodded sadly. I sank back onto the pillow. Minutes passed, and I thought how very unexciting was the struggle against death. Unexciting, but also undemanding. Why worry? I dozed off again, maybe for only a minute, when the boy shook me awake.

'You want a priest?' His voice had a slight tremble in it – I don't suppose he wanted to watch me expire – and, fighting my tiredness, I propped myself up by the elbows.

'Listen, you remember the sov. Would you do me a favour in return?' He nodded, and I asked him if he knew Clarendon Square in Somers Town. No, he didn't, but when I described the Polygon to him his eyes flared in recognition.

'The white one, like a circle.'

'Yes, the one like a circle. Number 29. A woman called Roma lives there. Can you – just tell her that David Wildeblood asked for her, and that –' I didn't know what else to say. 'Tell her I've been hurt.'

He stared at me dumbly a few moments longer. I asked him to repeat the names and the address I'd mentioned, and he got all three. Then I lay down, eyes towards the ceiling. When I turned my head again the boy was gone.

I drifted in and out of consciousness. I knew it was better to try and stay awake, but my fevered body writhed beneath a continuous assault of night frights, a horrible lurching train of faces and figments stalking unbidden across my dreams. Foremost among them Elder, his aspect – half-horse, half-human – glowering over me. Twice, at least, I was startled into waking by the chattering of my teeth. From the street below came shrieks, and the oaths bandied by midnight drunkards; even their racket was preferable to the phantasmal terrors rioting through my beleaguered brain. My breathing had become stertorous, ragged in my chest, and I thought, with regret but no anxiety, that *this* was how it was to die. Perhaps I already heard them on the stair, but my memory of their approach was the glimmer of a lamp at the door. As I peered, a boy's thin face coalesced through the grainy dark. Behind him I saw a woman in black – Roma, it had to be Roma – and next to her a man. And at the sight of him I realised my mistake in forgetting to tell the boy: don't bring the police.

19
Le strade

Un di, felice, eterea,
Mi balenaste innante
E da quel di tremante
Vissi d'ignoto amor . . .

That song again. They are singing it everywhere at the moment. I get
up from my desk and step onto the balcony, the soles of my bare feet
roasting on the smooth tiles. Down below, on the other side of the
street stand the organ-grinder and his mate, the latter's voice a surpris-
ingly mellow baritone. A hand shields his eyes as he looks directly up
at me: our gazes meet and, possibly embarrassed, he dips his head in
an ingratiating little bow. His face seems familiar. At this hour of the
morning the sun makes dramatic angles of shadow on the rearing walls
of these narrow old streets. In mediaeval times the city strutted on the
stage of European trade. Its name – I dare not write it down, for reasons
you will hear. Suffice to say, Italy, to the north.

Perhaps I should be more cautious, given recent events, only the
temptation to describe it is irresistible. The three and a half years I
have resided here have been the happiest of my life. At first I thought
I was merely charmed by the quality of its light, the soft way it falls
on things and seems to enhance them. Even the motes of dust it
shows teeming on the threshold of the shuttered room where I write,
even they please the eye. But then I found myself half in love with
the place itself, the vertiginous tenements and their huge oak door-
ways, the paving blocks placed diamond-wise, the smell of roasted
chestnuts and cigars, the portraits of *La Madonna* tucked into niches,
the metallic strains of organ music, and – what most reminds me of
Somers Town – the ceaseless theatre of buying and selling. On
market days you cannot walk the length of this street without being
importuned by at least half a dozen sellers. When I say '*grazie*' to
any of them the reply always comes: '*niente*'. Some mornings you

have to dodge around the donkeys, and the goats, tinkling and bleating, just to get fifty yards.

Down below the man has finished the song but still lifts his gaze up here, and now I realise that I have seen him and his organ-grinder before. Yesterday they were loitering outside on the piazza whilst I drank my noonday *caffè latte*. A week or so ago this coincidence would have gone unnoticed by me – there are many such *musicisti* wandering hereabouts – but that was before I knew I was being tracked. The man is whispering to his organ-grinder, who nods and glances up here for himself. If these two are indeed spies they are the least subtle of their trade I have yet encountered. I lean down and shout to them, '*Eh, suonane un'altra. Ecco una moneta!*' I find a soldo in my pocket and flip it down; the man, in a flash, snatches it out of the air, like a frog swallowing a fly. Obediently, they start up again, this time a song I've not heard before. It sounds like a funeral dirge.

I could not calculate how many hours I have frittered away leaning my elbows on this balcony rail, watching the life of the street drift by. Frittered? No. Time wasted purely in enjoying oneself is not wasted time. Small things delight me, like the wicker baskets that people lower on ropes from the windows, with the costers waiting on the pavement to load them. Vertical trading! And the different pace of the passers-by. Monks and other clericals step purposefully, like carriers of secret news. Tiny shuffling ladies in black, their faces tan and wrinkled as walnuts. The sauntering notaries and clerks, document cases under their arms. Nobody hurries. Sometimes I see the boy, returning from Mass or the market, stooping to stroke some dust-furred cat (more cats than clerics in this city). His mother will pause to wait for him. They never think to look up here.

I have just been down to the street. I wanted to have a closer look at those musicians, but by the time I emerged they had gone. I fear they too were posted there to watch me. Is my idyll of anonymity unravelling?

But perhaps you wonder how I came to be here at all. Who pulled me from the brink in that miserable dosshouse? Roma, of course. The Irish boy must have made all haste to the Polygon, and having impressed on her the seriousness of my condition offered to conduct her back to Seven Dials. The man who accompanied her was not a policeman, as I thought. She had had the providence to roust out an old ex-surgeon whose hand (thank God) was not yet tremulous with drink. By his ministrations the lead ball was excised and the danger averted, though I had lost some blood. He advised Roma not to move me, so for the next few days she installed herself at my bedside, administering broth and laudanum, with the boy on hand as her willing orderly.

She had saved my life, but that was only the start. For my life would not have been worth saving if the pursuing furies of Elder and co. had managed to track me down. First, she visited my lodgings in Islington and passed off a story to Mrs Home about my being in a sanatorium, and would it be possible to retrieve some of Mr Wildeblood's things in the meantime? A payment of four weeks' rent in advance secured her admission to my rooms, where she packed up my few clothes in a travelling bag. A glance from the top window onto the street confirmed my warning: a man was watching the house. Fortunately she had kept a cab waiting, and before the spy could intercept her on the pavement she was back in the vehicle and on her way.

Once I could stand up and walk about, we discussed ways of escape. London was no longer safe for me. Roma had already seen an artist's impression of my face on a handbill at King's Cross police station, and even in a low milieu like Seven Dials there were narks on the lookout to turn you in. I had to get out before the net closed, and Roma somehow arranged that, too. One evening towards midnight a trap was waiting to drive me from the dosshouse (on Shelton Street, I latterly discovered) to Rotherhithe, where a skiff carried me down-river to Gravesend. I was billeted in the upper room of a tavern and told to wait, which I did, for three days, staring at the sluggish flow of Thames trade through the window's distorting glass. At night the wind rattled at the leaded casements. On the evening of the fourth a knock sounded at my door. I opened it to find Roma. She walked in, and threw off her winter cloak in a businesslike way.

'You look half perished – here,' I said, and went to my table to pour a tot of brandy. She took a sip, and went to the window. She stood there, lost in thought for a few moments, then turned to me.

'You should get your things together. There's a steamer calling here on its way to Rotterdam. Here's the ticket – they won't trace it to you.'

I joined her at the window, and we gazed out at the river glimmering in the dark. The lantern light on a tug bobbed past. If I was going to ask her, it had to be now. 'Why have you done this for me?'

'What d'you mean?'

'All this. Saving my life. Saving me from arrest. Getting me out.'

She shrugged, and looked away. 'I wanted to.'

'But that day of the funeral, you said you cursed the day I came into your life. I thought you hated me, utterly.'

Head still bowed, she said something, but so quietly I couldn't hear it. 'I beg your pardon?'

After an agonised pause, she replied, 'I said, I'm here, ain't I?' Then she did look at me, and said, almost angrily, 'How could I hate you?'

I wasn't sure whether her question was in fact a declaration. I took hold of her hand, lightly, and wondered if she could sense my heart trying to punch a hole though my chest. 'I used to hold conversations with you in my head – can you imagine? I'd daydream all the things I wanted to say to you, rehearse them, and listen to what you might say in reply. But then once I was in your company I couldn't seem to . . .'

'Why not?'

'I think I was scared of you. Still am.'

She smiled. 'What sorta things did you mean to say?'

'Well . . . the main thing was – how very ardently I admired you.'

'That day we saw the butterfly and walked through those woods – d'you remember? – I thought you might say something then. And when you didn't . . . well, I went back to thinkin' . . .'

'Back to thinking what?'

'You were sweet on *her* – Kitty.'

'*Kitty?*' I said, startled. 'No! Why would you – She became a friend to me, of course. I *liked* her an awful lot . . .'

Her lips formed a thoughtful pout. 'Well, *she* was sweet on *you*. From the moment I set eyes on her –'

'No,' I said, shaking my head. 'What use was I to an heiress? We could never have been a match.'

'That's as maybe – but she was. I could tell.'

And now I thought back to my brief times with Kitty and felt less certain. The curious tone she took on that carriage ride. The eagerness with which she had implored me to dance that night. Had I missed the signs? Then her horrified expression on discovering me with a gun pointed at her father . . . the memory stabbed at me before I could banish it.

'Feeling wistful?' asked Roma, who had been watching me.

'No. A little sad. She must loathe me after what I said about her father . . .'

'I wouldn't be so sure. You don't know a woman's heart.'

I searched her face avidly. 'That much I would have to admit. Yours has been a mystery to me.' I took her other hand, and held them in a clasp. I felt a trembling in her. She said, 'You ought to get ready. There's a boat on its way.'

'Roma – please – won't you come with me? I need you.'

'You don't need me,' she said, shying away.

'But I do. I don't see any good in life if it hasn't got you in it.'

She gave me a sidelong look, considering. 'What would we do? I don't know anythin' but this. How would we survive?'

'We'd have each other,' I said, willing her to agree. 'We could go to Italy – you could see where your family came from!'

She nodded, but her eyes glistened with sadness. Distantly, from the river, came the lowing of a ship's horn. She gently unloosed her hands from my grasp. 'I'm sorry. Honestly I am,' she said, and I believe she was.

I packed up my few possessions whilst she fastened her cloak, neither of us speaking. After settling up with the tavern-keeper – I never learned his name – we walked out into the raw, damp night. The riverbank path was unpeopled at this hour. She walked with me as far as the stairs, at the foot of which a small rowing boat waited. The oarsman raised his lantern to me, and I signalled in return. The steamer had dropped anchor in the middle of the river, awaiting boarders. I turned to Roma, and lifted my hat.

'Shall I write to you?'

'I hope that you will,' she said. At that moment I contemplated throwing myself at her knees and begging her not to forsake me. What did I have to lose?

'Goodbye then,' I said, my tongue as dumb and leaden as that anchor on the riverbed.

She nodded slightly, and said, 'God bless you, David.' It was the first time I had ever heard her say my name: the first, and I supposed the last. I descended the rain-slick stairs to the landing, and stepped onto the boat, which rocked and righted itself before the man began to ply his oars through the cold black deep. We had nearly reached the steamer when my resistance broke and I looked back. I could see her pale face beneath the hood of her cloak, watching, from a point that seemed as remote and irreclaimable as the past itself.

My journey to this place needs no describing. I did not care to linger in the Low Countries, or in Germany or Switzerland for that matter. Italy was always my destination. No trace of my identity will be found on passenger lists or in foreign lodging houses. Since leaving England

I have lived under the name of William Duckenfield, a private tribute to my one-time companion in the workhouse. I have a feeling he would be amused by the appropriation.

Having roamed about in the north I stopped at this city, and after three weeks in residence knew that it was my home. My skin has darkened – this is my fourth summer here – and my hair has gone a strange tawny hue beneath the sun. Wearing a beard that is heavier since Somers Town, I appear to have assumed, unwittingly, a disguise. I now have Italian good enough to be able to do some teaching at the local school, where the pupils call me 'Signor Weel-yam'. A few months ago I started to write a memoir of my experiences in Somers Town, though I wondered if I were too easily diverted – so much pleasanter just to watch the world pass under this balcony. Now there are more sinister distractions.

I had convinced myself that, after three and a half years, Elder had given up his hunt. In the early days of exile I fancied that spies had been set on me, but nothing of consequence ensued. Perhaps he reasoned that I had no evidence of his wrongdoing, and that I would no longer be – what was the phrase? – a stone in his shoe. The few letters I have written to my father during these years always omitted a return address. I could not be sure that Elder wouldn't try to finagle information from him.

But an incident just a week ago has put me on guard again. In the days prior to it I had conceived a suspicion that I was being followed. I have resided here long enough to spot outsiders from a distance, and the fellow I first saw hovering amongst the crowds at the *duomo* one forenoon I identified straight away as *inglese*. If not from their clothes you can tell from their pallor. But this one was not the usual Cook's tourist type who peers up at the stained glass and helplessly attracts beggars. He was not sweating into his linen or objecting to the price of his guide. I walked once around the echoing nave, stopped to light a candle (I have taken on Romish tendencies) and waited for ten minutes before returning to the entrance. He was still there. No matter, I said to myself, and left the place.

Two hours later I emerged from lunch at the Caffè G— and saw my man lounging by a fountain, apparently taking the sun. Very well: let us see which way the cat jumps. I bent my steps west across the piazza, strolled through a little market and then ducked into a warren of lanes where the noise of workshops boomed in the air. Without looking back I sensed a shadow in my wake. Turning a corner I made a quick dart into an open courtyard. Sure enough, I spied him walk past, stop and look around in puzzlement. I had taken a seat in the yard, pretending to be about my business, when he eventually came through the door himself. He started on seeing me.

'*Ti posso aiutare? Sei perso?*' I asked him. He stuttered out a few apologetic phrases, and I wondered if I could pass myself off as a native. I pointed to a brass plaque on the wall – *dentista* – and explained, in genial Italian, that I was waiting for the man. Had a toothache all week. I reckoned it best (here I opened my mouth and mimed a violent tug) to pull the damned thing out. Stop it bothering me for good, I added.

He squinted at me in uncomprehending anxiety. Possibly the mimicking of the dental extraction troubled him. '*Mi dispiace*,' he muttered, and withdrew.

There is a shop a few streets from here which displays in its window a glass case full of pistols. Attached to the case is a little placard, announcing, without a trace of irony, *Variato assortimento in corone mortuarie* ('Varied assortment of funeral wreaths'). It makes me smile every time I see it.

A few days later the *inglese* was on the prowl again. My Italian hadn't fooled him. This time I would not be so accommodating. I wandered for a while, just to lull him, then turned towards the river. A little-used towpath invisible to the street traffic above would be the place – that is, the place to dispose of someone. It was late afternoon as I dropped down there, my footsteps ringing on the lonely flags. A leary man would have tumbled to the danger of following a mark to a riverbank; my fellow was far too complacent.

I heard his steps as he entered the shadowed walkway beneath the bridge. I let him pass, then on stockinged feet (my little precaution) crept up behind him. He jumped as he felt the knife pressed against his jugular, and groaned in fear as I walked him the few paces to the river's edge.

'*Mi dispiace*,' I said in greeting, then changed to our own tongue. 'Let's have this done with. Who sent you?'

He hesitated, until I nicked his flesh with the blade. Then he stammered it out: 'The party's name is Elder.'

Strange to hear it again – and somehow inevitable. 'Not a man to have trusted, my friend,' I said softly, and readied myself for the fatal swipe. He sensed it, and cried, 'No, no – my office told me it was a *lady*, not a man!'

'*What?*'

'I didn't meet the client – I rarely do. They said her name was Catherine Elder.'

Keeping the blade tight at his throat I used my other hand to dip into his coat pockets. His travel documents revealed him as one Philip Tarlton. His employers, whose name I recognised, operated from two addresses, one at Cheapside, the other off Pall Mall. Amongst the papers was a folded sheet, its ragged edge indicating it had been ripped from an album. I opened it, and saw a pencil sketch of a face – my face. It was dated June '82, in Kitty's hand. I had never seen it before. I asked him *why* she had sent someone after me, but he swore on his life he didn't know. He had no message. His brief was to find me, that was all.

My mind raced. I didn't want to be found, by Kitty or by anyone else. The solution to ensuring that was clear: a quick flick of the blade, a discreet splash as his body disappeared into the river. Even if they fished him out at some point, they would be a long time tracing his identity. Without papers his connection to me was – *niente*. Perhaps he heard something in my sigh, because when he next spoke his tone was meekly imploring. 'Please. Sir, I have a wife and child. I beg you. I shall reveal nothing of your whereabouts – I *swear* it.'

It would be so much safer to kill him. I know it, and so does he. And this would be the moment. Taking him by the scruff I force him to his knees, so that he is only inches from the drop into the river. My knuckles whiten around the knife's handle. I wish he hadn't told me what he just did . . .

He is trembling as I crouch down beside him. 'Well, Mr Tarlton. Listen to me carefully. I too have a wife and child. Their safety and well-being are my dearest concern. Should I ever suspect that you or your employers have endangered them, in any degree, I will come and find you.' I lift the blade to within half an inch of his eyeball. 'And I swear you'll not have the chance to beg for your life a second time.'

I do not want his thanks, though he is tearfully eager to bestow them on me. I dismiss him with a look, and listen as his steps quicken into a run along the towpath. Kitty's pencil portrait is still in my hand.

The blame is mine, I own it. I can trace it back to a moment, two months ago, whilst I was having my hair cut. The barber, Rocco, a tall, taciturn cove with a conquistador beard, did the same thing as always after he had wristily cast the sheet over my seated form. He handed me an English newspaper. It was an edition of *The Times*, from ten days before. (All the English come here, Rocco shruggingly told me.) I sat there, half absorbing the newsprint, when a name sprang out from the Announcements column, *ELDER, Catherine, only daughter of Sir Martin Elder* . . . It seemed that she was engaged to be married, which meant that her previous affianced, Douglas, had failed to lead her down the aisle. It rejoiced me to think that Kitty, by whatever means, had escaped the ruddy-cheeked brute.

The news was still preoccupying me when, a few days later, I was mooching about a market and happened upon a stall offering multifarious gewgaws for sale. My eye fell upon it instantly: a paperweight monkey, daintily carved from ivory. It recalled a certain primate whose disobliging behaviour had once, inadvertently, saved my life. I asked the stallholder how much he wanted for it, and paid him without haggling. Back in my rooms I had another long stare at the thing before swaddling it in tissue paper and making a parcel of it. I wrote the briefest note of congratulation to Kitty, without signing it; I felt sure she would know from whom it came. Obeying a cautious instinct, I took the package to a post office on the outskirts of the city and wore a slouch hat over my brow to prevent anyone there taking a close look at me. The address on the label was for Kensington Palace Gardens, London, a house that still returns to me in dreams. The clerk took it, I paid him, and left.

I see that it was imprudent. A provincial post office would seldom handle a package bound for *Inghilterra*, let alone a fashionable address in London. With or without my hat I would have been noticed, by somebody. And why send Kitty a gift in any case? If she thought of me at all it would very probably be with anger and disgust at my behaviour towards her sire. Or did some of the old affection linger in her heart for me? I would never know. I dispatched the thing as one might cast a stone into the sea, without thought of consequence. My mistake. Kitty has sent a man in search of me, the hireling of an agency that deals in cases of missing persons. Why? Philip Tarlton was no assassin, but he would have little trouble contracting one around here. Or did Elder somehow get wind of Kitty's secret commission and pervert it to his own use?

Whatever the reason, I am at present comprehensively alarmed. Those two street musicians I saw earlier today have been watching me, I feel certain of it. Tarlton is a professional and, in spite of his close shave, might easily have set them onto me. The way they hurried off before I could get down to the street . . .

I am humming that song – it has taken up residence in my head – when I hear footsteps slap on the tiled stairs. A man's. This tenement shares a common courtyard and entrance. The tall oak door, with its gigantic iron fanlight, is open all hours of the day – anyone can come and go. A knock at the door.

'*Signora?*'

I go to open it, then stop. *Signora*. Nobody comes up here without an invitation. And my next thought is: They know she lives here. They will get at me through her. I feel my whole body tense and close, like a fist. He knocks again, and I hear his hesitation before he retreats back down the stairs. I silently open the door and sneak onto the landing in time to catch his face as it vanishes down the stairwell. A lean fellow with a swarthy, stubbled face; something crafty about the eyes that unnerves me. I should follow him, but I'm still barefooted. I dash back in and haul on my shoes, then hurtle down the staircase and into the courtyard. The big door stands open. On the street I look this way and that, but it's a market day, and the crowds ambling along have swallowed any trace of him.

The bells from the nearby church ring eleven – no, twelve o'clock. Midday. They ought to be back by now. I look up, distractedly, to find that it's a beautiful day. The sky is a deep cornflower blue on which the clouds have been spread, like fresh laundry. A feather-light breeze riffles through the long-suffering streets. And I am in a panic. I join the drift of folk dawdling towards the market, where I know she will be. I hear singing from somewhere – is it those shifty musicians? I find myself hurrying, dodging between people ('*scusi, scusi*'), my steps light with dread. I am convinced that Elder's spies have come to snatch away my wife and child. The market's hubbub encloses me; faces loom and pass, one stranger after another, not caring. And then a voice startles me.

'David?' It is Roma, staring at me in puzzlement. She is wearing a faded black cotton dress and a mulberry-coloured headscarf. She seems to have been in the middle of a purchase, because a coster piling oranges on his scales has paused too, interested in her distraction. The boy is at her side, gazing fixedly at a bird in its cage. He could almost be in a trance. 'What's the matter?'

'Nothing,' I reply, relief flooding me. 'I only wondered where you'd got to.'

Roma stares at me, searching for a clue to my odd behaviour. 'I took his nibs for a walk in the park, then we came here. Like we always do.'

She touches my shirt, which is damp with sweat. 'What *is* the matter?'

she asks again. I have told her nothing of my suspicions – nothing of my encounter with Tarlton, of the musicians outside our window, of the fellow who has just been knocking at our door.

I put on a smile, spreading my palms and hunching my shoulders in the exaggerated manner of the locals. '*Niente.*'

She gives one of her choked-off laughs. My Italian shrug never fails to amuse her. She picks up the boy, and fits him against her hip. I take her laden basket from the coster ('*Grazie!*'). We start walking back home.

Roma. Yes: Roma. She decided the matter, not I. Once I was settled here I wrote to her, as promised, though without daring to renew those avowals I made that winter's night on the river at Gravesend. I simply recounted the story of my journey, and how I had chosen this city as home. Perhaps that was my way of asking her, though I wasn't conscious of it at the time. I recall the shock – the shock of delight – on reading her reply, in the thick-nibbed cursive I had not seen before. *I have thought of that night, when you asked me to come away with you. It seemed impossible to me then. But in the weeks since you left, your words have kept with me, and it seems not impossible at all. If you wish it still, then tell me, and I will come . . .*

No expressions of love or longing followed. That has never been her way. But she did come.

As we near our home, I am outwardly all smiles; inside, I am taut with consternation. Adopting a casual tone, I ask her if she has ever considered leaving the city – for a quieter place, perhaps.

'I like it here,' she says mildly. 'Why should we move?'

'Well . . . there's a whole country to discover. Would you not like to see the town your grandparents came from?'

She ponders this in silence for some while, then turns a curious look on me. 'Are you not happy here?'

The question takes me by surprise. 'Yes . . . that is, I'm happy to be wherever you are. And he is.' I nod to the infant. 'But it doesn't have to be in this city. We could find somewhere else.'

She stops, and takes a breath. 'David. This is our home. I don't want to live anywhere else. If you'd only tell me what's wrong – you've been as jumpy as a cat these last days.'

She searches my face, waiting for me to confess. When I say nothing, she gives a sad little shake of head and walks on. I cannot tell her. I don't want to frighten her for the sake of mere inklings.

Children are playing on the street outside our front door. Roma puts the boy down and enters the high-walled courtyard, a cool refuge from the noonday sun. As I follow within I see the silhouette of a seated figure, who rises to meet her. It's the crafty-eyed fellow who knocked at our door, returning to – what? My hand is already on the knife concealed in my back pocket, and as I close the distance between him and Roma I have a sudden presentiment of thrusting the blade in his neck and twisting it, the dark blood spurting from him in great gouts as he collapses to the ground. And just as I am about to interpose myself I hear her talking to him: they know each other. She is thanking him for something. I leave the knife in my pocket.

She tells me, in Italian, that this is Signor Riva, a carpenter who works nearby. We shake hands, then he picks up the wooden stool he's been sitting on, and hands it to me, with a grin. It looks new.

'For me?' I say, confused.

A gift from your wife, he explains. '*Fatto di quercia – il migliore.*'

I look to Roma, whose mouth is curved in a rueful smile. 'That balcony is too narrow for a chair, so I asked him to make you a stool. Now you can sit and watch the street to your heart's content.' Perhaps I look rather dumbfounded, because she then says, 'D'you like it?'

'*Si. Bellissima!*' I say, and she exchanges a satisfied look with the carpenter. It is indeed beautiful, but what makes it precious is that she took the trouble just for my sake. Can I continue to doubt that she loves me?

Later, now seated, I am back to watching the street. I've told Roma that I may begin to eat and sleep out here, too. I have just been listening to her and the boy singing together: no sound I love better. They come onto the balcony, and he totters over. He has his mother's olive skin and serious expression, which I will do almost anything to provoke into gaiety. He watches with solemn eyes as I pare an apple. I hold out a thin translucent slice, which he immediately puts in his mouth. He makes an odd humming sound as he chews.

'Doogheno or dabheno?' I ask him.

He pauses, then says, 'Doogheno.'

He doesn't yet know who taught *me* the word, but he will recognise the name when I eventually tell him. How could he not? It is his own.

Acknowledgements

My sincere thanks to Dan Franklin, Tom Drake-Lee and all at Cape; likewise to Rachel Cugnoni, Laura Hassan and all at Vintage; and to my agent Anna Webber at United Agents. I am very grateful to Doug Taylor, whose close reading of the manuscript was, in Flaubert's words, *severe mais juste*. Katherine Fry was exemplary in her beadiness. Thanks also to Mike McCarthy and to Rupert Christiansen. *Grazie* to Tara Hacking and Anna Murphy.

Two colossi of nineteenth-century journalism cast monumental shadows over this novel: Henry Mayhew's *London Labour and the London Poor* and Charles Booth's *Life and Labour of the People of London*. Brief acquaintance with either will reveal how much I have depended on them. I am also indebted to Sarah Wise's *The Blackest Streets*, a brilliant study of the vanished Nichol, which gave me the idea for a plot.

I am extremely fortunate to have in Rachel Cooke a loving helpmeet, an excellent reader and a constant bucker-up.